Alarms and Diversions

JAMES THURBER

PENGUIN BOOKS

in association with Hamish Hamilton

Penguin Books Ltd, Harmondsworth, Middlesex
AUSTRALIA: Penguin Books Pty Ltd, 762 Whitehorse Road,
Mitcham, Victoria

—

First published in Great Britain by Hamish Hamilton 1957
Published in Penguin Books 1962

—

—

Made and printed in Great Britain
by Cox and Wyman Ltd,
London, Reading, and Fakenham
Set in Monotype Times

—

Most of the material in this book originally appeared
in the *New Yorker*

for HELEN

Contents

Foreword

THE pieces in Part I of this collection appear here in book form for the first time. All of them but one were written in the past two years or so. The exception, 'Two O'Clock at the Metropole', was written twenty years ago as one of a *New Yorker* series called 'Where Are They Now?' This account of the Herman Rosenthal murder of 1912, like the story of the trial of Willie Stevens, 'A Sort of Genius', has been rewritten to place it in proper perspective. There is no longer a question as to the mundane whereabouts of the principal figures in these cases, for most of them died some time ago, or disappeared from public view and the records of the police. The two murder stories seem to belong to the present period of journalistic journeys into the tragic American past.

Many of these pieces, new and old, have been rewritten to some extent, mainly to bring them into accord with the changes wrought by time, the accumulation of new material, and certain shifts of viewpoint due to experience and the fruits of meditation. The piece about my mother, 'Lavender with a Difference', had to be put, sorrowfully, into the past tense. I have tampered with 'Daguerreotype of a Lady' only to include the incident about Mrs Detweiler's ghost, which I had unaccountably forgotten.

'The French Far West' was originally written for the old New York *Sunday World*, and done over later for the *New Yorker* under another title, 'Wild Bird Hickok and His Friends', but I have restored the original title as being more suitable for my old and exciting adventure in the Gallic translation of American nickel and dime novels. The backward glance at *Punch*, a stoutly durable weekly which has had its highs and lows, like any other, may serve one good purpose in proving that the friendship of Great Britain and the United States has survived more than one acrimonious family squabble. *Punch* and the *New Yorker* have exchanged parodies in the recent past, with no holds barred and no bones broken. I predict that the two weeklies, like the nations they represent, will continue more in amity than in dissension, but, I hope, always with the healthy give and take that marks a sound friendship.

'The Last Flower', originally published by *Harper's* as a book in itself, is included here in its entirety.

Most of the material in this book originally appeared in the *New Yorker*. 'There's Something Out There!' and 'The First Time I Saw Paris' were first published in *Holiday*, and 'My Own Ten Rules for a Happy Marriage' is reprinted from the *Cosmopolitan*. In the two years I spent on the trail of the Loch Ness monster I got invaluable help from many British newspapermen. I especially want to thank William Hardcastle, of the London *Daily Mail*, who made constantly available to me his newspaper's voluminous files on the subject. A. R. MacElwain, Frank Rizza, and Nora Sayre were also of great assistance.

My grateful thanks go to Simon & Schuster and Harcourt, Brace for their gracious permission to let me reprint from their own books of mine much of the material that appears herein, and detailed acknowledgement of their kindness appears on another page.

J. T.

West Cornwall, Conn.

The ladies of Orlon

SURGICAL science, still achieving, still pursuing, has successfully replaced a section of the femoral artery in a human leg with a tube made of nylon, and the medical profession confidently prophesies for the near future a practicable aorta made of the fabric known as orlon. We are all so used to the heart as a lyrical organ, made of the stuff that breaks, that a metaphorical shift to a heart made of the stuff that tears, or rips, or has to be hemstitched, may have a strange and disastrous effect on writers and composers. It has already had its effect on me, getting into my daydreams and nightmares. In one of the latter, a bearded doctor, fiercely grinning, asked me, 'Do you know how to tell your wife from the children's toys?' and startled me wide awake just before dawn. This fragment of dream was probably the associative product of the orlon surgical technique and Eugene Field's creatures of gingham and calico. (It wasn't until later that I heard about the new orlon-filled toys.) All I need to make a chaos out of my already tormented nights is a dream world of patchwork girls, indestructibly fabricated females with a disconcerting froufrou deep inside their organdie in place of the old-fashioned pulse beat.

One night, I dreamed I was at this party. A young lady had been carelessly flung on to the sofa beside me, her long legs loosely intertwined and her stuffing showing plainly at one shoulder seam. 'You're losing your sawdust,' I told her anxiously. 'Nonsex,' she said, and I suddenly realized that she and all the other women guests were dolls. Such a dream could be construed as meaning that I have reached the time of life when I seek to deny the actuality of the American Woman and to reduce her to the level of an insentient plaything. Actually, the latent meaning of this dream goes far deeper than that, and consists of a profound anxiety on my part as to what would happen to our world if the stature of Woman decreased.

A lovely woman with a taffeta xiphisternum might conceivably make this artificiality a part of her mysterious allure – I have known the kind of lady whose charm could even take the ugliness out of a thrug sutured with silk to her thisbe – but a gentleman of like kidney, let us say, could surely never regain the position he held in our competitive society before his operation. Man is used to being repaired with silver plates and pins, and it is doubtful whether his ego could long sustain a body consisting largely, or in part, of dress material. It may be, then, that a gradual textilization of the human species is one of the desperate strategies of Nature in her ceaseless effort to save our self-destructive race from the extinction of which it seems so massively enamoured. Nature and I have long felt that the hope of mankind is womankind, that the physically creative sex must eventually dominate the physically destructive sex if we are to survive on this planet. The simplest things last longest, the microbe outlives the mastodon, and the female's simple gift of creativity happily lacks the ornaments and handicaps of male artifice, pretension, power, and balderdash.

Nature (I do not say God, because I think protective Providence washed Its hands of us long ago) realizes that we have to be turned into something as durable as the toughest drygoods if we are to endure the wear and tear caused by the frightened tempo of our time. Men and women – the former because they think the Devil is after them, the latter merely to hold their own – make the revolving doors of our office buildings whirl at a dangerous and terrifying rate of speed as they rush lickety-split to their lunches, return hellbent to their desks, and fling themselves recklessly homeward at twilight to their separate sorrows. It is the men who are the casualties of this pell-mell, the men who are caught in the doors and flung to the floors, and it is the women who pick them up, or at least it is the women who pick *me* up. Once the ladies have become compounded largely of bland but durable textiles, they will outlive the once stronger sex even more easily than they do now. Nature, prefiguring the final disappearance of the male, has aided science in solving the problem of the continuation of the human being with her usual foresight, by establishing the ingenious, if admittedly stuffy, technique of artificial insemination. It is only a question of time before the male factor in the perpetuation of the species becomes a matter of biological deep freeze, an everlasting laboratory culture, labelled, controlled, and supervised by women technicians.

The male, continuously preoccupied with his own devices and his own mythical destiny, polysyllabically boasting of his power and purpose, seems blithely unconscious of the conspiracy of Nature and women to do him in. He does not seem to know that he is doomed to go out like a light unless he abandons the weapons and the blue-prints of annihilation. Woman says little about it, but she does not intend to be annihilated by Man, even if she has to get rid of him first to save herself. This is not going to be as difficult for her to face as one might think, for her ancient dependence on the male began slowly to turn into disdain about A.D. 1835, according to Dr Rudolph Horch, who makes the astounding statement that the female's sexual interest in her mate has decreased seventeen and two-tenths per cent since September 1929. The female has greater viability than the male, Dr Horch reminds us, and the male knows this when he puts his mind to it, which he naturally does not like to do. I once asked a distinguished obstetrician which he would rather be called upon to deliver, male quintuplets or female quintuplets. He began with the usual masculine circumlocutions, pointing out that there are no dependable statistics, on a large scale, dealing with the relative viability of the sexes. 'Let me put it this way,' I said. 'Two women are about to give birth to quintuplets, and by means of some hypothetical prescience it has become known that one is going to have five boys and the other five girls. Which would you rather deliver if you were called upon to make a choice?' 'The girls,' he said.

It may come down, in the end, to a highly dramatic sex crisis. Man is forever discovering some new and magnificent miracle weapon or miracle drug, and it is possible that he may soon stumble upon an undreamed-of mineral, of which there will be just enough in the world to create a drug that could cure everybody of everything or to manufacture a bomb capable of blowing the planet into fragments the size of Cuba. The ultimate struggle for possession of the precious material would divide men and women into two warring camps. I have the confidence to believe that the creative females would defeat the destructive males and gain control of the miracle substance.

I no longer see the faces of men and women at the parties I attend, or in the streets I walk along, or the hotel lobbies I sit in, but I hear their voices more clearly than ever. The voices of the women, it seems to me, have taken on a new and quiet quality – a secret conspiratorial tone, the hopeful and reassuring note of a sex firmly dedicated to the principle of not being blown into fragments. For centuries Woman has been quietly at work achieving her present identity. Not many years ago the *Encyclopaedia Britannica* listed nothing under 'Woman', but merely said 'See Man'. The latest Oxford English Dictionary, however, gives woman twelve columns to man's fifteen. The development of her name from Old English through Middle English to Modern English is fascinating to trace in the O.E.D. She began as 'wife', became 'wifman', and underwent seventeen other changes until the word 'woman' came into use about the year 1400. Most writers, glibly discussing the origin of the word over their brandy, contend that it derives from the derogatory phrase 'with man' or the physiological 'wombman'. They don't know what they are talking about. Earlier male writers, equally mistaken, declared the word derived from 'woe to man' or 'wee man'. Some of them were serious, others merely kidding, in the immemorial manner of the superior male.

I'm glad to report that the feminist Flecknor took a fairer view in 1653 when he wrote: 'Say of Woman worst ye can, what prolongs their woe, but man?' In the past three hundred years the importance of women has often been derided by men, from J. Clarke's 'A Woman, asse, and walnut-tree, the more you beat the better be' to Noël Coward's 'A woman should be struck regularly like a gong.' But there were wiser men who spoke of the female of the species with proper respect, and even fear. It was Congreve who wrote the almost invariably misquoted 'Heav'n has no Rage, like Love to Hatred turn'd, Nor Hell a Fury, like a Woman scorned,' and in 1835 Hook recognized the stature of the female with 'A girl of seventeen is a woman, when a man of seventeen is a boy.' Thirty-two years later, English law under Queen Victoria formally defined the female: 'Woman shall mean a Female of the Age of Eighteen Years or Upwards', and twenty years after that the British female legally became a woman at the age of sixteen while males of the same age were still regarded as schoolchildren.

It was in the 1890s that the old-fashioned dependent woman was scornfully rejected by her own sex as the 'cow-woman', and 'new woman' and even 'new womandom' came into common and spirited use. Ninety years before that decade of the self-assertive woman, J. Brown had arrogantly written, 'No ecclesiastical power can reside in a heathen, a woman, or a child'. Fortunately for his peace of mind, he didn't live to see the female become the residence of practically any power you can name. She is now definitely here to stay, whereas the decline of the male, even the actual decadence of the insecure sex, has been observed by alarmed scientists in a score of other species. A certain scorpion, for example, disappears with his mate after a ritualistic courtship dance, and is never seen again. The female, though, emerges from the honeymoon, fit as a fiddle and fresh as a daisy. And there is a certain female fish in the waters of the sea who has reduced the male to the status of a mere accessory. She actually carries him about with her, for occasional biological use, in the casual way that a woman carries a compact or a cigarette lighter in her handbag. There are dozens of other significant instances of the dwindling of the male in the animal kingdom, but I am much too nervous to go into them here. Some twenty years ago, a gloomy scientist reported, 'Man's day is done.' Woman's day, on the other hand, is, by every sign and token, just beginning. It couldn't happen to a nicer sex.

In case you have always wondered why the *o* in women is pronounced differently from the *o* in woman, the Oxford Dictionary has a theory about that, as about everything else. The change is the result of the associative influence of certain other pairs of words, singular and plural, such as foot and feet, and tooth and teeth. The women will now please keep their seats until the men have left the auditorium. They need, God knows, a head start.

The first time I saw Paris

WHAT I saw first of all was one outflung hand of France as cold and limp as a dead man's. This was the seacoast town of Saint-Nazaire, a long while ago. I know now that French towns don't die, that France has the durability of history itself, but I was only twenty-three then, and seasick, and I had never been so far from Ohio before. It was the dank, morose dawn of November 1918, and I had this first dismal glimpse of *France la Doulce* from the deck of the U.S. Transport *Orizaba*, which had come from the wintry sea like a ship out of Coleridge, a painted ship in an unreal harbour. The moist, harsh light of breaking day gave the faces of the silent staring gobs on deck a weird look, but the unreality was shattered soon enough by the raucous voice of a boatswain bawling orders. I had first heard this voice, strong enough to outshout a storm, snarling commands at 'abandon ship' drill: 'Now, light all lanterns!' and 'Now, lower all lifeboats!' I had been assigned to a life raft that was rusted to the deck and couldn't be budged. 'Now, what's the matter with Life Raft Number Six?' the boatswain had roared. A sailor next to me said, 'She's stuck to the deck, sir.' The boatswain had to have the last word and he had it. 'Now, leave her lay there!' he loudly decreed.

The *Orizaba* had taken a dozen days zigzagging across the North Atlantic, to elude the last submarines of the war, one of which we had sighted two days before, and Corcoran and I felt strange and uncertain on what seemed anything but solid land for a time. We were code clerks in the State Department, on our way to the Paris Embassy. Saint-Nazaire was, of course, neither dead nor dying, but I can still feel in my bones the gloom and tiredness of the old port after its four years of war. The first living things we saw were desolate men, a detachment of German prisoners being marched along a street, in mechanical step, without expression in their eyes, like men coming from no past and moving toward no future. Corcoran and I walked around the town to keep warm until the bistros opened. Then we had the first cognac of our lives, quite a lot of it, and the day brightened, and there was a sense of beginning as well as of ending, in the chilling weather. A young pink-cheeked French army officer got off his bicycle in front of a house and knocked on the door. It was opened by a young woman whose garb and greeting, even to our inexperienced eyes and ears, marked her as one of those females once described by a professor of the Harvard Law School as 'the professionally indiscreet'. Corcoran stared and then glanced at his wristwatch. 'Good God!' he said. 'It isn't even nine o'clock yet.'

The train trip down to Paris was a night to remember. We shared a sleeping compartment with a thin, gloved, talkative Frenchman who said he was writing the history of the world and who covered his subject spasmodically through the night in English as snarled as a fisherman's net, waking us once to explain that Hannibal's elephants were not real, but merely fearful figments of Roman hallucination. I lay awake a long time thinking of the only Paris I knew, the tranquil, almost somnolent city of Henry James's turn-of-the-century novels, in which there was no hint of war, past or approaching, except that of the sexes.

Paris, when we finally got there, seemed to our depressed spirits like the veritable capital city of Beginning. Her heart was warm and gay, all right, but there was hysteria in its beat, and the kind of compulsive elation psychiatrists strive to cure. Girls snatched overseas caps and tunic buttons from American soldiers, paying for them in hugs and kisses, and even warmer coin. A frightened Negro doughboy from Alabama said, 'If this happened to me back home, they'd hang me.' The Folies Bergère and the Casino de Paris, we found a few nights later, were headquarters of the New Elation, filled with generous ladies of joy, some offering their charms free to drinking, laughing, and brawling Americans in what was left of their uniforms. At the Folies a quickly composed song called '*Finie la Guerre*' drew a dozen encores. Only the American M.P.s were grim, as they moved among the crowds looking for men who were AWOL, telling roistering captains and majors to dress up their uniforms. Doughboy French, that wonderful hybrid, bloomed everywhere. '*Restez ici* a minute,' one private said to his French girl. '*Je* returny *après cet* guy partirs.' *Cet* guy was, of course, a big-jawed military policeman set on putting a stop to non-regulation hilarity.

'I do not understand the American,' a Casino girl told me. 'They fight at night with each other, they break mirrors, they become bloody, they say goddamn everybody, and the next day what do you think? They are in the Parc Monceau on all fours giving little French children a ride on their backs. They are marvellous. I love them.'

The Americans have never been so loved in France, or anywhere else abroad, as they were in those weeks of merriment and wild abandon. When, late in 1919, most of our soldiers had sailed back home, *La Vie Parisienne* had a full-page colour drawing of an American officer over whose full-length figure dozens of lovely miniature French girls were rapturously climbing, and the caption ruefully observed: 'The hearts of our young ladies have gone home with the Americans.'

My trunk had stayed on the *Orizaba*. Corcoran and I had been the only two civilians on board, and transports were not used to unloading non-military baggage. All I had was the clothes I wore – my hat had been claimed as a souvenir – and I set about the considerable task of buying a wardrobe, paying what amounted to five dollars for B.V.D.s at the Galeries Lafayette. A suit I bought at a shop deceptively called 'Jack, American Tailor' is packed away in the modest files of secret memory. It might have been made by the American Can Company. I tried on hats for an hour in a shop on the Avenue de l'Opéra, upon whose civilian stock the dust of four years of war had settled. There were narrow-brimmed hats, each with a feather stuck on one side, that made me looked like Larry Semon, movie comic of the silent days, and some that would have delighted that great connoisseur of funny hats, Mr Ed Wynn. They were all placed on my head with an excited '*Voilà!*' by the eager salesman, and they were all too small, as well as grotesque. In one of the famous black, broad-brimmed hats, long and lovingly associated with the painters and poets of Bohemian Paris, I looked like a baleful figure attending the funeral of Art. I nearly broke the salesman's heart when I turned down a ten-gallon white Stetson he had dug up out of the cellar. So I went through that cold, dank Paris winter without a hat.

I had bought a cane, which in Columbus would have identified me as a lounge lizard of dubious morals, and I acquired enough boulevard French to say, '*Où est la Place de la Concorde?*' and to reply to '*Voulez-vous une petite caresse?*' My *tout ensemble* was strange, but not strange enough to deceive doughboys and gobs wandering along the Champs-Élysées, homesick and disconsolate after the elation died down. I helped them decipher the small red-and-black French-English dictionaries they carried and told them that, contrary to their invariable conviction, they would not be stuck in 'this godforsaken city' forever. Once I translated, for a puzzled demoiselle, a mysterious note she had got through the mails from a doughboy who had returned to her one day before *cet* guy had partired. It began, 'I am in a place I cannot leave.' I managed to explain to her that her boy had been jailed for being absent without leave. I gathered that he had been, when on the loose, a great lover, fighter, and piggy-back rider, like the others. 'I wish to cry on your shirt,' his girl friend told me, and she cried on my shirt. That astonished shirt, stained with Lacrimae Puellae 1919, must have cost a lot, but all I remember is that the amazing French shirt-tail reached to my knees.

When I got to France, the franc was worth almost a quarter, but pretty soon you could get fourteen francs for your dollar, and since prices didn't rise as rapidly as the franc fell, the $2000 annual salary of a code clerk began to mean something. One amateur speculator among us, certain that the franc would come back with all the resilience of Paris, bought up francs and was wiped out when *la chute* continued. In my nearly forty years off and on in France I have seen this coin of a thousand values vary from 5.30 to 350. 'It will be as worthless as dandelions,' a dour concierge predicted in 1919, but she was wrong.

'*Ah, ces américans,*' sighed a Folies girl one evening. '*Quels hommes!* They are such good bad boys. They wish to spend the night, even the week-end.' She went on to explain how this complicated the economic structure of one in her profession. She was used, in the case of other foreigners, to a nightly transference of paid affections as neatly manoeuvred as the changing of partners in a square dance. 'These Americans are men born to marry,' my informant went on. Many of them – thousands, I believe – did marry French girls and took them home to an astonished Brooklyn, a disapproving Middle West, and occasionally more amiable regions. I read somewhere in 1928 that about 75 per cent of these wartime marriages had ended in the return of the brides to France. One of those who stayed wrote me a letter a quarter of a century ago in which she said, dolorously, 'There is not the life in Detroit. It is not Paris. Can you send me some books in French?' She had married a great big good bad American Army lieutenant. I sent her, among other books in French, the poems of Mallarmé and the book Clemenceau wrote after the war. I often wonder what finally became of another girl who married a sailor and went to live in Iowa, and what they thought of her English out there. She had learned it all from the plays of Shakespeare and it was quaint and wonderful to hear, but definitely not for Iowa. 'How goes the night?' she asked me once, straight out of *Macbeth*, to which I was proudly able to reply, 'The moon is down. I have not heard the clock.' This Gallic Elizabethan had given up working for a few francs a week in a garment factory for a more lucrative and less monotonous career. Once I met her by appointment, and in pursuit of my sociological studies, on the terrace of the Café de la Paix, where, over vermouth cassis, she explained that she was going to meet, in half an hour, an American captain whom she had comforted one night long ago when he didn't have a sou. It seems he had promised to meet her at the café and pay his debt of gratitude, and he had written her from somewhere and fixed an hour. 'He will be here,' she said confidently, and she was right. A quiet, almost shy good bad boy, he slipped her a sealed envelope while I studied the passing throng in which, true prophecy has it, you will see everybody you know if you sit at your table long enough. I still remember that what he ordered was chocolate ice-cream.

The City of Light, during most of 1919, was costumed like a wide-screen Technicolor operetta, the uniforms of a score of nations forming a kind of restless, out-of-step finale. The first Bastille Day celebration after the war was a carnival that dazzled the eye and lifted the heart. Chairs at windows of buildings along the route of march cost as much as fifty dollars, and stepladders on the crowded sidewalks could be rented for fifteen dollars. At night, in a thousand 'tin bars', as our men called bistros, and in more elaborate *boîtes de nuit*, the Americans often changed the pre-war pattern of Paris night life by fighting among themselves, or singly, in pairs, or in groups, the Anzacs, the waiters, the management, the *gendarmerie*, or whoever was looking for action. Chairs and bottles were thrown, and mirrors cracked from side to side. There was a conviction among Americans, more often false than true, that they were always overcharged, and this was the chief provocation for trouble, but high spirits, the irritating factor of unfamiliarity, triple sec, and a profound American inability to pick up foreign languages easily, often led to roughhouse. A civilian I knew who hailed from New Jersey, and constantly and profanely wished he was back there, asked me one morning how to say in French, 'I demand the release of these Americans.' It turned out that no Americans he knew were in durance anywhere. My unilingual companion simply planned to go out on the town that night with some compatriots and wanted to be prepared, in case his detachment was overwhelmed by the authorities in some bar. Like me, he worked at the Embassy, then on the rue de Chaillot, and he had a code-room pass which he proposed to wave while shouting his command. I told him the French were always aroused, never intimidated, by civilians shouting orders, especially if they flaunted mysterious and doubtful official credentials. He would be taken, I told him, for the most despised of creatures, the *mouchard*, or police spy. Not the next morning, but a few days later, he showed up with bruised knuckles and a swollen jaw. 'You were right,' he admitted meekly.

Paris had been down on her knees, but now she got back on her feet, surely and resolutely, in the noble tradition of the world's most spirited city. Montmartre, when I first walked its deserted silent streets, had seemed down and out for good, but by New Year's Eve 1918 it had begun to function, and before long the Moulin Rouge and the Chat Noir were gaily crowded again. Excellent food, the great pride of Paris, was naturally slow in reaching the tables of the famous restaurants, but I took an American Red Cross girl to Voisin's not many weeks after I arrived, and it seemed to have gone through the war as if nothing worse than a storm had passed. This was the quietly elegant restaurant celebrated for its calm, almost austere, survival of the Siege of Paris in the war with Prussia, when, undaunted by dwindling supplies, it served up the tender cuts of some of the more edible animals of the zoo. I remember being shown one of the remarkable and touching menus of those war years. I have forgotten just when it closed its doors forever, but in 1938, while accompanying my wife on a shopping trip, I was suddenly overcome by a curious and haunting sense of the past in a woman's glove store. Recognition flowed back like a film developing, and I realized that I stood within a few feet of where the American girl and I had sat for lunch one day. It was like meeting an old beloved friend who has undergone a sorrowful change and no longer knows who you are.

Paris during the months of the Peace Conference would have delighted Hadrian, Playboy of the Roman Empire, who enjoyed colourful spectacles brought together from the corners of the world. When President Wilson drove down the Champs-Élysées, more people watched and cheered, more flags were waved, more eyes were bright, than I have ever seen in one place at one time. The way from there had to be down, because there was no higher place to reach, and the international highway of acclaim never runs straight and smooth very far. There had been, even on the day of armistice, voices that did not shout '*Finie la guerre!*' but solemnly warned, '*Maintenant ça commence.*' But these prophets of predicament and peril were lost sight of in the carnival. I didn't hear them myself; I was too busy, between coding and decoding telegraphic messages, watching Premier Paderewski arriving at his hotel, catching glimpses of Herbert Hoover sitting erect in the back seat of his big Cadillac, identifying the impressive head of Lloyd George at one of the restaurants in the Bois de Boulogne. At the Casino de Paris, the famous straw hat and lower lip of Maurice Chevalier, not long before turned thirty, attracted crowds as his rising star dimmed a little the light of the great Mistinguette. He did a wonderful burlesque of an American gob, by turns melancholy and gay, excited and bewildered, taking the edge off Mistinguette's singing of 'For Me and My Gal', a song the French loved. The Americans, of course, were singing 'Smiles' and 'Hindustan', and then a song of which someone had sent me a recording from America, 'Dardanella'. I remember taking the Red

Cross girl to dinner at Noël Peters, where a trio of piano, violin, and cello played many pieces, only one of them American. After brandy I had requested an American song, and the pianist finally dug up the sheet music of 'Good-bye My Bluebell'.

Everybody went out to Versailles, where the famous fountains had been turned on for the first time in years. All kinds of devices were used to get into the Hall of Mirrors. Never had so many fake passes been so elaborately contrived, but few of them worked. And through it all the Battle of Paris went on. Souvenir hunting by Americans reached a high point. They took things out of niches and tried to pry things loose from plinths, to add to the relics of war brought back from the front, including ornamental vases made by French soldiers out of the casings of French ·75s. I got one of these at Fort Vaux outside Verdun, which had been stormed and taken and retaken so many times. Verdun had been the farthest north reached by me and another Embassy clerk in the week before Christmas 1918. We had gone by train as far as the town of Vierzy, where my companion searched vainly for the grave of a friend from Illinois who had been a marine. Another marine from the Embassy guard, talking and dreaming of his ranch in Montana, had gone with us as far as Vierzy, mainly to find an open space in which he could practise firing a Luger he had picked up somewhere, but he would have no part of our plan to walk through the battlefields, day after day, as far as Soissons and Verdun. Up there we paid our way into Fort Vaux and the underground city of Verdun with American cigarettes. I often consume again, in fantasy, the light omelet, *pain de famille*, and good white wine served to us by a young French farmer and his wife who were bravely rebuilding their home in one of those landscapes of destruction so poignantly painted by the late English artist Paul Nash. It took long argument to persuade the couple to take money for the meal.

In our trek through the battlefields, with the smell of death still in the air, the ruined and shattered country scarred with ammunition dumps and crashed planes, we came upon the small temporary cemeteries arranged by the Graves Registration Service, each with a small American flag, such as the children of Paris waved at President Wilson, nailed to a post and faded by the rain and wintry weather. In one of these cemeteries my companion, a Tennessee youth, only a little taller than five feet, began singing 'The Star-Spangled Banner' with his hat over his heart, and went on singing it in a sudden downpour of rain, for the anthem, once started, must be finished. He was loaded down with junk on our way back, most of which he had to abandon. He mourned his failure to wrench an ornamental iron gate from the entrance to a shattered château. The only thing I brought back, besides the vase, was the identification papers of an Algerian soldier named A. Mokdad, which were lying on the ground, punctured by two machine-gun bullets. Detachments of French labour battalions were trying to clear up the wreckage here and there, a task that seemed hopeless. But the French soldiers were tough, determined men. By the light of a Very shell one night in Soissons we had seen a company of *poilus* marching through the mud, singing 'Madelon'. In the muzzles of some of their carbines flowers from God knows where had been stuck. The soldiers looked enormous and indomitable, and it is good to know that one or two French painters of the time did justice to their stature, painting them to look like the rocks they were. Contrary to the prewar American notion of Frenchmen as small and dapper, there were scores of d'Artagnans in the armies of France for every Aramis – and he was tough enough himself.

Back in Paris, I made a brief survey of the souvenirs collected by Americans I knew. One man had brought from somewhere a machine-gun, which he kept in his hotel room and left there when he went home. Legend had it that the upraised sword of the equestrian statue of George Washington in the Place d'Iéna had been replaced nine times, and one over-enthusiastic vandal had been arrested while attempting to take one of the gilt cherubs from the superstructure of the bridge of Alexandre III across the Seine. A sailor I know collected, with the aid of chisel and screwdriver, ornate locks from old doors and gates, and his trophies must have weighed a good hundred pounds. A doughboy who fancied bronze and marble busts in museums was less successful. It was rumoured, in the days of the Great Hunt, that not more than five servicemen were admitted to Napoleon's tomb at one time. Everybody heard, and retold, the wonderful myth of the bold and enterprising soldier in the Louvre who had got away with the arms of the Venus de Milo and the head of the Winged Victory.

I have nothing tangible to remind me of those tangled days, the Verdun vase and the papers of A. Mokdad having long since disappeared. The vase, wherever it is, must still bear the deathless hammered-out name 'Verdun'. From a separate trip to Rheims I brought back nothing but chill memories that still turn up now and then in nightmares. I see the vacant staring space from which the rose window of the cathedral had been carefully removed in time, and the gaping hole in one wall of the edifice, made by a shell hit. This great city of the Champagne country was all but deserted when I was there, and a walk through its streets was a walk on the moon. The disappearance of one wall had revealed a bedroom that looked like a dismal abandoned stage set. The works of a printing shop, its machines and type, were scattered across a street. The façade of a theatre had been ripped off, revealing a crumbling stage, while empty seats and boxes, unharmed except by weather, gave the beholder the feeling that cast and audience had fled in horror during the showing of some kind of extravaganza in hell. And in Paris, so near in space, seemingly so far away in time, morbid visitors, looking for the effects of war, asked where they could find the church upon which a shell from Big Bertha had made its terrible direct hit.

All of us went to the grand opera many times, my own first visit being to hear *Aïda* and to see the *haut monde* of Paris once again in evening clothes, glittering up and down the marble staircases between acts. Someone pointed out René Fonck in the crowd, and I still remember the ribbon of the great airman's Croix de Guerre, as long as a ruler to accommodate all the palms he had won. There is a timelessness about grand opera in Paris, and except for the uniforms, there was no hint that the greatest war in history had come so recently to an end. I paid a dollar that night for a pack of American cigarettes, but this was not my most memorable financial transaction. A week or two after our arrival Corcoran and I had paid a dollar apiece for fried eggs, and almost as much for marmalade.

I sometimes ate with the doughboys, who never got used to French food, and groused about American Army grub. In Verdun one day we ate Army beans and the rest of the rations, using borrowed mess kits. 'Look at them guys eat that stuff,' one private said. 'I'll be damned if they don't like it.' We also liked the wheat cakes with genuine maple syrup served at an Army kitchen set up in the basement of the Crillon, the de luxe hotel in the heart of Paris which had been taken over by the Americans.

I saw no doughboys or gobs at the opera, but they crowded into the cinemas when they opened, to watch the American films of three actors popular with the French – W. S. Hart ('*le roi du ranch*'), Harold Lloyd, known as '*Lui*', and Douglas Fairbanks *père*, lovingly called 'Doogla' by the French.

When I finally sailed back home, sixteen months had elapsed since the Armistice, and the Brave New World was taking on its disillusioning shape. Theodore Roosevelt had died in 1919, which marked in its way the end of an era, and Woodrow Wilson had come down from his dizzy pinnacle of fame and hope, and was on his way to his own dismayed and frustrated end. Before long a celebrated room was to be filled with smoke out of which a political magician named Harry M. Daugherty would produce the shadowy figure of Warren Gamaliel Harding and the misleading motto of 'Return to Normalcy' in a period of flagpole sitting, non-stop dancing, Channel swimming, ocean flying, husband murder, novels of disenchantment, and approaching financial chaos. I reached New York still without a hat. It was March and blustery in New York, and one of the first things I did was to buy one. It fitted my head, and seemed to my repatriated eye extremely becoming. It wasn't until later that day that I looked inside the hat to see the mark of the maker. I quote from a piece I wrote in 1923 for the Columbus, Ohio, Sunday *Dispatch*: 'Something inside the crown caught my eye. I looked more closely. "*Fabriqué par Moissant et Amour, 25 Avenue de l'Opéra, Paris,*" it said.'

Paris, City of Light and of occasional Darkness, sometimes in the winter rain seeming wrought of monolithic stones, and then, in the days of its wondrous and special pearly light, appearing to float in mid-air like a mirage city in the Empire of Imagination, fragile and magical, has had many a premature requiem sung for the repose of its soul by nervous writers or gloomy historians who believe it is dying or dead and can never rise again. Paris, none the less, goes right on rising out of war, ultimatum, occupation, domestic upheaval, cabinet crises, international tension, and dark prophecy, as it has been in the habit of doing since its residents first saw the menacing glitter of Roman shields many centuries ago. Recently in the New York Sunday *Times* John Davenport sang sorrowfully of the Paris of today as a dying city, a city of ghosts, but his funeral arrangements were laughed off by, among others, a South Carolina reader who protested, 'It is not Paris but an Anglo-American myth that is dying.'

The Americans and English have never become an integral part of the anatomy of the city, which is forever French. Its visitors come and go, hopeful or despondent, comfortable or uneasy, looking in the wrong places for the pulse of the city, feeling in the wrong places for the throb of its heart. I have been in and out of Paris half a dozen times from 1920 to 1955, and I have had my moments of depression and worry about the great city, but I have never felt that I was sitting up at night with a fatally sick friend. I have seen her moods shift from confidence to despond, for Paris is a lady of temperament and volatility, but I have never felt she was mortally languishing, like a stricken heroine of grand opera.

I enjoy arguing with Parisian friends about the true gender of their fair city, pointing out that 'feminine', in my lexicon, means neither frail nor frivolous, neither capricious nor coquettish, but female, and summing up with this sound paraphrase of Kipling: 'The female of the cities is far tougher than the male.' In my observation, the female of any species is not, in Simone de Beauvoir's pallid phrase, the Second Sex, but the First Sex, of which the Second is luckily born. Frenchmen jump too easily to the inference that 'lady', when applied to Paris, means *poule de luxe*, or that what we feminists have in mind is the gay figure evoked when Monsieur Chevalier sings '*Paris, elle est une blonde*'. What we really mean is Woman in the sense and stature, the sign and symbol, in which she is represented everywhere you look in Paris, from the celebrated statue of the fighting French woman called *Quand Même*, in the Tuileries, to the monumental figure on one side of the Arch of Triumph. Or take the statues in the Place de la Concorde representing eight great provincial cities of France, all of which are depicted as women. Perhaps the finest, that of Strasbourg, was shrouded in black when I first beheld it, but I was happily on hand when the lady was joyously stripped of her mourning after Strasbourg had been restored to France.

Street rioting has broken out in the streets of Paris from time to time, for Paris does not repress her anger any more than she suppresses her desires, and windows are smashed and buildings are burned, and now and then someone is killed. Once in a while the United States has been the object of Parisian wrath – thirty years ago I witnessed a *rixe* or two, but never a real *bagarre* – because of our failure to write off the French war debt. There were those at the time who feared that demonstrators might overturn the statue in the Place des États-Unis of Washington and Lafayette shaking hands. It has been marked with chalk, but it will never be overthrown. Not far from these sculptured hands across the sea stands an equally solid monument to the 118 Americans who lost their lives in the service of France during the First World War, sixty-one of them in the Lafayette Escadrille. The granite tribute contains the indestructible names of Raoul Lufbery, Norman Prince, Kiffin Rockwell, Victor Chapman, and Alan Seeger.

This is the American quarter of Paris that I knew so well in the months after the Armistice. In front of what was once the chancellery of our Embassy at 5 rue de Chaillot, a statue of Rochambeau salutes the mounted image of George Washington in the Place d'Iéna not far away. It was indeed *bien américain* the time of my first visit, for Woodrow Wilson lived at No. 11 Place des États-Unis, and a short walk from there was the Avenue du Président Wilson and a *pension* filled with Americans from the Embassy. The streets were loud with American voices and bright with our uniforms, and marines sometimes played baseball in the rue de Chaillot. A bar advertised 'American cocktails' and Yanks sang our war songs, including the one with the line 'I'll bring you a Turk and the Kaiser, too', which may have inspired the wild notion in some of our men to invade Doorn and bring old Wilhelm back to America as the souvenir of souvenirs. Nearly twenty years ago I made a pilgrimage to the old Yank district, meeting French friends of mine who were still there, and reading the tablet placed near the door of the former chancellery by the

Paris Post of the American Legion, a small memorial perpetuating the myth that the late Myron T. Herrick was our Ambassador during the war of 1914–18. Actually he had been replaced in December 1914 by the late William G. Sharp, who served during all but four months of the war, but has gone unremembered and unmarked. Legend made Myron Herrick our wartime ambassador, and legend, from Barbara Frietchie to Mr Herrick, is more durable than fact.

The last time I saw Paris, or heard and sensed the city, since I was no longer able to see the old landmarks, was in the late summer of 1955, and I didn't get around to the once familiar places which, if you are there and interested in such a ramble, you can find more easily by following the Avenue Kléber out of the Place de l'Étoile toward the Seine and the Eiffel Tower. Here are the permanent pages of history, written in bronze and stone, of America in Paris, and they are worth a morning's walk and an hour's meditation.

The second time I saw Paris, in 1925, she wore a new gown and a different mood. The Americans had taken over the Left Bank from the Deux Magots to the Dôme and the Rotonde, and there were almost as many writers and artists as there had been doughboys and gobs. It was the era of Hemingway, Scott Fitzgerald, and John Dos Passos in Paris, and over the restless new American hive Gertrude Stein, prophetess of the Lost Generation, presided like a modernistic queen bee. But that is another memory, for another time.

À bientôt.

The psychosemanticist will see you now, Mr Thurber

I BELIEVE there are no scientific investigators that actually call themselves psychosemanticists, but it is surely time for these highly specialized therapeuticians to set up offices. They must not be carelessly confused with psychosomaticists, who study the effects of mental weather upon the ramparts of the body. The psychosemanticists will specialize in the havoc wrought by verbal artillery upon the fortress of reason. Their job will be to cope with the psychic trauma caused by linguistic meaninglessness, to prevent the language from degenerating into gibberish, and to save the sanity of persons threatened by the onset of polysyllabic monstrosititis.

We have always been a nation of categorizationists, but what was once merely a national characteristic is showing signs of malignancy. I shall not attempt to discover the incipient primary lesion, for I am not a qualified research scholar in this field. Indeed, for having had the impudence to trespass thus far I shall no doubt be denounced by the classificationists as a fractional impactionist (one who hits subjects a glancing blow), an unauthorized incursionist, a unilateral conclusionist, and a presumptuous deductionist. Our national predilection for ponderous phraseology has been traced by one authority as far back as the awkward expression 'taxation without representation' (unjust impost). It is interesting to note that the irate American colonists of that period in our history would be categorized today as 'anti-taxation-without-representationists'.

Not long ago, for the most recent instance in my collection, Senator Lyndon Johnson was described by a Washington newspaperman as a pragmatic functionalist, a term that was used in a laudatory sense. It isn't always easy nowadays to tell the laudatory from the derogatory at first glance, but we should be glad that this Democratic leader is not a dogmatic divisionary or an occlusive impedimentarian. The most alarming incidence of verbal pre-malignancy occurs, of course, in this very area of politics, but let us skip over such worn and familiar double-jointedisms as creeping Socialists, disgruntled ex-employees, ritualistic liberals, massive retaliationists, agonized reappraisalists, unorthodox thinkers, unwitting handmaidens (male), to name only a few out of hundreds, and take a look at excessive pre-war anti-Fascism, a colossal (I use the adjective as a noun, in the manner of television's 'spectacular') that was disgorged a few years ago. Here the classificatory degradationists brought a time element into what might be called the post-evaluation of political morality. The operation of this kind of judgement during and after the Civil War would have thrown indelible suspicion upon all the Northern patriots, including Abraham Lincoln, who wanted Robert E. Lee to take command of the Federal Armies in the field. They would be known today as 'over-enthusiastic pre-Manassas pro-Leeists'.

The carcinomenclature of our time is, to be sure, an agglomerative phenomenon of accumulated concretions, to which a dozen different types of elaborative descriptivists have contributed – eminently the old Communist intellectuals, with their 'dialectical materialists', 'factional deviationists', 'unimplemented obscurantists', and so on, and so on. Once the political terminologists of all parties began to cross-infect our moribund vocabulary, the rate of degeneration became appalling. Elephantiasis of cliché set in, synonym atrophied, the pulse of inventiveness slowed alarmingly, and paraphrase died of impaction. Multiple sclerosis was apparent in the dragging rhythms of speech, and the complexion of writing and of conversation began to take on the tight, dry parchment look of death. We have become satisfied with gangrenous repetitions of threadbarisms, like an old man cackling in a chimney corner, and the onset of utter meaninglessness is imminent.

The symptoms of this ominous condition show up most clearly in the tertiary stage of 'controversial figure'. The most complicated specimen of this type of modern American is the man of unquestionable loyalty, distinguished public service, and outstanding ability and experience who has nonetheless 'lost his usefulness'. Actually, this victim of verbositosis has not lost his usefulness, his nation has lost it. It doesn't do the national psyche any good to realize that a man may be cut off in the full flower of his usefulness, on the ground that that is not what it is. I trust I have made the urgent need for psychosemanticists apparent, even though I have admittedly become contaminated in the process, and I doubt whether my own psychosemanticist, after treating me, will ever be able to turn to my wife and say cheerfully, 'Madam, your husband will write clearly again.'

Before visiting my hypothetical psychosemanticist for a brief imaginary interview, I feel that I should get something reassuring into this survey of depressing ailments of the tongue. We have, then, cured, or at least survived, various incipient mouth maladies in the past. There was a moment when 'globaloneyism', growing out of the Timethod of wordoggle, seemed likely to become epidemic, but it fortunately turned out to be no worse than a touch of pig Latin or a slight case of Knock, Knock, Who's There? Congress was not prepared to adopt the telescoping of words, which takes both time and ingenuity, and unless an expression becomes absorbed by Congressionalese, it has little chance of general survival. This brings me to what may easily be the direct cause of my being bundled off to the psychosemanticist's before long: the beating the word 'security' is taking in this great, scared land of ours. It is becoming paralysed. This is bound to occur to any forceful word when it loses its quality of affirmation and is employed exclusively in a connotation of fear, uncertainty, and suspicion. The most frequent use of 'security' (I hate to add to its shakiness with quotation marks, which have taken on a tone of mockery in our day) is in 'security risk', 'weakest link in our chain of security', and 'lulled into a false sense of security'. Precision of speech and meaning takes a small tossing around in the last of those three phrases. 'Lulled' is actually what happens to a nation after it has been argued, tricked, manoeuvred, reasoned, coaxed, cajoled, or jockeyed into a false sense of security, but the inflexibility that has descended upon us has ruled out the once noble search for the perfect word and the exact expression. What Eric Partridge calls 'a poverty of linguistic resource' is exemplified by the practically exclusive use of two verbs in any public-forum discussion of national security. It is threatened or it is bolstered; I never heard of its being supported, reinforced, fortified, buttressed, or shored up, and only very rarely is it menaced, endangered, or in jeopardy.

The word 'insecurity,' by the way, seems to have been taken over by the psychiatrists as their personal property. In politics, as in penology, 'security' itself has come to mean 'insecurity'. Take, for example, this sentence: 'He was considered a "maximum security" prisoner because of his police record and was never allowed out of his cell block.' Similarly, 'security data' means data of the kind calculated to scare the living daylights out of you, if not, indeed, your pants off. I could prove that 'maximum', in the case of the prisoner mentioned above, really means 'minimum', but I don't want to get us in so deep that we can't get out. The present confused usage of 'security' may have originated with the ancient Romans. Anyway, here is what Cassell's Latin Dictionary has to say about *securitas:* 'I. *freedom from care.* A. In a good sense, *peace of mind, quiet*, Cic. B. In a bad sense, *carelessness, indifference*, Tac. II. Transf., *freedom from danger, security*, Tac.'

A vital and restless breed of men, given to tapping our toes and drumming with our fingers, infatuated with every new crazy rhythm that rears its ugly beat, we have never truly loved harmony, the graceful structure of shapes and tones, and for this blindness and deafness we pay the awful price of continuous cacophony. It gets into language as well as music; we mug melody for the sake of sound effects, and the louder and more dissonant they are, the better we seem to like them. Our national veins have taken in the singing blood of Italy, Wales, Ireland, and Germany, but the transfusion has had no beneficial effect. Great big blocky words and phrases bumble off our tongues and presses every day. In four weeks of purposeful listening to the radio and reading the newspapers I have come up with a staggering list, full of sound and fury, dignifying nothing: 'automation', 'roadability', 'humature', 'motivational cognition' (this baby turned up in a series of travel lectures and was never defined), 'fractionalization', 'varietism', 'redesegregation', 'additive', 'concertization' (this means giving a concert in a hall, and is not to be confused with cinematization or televisionization). The colloquial deformity 'knowledgeable', which should have been clubbed to death years ago, when it first began crawling about like the late Lon Chaney, has gained new life in recent months. It is a dented derby of a word, often found in the scrawny company of such battered straw hats as 'do-gooder', 'know-how', 'update', 'uptake' (I recently uptook the iodine uptake test for thyroidism), and others so ugly and strange I can't decipher them in my notes. One of them looks like 'de-egghead', which would mean to disintellectualize or mentally emasculate – a crippling operation approved of by an alarming number of squash-heads, in Washington and elsewhere.

During my month of vigil and research, I heard an able physiologist who has a radio programme say, quite simply, 'We do not use up all the food we take in.' He wasn't allowed to get away with that piece of clarity, however. 'Ah,' cut in his announcer, for the benefit of those no longer able to understand simplicity, 'the utilization factor!' I turned from this station to a droning psychologist, just in time to hear him say, 'The female is sometimes the sexual aggressor.' Here a familiar noun of mental illness and military invasion was clumsily at work beating in the skull of love and a verbal bung-starter. The sweetheart now often wears the fustian of the sick man and the Caesar. In the evening, I tuned in on one of the space-patrol programmes that gleefully exude the great big blockyisms. 'Your astrogation bank will tell you!' cried the captain of a space ship to another interplanetary pilot, meaning his navigational instruments. In a fairy tale, an astrogation bank would be a 'star panel', but the quality of fairy tale is nowhere to be found in these dime novels of the constellations.

One Sunday morning, my head aching with 'kiss-close' and 'swivel-chair-it', meaning, I guess, 'at kissing distance' and 'maul it over in your executive brain', respectively, I stumbled upon a small radio station that had been captured by a man of God, ominous and squealful, who was begging his listeners to live on their knees, not as slaves but as supplicants. This particular fundamentalist, or maybe it is fundamentalitarian, had probably never heard of the great protest 'I would rather die on my feet than live on my knees.' But these yammering eschatologists, and many of there followers, have even less respect for the glory and grace of English than the unsaved politicians. 'Let us cease to sugar-coat, let us cease to whitewash, let us cease to bargain-counter the

Bible!' the speaker implored us. He finished second in vulgarity, I regret to say, to a reverend I had heard earlier in the year, who shouted, 'I didn't cook up this dish, God cooked it up. I'm just dishing it out to ye!' The line between holiness and blasphemy becomes even thinner when some of the lay testimonialists begin ranting. 'I own a shoe store in New Jersey,' one of them confessed, 'but Jesus Christ is my senior partner.'

A recent investigation of the worries and concerns of five thousand selected Americans revealed that we are preoccupied almost wholly with the personal and private, and are troubled only mildly by political anxieties, including the danger of war, the state of civil liberties, and the internal Communist threat. This does not come as a surprise to me, since the nature of our national concern about Communism is proved to be personal by such expressions as 'anti-anti-Communists' and 'anti-anti-anti-Communists'. The first actually means men who are against men who are against Communists, and the second, when you unravel it, means men who are against men who are against men who are against Communists. In these wonderful examples of our love of formidable elaborationisms, concept and doctrine are put aside, and personalities take their place. What we have left is pure personalism – a specific reactionary who is against a specific liberal who is against Senator Malone, let us say. The multiplicity of prefixes, another sign of linguistic poverty, was touched with a fine and healthful irony in Quincy Howe's invention of the phrase 'ex-ex-Communist'. (Many will claim that for their own, but Mr Howe got to it first.) One would think that Americans would be worried, or at least concerned, by a man who may have ceased to be a man who may have ceased to be a Communist, but the Worry Research I have mentioned shows that this isn't so. We are worried about health, family matters, and money, and we have no time for a man who may be lying about lying. Incidentally, a fairly new advertising slogan, 'The portable portable', fits neatly into modern jargon: the typewriter that you can carry that you can carry.

While I was exploring the decline of expression in America, I spent a week in a hospital. Medical science has done much for humanity, but not in the area of verbal communication. It should undergo a prefectomy, and have some of its prefixes taken out. I should like to see the 'semi' removed from 'semi-private', a dispiriting word that originated in hospitals; there must be a less depressing way of describing a room with two or more beds. I am also for taking the 'sub' out of 'sub-clinical', and starting all over again with the idea in mind of making the word mean something. Incidentally, I discovered at the hospital the difference between 'to be hospitalized' and 'to become hospitalized'. The first means to be placed in a hospital, and the second has two meanings: to get so that you can't stand it in the hospital any longer, and to like it so much there that you don't want to leave.

Lying in bed brooding over these matters, I turned on the radio and heard an American describe another American as 'an old-time A.D.A. type of anti-Jeffersonian radical' – a beautiful specimen of bumblery. Sir Winston Churchill, in the exhilarating years of his public life, turned out many phrases as sharp as stilettos – for one example, 'squalid gamin'. But you can count on your fingers the Americans, since the Thomas Paine of 'the summer soldier and the sunshine patriot', who have added bright, clear phrases to our language. If you can bumble an opponent to death why stab him seems to be the general feeling among our politicians, some of whom have got through the twelve years since the war ended with only five adjectives of derogation: naïve, hostile, unrealistic, complacent, and irresponsible. All these slither easily, if boggily, into bumblery, and the bumbler is spared the tedious exercising of his mental faculties.

The day I got dressed and was about to leave the hospital, I heard a nurse and an interne discussing a patient who had got something in his eye. 'It's a bad city to get something in your eye in,' the nurse said. 'Yes,' the interne agreed, 'but there isn't a better place to get something in your eye out in.' I rushed past them with my hair in my wild eyes, and left the hospital. It was high time, too.

When and if I find a reputable psychosemanticist, I want to take up with him something that happened to me one night more than two years ago. It may be the basis of my etymological or philological problems, if that's what they are – words, especially big ones, are beginning to lose their meaning for me. Anyway, I woke up one summer night, from a deep dream of peacelessness, only to realize that I had been startled by nothing whatever into a false sense of insecurity. I had a desperate feeling that I was being closed in on, that there was a menace in the woods behind my house or on the road in front of it, watchful, waiting, biding its time. A few weeks later I bought a ·38-calibre Smith & Wesson police revolver, which startled my wife into a genuine sense of insecurity. She hid the gun somewhere, and the cartridges somewhere else, and I still don't know where they are. I have often thought of telling my psychosemanticist about it, and I sometimes have the feeling that I did call on him and that the interview went like this:

'Doesn't your wife's hiding the gun worry you?' he asked.

'No,' I said.

'It would me,' he confessed.

'It would *what* you?' I demanded.

It seemed to disturb him. '*What* would what me?' he asked cautiously.

I suddenly couldn't think of a thing. I didn't even know what what was, but I had to say something, so I said something: 'Ill fares the land, to galloping fears a prey, where gobbledygook accumulates, and words decay.'

About two years ago a wistful attempt was made by some Washington bureau to straighten out the governmentalization of English. Directives were sent to the various departments demanding, among other things, the elimination of 'finalize'. It was as hopeless as asking a tiny child to drop its popsicle and bathe the St Bernard. Izationism is here to stay. It appeals to bureaucrats and congressmen because of its portentous polysyllabification. Politicians love it the way they love such expressions as 'legislativewise'. Lord Conesford, stout defender of the Queen's English, recently paraphrased Churchill's 'Give us the tools and we will finish the job' by Washingtonizing it like this: 'Supply us with the implements and we will finalize the solution of the matter.'

Webster's Unabridged, to my sorrow, recognizes such mastadonisms as 'psychologize' and 'physiologize' and, a prime favourite of congressmen, 'analogize'. It was, however, the physiologist I have already mentioned who classified those of us who are still up and about as 'the non-institutionalized'. This is a piece of bungalorum calculated to give even the healthiest men a sense of monolithic insecurity. 'Non' has an insidious way of creeping into izationisms. A piece of journalism was described on the air not long ago as 'absolutely non-fictionalized'. This negationization of what once could be described as verbal communication caused a Scot of my acquaintance to ask me, 'Have you nothing that is positively American? It seems to me that everything one hears about in America is un-American.' This abused and imprecise arrangement of letters seems bound to lose its proud A before long and to end up as 'Un-american'. President Eisenhower might well add to his imperatives the necessity to speak and write in such a way that we can be understood by the English-speaking peoples as well as the other races of a world that stands in grave need of clarity, accuracy, and sense.

The conspiracy of yammer and merchandising against literate speech reached a notorious height in 1956 with a singing commercial for a certain cigarette which we were told 'tastes good like a cigarette should'. I have one or two suggestions for the Madison Avenue illiterates in the grey flannel suits. The first is a slogan for a brewery: 'We still brew good like we used to could.' The second is an ad for some maker of tranquillizing drugs:

> Does he seldomly praise you any more? Those kind of husbands can be cured of the grumps with Hush-Up. So give you and he a break. Put Hush-Up in his food. It don't have no taste.

And now, for God's sake, let's go out and get a breath of fresh air.

It's Your Mother

I WAS listening to the radio the other day, alone in a hotel room, when a young woman began singing 'Come On Out, Edward, I Know You're in There', which may or may not be as depressing as 'Open the Door, Richard' of some years back. I don't know, because I hastily twisted the knob, hunting for normal human companionship, and found it on a five-minute programme on WOR called 'It's Your Baby'. The narrator of the programme, a man named Dan McCullough, was broadcasting helpful hints from young mothers, and I arrived just in time to learn about 'the thunder game'. This ingenious diversion, invented by the mother of a little girl, is intended to allay a baby's inherent fear of the loud noises accompanying electrical storms. 'When there was a clap of thunder,' narrated Mr McCullough, 'she [the mother] imitated it with her hands, crying "To-Roooomba!" Soon her child was doing the same, and instead of being afraid of thunder, looked forward to the next rumble.'

Always wary of the tendency of our time to oversimplify problems, especially where little girls are concerned, I began to pick flaws in the thunder game. I have never heard anyone imitate thunder very well, and I doubt if even Paul Douglas could bring it off, because there is a lot more to it than "To-Roooomba". In a first-rate electrical storm the lightning flash is usually followed by a tremendous splitting sound as if the house next door were being riven in two, and there is no way to imitate this unless Mama begins smashing the furniture. Babies are born with a love of destructiveness, to be sure, but they learn early to associate it with Daddy. Mother represents, as we all know, the Great Security, and there is always the danger, if she lets herself go in any kind of wild abandon, that Baby will begin to identify her with the powers of darkness.

I have had more experience with dogs in thunderstorms than with babies, but I have never owned one silly enough to be enticed into making sport of the growling monster of the menacing skies. My female French poodle, now going on fifteen, is as terrified of thunder as she was in 1941, and so, come to think of it, am I. She wedges herself under a bed when the rumbling starts, and if I went 'To-Roooomba!' and clapped my hands, she might never come out again. I made a couple of hasty mental notes on the thunder game, and went back to Mr McCullough. He was now describing another, much more involved pastime for mother and child. 'Then there was a mother whose baby would cry violently if she attempted to leave him at home while she went out,' said Mr McCullough. 'This is a fairly common baby fear. Baby thinks Mother, his closest link to security, will never return. This mother played the game of "bye-bye" with her baby. She left the room, and when Baby became fearful and was about to cry, she made her reappearance with a big smile. Doing this many times, with longer periods between leaving and coming back, made Baby realize that Mother would eventually return with a happy greeting for him, and his fears disappeared.'

Surely even the merriest baby must tire of a whole morning or afternoon of bye-byes and greetings, and the smarter tot might conceivably gain the disturbing impression that Mama's rocker is not as sound as it should be. This game reminds me of an old Joe Cook routine in which that famous comedian, dressed in white tie and tails, attempted to say good night to his butler before going out to some formal function. As I remember it, it went like this: 'Good night, Harkins,' 'Jolly times, Joe,' 'Jolly times, Harkins,' 'Good night, Joe,' 'Good night, Harkins,' 'Jolly times, Joe,' 'Jolly times, Harkins,' and on and on, in a memorable series of frustrated exists.

The bye-bye game has other faults, which might turn out to be not merely tedious but serious. Both mother and child might learn to like the period of separation better than the period of reunion, and this could give Mama ideas about the advantages of playing the game on a more adult, if not more mature, scale. I can see Alice, let us call her, suddenly saying 'Bye-bye' to her husband, George, during one of his political harangues in the living-room after dinner, and going upstairs, to be gone five minutes, and then ten, and then twenty. George, who loves to hear himself talk, gets more and more adjusted to these disappearances, and so, when she doesn't reappear at all to listen to his analysis of the 1960 quandary of the Democratic Party, he begins to realize that he doesn't actually need her. Upstairs, meanwhile, his spouse, having made a similar discovery, is quietly packing a bag. Of course, she is going to have to take Baby with her when she slips downstairs and out the back door, and this may not be as easy as it sounds, especially if Baby gets the idea that Mama wants to play the bye-bye game again. I am not a pediatrician or a child psychologist, but I should not recommend the bye-bye game or the thunder game to every mother and child. In the case of the latter game, it has suddenly occurred to me, Baby might quite naturally begin to believe that her parent was able to cause the jolly thunder at will, and I need not diagram the tearful dilemma that would follow the infant's cruel disenchantment. Let's face it, mothers: there *is* no dependable method of making life with Baby a heaven on earth.

Twenty years ago (to change the focus but not the subject), I knew the father of a two-year-old girl, knew him very well, and I vividly recall what happened to the poor chap when he was left alone with his daughter one evening and had to give her her supper and put her to bed. All she would eat was the ice-cream he had recklessly promised her for dessert, and his efforts to sell the yum-yum game to the little girl were disastrous and pitiable. He got himself full of whatever glop it was the child was supposed to eat, and his gorge set a new high as a result. The little girl was not only willing but delighted to let her father clean up the banana squush, or corn moisties, or whatever it was.

A worse ordeal was still ahead of the stricken fellow, who had never before tackled the formidable task of getting his small daughter into one of Dr Radway's magical one-piece sleepy-time nighties, or whatever the hell they were called. He still remembers unfastening something and beholding the garment fall to the carpet, where it lay like a great, complicated dead butterfly. 'Lie down on that,' he said to his daughter desperately. (He had once tried to put the tyre chains on his car by spreading them out on the roadway and trying to back into them, and the little girl may have remembered the consequences.) 'You don't do it that way,' she said scornfully. He broke down completely at this. 'Come on, for

God's sake,' he wailed, 'be a sport. Lie down on that thing.' She just stood there. Her father finally got her into one of his own clean shirts. It came down around her ankles and proved to be a great success and a wonderful solution of a knotty problem, although it must be admitted that the child's mother didn't think very highly of it. It also had what could be called a disturbing after-effect, for when the little girl got into her teens, she was more interested in wearing her father's shirts than any garments of her own. He sometimes accuses himself of having started this fad, for fad it has become, on a national scale. All teenage girls, I understand, would rather wear their fathers' shirts than the ones actually created for them by manufacturers. Why they insist on wearing them *outside* their blue jeans, nobody seems to know, but the fashion has the nation in its grip, and nothing can be done about it now.

'It's Your Baby', so far as I know, gets no helpful hints from fathers, but I shall pass one on to Mr McCullough for what it may be worth. I learned about it from a young mother who lives in Bermuda. In order to keep her little girl occupied for an hour or so around dawn, so that she could get a little more sleep herself, this parent hit on the idea of spreading twenty graham crackers, in five rows of four crackers each, in front of the child in its crib. In this way, the baby can have its game and eat it, too. A diet consisting, in part, of some seven thousand graham crackers a year does not seem to have had a bad effect on this baby, and the National Biscuit Company will probably love the idea of the cracker game.

Mr McCullough, to get back to our narrator, ended the programme I was listening to as follows: 'And this is Dan McCullough advising mothers never to lose their sense of humour; like the mother who was trying to make her stubborn child eat. She ran out of patience finally, and said, "Look, honey baby, eat. Make believe it's sand."' If your own baby prefers caterpillars to sand, or some other tidbits, such as buttons or small pieces of coal, these can, of course, be substituted. As simple as that, Mother.

Some of us senescent students of the domestic scene worry about Mama's plans to rid the infantile consciousness of even the most natural anxieties, the very roughage of mental diet, and replace them with fake and gaudy reassurances. We are afraid that America may become a nation of tranquillizationists, living in a fool's Euphoria, with an incantation for every sorrow, and a magic wand for every menace. Already we have multiple miracle pills for most of the darker states of mind, and if we don't look out, our children may reach the end of life by detour and bypass, quit of scars and tears, the badges and honours acquired by going through it the hard way.

It is better to let Junior and Baby learn that farewells are sometimes sad, and that thunder growls and doesn't chortle, and flashes a dagger and not a smile. It won't hurt Mama, either, to face the challenging difficulties of explaining the true nature of the perils that beset us. I am glad that I am only a husband, father, and grandfather, whose job it is to win the bread. At least I escape the far harder task of demonstrating that Santa Claus does not exist even though you can see him, and that the wolf at the door is real even though you can't see him.

Two o'clock at the Metropole

JUST a few minutes before two o'clock on the hot, sticky morning of Tuesday, 16 July 1912, a man sauntered up to a table in the café of the old Hotel Metropole on Forty-third Street near Broadway and spoke to another man who sat there. 'Somebody wants to see you outside, Herman,' he said. In that casual sentence was spoken the doom of the famous and flourishing Hotel Metropole; it closed its doors not long afterwards because of what happened in the next minute. The man at the table got up and walked briskly out on to the street, the other man following him. The one who had been addressed as Herman stood under the bright lights of the hotel's marquee, looking around for whoever it was wanted to see him. He didn't have to wait long. Four short dark men jumped out of a grey automobile standing at the kerb, closed in on him, and fired six shots. That was the end of Herman Rosenthal, the gambler, and the beginning of one of the most celebrated murder cases in our history. Two days before this happened, Rosenthal had become known to the reading public. The *World* had printed an affidavit of his on that day charging that a police lieutenant named Charles Becker had exacted 'protection money' from him and had then raided and closed his gambling house. It had also been intimated in the newspaper that Rosenthal would go before the grand jury and involve Becker even more deeply in corruption.

The murderers hadn't bothered to remove or obliterate the licence plates of the grey touring car, because, as it transpired later, they had been told that 'the cops are fixed' and nobody would do anything to them on account of their little job. But they reckoned without the *World*, District Attorney Charles S. Whitman, and a man named Charles Gallagher, a cabaret singer, who had just happened to be passing by. Gallagher caught the licence number of the car: 41313 N.Y. He went immediately to the West Forty-seventh Street police station, reported the number, and was instantly thrown in jail for his pains. His information might have been completely ignored (the police had licence numbers of their own to report, all of them wrong) had not a *World* reporter rung Whitman out of bed. The District Attorney got to the police station at three-twenty-five in the morning, learned about Gallagher, demanded his release, and got men to work on that licence number. Before dawn the driver of the grey car, a man named Shapiro, was arrested in his bed in a room near Washington Square. Shapiro told Whitman his car had been hired that night by a man known as Billiard Ball Jack Rose.

Born Jacob Rosenzweig, in Poland, Jack Rose, thirty-five years old, was known in certain circles as the slickest poker player in town and as graft collector for Lieutenant Becker, head of the Strong Arm Squad, which, among other things, 'looked after' gambling joints in the city. There were hundreds of such places. A very popular one, on the second floor of a building at the north-west corner of Forty-second Street and Sixth Avenue, was run by a suave gentleman called Bridgie Webber. Rosenthal's place was near by, at 140 West Forty-fifth Street. The Forties writhed with gambling joints running wide open. They all paid tribute to Charles Becker. His salary was only $2,200 a year, but it came out later that he had, in one-nine-month period, banked almost $60,000. All his graft money was collected for him by Baldy Jack Rose (he had several nicknames). Becker lived in a mansion of a house he had built on Olinville Avenue in the Bronx. It still stands there; Judge Peter Sheil lived in it until his death some years ago, and his widow died there last fall.

Two days after the assassination, Rose turned up at Police Headquarters, and the case's most unusual figure thus made his formal advent. Soft-spoken, a snappy dresser – his ties and shirts and socks always matched – Rose's physiognomy was not unlike that of Peter Lorre, in Lorre's more familiar make-up. Rose had not a hair on his head; even his eyebrows and eyelashes were gone, the result of typhoid in infancy. He admitted, lightly, that he had hired Shapiro's car; he had hired it to go uptown and visit a relative. He was put in a cell in the Tombs, where he was shortly joined by two other suspects, Bridgie Webber and another gambler named Harry Vallon. Webber had sent the widow

Rosenthal $50 to help toward the funeral of Herman. All three men protested their innocence; they all had alibis.

The Rosenthal murder case bloomed blackly on the front pages of all the papers. Here was a more exciting story than even the story of the *Titanic*, which had sunk three months before. Various curious characters began to come into the case, enlivening it. There was a tough gangster chief named Big Jack Zelig (it was at this time that the word 'gangster' was coined). There was a strange, blinking little man named Sam Schepps. One week after the murder, the harried Whitman, who was to become Governor because of his prosecution of this case, announced he would give immunity to anyone who named the 'real culprit'. Rose, Webber, and Vallon, all good poker players, knew when it was time to quit bluffing. They made prompt confessions. They charged that Lieutenant Becker had commissioned them to arrange the murder of Herman Rosenthal. They told who the actual killers were, the men for whom Rose had hired the car, and four unforgettable names were added to the annals of American crime: Lefty Louie, Gyp the Blood, Whitey Lewis, Dago Frank. We can dismiss briefly this infamous quartet, each of whom appears to have got $250, a big price at the time, for croaking Rosenthal. They were henchmen of the gang leader, Big Jack Zelig, who obeyed Becker but hated him. People were eager to hear a gangster chief testify, but they never got the chance; just as the case was about to come to trial Big Jack Zelig was found one day shot to death. So was the proprietor of a small café who had squealed on Dago Frank, the first of the four killers to be found and arrested. But Rose, Vallon, and Webber lived to testify; the District Attorney saw to it that they were carefully guarded. They lived in style in their cells. Lefty and Gyp and Whitey and the Dago were convicted in November 1912 and speedily sentenced to death, although they weren't executed until a year and a half later. It was Becker, and not the four gunmen, who most interested the public – and Whitman. The case against the big, suave policeman was harder to prove.

Becker's first trial took place three months after the murder. Billiard Ball Jack Rose, neatly dressed in a dark blue suit, his shoes brightly shined, was the State's star witness. He told the jury that Becker had said to him, 'Have Rosenthal murdered – cut his throat – dynamite him – anything!' Rose testified that Becker had advanced Rosenthal the money to open up his gambling house, had quarrelled with him, and finally raided the place. Rosenthal, unable to interest Whitman at the time, had taken his plaint to the *World.* Things looked black for Becker, but the testimony of the three gamblers who had turned State's evidence was, under the law, not enough to convict. There had to be a corroborating witness, somebody entirely outside the crime. It was here that Sam Schepps, a cocky little man peering through spectacles, was brought forward by the State. Rose had told about a remarkable meeting, held in a vacant lot far uptown in Harlem and attended by himself, Vallon, Webber, and Becker, at which, Rose said, the police lieutenant had commanded them to get rid of Rosenthal. Schepps, a kind of hanger-on and toady of the gamblers, had witnessed this meeting, it was claimed, but at a distance. He swore he had had no idea what the four men were talking about; he had merely seen them talking together. On this extraordinary evidence about an extraordinary conference, Becker was sentenced to death. His lawyers appealed. Sixteen months went by, and then the Court of Appeals rejected the decision of the lower court, attacking the reliability of Schepps's testimony, declaring that he was obviously an accomplice of the three gamblers.

On 6 May 1914, almost two years after Rosenthal's death, Becker went on trial again. At this trial a defence attorney turned on Rose and said, sharply, 'When you were planning this murder, where was your conscience?' Rose answered, agonizedly but promptly, 'My conscience was completely under the control of Becker.' That seems to have been the truth about Baldy Jack Rose. Like many another gambler, and many a gangster, he lived in abject fear of the cold, overbearing, and ruthless police lieutenant. It was dangerous to cross Becker; he had railroaded dozens of men who had. Becker's lawyers claimed the gamblers had killed Rosenthal on their own, afraid of what he might reveal about them. Nobody much believed this. At this second trial – presided over by the youngish Samuel Seabury – a new corroborating witness was somehow found, a man named James Marshall, a vaudeville actor. He testified he had seen the gamblers and the lieutenant talking in the vacant lot on the night in question. His testimony was accepted; the defence failed to break it down. Becker was sentenced to death again, and this time the higher court did not interfere. He was executed, a maundering, broken hulk, on 30 July 1915, a little more than three years after the slaying of Herman Rosenthal. Charles S. Whitman was then Governor of New York. He was considered criminally libelled by the inscription on a silver plate which Mrs Becker had placed upon her husband's coffin. It read:

CHARLES BECKER
Murdered 30 July 1915
by
GOVERNOR WHITMAN

The plate was removed by order of Inspector Joseph Faurot, and the police lieutenant's widow replaced it with one bearing only his name and the dates of his birth and death. The *Lusitania* had been sunk two months earlier, and the memory of Becker was soon lost in the files of newspapers preoccupied with headlines of war.

Whitman, after retiring from politics, returned to the practice of law. He died of a heart attack in 1947, at the age of seventy-eight. Sam Schepps and Bridgie Webber died more than twenty years ago. What happened to James Marshall, the vaudeville actor, and to Charles Gallagher, the carbaret singer, it would be hard to find out. Webber, after the trials, went to live in New Jersey. He became, finally, vice president and secretary of the Garfield Paper Box Company of Passaic. He had lived in Fair Lawn, New Jersey, and worked in Passaic for twenty years as William Webber, a man without a past, until, in 1933, he appeared as a witness in a trial over there. A lawyer asked him on the stand if he was not the Bridgie Webber of the Rosenthal case. He admitted that he was. It seems to have made little difference to his friends and business associates. He died on 30 July 1936. There may have been some, reading of his end, who found ironic significance in the fact that Charles Becker also died on 30 July, twenty-one years before.

Jack Rose did not withdraw from the view of men after the files of the Rosenthal-Becker case were closed. He preferred to be called simply Jack, and discouraged the use of the nicknames that had made him notorious, but he did not sulk in the shadows of life or attempt to disguise himself. He wore a cap to cover his baldness, but scorned the use of a toupee. He came boldly out into the open during the war years, and went from camp to camp lecturing soldiers on the evils of gambling and other vices. He lived in a fourteen-room house in a quiet suburban community with his wife and two sons, and when he wasn't lecturing on 'Humanology', which he said meant the science of being human, he exhorted the children of his neighbourhood to lead clean lives, and told them how he had ended up in reform school as a bad boy, where he first made contact with the underworld. He acquired a Chautauqua air, and the ardent platform manner of a reformer. His Humanology Motion Picture Corporation, founded in 1915, ended in failure two years later, but not until after he had produced six pixtures based on the poems of his idol and friend, Ella Wheeler Wilcox. He liked to display a jewelled ring he wore, which Mrs Wilcox had left him in her will. 'She got the ring from an Indian rajah she met on this world tour,' he said, proudly.

Jack Rose was an able and energetic businessman, and Humanology Pictures, more an expiation than an enterprise, was one of his few failures. Before he came to New York in the Becker régime, he had had a varied career in Connecticut. He ran a hotel in Bridgeport for a while, promoted prizefights in Hartford, managed the Danbury baseball team, and became part owner of the Norwich baseball team, gambling and playing the races on the side. Rose never had any trouble getting financial backing. His principal and most successful business venture after the trials was the establishment of a chain of roadside restaurants between Milford, Connecticut, and Lynbrook, Long Island. The restaurants were large and impressive and well run. 'The largest one seats 248 persons and can serve 3000 meals a day,' he liked to boast. He supervised the planning of sunken gardens, and planned a twelve-piece orchestra for his favourite unit in the chain. Most of his customers didn't know who he was, and he was satisfied with that. He never brought up his past except in his talks to the soldiers and the children. If a reporter called on him, as one did occasionally for a Sunday feature story, he was not evasive, but answered questions directly. What he mostly wanted to talk about, though, was some new gadget he was installing, such as a hamburger machine, which he liked to show off to visitors. He rarely came to New York and, when he did, avoided his old haunts, and made his headquarters at the uptown millinery shop of a relative. If anybody recognized him and wanted to talk, he would talk. Billiard Ball Jack Rose's adjustment to life was never achieved by the manager of one of his restaurants, Harry Vallon. Vallon and his wife lived obscurely, refused to talk about themselves, and would hastily disappear if the subject came up. Once when Vallon dropped in on Jack at the main restaurant, he was introduced to a New York reporter. He turned on his heel without a word, hurried out to his car, and drove away.

Jack Rose died 4 October 1947 at the age of seventy-two, a few months after the death of Whitman. Nobody knows what became of Harry Vallon. The files of the *Times*, the *Herald Tribune*, and the Associated Press contain no mention of Vallon after the middle thirties. The Police Department has no record of him, either, since that time. If alive, he would be in his eighties, but it is likely that he died obscurely, possibly under an assumed name, where and when nobody may ever find out.

John's Chop House, which had occupied the site of Rosenthal's place at 104 West Forty-fifth Street, is no longer standing. The Sixth Avenue Urban Garage, Inc., completed on 15 November 1955, is located at 104 now. Nobody there ever heard about the notorious gambling house, or of the gambler who became one of the most celebrated figures in the annals of New York crime.

Get thee to a monastery

'TONIGHT we shall discuss the demasculinization of the theatre of our time,' said Dr Bach, 'with a gloomy glance at the near future, when the stage will have become completely womanized.' Dr Bach was an obdurate selector of themes for discussion, and hc did his selecting with a pontifical air of authority and finality. We were sitting, this particular night, on the lawn of a guesthouse in Bermuda, where we had come, he from Boston and I from New York, to get away from television. I never found out what Dr Bach was a doctor of, because he never gave me the chance to ask. He was a man in his late sixties, possibly a retired professor of philosophy, fond of dressing for dinner in a white dinner jacket and of sitting around until midnight over brandy and cigars, selecting subjects of conversation and pulling them apart until all the petals were gone and nothing was left but the stem. I had the feeling of listening to lectures rather than of taking part in post-prandial exchanges of opinion, and Dr Bach's allusions to 'our little talks' were something in the nature of a distortion of our summer evenings in the Fairy Isles.

'I overheard the young lady on your left at dinner,' said Dr Bach, 'remarking that she had seen the original company of *The Male Animal* with Gene Tierney. Now, you and your collaborator, subconsciously aware fourteen years ago of the imminent feminization of Broadway, not only selected an aggressively masculine title for your comedy but actually filled the play with obtrusively male characters and only a hint of females, rather sketchily and ineptly drawn.' I squirmed a little in my chair, but seeing that I was about to speak, Dr Bach raised his hand for silence and went on. 'In spite of your manly efforts on behalf of the dramaturgic survival of your sex, we observe that your little farce will be remembered, if it is remembered, as a 1940 vehicle for Miss Gene Tierney. Edmund Kean, of course, would have strangled the young lady at your table. I refrain from describing what he might have done to Miss Tierney, had he played in support of her in your little comedy as Professor Jimmy Turner.'

I did get in a word at this point. I said, 'Tommy.'

Dr Bach held up his hand again. 'Kean is only a fading memory now,' he said, 'like Lemaître and the last of the great male actors, John Barrymore. You will think I have not heard of Brasseur, the violently energetic French actor who recently revived the male in the Continental theatre, but I remind you that he was playing Edmund Kean in the new version of Alexandre Dumas's melodrama about that great Englishman. In a word, his was but a momentary backward glance at an ancient hurricane long since blown over, a phenomenon of fad, full of sound and fury, signifying nothing. The vigorous Brasseur will have been forgotten long before the ladies have ceased to babble about the public disturbance created by Miss Katharine Hepburn in Shaw's *The Millionairess*.' Dr Bach settled back in his chair, sipped his brandy, and gave his cigar a flourish. The overture had ended and he was about to raise the curtain on the play of his present argument.

'It is true,' said Dr Bach, 'that the Broadway critics, during recent seasons, have written of actresses as if they were superhuman geniuses, at once golden and edible, ineffable and endlessly describable, impalpable and all over the place, in the manner of men who had never seen a woman before, let alone a play. But we must seek further back for the true causes of the disease that I can only call Actressissima. The fault lies, ironically enough, with the male playwrights, who have women-chanted the modern theatre. They have all been specialists in the de-masculinization of the stage. Let me tick off a few, at random.'

I could tell by his expression that he was not going to tick off anything at random but recite something he had rehearsed ever since he had eavesdropped on the young lady at my table. 'Ibsen explores the condition of Woman,' he said, waving his cigar at an imaginary enrapt audience of scholars. 'Shaw exposes the nature of women, Barrie exalts the virtues of ladies, Maugham exhibits the vices of females, Barry exploits the talents of actresses.'

It seemed so pat and studied that I cut in rather sharply, hoping to throw him off balance, with 'How about Williams?'

He aimed his cigar at me as if it were a pistol. 'Let us not discuss baseball,' he said testily. 'I detest baseball.'

I sipped my brandy and said, 'I mean Tennessee Williams.'

He realized that he had to deal with it, and he dealt with it, I think, rather neatly, considering the fact that not every verb begins with 'ex'. He said, 'Williams exhumes the dead dreams of the weaker sex.'

I let my companion dangle in what was for him an unusually long silence – perhaps a dozen seconds, during which I suppose he was trying to fit Chehov and O'Neill into his tidy game of definition. 'It seems to me,' I began finally, 'that – '

'Not at all,' he said abruptly. 'I have been considering the staggering price the male playwrights may have to pay, in the end, for their preoccupation with various phases of the female. Their names are likely, unless I am greatly mistaken, to become entirely forgotten, and this is intolerable to the masculine ego. Something will have to give, probably the masculine ego, and we shall be reduced to the stature of chipmunks. Even now, many a person who knows who played Hedda Gabler does not know who wrote it. I chanced to be in the lobby of the theatre between acts during Blanche Yurka's production of *Hedda*, and I overheard two distinguished New York critics discussing the play, if you could call it discussing the play. "She isn't Emily Stevens," said one of them. The other thought a moment and said, "No, she isn't Emily Stevens." Now, the criticism of a drama in terms of who the actress playing the title role *wasn't* should have stood out for me as a clear portent of what was to come. To be sure, there had been many earlier warning signs, most of them undoubtedly familiar to you: the practice, or convention, of changing Peter Pan into a girl onstage, to say nothing of making a female out of Jim Hawkins in *Treasure Island* and, eminently, the fact that the most aggressively virile of all creatures, the barnyard cock, is forever identified with the gentlest of virgin actresses.'

I decided it was my turn to wedge in a sentence or two. 'Men are more interesting than women,' I said, 'but women are indubitably more fascinating, and possibly more amusing. This may account for the playwrights' immemorial dedication to an examination of the opposite sex.'

'You are missing the point,' said Dr Bach sharply. 'The absorption of male playwrights with the female is merely a further evidence of their blatant ego. They believe that only the masculine mind is capable of comprehending the intricacies of the feminine nature and of presenting to the world Woman's despair and eventual doom. It is a fine piece of irony that, in so reasoning, the playwrights have succeeded in writing their own doom.' He finished his brandy and set down the glass on the table that stood between us. I splashed more brandy into it, and now that I had got my foot in the door of the discussion I found something else to say. 'There can be no doubt – ' I began, but he waved it aside with his cigar. 'You used the word "immemorial" rather loosely,' he said. 'There was a long time, an epoch even, during which the male character and actor properly dominated our theatre. I refer to the era of the matinee idol, a term that aptly represents the decline of such giants as the ones I have already mentioned. I remember when the actress was kept sternly in her place. I remember David Warfield in *The Music Master*, Otis Skinner in *Mister Antonio*, William Hodge in *The Man from Home*, Henry Miller in *The Great Divide*, William Faversham in *The Squaw Man*, H. B. Warner in *Alias Jimmy Valentine*, John Drew in *Rosemary*, Robert Edeson in *Strongheart*, Dustin Farnum in *Cameo Kirby*, Maclyn Arbuckle in *The Round Up*, Douglas Fairbanks in *Hawthorne of the U.S.A.*, and even, God save my soul, Cyril Scott in *The Prince Chap*, and Guy Bates Post in *Omar, the Tent Maker*. The male persisted even into the nineteen-twenties. There was Robert Ames in *The Hero*, Frank Craven in *The First Year*, Harry Beresford in *The Old Soak*, and a few others, including a young friend of yours in *The Poor Nut*. Who remembers, for example, the name of the lady who played opposite Glenn Hunter in *Merton of the Movies*?'

I had him there and moved in quickly. 'I do,' I told him. 'Florence Nash.'

He almost dropped his cigar, and then became absorbed in a long study of the brandy in his glass.

'You left out some old classics,' I reminded him. 'The gentlemen who figured so prominently in *Secret Service*, *The Passing of the Third Floor Back*, *The Servant of the House*, and, of course,

Cyrano de Bergerac. There was also, later on, Joseph Schildkraut in *Liliom*.'

He turned ponderously in his chair and gave me a cold stare. 'It was Eva Le Gallienne in *Liliom*,' he objected. 'I was coming to her. The twenties marked the beginning of the end of men in the theatre. Consider the body blows they had to endure at the time: the Kikis, the Lulu Belles, the Miss Lulu Betts, the Saint Joans, the Mother Goddams, and the Miss Thompsons. This is a casual conversation we are having, not a precise calendar. It may be that man's day upon our stage began to bleed to death when the Reverend Davidson cut his throat on Pago Pago.'

We sat in silence for a long moment, contemplating the bleeding to death of the theatrical male. 'We have skipped a little lightly over William Gillette,' I put in.

He took a long drink of brandy this time, glanced at me as if I wasn't there, and observed, 'William Gillette as an actor died in *Dear Brutus* at the hands of an eighteen-year-old snippet named Helen Hayes.'

I thought he was going a bit too far, but I didn't say anything. His face took on a faint shade of uneasiness, and as I watched him, I wondered if his agile memory had suddenly stumbled upon the gallant stands put up by the embattled Male in *What Price Glory?*, *Journey's End*, and *The Front Page*. If he had disinterred these brave members of a vanishing sex, he said nothing about it, and I let the plays pass without mention.

'Man's interest in Woman,' I began, catching my companion's pontifical note, 'is superficial and momentary at best. I have been thinking about a discussion I had with half a dozen gentlemen some twenty years ago in a place called Tony's. Someone had posed the question "With what person, alive or dead, would you like to spend your last evening on earth?" Only one man present chose a woman. All the others selected men, for the dangers they had known, or the shut-outs they had pitched, or for the things they had written, composed, invented, discovered, or got away with. I recall that Mike Romanoff selected Oswald Spengler, possibly preferring intellectual stimulation at the end, however dismal, to spiritual comfort, and that a moody Irishman, up to his ears in rye, simply said, "Old Overholt," and closed his eyes.

Someone, I believe, said he would like to pass his final hours in the company of the captain of the *Mary Celeste* to find out, as he put it, what the hell happened.'

Dr Bach looked at me with a faint sign of interest.

'Who selected the woman?' he asked.

I suppose I blushed a bit. 'I did,' I told him. 'Raquel Meller.'

Dr Bach gave a small start, as if I had thrown something at him. 'Let us keep this discussion out of the realm of emotional involvement,' he suggested.

'I never met the lady,' I said a little stiffly. He had a comment for that, as he had for everything. 'Let us not get into the unattainable,' he commanded. 'Men have got into the unattainable and never returned.'

It was fun to embarrass my friend. 'I was also in love with Irene Fenwick and Marie Doro,' I said. 'They were both unattainable. None the less, I managed somehow to find my way back.' He treated all this with a heavy cold silence, tossed away his cigar, and brought out a fresh one. I held out my lighter and clicked it several times, but it wouldn't work. He found a match and a new tangent.

'A sensitive ex-lieutenant of police with whom I was at Harvard,' he began, 'persuaded me to accompany him not long ago to a performance of something called *Gigi*, an Americanized French bibelot from which all the Gallic essences were strained, so that what I endured for two hours and a half seemed like some overlaboured preparation for a junior prom. I had been informed that the star, an English child, possessed a new and undreamed-of something or other. Since I had decided that this miraculous gift was probably some kind of visual illusion, I sat through the piece with my eyes closed. In the play, the young girl romps with a man of the world, and during this scene, I was later told, love suddenly came to them both. Now, I have lived in France, and I am deeply aware that love in that realistic nation is not an accidental by-product of rumpus. Since I couldn't see what was going on, nothing whatever came across the footlights to me except the sounds of romp, and there's enough of that in real life to satisfy me. During a curious ten-second silence, representing the holy stillness of dawning perpetual rapture, I was about to shout "Get on with it!"

when my intuitive companion arrested me. I was in bed and asleep by eleven-twenty that night, the ineluctable magic of the little girl having eluded me completely. She is, I understand, the greatest of the Hepburns, as Shirley Booth is the greatest of the Booths.' He took, for the first time, a dollop instead of a sip of his brandy.

'Miss Booth comes across the footlights to me,' I said defensively, 'by a kind of magic I have never encountered in any other actress. She could play anyone from Snow White to Mrs Grover Cleveland.'

'Pish,' said Dr Bach. 'The damnation has descended upon you. You have caught the sickness of our age. I can see the female *Zeitgeist* hovering about your head and whispering in your ear. You stand in peril, sir, of becoming one of those writers who serve as literary eunuchs at the courts of the Misses Ethel Merman and Judy Holliday. It makes no difference, the critics say, what is written for them or who writes it. The ladies turn even the most senescent drivel into their peculiar jewels and gold, we are solemnly informed. Would God that Joseph Jefferson were still alive, or Mansfield, or even Nat Goodwin! I sat there at *Gigi* praying for the entrance of Ed Wynn or W. C. Fields with his kadoola-kadoola, but I have apparently not deserved these blessings even from the generous and merciful God that we all know is concerned with our every distress.' The tree toads across Pomander Road occupied the moment with their melancholy warnings.

'You find women less bearable than I do,' I observed at last. 'What I mean to say is that the element of personal taste enters into everything, with its magnifying glass and its automatic simplifier.' I was beginning to feel the brandy all right. 'I confess there was not a single moment,' I went on, 'when I cared what happened to Sabrina Fair, but on the other hand, I still wake up at night hoping that little Sheba will come back.'

'Posh,' said Dr Bach. 'You are talking like a dogman, not a calm, disinterested critic of the ladies of the theatre. Calmness and disinterestedness have, of course, disappeared almost without a trace. Now that every play is either a dismal failure or what is called, I believe, a smasherino, a theatrical exhibit is either "terrible" or "sublime". Humour is seeping out of critical appraisal, too. No longer is there a reviewer capable of saying that such-and-such a female performer tears a passion to titters.'

'Tatters,' I corrected him.

'Titters,' he insisted. It was obviously a gag that he enjoyed, and I paid it the tribute of a short laugh. He finished his brandy and sighed and put the glass down again, but waved the bottle away when I picked it up. 'Now that the New York critics have reached the top of Mount Everest,' he said sourly, 'having scaled Mount Fulsome with a mighty burst of rhetoric, to reach Summa Cum Laude at last, from where the tiny tattered banners of Bernhardt and Réjane may be seen faintly waving far below the bright and deathless colours of Miss Audrey Hepburn, we may perhaps hope for some kind of respite and repose, since there is no longer any place to go but down. Unless, of course, another English or French or perhaps Portuguese young woman appears suddenly from the regions which are holy land. Leaving aside the ecstasies of Poe and the excesses of Andrew Marvell, there has been nothing in all the range of my reading to compare with the critical exaltation of the Misses Booth, Hepburn, Jeanmaire, and Rosalind Russell since the late Joseph Hergesheimer, in an old issue of the *American Mercury*, compared the charms of the April moon unfavourably with those of Miss Lillian Gish.' He gave brooding attention to the glowing end of his cigar. The tree toads filled the interval with their mournful chant of 'Sweet, sweet, sweet.'

'What about the future?' I asked finally. 'You were going to take a gloomy glance at the future of the theatre.'

Dr Bach made a little gesture of annoyance. 'The future's dark indeed, sir,' he said. 'There will always be, I suppose, revivals of Shakespeare, mostly *As You Like It* whenever a new lady genius of unique magic and lovely legs comes out of Surrey or Marseille or Des Moines to send the transfigured critics to their eager and abused typewriters, but the great tragedies of the Bard, the wondrous kings and princes, the Falstaffs and Hamlets, have probably already strutted their final hour upon the boards. I have no doubt that the young lady at your table could tell you the name of the Cordelia who was so ably supported in the most recent production of *Lear* by Mr Louis Calhern. Our young admirer of the histrionic talents of Miss Tierney could never have seen Wolheim and Boyd in the Anderson-Stallings classic, but her mother has surely told her the name of the actress who dominated the play in the role of

Charmaine.' He was labouring his point now, but I decided to let him have a free rein, and he had it. 'I am thinking,' he said, 'of what the future playwrights, probably lady playwrights, will do to *Macbeth* or *The Tragedy of Lady Macbeth* in ten years to come, when they rewrite it to make room for the actresses of tomorrow. King Duncan, in this feminized version, will have a queen, thus affording a part for some new Judith Anderson or Tallulah Bankhead who is now in her teens somewhere in Connecticut or New Jersey. I can hear her saying to Duncan, as he twitters of swallows and St Martin's summer, "Thinkst thou I would let thee spend the night in these damp and hollow corridors alone with this crown-crazy twain?" Fleance will become Florence, a change of sex which would admittedly account for this character's now dubious escape from the assassins.' He tossed away his cigar and watched it expire in the damp night grass.

I felt myself dozing and cut in on his gloomy prefigurings in order to stay awake. 'Perhaps it will be Lady Banquo and not Banquo,' I suggested, 'who appears to Macbeth in the famous banquet scene. After all, "Never shake thy gory locks at me" has always sounded to me like a line addressed to a female; otherwise it would surely be "Never shake thy gory beard at me." I have always doubted that a staunch Scotsman in a crowded and well lighted hall would get the chattering jitters at sight of a dead man, but the apparition of a dead and bloody lady is something else again.'

I poured myself more brandy, and he held out his glass impatiently. 'Let us not – ' he began, but I interrupted him. I felt it was my turn. 'Then there is that duel between Macbeth and Macduff,' I said. 'I have always felt that "Macduff was from his mother's womb untimely ripped" is completely out of place in a mortal combat with broad-swords fought by two powerfully built medieval warriors. Such men would surely not discuss a Caesarean section at a moment like that. Lady Macduff and Lady Macbeth, on the other hand, scratching and pulling hair, would give the line verisimilitude.'

He gulped his brandy and said irritably, 'We have had too much to drink.' He stood up. I was about to say something in conclusion, but realized I would have to let him have the last word. '*Macbeth* is a rough-and-tumble mystery show, suitable for the kiddies and for television. The king should be played as if he were afraid someone was about to play Sam Spade. No one in his right senses, man or woman, would kill a king in a bedroom. The place to kill a king is on a heath. You can blame it on witches or the weather, or a horse with a loose shoe. It is the *Hamlet* of the future that mainly concerns and disturbs me. Some little doxy from Holland, who has run up like a weed overnight in the grandeur and glory of transcendent ability, will insist that the immortal drama be revised in order to build up the part of Ophelia at the expense of the mighty periods of the forlorn prince.' We began to cross the lawn slowly, toward the welcoming arms leading up to the porch of the guest-house. At the foot of the steps, he turned and gazed at me. 'I can see from here where the change will begin,' he said. 'When Hamlet says to the deranged idiot, "Get thee to a nunnery," the magic little Dutch girl will turn upon him and cry, "Get *thee* to a monastery," and he will exit, flinging roses, and blowing the time upon dandelion clocks.' He had mercifully not heard, I felt sure, about Siobhan McKenna and the strange story of her desire to play the Prince of Denmark. I did not tell him, for fear that he might have a fatal stroke, upon the spot.

He stood a moment, motionless and wordless; then he said, 'The rest in silex,' and began a tremulous ascent of the curving steps. In the hall inside we shook hands, an inevitable part of our nightly ritual, to go our separate ways to bed.

'Good night, sweet Prince,' I said, 'and flights of angels sing thee to thy rest!'

He turned on me and glowered. 'I shall not sleep,' he said pettishly. 'I propose to proceed to the kitchen and brew myself a large pot of strong coffee.'

I gave his apt pleasantry of a moment before, about the silex, a belated but appreciative tribute of laughter. He bowed slightly and murmured something I didn't catch. 'How about tomorrow night?' I asked.

'Tomorrow night,' he said over his shoulder as he walked toward the rickety old stairs leading to the first floor and the kitchen, 'our little talk shall deal with the appalling decline in our time of something or other, I haven't decided what.' I reached the door of my bedroom and opened it. He stood for a moment at the top of the steps, his back toward me. 'Snippets!' he said, as if to himself. 'Moppets!' He descended slowly and cautiously the steep staircase that had been built more than three hundred years before Audrey Hepburn was born. I heard the kitchen door closing behind him.

A holiday ramble

Now that the reflective years are upon me, I spend considerable time in my study chair, and the avenues and byways of meditation take me into curious but familiar places, inhabited by all kinds of persons, from the immortal to the forgotten. One of the forgotten, except by a few historians and other scholars, and me, is Colonel Thomas Hamilton, of His Britannic Majesty's armed forces. Thomas Hamilton visited the young United States in the early eighteen-thirties and went back to England to write a book about our ancestors, entitled *Men and Manners in America.* It seems to me that *Americans Have No Manners* would have been a more apt title for the Colonel's book, which was first published in 1833, just one year after Mrs Trollope's famous attack on our flaws and foibles and females. It was, as literary historians know, an era of thrust and parry across the Atlantic, and the English had the best of it until Nathaniel Hawthorne slashed back at them with his *Our Old Home*, in the eighteen-sixties. Colonel Hamilton was not only more fastidious than the other social critics on either side, he also had the queasiest stomach, and the year he spent among us could well be described as perfectly dreadful. He was repelled by almost everything he saw and heard, from the way Americans 'drink' boiled eggs to the grammar and the personal habits of President Andrew Jackson, a soldier whose fame is likely to outlive the Colonel's by a good ten thousand years, if there is that much planetary time left.

I looked up the Colonel's book in my library the other day and found it buried between *Sybil's Garden of Pleasant Beasts* and Francis Winthrop Palfrey's *The Antietam and Fredericksburg*. (I've got to get at that shelf one of these days and separate the blood from the fantasy.) I began rereading some passages I had indignantly marked in the Hamilton book nearly twenty years ago. My copy of *Men and Manners* is a later edition, published in 1843, and in it Hamilton really let himself go. In telling about the first of a couple of informal calls he made at the President's home.

the British officer wrote, 'He chews tobacco, and kept rolling an enormous quid about in his mouth. He makes sad mistakes, too, in grammar, and asked me about my servitude in the army. The house was dirty, and gave you the impression of a large, ill-furnished, and ill-kept hotel.' Of his second visit (I don't know why he kept going back) the Colonel wrote, 'The conversation for the first quarter of an hour was about the state of his bowels, the failure of calomel, the success of salts.' The Colonel also had ungallant things to say about American ladies and about what he regarded as the slovenly carriage of our West Point cadets, and he took a few stabs at our politicians and statesmen. He was appalled by attacks on their character in the public prints. 'The candidate for Congress or the Presidency is broadly asserted to have picked pockets or pocketed silver spoons,' the Colonel wrote. I think it was in 1940 that I encountered a repercussion of this statement in, of all places, one of Ralph Waldo Emerson's essays. The American poet and philosopher in this essay tells about calling on William Wordsworth in the summer of 1833, or just about the time the Colonel's book was being talked about in England. Here is what Wordsworth told his visitor: 'My friend Colonel Hamilton, at the foot of the hill, who was a year in America, assures me that the newspapers are atrocious, and accuse members of Congress of stealing spoons.' This constitutes the only piece of nineteenth-century literary research I have ever done, and if I have gone considerably out of my way to get it in, I trust that I shall be forgiven.

The great poet's friend and neighbour who lived at the foot of the hill, among the trodden ways, so long ago, happened to be in New York City during the celebration of Evacuation Day, more than a hundred and twenty years ago. This holiday, now as forgotten as the mocking Colonel's satire, celebrated, 'in profuse and patriotic jollification', the departure of the British Army at the end of the Revolutionary War. Evacuation Day was first celebrated in 1783, and the jubilation began with the official raising of the American flag at the Battery, where once the British colours had boldly flown. This ritual was continued every year until 1847. By that time, the tumult and the shouting had long since died down and the significance of the occasion was growing dim. Besides, the chill of late November in the city must have taken the edge off an outdoor show of patriotic fervour as the decades rolled by. Furthermore, the flag that had been raised at the Battery for so many years got burned, I don't know how, and this seems to have formed a good excuse for summer soldiers and sunshine patriots to stay home and drink their rum or Madeira in front of the fireplace. Those two beverages, as you shall see, symbolized for Colonel Hamilton labour and the leisure class. The celebration he witnessed was a kind of double feature, and I'll let the Colonel take it from there. 'On the present occasion,' he wrote, 'it was determined, in addition to the ordinary cause of rejoicing, to get up a pageant of unusual splendour, in honour of the late revolution in France. This revolution, I was informed, originated exclusively in the operative class, or *workies*, as they call themselves, in contradistinction to those who live in better houses, eat better dinners, read novels and poetry, and drink old Madeira instead of Yankee rum. The latter and more enviable class, however, having been taught caution by experience, were generally disposed to consider the present congratulatory celebration as somewhat premature. Finding, however, that it could not be prevented, they prudently gave in, and determined to take part in the pageant.' (Karl Marx was about fifteen years old when the Colonel's book came out, and I don't suppose he ever read it; if he had, the term 'workies' might have given him a stroke and saved the world most of the hell it is going through now.)

Our dashing Colonel, who was the author of a novel called *Cyril Thornton*, fancied himself as a colorist in prose, and he did noisy justice to the Evacuation Day parade, even dropping in a little Greek, which I mercifully omit from his description: 'At length the sound of distant music reached the ear; the thunder of the drum, the contralto of the fife, the loud clash of cymbals, and, first and furthest heard, the spirit-stirring notes of the trumpet. . . . On they came, a glorious cavalcade, making heaven vocal with sound of triumph, and earth beautiful with such colouring as nature never scattered from her pictured urn. And first appeared, gorgeously caparisoned, a gallant steed bestrode by a cavalier, whose high and martial bearing bespoke him the hero of a hundred fights. . . .' There is a great deal more of this, but let us turn for a moment to another writer's comments on the long lost holiday.

The late George Templeton Strong was one of many old Madeira drinkers, or non-workies, who deplored the passing of Evacuation Day. His diary sorrowfully traces its decline. In 1835, he made this entry: 'Glorious Evacuation Day . . . it allows us to kick up our heels all day at our leisure.' Clearly, the jugs were still being brought out, more than fifty years after the first flag-raising ceremony. On 23 November 1836, Mr Strong yelped, 'Diabolical outrage! They are not going to give us Evacuation Day – horrible! We shall have to take it!' Six years later, in 1842, he wrote, 'It a'nt the Evacuation Day of ten years ago – its glories have departed and nobody thinks about it now.'

Many a regional holiday, I have no doubt, has bloomed and gone to seed in America, leaving only a faint trace in the pages of old diaries and almanacs. Repudiation Day, for example, was once a time of riotous carryings-on in Frederick, Maryland, and the surrounding county. On 23 November 1765, about eight years before Barbara Frietchie was born, that proud and valiant county was the first to repudiate the British Stamp Act, levied by England under King George III. I don't know how long this great day was wildly celebrated, but it is probable that the hell-raising, in its hey-day, outdid the noise of Evacuation Day farther north, for New York celebrated a departure, but Maryland remembered an injustice. (Thanksgiving would have joined these two dead holidays in 1859 if the aldermen of Washington, D.C., had had their way. They voted, seven to five, to abandon the Day on the ground that it promoted 'drunkenness and disorder', and had been established by 'New England people' and, the insinuation was, you know how *they* are.)

The Stamp Act the Marylanders couldn't abide placed a tax of one shilling on every pack of playing cards and ten shillings on every pair of dice. No American could long tolerate any such tampering with his games of chance or skill. The Repudiation Act roared that 'all proceedings shall be valid and effectual without the use of stamps.' After that, a gentleman was on his own, and what he did with cards or dice was no affair of the royal government. What the American Housewife did about tax-free gambling was a private matter, and history has not recorded it. There were surely only a few doxies in the colonies who played cards for profit, and probably none at all addicted to dice. It is different today, and has been ever since the Girl of the Golden West cheated the sheriff at poker and won the life of her lover. Once I played cards with my wife at a café in France. The proprietor wandered over to our table and asked if he could examine the ace of clubs. I picked it out of my wife's full house, with which she had just beat my two pair, and let him see it. He handed it back, bowed, smiled graciously, begged a thousand pardons, and went away. We looked at the ace of clubs together. It bore a stamp showing that the French tax on playing cards had been paid – without rioting in the streets, the deposing of a cabinet, or the firing of a single shot. *Par exemple!*

Here I am, somewhat to my own surprise, in modern France, after starting from New York in 1783, but this is a casual journey, and we shall now visit Ohio momentarily on our way toward the future. They used to celebrate the birthday of President McKinley out there, on 29 January, and all the gentlemen of the city burst into bloom that day, each one wearing a red carnation, the late President's favourite flower, in his lapel. Oh, I suppose there were a few followers of William Jennings Bryan whose coats were not in blossom. The day had been forgotten before I reached long trousers, and you could no longer tell a Republican from a Democrat on sight.

This brings us to the future, a vast, untrammelled domain, where a man's freedom of thought and action is secure, since nobody has yet devised a method of convicting anyone for what he is probably going to think or do. Several undeclared holidays that might well fit into the American years to come have occurred to me during my contemplations.

Liability Day, for example, could be set aside – say, in January – as the one day of the year during which senators and congressmen would be deprived of immunity and could be sued for libellous remarks made on the floor of the Senate or House. On this day, the kind of senator or congressman that boldly asserts he will be glad to repeat his remarks in private, and practically never does, would be given a chance to prove his courage in full view and hearing of his colleagues, the Press, and the visitors' gallery. I doubt whether anything will ever come of this suggestion –

unless, of course, it is added to my dossier in the files of the F.B.I.

I don't suppose anything will ever come of Immunity Day, either, but I shall outline my concept of it anyway. On this national holiday, all bars and saloons would be open from 12.01 a.m. until midnight, and our present habit of accusing virtually everybody of practically everything would be not only encouraged but officially condoned. This annual occasion should have a salubrious psychological effect upon the populace by legally releasing inhibitions and repressions. Many persons, in our era of fear and hysteria, are afraid to say what they think about public figures and national affairs, and have become neurotic victims of ingrown reticence, no longer able to tell discretion from timidity, or conviction from guilt. A day of freewheeling criticism would cut down the work of the psychiatrists, thus enabling them to take time out for lunch. On Immunity Day, any citizen could say anything he wanted to about anything or anybody, even Formosa and Chiang Kai-shek, without danger of being hauled to the lockup. This might eliminate – for one day, at least – such incidents as the arrest of a lady and gentleman a year or so ago for discussing the Chinese situation in a public restaurant in Houston, Texas.

Fact Day, to be celebrated on 21 June, a week after Flag Day, should be a day on which only the proved is tolerated, but the truth must, in every instance, be constructive and favourable to those who are criticized. If you know anything good about anybody, it should be generously spoken on Fact Day, without a sniff, leer, wink, or raised eyebrow. Fact Day speakers at rallies or banquets or open-air meetings should attempt to revive in the minds of their listeners the old, abandoned American assumption of innocence, pointing out that guilt is not a matter of guesswork or conjecture, but of proof.

National Misgiving Day, to be held on the last Thursday of October, a month before Thanksgiving Day, could be the occasion for the assembling of American families for the purpose of pooling and enunciating their accumulated doubts, suspicions, and apprehensions, with a view to throwing out, in sober family council, any that may have grown out of mistaken identity, bad telephone connexions, hearsay, conclusion jumping, change of life, hyperthyroidism, cussedness, political ambition, malice, animosity, pride, envy, anger, or temporary or permanent loss of mind, grip, or bearings. Misgivings that turn out to be well founded should be carefully examined and appraised by the elder and soberer members of households before they are telephoned to the F.B.I., told to the corner druggist, or passed on to United States senators. Misgiving Day would give the faltering American family a nationally sponsored reason to reassemble and to get to know each other better.

Emergence Day, which could be coincidental with Groundhog Day, would direct nationwide attention to persons who have been falsely accused of undermining or overthrowing, and have holed up in their houses or apartments with the blinds pulled down, the doors locked, and the telephone disconnected. If they have been wrongfully shadowed or tailed and, on emerging, see their shadow or tail, they shall have the right and duty to point out such shadow or tail to the constabulary or other duly constituted authorities, who must then put a shadow on the tail, or a tail on the shadow, and trace it to its lair, or liar. Games for Emergence Day parties instantly suggest themselves, but I shall leave the working out of the rules for such games to persons better qualified for merriment than I am. Nobody would be arrested on Emergence Day for anything he had not done or for anything he had once thought.

It is not my intention to urge the reinstatement of Evacuation Day as an annual occasion for fun and games or rum and Madeira in New York City, since I believe that New Yorkers can get along on the Fourth of July in their celebration of the defeat of the British. The old, lost holiday has, however, given me an idea for Evaluation Day. J. Edgar Hoover and the F.B.I. properly and soundly object to the evaluation of dossiers on suspected persons by the police or other investigatory organizations, but this has left many of us with what might be called moist qualms. These come from too much worry about who is going to do the evaluating, and we who are susceptible to the galloping jumps or the chattering jitters sometimes have nightmares about going through life completely unevaluated. In my own anxiety dream, I am caught with a Russian passport while wearing only the top of my pyjamas, usually in the lobby of the Hotel Sheraton-Astor. Just what will take place on Evaluation Day I have not yet worked out in my mind, and I think the arrangements should probably be left to some federal commission, appointed for the purpose. Don't ask me who is going to evaluate the evaluators. I don't know. I am just a writie.

*

After this piece appeared in the *New Yorker* in 1955, the late Henry Pratt Fairchild, Professor Emeritus of Sociology at New York University, wrote the editors as follows:

James Thurber, in 'A Holiday Ramble', makes one erroneously optimistic statement. He says:

> This brings us to the future, a vast, untrammelled domain, where a man's freedom of thought and action is secure, since nobody has yet devised a method of convicting anyone for what he is probably going to think or do.

It may be that nobody has devised such a method, but our legislators in Washington act as if they had. The Internal Security Act of 1950, commonly referred to as the McCarran Act, provides, in Sec. 104. (a), that during an emergency the Attorney General or his representative is authorized to issue

> (1) a warrant for the apprehension of each person as to whom there is reasonable ground to believe that such person probably will engage in, or probably will conspire with others to engage in, acts of espionage or sabotage. . . .

and that such persons are to be confined in 'places of detention'.

Mr Thurber is not to be blamed. He is probably one of the 99 44/100 per cent of the population who do not know that we have such a law. They should.

'There's something out there!'

LOCH NESS, for the past quarter of a century one of the most famous places on earth, is a long, narrow slash of deep water cutting diagonally across Inverness-shire in the historic West Highlands of Scotland. Its sombre depths and rugged banks are rich in lore and legend, as befits a former part of the great medieval domain of Macbeth, and the dark dwelling, in this century, of the world's most publicized and controversial aquatic creature, the so-called Loch Ness monster, since 1933 familiarly known to millions as Nessie. After twenty-four years the fabulous riddle of the loch still remains unsolved, still attracts thousands of sightseers annually, fascinates investigators, bemuses scientists, inspires in most of its Scottish hosts a quiet pride of possession, but in others a dour embarrassment. The monster has been seen again this year, the first time on 11 March, by a police constable and a schoolmaster, whose experience was reported in the staid pages of *The Times* of London, which had recognized the possible existence of Nessie in December 1933, seven months after its début in the picturesque loch-laced region of heath and heather, burn and glen and strath, peat and barley, castle ruins, and ancient forts that once guarded the Great Glen. Loch Ness is also associated with Bruce, Bonnie Prince Charlie, and the ships of Cromwell. Johnson and Boswell stopped there on their way to the Hebrides, and Robert Burns visited the loch and described it in verse.

Since the cry 'There's something out there!' was first raised on the lochside in the troubled spring of 1933, the Thing in the Loch has bobbed up month after month (except for a few longer wartime intervals) in the water and in the newspapers and periodicals of six continents. It has been written about seriously, sensationally, and sceptically, facetiously, indignantly, and even angrily. Cartoonists of many countries have used it for the subject of everything from sardonic silly-season whimsey to savage political satire. Although Nessie has not been, and may never be, 'received into the scientific category of Natural History', to quote one cautious London zoologist, it has taken a permanent and conspicuous place in the long gallery of weird mysteries and wild alarms that extends from the Beast of Revelation to the flying saucers of the atomic era, and includes such ancient and fantastic British exhibits as the Questing Beast of the Arthurian legends, whose noise was 'like unto the Questyng of XXX coupil of houndes', and the bunyip of Australia, reputed to seize and carry off wicked adults and incorrigible children. In our time, only Bhanjakris, the Abominable Snowman of Asia, approaches the grotesque stature of Nessie's fame, but the Himalayan mountain monster's scrapbook of Press clippings is by no means so thick or varied, even though it was first sighted by Western eyes as long ago as 1899, thirty-four years before Nessie made its advent in the loch. (It became a contemporary of Nessie when it was seen by the Everest Expedition of 1936.)

Fourteen hundred years earlier than Nessie, or five centuries before Shakespeare's gory thane of Glamis and Cawdor murdered his way to royal power, there had been a wondrous tale of some enormous and mysterious animal in the complicated waters of the loch, whose tributaries include eight rivers and forty brooks. One Adamnan, in his Latin biography of St Columba, abbot of Iona, related how that holy man, encountering the dreadful creature about to seize a Pict, raised his hand and commanded, 'Touch not that man! Begone at once!' Whereupon it bewent, sinking tamely to its secret lair at the bottom of the river Ness.

It appears likely that this ancient legend was unknown to the couple who on 14 April 1933, while driving on the north shore of Ness, were attracted by a violent commotion in the loch, and watched a long, dark, humped body travel through the water at high speed and then suddenly dive, leaving in its wake a furious swirl of foam upon the surface. On that now celebrated April day, John Mackay, proprietor of the Drumnadrochit Hotel, was driving his wife home from Inverness on the motor road that runs for thirty miles along the northern bank when Mrs Mackay got what is generally conceded to be the first look at the great phenomenon. Others, to be sure, claim to have been first witness, including the distinguished Sir Compton Mackenzie, who insisted to me in Edinburgh in 1955 that he had glimpsed the thing on 13 April.

The author of *Sinister Street* and more than eighty other books now in his seventies, staunchly contends, against an imposing weight of contradictory evidence, that what he and the Mackays saw was only a large wounded grey seal.

A fortnight after their experience, the Mackays related what they had seen to their old friend Alexander Campbell, water-bailiff of Fort Augustus and local correspondent of the Inverness *Courier*. It was Mr Campbell who dubbed the creature 'The Loch Ness Monster' in his story for the *Courier*. Then, on 11 May 1933, Alexander Shaw and his son Alistair, standing in front of their house a hundred and fifty feet above the water on the south shore, saw something, again long and dark and humped, five hundred yards out, heading toward Urquhart Bay. A dependable count is impossible to obtain, but the monster was reported at least thirty-three times in 1933, and more than twice as often the following year, by which time a regular coach service was running tourists out from Inverness, thousands of motor cars from London, Glasgow, Aberdeen, and Edinburgh drove slowly along both banks, and hundreds of excited picnickers from everywhere thronged the banks in good weather. Trees had been cut down and underbrush cleared away in the building of new motor roads, and long areas of the loch, once screened from view, were now visible.

During Nessie's hey-day, the six years preceding the Second World War, the crowded hotels and shops of Loch Ness flourished mightily. Every second cottage was turned into a teashop, hotels were full up from Whitsuntide until late October, Bed and Breakfast signs appeared on hundreds of homes, and the loch was restlessly spangled with motor launches, private yachts, rowboats, and canoes. By 1936 there was a heavy tangle of traffic from dawn to dusk along the more than sixty miles of new motor roads that encircle the loch. Newspapermen and photographers were assigned to the story singly, and in pairs, and in groups, by the newspapers of the British Isles and the Continent. Millions of words were printed, and the literature of the Loch Ness monster is now vast, unorganized, and bewildering. It takes ten hours to read through the *Daily Mail*'s monster clippings. Scores of pamphlets on the subject appeared, and a number of books, including a 221-page volume, *The Loch Ness Monster* (1934) by the late Lieutenant-

Commander R. T. Gould, R.N., and *The Rival Monster*, a 1952 satire by the doubting Sir Compton, in which a flying saucer kills the monster. The latest book, *More than a Legend*, by Constance Whyte, was published only last April. The author is the wife of the manager of the Caledonian Canal, whose seventeen locks and the River Ness give the monster's lair access to firths and the open sea at the north-east end.

Twenty years ago, while leisurely touring the British Isles with my wife, I drove up one July evening to a small inn on the loch-side. I had not given the monster story any study, or much thought. American newspapers, wary of tall tales since the era of Paul Bunyan and the years of P. T. Barnum, had approached the story lightly, somewhat in the manner of coloured postcards by Tuck in Britain which showed anglers pulling gigantic fish and dragons out of the loch. The New York *Herald Tribune*, in an editorial in 1933, had quickly dismissed the whole business as a tourist trap. Seven years later, Goebbels devoted a double page in the *Hamburger Illustrierte* to Nessie, 'exposing' it as a myth, a summer-season invention of hotels and tourist agencies. He ignored two skilfully faked photographs of the captured monster, which had been published in one of his own Berlin papers in 1934, one of them depicting Nessie being hauled out of the loch and the other showing it on public exhibition in Edinburgh. In 1940 Mussolini's paper *Popola d'Italia* declared the monster had been destroyed by a direct hit 'during the intensified bombing of Britain'. At about the same time a Tokyo journal, unaware of this bravura boast, informed its readers that the Thing was prowling the very heath on which Macbeth had encountered the Weird Sisters.

My wife and I had driven some ten miles of one bank without seeing anything unusual in the water. It was still and warm when we arrived at the inn. Two bagpipers were playing Scottish airs near the water's edge. That night I ventured to suggest to the inn-keeper that the monster might have been nothing more than a pair of itinerant musicians who had floundered into the water, bag-pipes and all. My host viewed my levity with polite resentment. 'There's something out there, you know,' he said quietly, but with unmistakable conviction. He had never seen the monster himself, but he knew a number of persons who had, one of them a nun, two of them priests. These three had taken their experiences calmly, but had declined to be interviewed by journalists. I was later to learn that a number of other eyewitnesses, mainly residents of Inverness-shire, carefully avoided publicity about what they had seen.

The next morning, up early, we drove almost all the way around the Loch Ness banks, but again saw nothing but boats on the brooding water. 'The loch itself oppresses me as much as it did when I first saw it twenty years ago,' wrote the *Daily Mail*'s Percy Cater in 1953. (Two decades earlier he had been the first Fleet Street reporter on the scene.) 'It remains as enigmatic as the face of Mona Lisa. . . . Its surface, suggestive of its sinister deeps, is as forbidding as anything I know. . . . In this harsh landscape it is easy to think of strange goings-on in the loch.'

Ness, one of Scotland's many lochs, is the largest body of fresh water in the British Isles, twenty-four miles long, nearly two miles across at its widest, with a maximum depth of 754 feet. It is estimated to contain 263 billion cubic feet of water, or three times as much as romantic Loch Lomond. In shape it somewhat resembles Bermuda, from St George's to the tip of Somerset, and its area is not a great deal smaller. Situated in the foothills of the Grampians, it is alternately primitive and populated, a holiday resort of villages and hotels and cottages, with long high stretches of green hills that seem wild and remote from civilization. The loch's surface, more than fifty feet above sea level, never freezes over. It changes moods with the weather, from the tranquil blue of the Mediterranean to a dark imitation of the sea. Legend holds that there are vast subterranean caves far below the surface, but divers have never verified this. Not many have been able to descend very far and one, seeking to recover the jewels worn by a woman drowned in the loch, is said to have returned hastily to the surface, gibbering of strange sights and menacing creatures. The loch teems with salmon, trout, eels, and many another living thing. Superstition has also stocked it with kelpies, water beasts out of Gaelic myth, equine in form, reputed to seize and drown swimmers. The loch, according to another legend, never gives up its dead and, despite police records of recovered bodies, this old belief will not die.

Controversy, when I returned to Scotland in 1955, was as strong as ever, and two basic and opposed theories separated the believers from the scoffers: on the one hand, multiple witness, and on the other, mass hallucination. There was also a faction of optical illusionists who based their hypothesis on the strange tricks played upon the eye by the changing moods, the shifting lights and shadows, and the deceptive distances of the loch. Hoax and hysteria had early begun raising their mischievous heads. One day in 1934, the veritable tracks of a hippopotamus were discovered on one bank near the water's edge. Casts of them were hastily made and shipped to the British Museum. They all turned out to be of the same four-toed foot, plainly a hunter's trophy that had fallen into the hands of some practical joker. Now and then strange contraptions were secretly slipped into the loch at night, home-made monsters built of logs or wooden chairs linked to miscellaneous junk with rope or wire. Weird amphibians, spawned in fears and fancies, prowled the lochside at night, one of them resembling an enormous horse with eyes as bright as car headlights. One morning the skeletal remnants of a voracious beast's midnight meal were found on the shore, but they proved to be butcher-shop bones arranged by a waggish human hand. Despite the exposure of hoaxes, there was a growing belief among crofters and other lochsiders that the monster was in fact an amphibian, with a habit of hunting the woods at night. Mrs Whyte flatly states her conviction that *an Niseag*, as she calls Nessie, does come out of the water and cross the road. She cites the experience of a motor-cyclist named Grant, a man of steady nerves and good reputation, who almost bumped into the creature, on a moonlit night in January 1934, as it 'crossed the road in two bounds and plunged into the water'. He called it an unknown hybrid, fifteen to twenty feet long. Six months earlier a Mr and Mrs Spicer had had a similar encounter in early daylight with a thing that also crossed the road, in front of their car, its long neck, like an elephant's trunk, undulating and forming several arches. Their account had been accepted as bona fide by Commander Gould. Unbelievers promptly named this animal a grey seal, a sea lion, or a walrus, but Grant and the Spicers vehemently insist that what they saw was of loathsome texture and unique slimy appearance, with a small head and curious oval eyes, and their description conforms to that of an English engineer who, about the same period, had watched an enormous hybrid in the water near the shore at dawn.

All sorts of speculations and suppositions have been advanced by those who refuse to believe in an unknown beast: the creature is Sir Compton's amphibious grey seal, or a school of playful salmon (two of the most persistent assumptions), a shark, a killer whale, a giant squid, a diving crested grebe or a green cormorant, an otter with a fish in its mouth, a ribbon fish, a salamander, a romping of boisterous porpoises, a flight of wild geese skimming the loch's surface, even a prehistoric Plesiosaurus which had survived the Mesozoic Age – this was once a long creature with four short legs that could be used for paddles in swimming. Believers in the survival of outsize prehistoric monsters point to a gigantic 'bat bird', closely resembling a pterodactyl, which explorer Ivan Sanderson beheld a few years ago swooping above an African river, showing the long gleaming teeth of its massive lower jaw.

An oldster claimed that the monster was a German airship that had plunged into the loch in 1918 and kept rising and sinking. One group of theorists stuck to the notion of a long hollow tree trunk, inhabited by underwater creatures, which surfaced when they left it and submerged when they returned from food forays. Others mentioned mirages or the possibility of phenomena caused by subterranean gases, blasting, rock faults, and earth tremors. In November 1950 the Portsmouth Naval Station's School of Torpedos and Mines 'exploded the myth' with pontifical authority by revealing that a chain of mines had been planted in the loch during the First World War. This pronouncement was soon forgotten with most of the other suggestions, including one about a small boy's pet crocodile which had escaped into the loch many years before. Old wives' tales and those of ancient mariners recalled unexplained disturbances in Ness or other lochs in 1872, 1893, 1903, and 1923.

One candidate for the title of Loch Ness monster which has been curiously neglected is the oarfish (*Regalecus glesne*). It reaches a length of from twenty to thirty feet, can live longer than twenty years, is known to swim occasionally on the surface, and 'when it swims, it throws its elongated body into great serpentine curves'.

When the oarfish is excited it raises a crest, or mane, consisting of the anterior rays of its long dorsal fin. It is noteworthy that at least fourteen separate reports have described the loch creature as 'having a mane like a horse's'. A few years ago an alleged oarfish thirteen feet long was pulled out of nearby Loch Fyne. Against the oar's validity as the true monster are its narrowness of body, its silvery colour, and the coral redness of its fins. But the primary argument against the oarfish is its supposed allergy to fresh water. A conger eel can live in either salt or fresh or brackish water, but zoologists doubt that the oar has such a power of accommodation, though none has adduced positive proof. The assumption that Nessie was lochborn is supported by the admitted difficulty any large creature would have in reaching Loch Ness from the open sea. Commander Gould, however, defended the possibility after a careful study of the River Ness, which leads to Beauly Firth. He figured that a sea creature the size of Nessie could manage the passage, at night and unseen, when the water is in spate, in January or February. It was his respected opinion that brought about Nessie's first appearance in *The Times* of London.

Just five years ago a 'wake monster' was added to the lively conjectures of conclusion jumpers. This ingenious conception of Nessie grew out of the loch's most terrible disaster, the tragic destruction of John Rhodes Cobb's celebrated jet-propelled powerboat, *Crusader*, which was streaking at more than two hundred miles an hour over a measured mile on 29 September 1952, seeking a new world's record, when it struck a wave band set up by another boat, nose-dived sharply, and was literally blown to bits like an exploding bomb. Such wave bands, long and narrow, expire harmlessly on beaches, but are reactivated when trapped between sheer cliffs at water's edge on either bank, as is often the case in Ness, and may lash back and forth in antic force for nearly half an hour after the passage of a vessel. The 'wake monster' is worthy of mention as an outstanding instance of the continuing reluctance of sceptics to admit that the Thing in the loch is alive.

We come now, in this court of lore, to the witnesses for the defence of a living Nessie, those orthodox believers, impressively numerous, whose consistent testimony over a period of twenty-four years forms the classic description of Nessie as something strange, enormous, and alive, elongated (from twenty to fifty feet), capable of sinuous, hump-producing behaviour and a surface speed of twenty knots or more, given to unpredictable appearances and reappearances, usually in still, warm weather, and sudden submergings which leave in its wake a foaming agitation.

Well over a thousand persons, according to the *Daily Mail*, have watched, or glimpsed, the wonder in the water, whose recorded appearances have now reached a total of more than three hundred. It has been seen for less than a minute by some observers, for nearly an hour by others, lolling on the surface occasionally, or 'sun-bathing', but for the most part undulating rapidly over the surface of the loch in short spurts, or in cavortings that keep it visible for several hundred yards. Its disappearances have usually been followed by at least one re-emergence. Commander Gould, arriving at his own hypothetical measurements by averaging those of fifty-eight witnesses he interviewed in 1933 and 1934, figured that Nessie is about forty-five feet long. The central part of the body he estimated to be twenty feet in length, with an active ten-foot tail, and a fifteen-foot snakelike neck surmounted by a head resembling that of a sheep or a small horse or cow. Its main body has often been described as being like 'an upturned rowing boat'. (In Britain such a boat is often fifteen feet long.) Nessie is possessed of 'inviolable mutism' – a phrase invented by the late William Bolitho to describe the vocal silence of Harpo Marx. No witness has ever heard it make any sound except that of the swirling waters. In this it conforms to the nature of its famous cousin, the sea serpent. The seal, by the way, is a notorious barker and the porpoise a celebrated chatterbox.

Let us now consider the testimony of three separate eyewitnesses notable for soundness, competence, and reliability – the first of them an experienced skipper in the sturdy tradition of Masefield's 'dirty British coaster with a salt-caked smokestack' – Captain William Brodie of Leith, master of the steam tug *Arrow*. This tug was plying the loch on 30 August 1938, when its captain and its crew, except for one fireman, sighted Nessie. Captain Brodie thereupon entered the following in his log: 'Sighted Loch Ness monster while close inshore about two and a half miles east of Castle Urquhart at 4.40 p.m. . . . In sight again for half a minute

4.50 p.m.' Later in an interview, Captain Brodie said that on its second appearance the monster travelled at great speed near the tug, displaying several humps as against the one or two he had observed first. It could not have been a whale, he said, or any other common creature, and his crew agreed. 'I did not believe in the monster and had not been looking for it,' Captain Brodie insisted. 'There can be no doubt of the monster's existence.'

We come next to Mr Ewan Fraser, former caretaker of Urquhart Castle. Mr Fraser, seventy-three years old, but with the keen vision of the lifetime lochside resident, had spotted the monster in July 1934, and did not see it again until 14 August 1954. This time he quickly called his neighbour, Maggie Macdonald, and her description of the monster, the standard one, coincided with his. At this very moment, it later transpired, the same manifestation had been watched by a Mackenzie and a Maclean, the latter having viewed it through a telescope.

Our third witness is the County Clerk for Inverness-shire, whose name does not appear in my records for the simple and persuasive reason, I think, that his title carries, for his fellow Scots, undeniable weight and authority. After he had reported seeing Nessie of the classic description in the early summer of 1947, the Inverness County Council on 3 May of that year officially recognized the existence of the monster in the loch. 'Now if an English county clerk had made the report,' said a council member, 'it could be rejected as dubious or unlikely, but when *our* County Clerk says there's something out there, there's something out there.'

It would take a Senate subcommittee investigating unlochian activities a good six months to question all the other witnesses for Nessie. Subpoenas would have to go out to scores of wearers of the tartan, to many a Ros, Cameron, MacFadden, Gray, Campbell, Alexander, Gillies, Graham, Blair, Fraser, Douglas, Gillespie, Scott, and Macdonald. (One Captain John Macdonald, it is true, who had made twenty thousand trips up and down the loch over a period of fifty years as skipper of a McBrayne steamer, resolutely held out for salmon at play, but he had retired well before April 1933.) The long panel of witnesses includes the nun, a major general, a rear admiral, a Member of Parliament, three doctors, a water bailiff, three bus drivers, a mining director, a vicar, four priests, and other clergymen, several policemen and teachers, a piermaster, several caretakers of lochside estates, a contractor, a number of businessmen, five workmen, a balconyful of hotel guests, and five woodcutters who, like the workmen and the guests, all saw it at once. No one could estimate the number of foreign visitors who may have watched the marvel in the water. At the end of October 1934 the visitors' book of one lochside hotel contained the names of guests from New Zealand, Chicago, Siam, the Sudan, Ceylon, Johannesburg, Paris, Ireland, Berlin, Gibraltar, the Punjab, Italy, Sydney, Melbourne, Hong Kong, Hamburg, Canada, Alexandria, South Persia, Tanganyika, Rangoon, Madras, Durban, Amsterdam, Vienna, Detroit, and New Jersey.

Nessie's famous humps, the most consistently reported feature of its morphology, are probably produced by what Commander Gould called its 'flexuous motion'. All observers have seen at least one, and a great majority have reported two or three. One man said he counted twelve, but this may be put down to the expected exaggeration of the overwrought, the romantic, or the untrained observer, one of whom placed the monster's length at ninety feet. The creature's undulations on the surface of the water are characteristic of all reports of sea serpents, whose existence in the salt waters of the world was ably argued by Commander Gould in an earlier book, *The Case for the Sea Serpent*. Scoffers point to the fact that the body of no such creature has ever been washed ashore anywhere. To this Commander Gould could only advance the probability that these enormous creatures sink to the bottom of the sea after death.

The pictorial record of Nessie, compiled haphazardly through the years, is interesting but disappointing. It comprises a number of hasty snapshots of something dark at a distance, some lengths of movie film, without close-ups or sharp definition, and a wide variety of sketches, made on the spot or drawn later from memory. There is no conclusive or even convincing evidence in any photograph of Nessie's exact conformation or true scientific category. Most observers did not carry cameras, and those that did were usually too startled to employ them properly or too excited to use them at all. Several golden opportunities to photograph the monster at close range appear to have been lost. A gentleman who swears he saw Nessie swallowing fish like a cormorant forty feet from shore had nothing with him but his retinas, and two priests out fishing in a rowboat, who saw the monster for many minutes less than fifty yards from their boat, had forgotten to bring a camera. The best-known photograph was taken in April 1934 by Mr Robert Kenneth Wilson, a surgeon of London's West End. It was reproduced in the *Daily Mail*, and hundreds of prints of it have been circulated. A few years ago this picture was admitted as Exhibit A in a B.B.C. television investigation of the case of Nessie, but the 'jury', after careful consideration in the best tradition of English justice, finally returned a verdict of 'not proven'.

Early on, as the English say, monster hunts were organized, and everybody from a naturalist and big-game hunter named M. A. Wetherell (the man who discovered the hippo's spoor) to a troop of Boy Scouts from Glasgow took a hand. Sir Edward Mountain, insurance magnate, in July 1934 stationed carefully selected observers at intervals of a mile along that length of bank between Urquhart Castle and Fort Augustus off which Nessie has been most often reported. Four of his men and one woman caught sight of Nessie that summer – one William Campbell saw it twice – and half a dozen photographs were taken, with no outstanding success because Nessie was always too swift or too far away. Captain D. J. Munro, R.N. (Ret.) established four observation posts, three on land and one afloat, manned by watchers equipped with telephoto and movie cameras, range finders, stop watches, and powerful binoculars. He also sold shilling shares, to defray expenses, in what he called Loch Ness Monster, Ltd, to be capitalized at fifteen hundred pounds. The record does not show how many shares were sold, but some of his men saw Nessie and one or two were able to snap pictures.

It wasn't long before the Loch Ness Fishery Board, the County Council, the Constabulary of Inverness-shire, and other Scottish authorities became alarmed by announced intentions to trap or kill the loch's mysterious resident, which is reputed to have brought more income to Scotland than any other single attraction except Scotch whisky. Two men threatened to stretch thin wires across the loch in the region of Nessie's favourite haunts, baited with a secret lure. A member of the Overseas Club of London planned to capture it in great nets or shoot it with a harpoon gun. J. E. Williamson, an American, said he would go down into the water and hunt for Nessie in his 'photosphere', a globe six feet in diameter at the end of a 400-foot steel tube. All manner of hydrophones and other depth-sounding equipment were brought to the loch, after an echo graph of something long, eighty fathoms deep, and presumably alive had been registered upon an asdic screen aboard a trawler. The world was closing in on Nessie. When rumours that a submarine would hunt it down were circulated, and there was wild talk of a mighty, electrified loch-wide wire net, the Loch Ness Fishery Board forbade the use of any nets, and higher Scottish authorities went into action to protect Nessie from capture, or death, or molestation. It had been well-established by now that the fantastic creature was not menacing to man, but afraid of him, a peaceable, even timid animal that wished only to be let alone.

In December 1933 Sir Godfrey Collins, then Secretary for Scotland, had issued instructions 'Forbidding any attack on the animal if sighted,' but monster hunts with great nets or lethal weapons continued to be talked about. The Brighton Aquarium had offered one thousand pounds for Nessie alive, and Bertram Mills, a circus proprietor, upped this to twenty thousand pounds. Then, in 1938, Sir Murdoch Macdonald, M.P. for Inverness, wrote to Lieutenant-Colonel John Colville, Secretary for Scotland, asking that the police be instructed to take 'immediate measures to safeguard the monster'. Thereupon Major A. C. Maclean, chief constable of Inverness-shire, ordered his men to be on the lookout for monster hunters who would deprive Scotland of its famous and harmless attraction. The only case of a leviathan more strictly protected than Nessie was that of Pelorus Jack, a huge grampus which for many years around the turn of the century used to pilot ships regularly through French Pass, Cook Strait, New Zealand. It became a national institution and was protected by a stern Order in Council of the New Zealand legislature.

Commander Gould, not only a naval officer of long experience, but also easily the best-implemented investigator of sea serpents, was not a man to jump to facile conclusions. He made no attempt to classify the loch monster with scientific exactness, but was content to set it down as an anomalous creature of the general nature and morphology of the sea serpent, which had probably fled into the loch from the sea to escape its natural enemy, the whale. In his book on sea serpents, his convincing list of sightings of water animals similar to Nessie by seafaring men, one of them later a commodore of the Cunard fleet, takes in an enormous creature frequently seen off Gloucester, Massachusetts, in 1817 and 1819, another observed in Loch Hourn (1872), and a third in the Kyle of Lochalsh in 1893. To these Dr Maurice Burton, Deputy Keeper of the British Museum's Department of Natural History, added the lau in his *Living Fossils* (1954). The lau inhabits Lake Victoria in Africa and is described as being from forty to one hundred feet long, with a thick body, a long neck, and a snakelike head. It has been viewed by officers of the Victoria-Nyanza steamers and explorers of standing.

Dr Burton, bearing in mind the multiple descriptions of Nessie's structure and deportment, visited the London Aquarium one day three years ago to observe the conger eels there, some of them five feet long. His vigil at tankside resulted in positive evidence that congers can swim on the surface, undulating latterly and producing humps that seem vertical, and leaving violent agitations of water when they dive. Sometimes, he found, only the tail was visible above the surface, or the long snake-like neck, or just the central part of the dark body, and as Nessie has been seen in all of these postures, Dr Burton ably argues the possibility of a conger attaining giant size.

When Nessie went unsighted from September 1939 until August 1940, many scoffmonsters declared this was proof that it had never existed except in the imagination. But no war year actually went by without a report of it in the water, and it was seen eleven times in 1941. The winds of interest and attention had shifted in the weather of war, holiday makers had departed, and only doctors' cars and official vehicles travelled the lochside roads.

Naturalists in Britain, wary of a long tradition of hoaxes, including spurious fossils of 'prehistoric man', have been disinclined to go out on a limb about the Thing in the Loch, since there is lacking any hide or hair, head or tail, of the enigmatic Whatever-it-is, and therefore many questions as to the monster's origin, ancestry, longevity, feeding habits, and sex life, often propounded, remain scientifically unanswered or even untackled. It is known that the conger, like other eels, is a bottom feeder and not a surface diner. The oarfish, like the sea serpent for which it has often been mistaken, has kept most of its habits a secret. There have been vague plans to introduce an oar into the loch and see what happens, but so far this project remains in what movie men call the talking stage. It may be that Walt Disney, who has twice visited Loch Ness, will give the monster the benefit of one of his thorough and fascinating natural history film documents. His New York office says that such a project is under consideration, but so far has only been roughly blocked out. It should be a notable undertaking, if it comes to pass – the champion photographer of *ferae naturae* versus the champion evader of the camera lens, in the contest of the century.

Whatever the enigma of Loch Ness may be, and whatever happens to it finally, it is assured of a double immortality: an everlasting place in the colourful and gaudy annals of the Scottish Highlands, and a permanent residence in the back files of *The Times* of London and perhaps a thousand other journals around the world. These annals and files are increased and enlivened every year by the addition of some new item: a caretaker claims he saw the monster drooling a blackish oily substance; a sailor asserts that the colour of its serpentine coils is yellowish; a college student insists he clocked it making sixty miles an hour; a posthumous report comes to light of a smaller monster seen one day, ten years ago, trailing Nessie at a distance of two hundred yards. This report of a second monster was made by two ladies of the Fraser family of Fort Augustus, who had requested that nothing be published about their experience during their lifetime, and nothing was.

The famous Riddle of the Loch still baffles investigators, but strange things continue to be found in the waters of the world. The most astounding of these was the 1938 discovery that the Coelacanth, a fish supposed to have been extinct for seventy million years, is still extant, in fine fettle and excellent health. Where it has been all this time is as great a mystery as the origin and nature of Nessie. It serves to indicate a depressing possibility that fish, which preceded man, may yet outlast him on this whirling globe. One far day another Nessie may rise to the sullen surface of the loch, scan the silent banks, and behold no living thing staring back at it – nothing furred, or feathered, or wearing clothes. But there are queer and present dangers to worry about. In this ominous era of guided missiles and unidentified flying objects, the cry most often heard is 'There's something up there!' A few years ago eerie green lights appeared high above Texas, and something large and blue and whirling is said to have pursued automobiles on high-roads in Oregon when dusk was falling. Only last April residents of Rhodesia twice saw a flock of flying lizards, each about thirty inches long, perhaps the great grandchildren of Mr Sanderson's gigantic 'bat bird'. And what is that strange object in the sky, high above the housetops there, oblate and luminous, moving so swiftly, whooshing so loudly, headed for Earth?

I don't know the answer to any of the mysteries of air, land, or sea, but the remarkable case of the Coelacanth has aroused hopes that Nessie, or one of its ilk, may yet be caught or cornered and classified. They seem to be as prevalent as witches in many parts of the planet. In addition to Nessie and the lau, there are the Skrimsl of the Icelandic fjords and the Ogo-pogo of British Columbia, and it may be that another country than Scotland will eventually be the first to admit one of these underwater monsters to the scientific category of Natural History. Meanwhile, I am betting on Scotland, for many centuries ago it was written 'In every loch there lives a dreaded beast.' Residents of the banks of all the Scottish lochs now keep a sharp, if furtive, lookout for such wonders of the water, and each loch has its ancient legend of 'a floating island' or some other strange upheaval from time to time. I have little knowledge of what may be in the other lochs of Scotland, but I confidently join Captain Brodie, Ewan Fraser, the County Clerk of Inverness-shire, and almost innumerable others in saying of Loch Ness, with unshakable conviction: There's something out there.

In conclusion, I am happy to be able to report that last-minute researches have definitely established at least one positive identification. The name of the County Clerk of Inverness-shire is Mr J. W. MacKillop.

The moribundant life, or, grow old along with whom?

THE English lady on my right at a summer dinner party in London two years ago lifted her fluent eyebrows in a finely shaded disapproval of my observation, over the *coupe framboise*, that most of the male American writers I have known are dead. She had taken it as a bit of gaunt and sepulchral levity, and she would have slapped my wrist gracefully with her fan if she had had one. Over the coffee, I persuaded her and the rest of those at table – there were eight of us – that I was not jesting but, rather, trembling, whistling in the dark as the moonlight of Jeopardy glinted on the marble and granite names of so many of my friends and acquaintances, all of them fellow-wordmen of my own generation. I defined my generation as consisting mainly of men born in the eighteen-nineties, but with an overlap of several years each way.

We had got on to the subject of the comparative longevity of writers in America and those living in Europe when someone mentioned that Laurence Housman had just celebrated his ninetieth birthday. Someone else then remarked that Bernard Berenson, an American, but of long residence in Italy, was also ninety. One of the gentlemen present, an English publisher, topped the others by reminding them that Eden Phillpotts, who was born in the year Lincoln removed General McClellan from the command of the Army of the Potomac, was ninety-three and writing television scripts for the B.B.C. The only elderly men of letters in America that I could think of offhand who were still alive were Robert Frost, Samuel Hopkins Adams, and Carl Sandburg. But I could reel off the names of thirty fellow-countrymen whose literary careers and physical being came to an end in their fifties or forties, and at least half a dozen upon whom, though still alive, one form or another of writer's cramp had fallen. I confessed, in the warmth of the wine, that I had recently frightened myself into a cold night sweat by running the list up to ninety-eight, including newspapermen and a few editors and publishers who had written something and died soon after.

The lady on my right – the one on my left was interested mainly in children under seven – asked me if it was true that Americans can only write in certain phases of the moon and in odd parts of the house, but before I could attempt an answer, an anecdote about Gordon Craig drifted on admiring laughter down the table. It seems it had been decided earlier that year to pay homage to the memory of Mr Craig on the fiftieth anniversary of the publication of his first book, whereupon his admirers discovered (I don't know why it surprised them) that he was alive and eighty-three.

Everybody at table knew that W. Somerset Maugham, at eighty-one, was still writing in his villa at Saint-Jean-Cap-Ferrat. A score of other writers, alive at the time and still writing in their seventies and eighties and even nineties, were mentioned, Bertrand Russell, Walter de la Mare, Max Beerbohm, H. M. Tomlinson, A. E. Coppard, Percy Lubbock, St John Ervine, Sir Compton Mackenzie, and A. A. Milne among them. In the two years since that dinner party, a few of these venerable authors have died, but 1955 was the high-water mark, perhaps the finest hour of elderly but sturdy English writing.

When I belonged to the English Club as a university freshman, more than forty years ago, we used to think vaguely of English authors as being one with sticks and stones and Tennyson, or as men of a fine *fin-de-siècle* Stevensonian fragility, who faintly called, with the doomed Dowson, for madder music and for stronger wine, and died before the *sommelier* reached the table, upon which lay a lovely lyric inscribed to a damsel of dream and writ in Bordeaux red. I woke up the morning after the dinner party realizing that the British authors who had ceased to be before their pens had gleaned their teeming brains were but drops in a lusty bucket of vast durability. I remembered that the aged Swinburne had given up the ghost only a year before the youthful O. Henry, in 1909, a year also attained by George Meredith, the modernness of whose *Modern Love* goes back to the first year of the Civil War. It was comforting to contemplate the host of British authors that had easily survived the white plague and the other perils of the strange decade of the *Yellow Book* and the green carnation. I got out of bed, with some effort at the age of sixty, and went through a few mild setting-up exercises, but it wasn't terribly reassuring to remind myself that I am a stronger man than Aubrey Beardsley was, or that I had lasted eight years longer than Thackeray, who once referred, in his forty-seventh year, to his 'old and decaying carcass'.

A few days later, I tottered over to the British Museum, half expecting to bump into H. Rider Haggard or Wilkie Collins on the way, to look up some more facts and figures on British and American authors. It didn't take me long to expand the list of British men of letters who had gone on a long, long time. Ernest Newman was eighty-seven then, and still writing a weekly column of music criticism. Lord Dunsany was seventy-seven, and capable of denouncing modern poetry in no quavering tones. John Cowper Powys, who I thought had disappeared from the earth about the same time as the Brevoort dining-room, was eighty-three, Sir Philip Gibbs was seventy-eight, John Masefield and Oliver St John Gogarty were seventy-seven, E. M. Forster and A. S. M. Hutchinson were seventy-six, Alfred Noyes was seventy-five, P. G. Wodehouse was seventy-four, and Frank Swinnerton was seventy-one. I turned to source books about American literary figures of my sex, and was delighted to find out that quite a few of them, born in the vintage years of the last century, were still above the green quilt. Percy Mackaye, eighty; Upton Sinclair, seventy-seven; James Branch Cabell, seventy-six; Carl Van Vechten, seventy-five; Clarence Budington Kelland and Stark Young, seventy-four; George Jean Nathan, seventy-three; and William Carlos Williams, seventy-two.

After my exploration of living Americans, I looked up the dates of some of the departed, and more or less illustrious, men of letters on our side. I hope that some researcher, with more years left than I have, will some day do a monograph on the curious viability, at home and abroad, of writers born in the eighteen-sixties. Owen Wister (*The Virginian*), born in 1860, lived to be seventy-eight; Hamlin Garland (*Main-Travelled Roads*), 1860, reached seventy-nine; George Ade (*Fables in Slang*), 1866, and Meredith Nicholson (*The House of a Thousand Candles*), also 1866, lived to be seventy-eight and eighty-one, respectively.

Booth Tarkington and Edgar Lee Masters, born in the last year of the writers' decade, attained the ages of seventy-six and eighty. There were others out of that special period, too – Finley Peter Dunne and David Graham Phillips – but they didn't do so well, reaching sixty-eight and forty-three, in that order. Violence ended Phillips's life; he was shot and killed one day in Gramercy Park, back in 1911. Born just this side of the viable decade, Gouverneur Morris lived to be seventy-seven, and Rex Beach seventy-two. This list of durables is incomplete, and I have no doubt that Indiana alone, seemingly the state of highest vitality, could add more names to those of Ade, Nicholson, and Tarkington.

I tottered back to my hotel, remembering, on the way, various writers of my own generation, and their youthful ghosts began getting between me and the sun. 'Look out,' a taxi-driver cried as I stepped into the street, 'and you'll live longer!' Look out for what, besides motor-cars, I wondered. I began piecing together out of memories of my lost colleagues the perils and threats, the mantraps and the pitfalls that had beset them in their short journeys from light to dark.

When I got back to my hotel, the lady who had sat on my right at dinner was there, looking anxious, and a bit surprised to find me up and about. I tried to look rugged, but she kept regarding me as if I were a flickering match. She had been worrying about my descending flame, she said, and had called to see if I was ready to depart. I told her, in the sitting room of my suite, from which the empty bottles and other debris of the night before had been removed, that I was still holding on, in spite of an ominous, unaccountable sound in my ears after my tenth or twelfth cocktail, something like Reginald Gardiner's imitation of a train, and a disturbing tendency of faces to recede dimly, float past me, accelerating their speed, and then come drifting slowly back.

'You all live too hard,' my companion said, 'as if life were chasing you.' And then she proved that she had been giving the situation of my generation serious thought. 'Even your common idioms are jumpy,' she continued. 'You say "Take it in your stride" and "Knock it off" and "Break it up" and "Drag it out" and "Pipe it down" and "Snap out of it" and "Step on it".

Your daily routine is so very like the two-mile-high hurdles of one of your field meets. You speak of the life hereafter, in certain of your titles, as if you were breaking your necks to get there – *Hell-Bent for Heaven*, *Heaven's My Destination*, and *One Foot in Heaven.* And it does seem that you never go to bed. Are you all afraid of the dark?'

'We never take it lying down,' I told her firmly. 'Each generation has its rituals and habit patterns. For us, every night is New Year's Eve, I'm afraid. It isn't easy for a writer's wife, returning home from her mother's early in the morning for another go at her marriage, to tell whether her husband is having a nightcap or an eye-opener, the last drink of the evening before or the first one of the day at hand.'

My friend sighed and made a small, impatient gesture. 'How do your wives stick it?' she demanded. 'And what keeps them ticking?' It was a hard question, and I turned it over for several moments. 'We have been accused of making a career of sex, a hobby of drinking, a havoc of marriage, and a tradition of divorce,' I began, 'but the wife of an American writer at least knows what she is getting into. We pick women for our mates who have great constitutional strength and are not twittery, even in the face of a charging rhinoceros. A writer's wife usually lasts until her husband begins addressing her by snapping his fingers or going "Psst!" This is an invariable sign that he is going through what we call change of wife in the male. In such a state the writer husband often uses expressions like "marry-go-round" and "welded blitz".'

My companion's gaze turned a little cold. 'It's all the fault of what you call the Scotch Fitzgerald era,' she said severely.

'Gin,' I corrected her, with an impatient gesture of my own, but she talked through it.

'You are not *really* afraid of the dark. Fitzgerald called the novel he liked most *Tender Is the Night.*'

'He also wrote *Taps at Reveille*,' I reminded her, 'and Hemingway wrote *Death in the Afternoon.* Vincent McHugh's *Sing Before Breakfast* is, of course, short for "Sing Before Breakfast, Die Before Night".' My guest's voice turned a little sharp. 'Pity you didn't beat Koestler to *Darkness at Noon*,' she said. I opened a bottle of Scotch, to keep up the reputation of my generation, and ordered tea for my visitor.

On my fourth highball, I began to brag a little about the achievements of Edgar Allan Poe. 'Poe,' I said, 'was perhaps the first great nonstop literary drinker of the American nineteenth century. He made the indulgences of Coleridge and De Quincey seem like a bit of mischief in the kitchen with the cooking sherry. O. Henry picked up the flagon where Poe had let it fall, and passed it on to us.'

'Don't romanticize it,' said my friend. 'There must be other factors than liquor involved in the brevity of your lives.'

I had to think that over for a while before replying. 'Senescence comes up gradually over here,' I began at last, 'but in America it pounces on writers like a catamount. This is another reason for our going through life, such as it is, at a dogtrot. I was once about to hand a quarter to a bewhiskered old scalawag who accosted me on the street when I recognized him; he had been a sophomore at Ohio State when I was a senior. There are many other terrors that should not be overlooked: the impalpable, the imponderable, the personal income tax, the mobile investigatory units of Congress, the bears under the bed, the green men from Mars, the cats sealed up in the walls, the hearts beating under the floor boards, the faces of laughing girls that recede, float past, and come back again.'

On my eighth drink, I tried in vain to think of an evening I had spent with any American writer at the end of which he or I had gone home. I recalled, instead, the night in 1934 when Scott Fitzgerald and I went on from 10 p.m. till eight in the morning, and I sketched in the highlights and the highballs for my shocked companion. 'We were both to blame that night,' I said, 'but it was mainly *my* fault the day in 1936 when Thomas Wolfe came to a cocktail party at my New York apartment. He stayed until nine in the morning, and was thoughtful enough to phone back an hour later to ask if he could return to apologize for having stayed so long. It is possible that our American custom of buying whisky by the case,' I added, 'may have something to do with our late hours.'

Upon this, my companion had a grave question for me. 'Do

not an American writer and his wife ever think to leave a party before midnight?'

'I wouldn't exactly say leave,' I told her. 'The process is more often one of being put out. On such an occasion, the writer and his mate take up at home where they left off at the party. This is known as bringing out the jugs with the wife. It is customary, in this ritual, to telephone, at three o'clock in the morning, an old friend and his wife. If, for some reason, they cannot appear, which is most improbable, their would-be host is likely, around five o'clock, to threaten to read aloud to his wife from whatever whisky-stained manuscript he may be working on fitfully at the time. To avert this, it is usually the wife's custom to deride the intelligence or sartorial get-up of some girl he was once incredibly fond of in his Greenwich Village years.'

'You may be a lost generation,' my companion sighed, 'but you are extraordinarily evident while you last.' I could tell from the way she accented her key words that she was beginning to feel her third cup of tea. Presently, she took flight on the mothy wings of a new eloquence. 'You are incurably competitive, all of you,' she went on, 'and a constant sense of competition is likely to burn men out in their middle years. You speak of the writing game and the publishing game. You know the score, you are forever throwing your highball past someone, and you say "Keep pitching", instead of "Good-bye".'

I had to cut in on her there. 'You are speaking of our fast ball,' I corrected her, but she motioned for silence.

'I fancy that even your reveries are competitive, that you dream not of the girls you have loved but of how you took them away from somebody else.'

'It's time for a toast,' I told her, 'to Edgar Allan Poe,' and I got up and opened a bottle of sherry and poured her some, after slugging my own next drink. I did not wish to diminish the lady's fascinated dismay. 'Here's to Poe,' I said, 'who found his manuscripts in a bottle.'

She sipped and I gulped. 'Please sit down,' she commanded. 'It takes a great deal out of a man to drink standing up. You always seem to ride pleasure as if it were an unsaddled giraffe. You go about your other relaxations in such a way that they seem the arduous involvement of a husband trying to wash a Venetian blind. It is hard to tell your conformity from your dissent, you hit them both so hard.'

I sat down reluctantly, for I had an urge to pace. 'Some twenty years ago,' I began, 'I composed, with a writer friend of mine, a parody of A.E. Housman that seems to fit in here somehow, if you would care to hear it.'

The lady gestured gracefully for more sherry, and I filled her glass. 'I think,' she said, 'that I can now stand anything,' and I began to recite:

Loneliest of these, the married now
Are hung with gloom along the vow,
And stand about the wedland drear
Dreaming dreams of yesteryear.

Now, of our twoscore years and ten,
Forty will not come again,
And take from fifty springs that many,
It only leaves us ten, if any.

And since to look at girls in bloom
Ten small years is little room,
From out the wedland we will go
And try to find the mistletoe.

My guest set down her unfinished sherry and rose to her feet. 'Grow your age, to use one of your own idioms,' she said. 'Rise quite above it. If poor, dear Henry James had lived in America instead of England, we should probably not have had *The Turn of the Screw*, to say nothing of the novels of his major phase.'

She was about to start for the door when I proposed another toast, this one solemn and sincere. 'I have decided to write a memoir of our so pleasant, if gruesome, conversation,' I said, 'and it has occurred to me that between the writing and the printing of the piece one or more of those we have mentioned, all in wonder and in awe, may have reached the top of that hill beyond which there is no going.' She picked up her glass again, and I touched it with mine, and gave my toast: 'God rest you tranquil, gentlemen, whom life did not dismay.'

After the lady had gone, I phoned downstairs to ascertain the phase of the moon, and found that it was not good for writing. Besides, there are no odd places to work in the suites of the Stanton Hotel. I decided to lie down, instead. After all, an American writer born as long ago as 1894 cannot get too much rest.

Merry Christmas

It didn't surprise me to learn that Americans send out a billion and a half Christmas cards every year. That would have been my guess, give or take a quarter of a billion. Missing by 250 million is coming close nowayears, for what used to be called astronomical figures have now become the figures of earth. I am no longer staggered by the massive, but I can still be shaken by the minor human factors involved in magnificent statistics. A national budget of 71 thousand million is comprehensible to students of our warlike species, but who is to account for the rising sales of vodka in this nation – from 108,000 bottles in 1946 to 32,500,000 bottles in 1956? The complexities of federal debt and personal drinking are beyond my grasp, but I think I understand the Christmas card situation, or crisis.

It disturbed me to estimate that two-fifths of the 1956 Christmas cards, or six hundred million, were received by people the senders barely knew and could count only as the most casual of acquaintances, and that approximately thirty million recipients were persons the senders had met only once, in a bar, on a West Indies cruise, at a doctor's office, or while fighting a grass fire in Westchester. The people I get Christmas cards from every year include a Yugoslav violist I met on the *Leviathan* in 1925, the doorman of a restaurant in Soho, a West Virginia taxi driver who is writing the biography of General Beauregard, the young woman who cured my hiccoughs at Dave Chasen's in 1939 (she twisted the little finger of my left hand and made me say Garbo backward), innumerable people who know what to do about my eyes and were kind enough to tell me so in hotel lobbies and between the acts of plays, seven dog owners who told me at Tim's or Bleeck's that they have a dog exactly like the one I draw, and a lovely stranger in one of these saloons who snarled at a proud dog owner: 'The only dog that looks like the dog this guy draws is the dog this guy draws.'

The fifteen hundred million annual Yuletide greetings are the stamp and sign of the American character. We are a genial race, as neighbourly abroad as at home, fond of perpetuating the chance encounter, the golden hour, the unique experience, the pre-war vacation. 'I think this calls for a drink' has long been one of our national slogans. Strangers take turns ordering rounds because of a shared admiration of disdain, a suddenly discovered mutual friend in Syracuse, the same college fraternity, a similar addiction to barracuda fishing. A great and lasting friendship rarely results, but the wife of each man adds the other's name to her Christmas list. The American woman who has been married ten years or longer, at least the ones I know, sends out about two hundred Christmas cards a year, many of them to persons on the almost forgotten fringe of friendship.

I had the good luck to be present one December afternoon in the living-room of a couple I know just as the mail arrived. The wife asked if we minded her glancing at the cards, but she had already read one. 'My God!' she exclaimed. 'The Spragues are still together! They were this really charming couple we met in Jamaica eight years ago. He had been a flier, I think, and had got banged up, and then he met Marcia – I think her name was Marcia.' She glanced at the card again and said, 'Yes, Marcia. Well, Philip was on leave in Bermuda and he saw her riding by in a carriage and simply knew she was the girl, although he had never laid eyes on her before in his life, so he ran out into the street and jumped up on the carriage step, and said, "I'm going to marry you!" Would you believe it, he didn't even tell her his name, and of course he didn't know her from Adam – or Eve, I guess I ought to say – and they were married. They fell in love and got married in Bermuda. Her family was terribly opposed to it, of course, and so was his when they found out about hers, but they went right ahead anyway. It was the most romantic thing I ever heard of in my life. This was four or five years before we met them, and – '

'Why are you so astonished that they are still together?' I asked.

'Because their meeting was a kind of third-act curtain,' said my friend's husband. 'Boy meets girl, boy gets girl – as simple as that. All that's left is boy loses girl. Who the hell are Bert and Mandy?' he asked, studying a Christmas card.

Another greeting-card category consists of those persons who send out photographs of their families every year. In the same mail that brought the greetings from Marcia and Philip, my friend found such a conversation piece. 'My God, Lida is enormous!' she exclaimed. I don't know why women want to record each year, for two or three hundred people to see, the ravages wrought upon them, their mates, and their progeny by the artillery of time, but between five and seven per cent of Christmas cards, at a rough estimate, are family groups, and even the most charitable recipient studies them for little signs of dissolution or derangement. Nothing cheers a woman more, I am afraid, than the proof that another woman is letting herself go, or has lost control of her figure, or is clearly driving her husband crazy, or is obviously drinking more than is good for her, or still doesn't know what to wear. Middle-aged husbands in such photographs are often described as looking 'young enough to be her son', but they don't always escape so easily, and a couple opening envelopes in the season of mercy and good will sometimes handle a male friend or acquaintance rather sharply. 'Good Lord!' the wife will say. 'Frank looks like a sex-crazed shotgun slayer, doesn't he?' 'Not to me,' the husband may reply. 'To me he looks more like a Wilkes-Barre dentist who is being sought by the police in connexion with the disappearance of a choir singer.'

Any one who undertakes a comparative analysis of a billion and a half Christmas cards is certain to lose his way once in a while, and I now find myself up against more categories than I can handle. Somewhere in that vast tonnage of cardboard, for example, are – I am just guessing now – three hundred million cards from firms, companies, corporations, corner stores, and other tradespeople. In the old days they sent out calendars for the New Year, and skipped Christmas, but I figure they are now responsible for about a fifth of the deluge. Still another category includes inns, bars, restaurants, institutions, councils, committees, leagues, and other organizations. One of my own 1956 cards came from the Art Department of Immaculate Heart College, in Los Angeles, whose point of contact with me has eluded my memory. A certain detective agency used to send me a laconic word every December, but last year, for some disturbing reason,

I was struck off the agency's list. I don't know how I got on it in the first place, since I have never employed a private investigator to shadow anybody, but it may be that I was one of the shadowed. The agency's slogan is 'When we follow him he stays followed', and its card was invariably addressed to 'Mr James Ferber'. This hint of alias added a creepy note to the holidays, and, curiously enough, the sudden silence has had the same effect. A man who is disturbed when he hears from a detective agency, and when he doesn't, may be put down, I suppose, as a natural phenomenon of our nervous era.

I suddenly began wondering, in one of my onsets of panic, what becomes of all these cards. The lady in my house who adds two hundred items to the annual avalanche all by herself calmed my anxiety by telling me that most of them get burned. Later, I found out, to my dismay, that this is not actually true. There are at least nine million little girls who consider Christmas cards too beautiful to burn, and carefully preserve them. One mother told me that her garage contains fifteen large cartons filled with old Christmas cards. This, I am glad to say, is no problem of mine, but there is a major-general somewhere who may have to deal with it one of these years if the accumulation becomes a national menace, hampering the movement of troops.

Ninety per cent of women employ the annual greeting as a means of fending off a more frequent correspondence. One woman admitted to me that she holds at least a dozen friends at arm's, or year's, length by turning greeting cards into a kind of annual letter. The most a man will consent to write on a Christmas card is 'Hi, boy!' or 'Keep pitching', but a wife often manages several hundred words. These words, in most instances, have a way of dwindling with the march of the decades, until they become highly concentrated and even cryptic, such as 'Will you ever forget that ox bice cake?' or 'George says to tell Jim to look out for the 36'. Thus the terrible flux of December mail is made up, in considerable part, of the forgotten and the meaningless. The money spent on all these useless cryptograms would benefit some worthy cause by at least three million dollars.

The sex behind most of the billion and a half Christmas cards is, of course, the female. I should judge that about 75,000,000 cards are received annually by women from former cooks, secretaries, and hairdressers, the formerness of some of them going back as far as 1924. It is not always easy for even the most experienced woman card sender to tell an ex-hairdresser from someone she met on a night of high wind and Bacardi at Cambridge Beaches in Bermuda. The late John McNulty once solved this for my own wife by saying, 'All hairdressers are named Dolores.' The wonderful McNulty's gift of inspired oversimplification, like his many other gifts, is sorely missed by hundreds of us. McNulty and I, both anti-card men, never exchanged Christmas greetings, except in person or on the phone. There was a time when I drew my own Christmas cards, but I gave it up for good after 1937. In that year I had drawn what purported to be a little girl all agape and enchanted in front of a strangely ornamented Christmas tree. The cards were printed in Paris and mailed to me, two hundred of them, in Italy. We were spending Christmas in Naples. The cards were held up at the border by the Italian authorities, agents of Mussolini who suspected everything, and returned to Paris. 'I should think,' commented an English friend of mine, 'that two hundred copies of any drawing of yours might well give the authorities pause.'

One couple, to conclude this survey on an eerie note, had sent out the same engraved Christmas card every year. Last time 'From John and Joan' had undergone a little change. Joan had crossed out 'John and'. Her friends wonder just how many of these cheery greetings the predeceased Joan has left. So passed one husband, with only a pencil stroke to mark his going. Peace on earth, good will to women.

A Gallery of Drawings

'I'm helping Mr Gorley with his novel, darling.'

'Everybody noticed it. You gawked at her all evening.'

'Why don't you get dressed, then, and go to pieces like a man?'

'I told the analyst everything except my experience with Mr Rinesfoos.'

'No son of mine is going to stand there and tell me he's scared of the woods.'

'Get a load of this sunset, Babe!'

'Bang! Bang! Bang!'

'It's Lida Bascom's husband – he's frightfully unhappy.'

Why do you keep raising me when you know *I'm bluffing?'*

'What do four ones beat?'

'Why don't you wait and see what becomes of your own *generatio*
before you jump on mine?'

'You were wonderful at the Gardners' last night, Fred, when you turned on the charm.'

'You haven't got the face for it, for one *thing.'*

'Here! Here! There's a place for that, sir!'

'Good morning, my feathered friends!'

'Ooooo, guesties!'

'My wife always has me shadowed on Valentine's Day.'

File and Forget

I WANT to thank my secretary, Miss Ellen Bagley, for putting the following letters in order. I was not up to the task myself, for reasons that will, I think, become clear to the reader. J. T.

Miss Alma Winege,
The Charteriss Publishing Co.,
132 East What Street,
New York, N.Y.

West Cornwall, Conn.
2 November 1948

Dear Miss Winege,

Your letter of 25 October, which you sent to me in care of The Homestead, Hot Springs, Ark., has been forwarded to my home in West Cornwall, Conn., by The Homestead, Hot Springs, Va. As you know, Mrs Thurber and I sometimes visit this Virginia resort, but we haven't been there for more than a year. Your company, in the great tradition of publishers, has sent so many letters to me at Hot Springs, Ark., that the postmaster there has simply taken to sending them on to the right address, or what would be the right address if I were there. I explained to Mr Cluffman, and also to Miss Lexy, when I last called at your offices, that all mail was to be sent to me at West Cornwall until further notice. If and when I go to The Homestead, I will let you know in advance. Meanwhile, I suggest that you remove from your files all addresses of mine except the West Cornwall one. Another publishing firm recently sent a letter to me at 65 West 11th Street, an address I vacated in the summer of 1930. It would not come as a surprise to me if your firm, or some other publishers, wrote me in care of my mother at 568 Oak Street, Columbus, Ohio. I was thirteen years old when we lived there, back in 1908.

As for the contents of your letter of the 25th, I did not order thirty-six copies of Peggy Peckham's book *Grandma Was a Nudist.*

I trust that you have not shipped these books to me in care of The Homestead, Hot Springs, Ark., or anywhere else.

Sincerely yours,
J. Thurber

PS. Margaret Peckham, by the way, is not the author of this book. She is the distinguished New York psychiatrist whose *The Implications of Nudism* was published a couple of years ago. She never calls herself Peggy. J.T.

Miss Alma Winege, *West Cornwall, Conn.*
The Charteriss Publishing Co., *3 November 1948*
132 East What Street,
New York, N.Y.

Dear Miss Winege,

In this morning's mail I received a card from the Grand Central branch of the New York Post Office informing me that a package of books had been delivered to me at 410 East 57th Street. The branch office is holding the package for further postage, which runs to a considerable amount. I am enclosing the notification card, since these must be the thirty-six copies of *Grandma Was a Nudist*. I have not lived at 410 East 57th Street since the fall of 1944. Please see to it that this address is removed from your files, along with The Homestead address.

Whoever ordered those books, if anyone actually did, probably wonders where they are.

Sincerely yours,
J. Thurber

THE CHARTERISS PUBLISHING COMPANY
NEW YORK, N.Y.

Mr James M. Thurber, *5 November 1948*
West Cornwall, Conn.

Dear Mr Thurber,

I am dreadfully sorry about the mix-up over Miss Peckham's book. We have been pretty much upset around here since the departure of Mr Peterson and Mr West, and several new girls came to us with the advent of Mr Jordan. They have not yet got their 'sea legs', I am afraid, but I still cannot understand from what file our shipping department got your address as 165 West 11th Street. I have removed the 57th Street address from the files and also the Arkansas address and I trust that we will not disturb your tranquillity further up there in Cornwall. It must be lovely this time of year in Virginia and I envy you and Mrs Thurber. Have a lovely time at The Homestead.

Sincerely yours,
Alma Winege

PS. What you had to say about *Grandma* amused us all. A. W.

Columbus, Ohio
16 November 1948

Dear Mr Thurber,

I have decided to come right out with the little problem that was accidentally dumped in my lap yesterday. I hope you will forgive me for what happened, and perhaps you can suggest what I should do with the books. There are three dozen of them and, unfortunately, they arrived when my little son Donald was alone downstairs. By the time I found out about the books, he had torn off the wrappings and had built a cute little house out of them. I have placed them all on a shelf out of his reach while awaiting word as to where to send them. I presume I could ship them to you C.O.D. if I can get somebody to wrap them properly.

I heard from old Mrs Winston next door that you and your family once lived here at 568 Oak Street. She remembers you and your brothers as cute little tykes who were very noisy and raised rabbits and guinea pigs. She says your mother was a wonderful cook. I am sorry about Donald opening the books and I hope you will forgive him.

Sincerely yours,
Clara Edwards
(Mrs J. C.)

Mr Leon Charteriss, *West Cornwall, Conn.*
The Charteriss Publishing Co., *19 November 1948*
132 East What Street,
New York, N.Y.

Dear Mr Charteriss,

I am enclosing a letter from a Mrs J. C. Edwards, of Columbus, Ohio, in the fervent hope that you will do something to stop this insane flux of books. I never ordered these books. I have not read *Grandma Was a Nudist.* I do not intend to read it. I want something done to get these volumes off my trail and cut out of my consciousness.

I have written Miss Winege about the situation, but I am afraid to take it up with her again, because she might send them to me in care of the Department of Journalism at Ohio State University, where I was a student more than thirty years ago.

Sincerely yours,
J. Thurber

PS. I never use my middle initial, but your firm seems to think it is 'M'. It is not. J.T.

THE CHARTERISS PUBLISHING COMPANY
NEW YORK, N.Y.

Mr James M. Thurber, *23 November 1948*
West Cornwall, Conn.

Dear Mr Thurber,

Mr Charteriss has flown to California on a business trip and will be gone for several weeks. His secretary has turned your letter of the 19th over to me. I have asked Mr Cluffman to write to Miss Clara Edwards in Columbus and arrange for the reshipment of the thirty-six copies of *Grandma Was a Nudist.*

I find, in consulting the records, that you have three times ordered copies of your own book, *Thurber's Ark*, to be shipped to you at West Cornwall, at the usual discount rate of forty per cent. I take it that what you really wanted was thirty-six copies of your own book and they are being sent out to you today with our regrets for the discomfit we have caused you. I hope you will be a little patient with us during this so trying period of reorganization.

Cordially yours,
Jeannette Gaines
Stock Order Dept

PS. You will be happy to know that we have traced down the gentleman who ordered those copies of *Grandma.*

Mr Henry Johnson,
The Charteriss Pub. Co.,
New York, N.Y.

West Cornwall, Conn.
25 November 1948

Dear Harry,

Since the reorganization at Charteriss, I have the forlorn and depressing feeling that I no longer know anybody down there except you. I know that this immediate problem of mine is not in your field, but I turn to you as a last resource. What I want, or rather what I don't want, is simple enough, Harry. God knows it is simple.

I don't want any more copies of my book. I don't want any more copies of my book. I don't want any more copies of my book.

As ever,
Jim

PS. It has just occurred to me that I haven't seen you for more than two years. Let's have a drink one of these days. I'll give you a ring the next time I'm in the city. J.T.

THE CHARTERISS PUBLISHING COMPANY
NEW YORK, N.Y.

Mr James Grover Thurber,
Cornwall, Conn.

26 November 1948

Dear Jim Thurber,

I haven't had the pleasure of meeting you since I had the great good luck to join forces with Charteriss, but I look forward to our meeting with a high heart. Please let me know the next time you are in the city, as I should like to wine and dine you and perhaps discuss the new book that I feel confident you have in you. If you don't want to talk shop, we can discuss the record of our mutual football team. You were at Northwestern some years ahead of my time, I believe, but I want you to know that they still talk about Jimmy Thurber out there.

Your letter to Harry Johnson has just come to my attention, and I regret to say that Harry is no longer with us. He went to Harcourt, Brace in the summer of 1947. I want you to feel, however, that every single one of us here is your friend, willing and eager to drop everything to do your slightest bidding. All of us feel very deeply about your having turned against your book *Thurber's Ark*. I note that in your present mood you have the feeling that you never want to see it again. Well, Jim, let me assure you that this is just a passing fancy, derived from a moment of depression. When you put in your last order for thirty-six copies, you must surely have had some definite use in mind for them, and I am banking on twenty years' experience in the book-publishing game when I take the liberty of sending these twenty books off to you today. There is one thing I am something of an expert at, if I do say so myself, and that is the understanding of the 'creative spirit'.

We have a new system here, which is to send our authors not ten free copies, as of old, but fifteen. Therefore, five of the thirty-six copies will reach you with our compliments. The proper deductions will be made on the record.

Don't forget our dinner date.

Cordially,
Clint Jordan

PS. I approve of your decision to resume the use of your middle name. It gives a book dignity and flavour to use all three names. I think it was old Willa Cather who started the new trend, when she dropped the Seibert. C.J.

THE CHARTERISS PUBLISHING COMPANY
NEW YORK, N.Y.

13 December 1948

Dear Thurber,

Just back at the old desk after a trip to California and a visit with my mother, who is eighty-nine now but as chipper as ever. She would make a swell Profile. Ask me about her someday.

Need I say I was delighted to hear from the staff when I got back about your keen interest in *Grandma Was a Nudist*? The book has been moving beautifully and its ceiling has gone sky-high. We're planning a brief new advertising campaign and I'd be tickled pink if you would be good enough to bat out a blurb for us.

Yours,
Leon

THE CHARTERISS PUBLISHING COMPANY
NEW YORK, N.Y.

Mr James M. Thurber,
West Cornwall, Conn.

15 December 1948

Dear Mr Thurber,

I hope you will forgive me – indeed, all of us – for having inexcusably mislaid the address of the lady to whom the thirty-six copies of *Grandma Was a Nudist* were sent by mistake. I understand that we have already dispatched to you at your home another thirty-six volumes of that book.

My apologies again.

Sincerely yours,
H. F. Cluffman

Mr H. F. Cluffman,
The Charteriss Publishing Co.,
132 East What Street,
New York, N.Y.

West Cornwall, Conn.
19 December 1948

Dear Mr Cluffman,

The lady's name is Mrs J. C. Edwards, and she lives at 568 Oak Street, Columbus, Ohio.

I have explained as clearly as I could in previous letters that I did not order thirty-six copies of *Grandma Was a Nudist*. If you have actually shipped to me another thirty-six copies of this book, it will make a total of seventy-two copies, none of which I will pay for. The thirty-six copies of *Thurber's Ark* that Mr Jordan has written me he intends to send to West Cornwall would bring up to one hundred and eight the total number of books that your firm, by a conspiracy of confusion unique even in the case of publishers, has mistakenly charged to my account. You may advise Mr Jordan that I do not wish to receive the five free copies he mentioned in his letter.

If your entire staff of employees went back to *Leslie's Weekly*, where they belong, it would set my mind at rest.

Sincerely yours,
J. Thurber

PS. I notice that you use only my middle initial, 'M'. Mr Jordan and I – or was it Mr Charteriss? – have decided to resume the use of the full name, which is Murfreesboro. J. T.

Mr Leon Charteriss,
The Charteriss Publishing Co.,
132 East What Street,
New York, N.Y.

West Cornwall, Conn.
27 December 1948

Dear Mr Charteriss,

I am sure you will be sorry to learn that Mr Thurber has had one of his spells as a result of the multiplication of books and misunderstanding that began with Miss Alma Winege's letter of 25 October 1948. Those of us around Mr Thurber are greatly disturbed by the unfortunate circumstances that have caused him to give up writing, at least temporarily, just after he had resumed work following a long fallow period.

Thirty-six copies of Mr Thurber's book and thirty-six copies of *Grandma Was a Nudist* have arrived at his home here, and he has asked me to advise you that he intends to burn all seventy-two. West Cornwall is scarcely the community for such a demonstration – he proposes to burn them in the middle of U.S.

Highway No. 7 – since the town regards with a certain suspicion any writer who has not won a Pulitzer Prize.

I am enclosing copies of all the correspondence between your company and Mr Thurber, in the hope that someone connected with your firm will read it with proper care and intelligence and straighten out this deplorable and inexcusable situation.

Mr Thurber wishes me to tell you that he does not want to hear from any of you again.

Sincerely yours,
Ellen Bagley
Secretary to Mr Thurber

THE CHARTERISS PUBLISHING COMPANY
NEW YORK, N.Y.

Mr James Murfreesboro Thurber, *28 December 1948*
72 West,
Cornwall, Conn.

Dear Mr Thurber,

I have at hand your letter of 19 December, the opening paragraph of which puzzles me. You send me the following name and address – Mrs J. C. Edwards, 568 Oak Street, Columbus, Ohio – but it is not clear what use you wish me to make of this. I would greatly appreciate it if you would clear up this small matter for me.

Sincerely yours,
H. F. Cluffman

PS. *Leslie's Weekly* ceased publication many years ago. I could obtain the exact date if you so desire. H. F. C.

THE CHARTERISS PUBLISHING COMPANY
NEW YORK, N.Y.

Mr James M. Thurber, *29 December 1948*
West Cornwall, Conn.

Dear Mr Thurber,

You will be sorry to hear that Mr Charteriss was taken suddenly ill with a virus infection. His doctor believes that he lost his immunity during his visit to the West Coast. He is now in the hospital, but his condition is not serious.

Since the departure of Miss Gaines, who was married last week, I have taken over the Stock Order Department for the time being. I did not take the liberty of reading your enclosures in the letter to Mr Charteriss, but sent them directly to him at the hospital. I am sure he will be greatly cheered up by them when he is well enough to read. Meanwhile, I want you to know that you can repose all confidence in the Stock Order Department to look after your needs, whatever they may be.

Sincerely yours,
Gladys MacLean

PS. I learned from Mr Jordan that you were a friend of Willa Cather's. Exciting!

Columbus, Ohio
3 January 1949

Dear Jamie,

I don't understand the clipping from the Lakeville *Journal* Helen's mother sent me, about someone burning all those books of yours in the street. I never heard of such a thing, and don't understand how they could have taken the books without your knowing it, or what you were doing with so many copies of the novel about the naked grandmother. Imagine, at her age! She couldn't carry on like that in Columbus, let me tell you. Why, when I was a girl, you didn't dare walk with a man after sunset, unless he was your husband, and even then there was talk.

It's a good thing that state policeman came along in time to save most of the books from being completely ruined, and you must be thankful for the note Mr Jordan put in one of the books, for the policeman would never have known who they belonged to if he hadn't found it.

A Mrs Edwards phoned this morning and said that her son Donald collects your books and wants to send them to you – to be autographed, I suppose. Her son has dozens of your books and I told her you simply wouldn't have time to sign all of them, and she said she didn't care what you did with them. And then she said they weren't your books at all, and so I just hung up on her.

Be sure to bundle up when you go out.

With love,
Mother

PS. This Mrs Edwards says she lives at 568 Oak Street. I told her we used to live there and she said God knows she was aware of that. I don't know what she meant. I was afraid this little boy would send you all those books to sign and so I told his mother that you and Helen were at The Homestead, in Hot Springs. You don't suppose he would send them there, do you?

And here, gentle reader, I know you will be glad to leave all of us.

A sort of genius

ON the morning of Saturday, 16 September 1922, a boy named Raymond Schneider and a girl named Pearl Bahmer, walking down a lonely lane on the outskirts of New Brunswick, New Jersey, came upon something that made them rush to the nearest house in Easton Avenue, around the corner, shouting. In that house an excited woman named Grace Edwards listened to them wide-eyed and then telephoned the police. The police came on the run and examined the young people's discovery: the bodies of a man and a woman. They had been shot to death and the woman's throat was cut. Leaning against one of the man's shoes was his calling card, not as if it had fallen there but as if it had been placed there. It bore the name Rev. Edward W. Hall. He had been the rector of the Protestant Episcopal Church of St John the Evangelist in New Brunswick. The woman was identified as Mrs Eleanor R. Mills, wife of the sexton of that church. Raymond Schneider and Pearl Bahmer had stumbled upon what was to go down finally in the annals of our crime as perhaps the country's most remarkable mystery. Nobody was ever found guilty of the murders. Before the case was officially closed, a hundred and fifty persons had had their day in court and on the front pages of the newspapers. The names of two must already have sprung to your mind: Mrs Jane Gibson, called by the avid press 'the pig woman', and William Carpender Stevens, once known to a hundred million people simply as 'Willie'. The pig woman died in 1931, but Willie Stevens went on living, until his death in 1942, with his sister, Mrs Hall, at 23 Nichol Avenue, New Brunswick.

It was from that house that the Rev. Mr Hall walked at around 7.30 o'clock on the night of Thursday, 14 September 1922, to his peculiar doom. With the activities in that house after Mr Hall's departure the State of New Jersey was to be vitally concerned. No. 23 Nichol Avenue was to share with De Russey's Lane, in which the bodies were found, the morbid interest of a whole nation four years later, when the case was finally brought to trial. What actually happened in De Russey's Lane on the night of 14 September? What actually happened at 23 Nichol Avenue the same night? For the researcher, it is a matter of an involved and voluminous court record, colourful and exciting in places, confused and repetitious in others. Two things, however, stand out as sharply now as they did on the day of their telling: the pig woman's story of the people she saw in De Russey's Lane that night, and Willie Stevens's story of what went on in the house in Nichol Avenue. Willie's story, brought out in cross-examination by a prosecutor whose name you may have forgotten (it was Alexander Simpson), lacked all the gaudy melodrama of the pig woman's tale, but in it, and in the way he told it on the stand, was the real drama of the Hall-Mills trial. When the State failed miserably in its confident purpose of breaking Willie Stevens down, the verdict was already written on the wall. The rest of the trial was anticlimax. The jury that acquitted Willie, and his sister, Mrs Frances Stevens Hall, and his brother, Henry Stevens, was out only five hours.

A detailed recital of all the fantastic events and circumstances of the Hall-Mills case would fill a large volume. If the story is vague in your mind, it is partly because its edges, even under the harsh glare of investigation, remained curiously obscure and fuzzy. Everyone remembers, of course, that the minister was deeply involved with Mrs Mills, who sang in his choir; their affair had been for some time the gossip of their circle. He was forty-one, she was in her early thirties; Mrs Hall was nearing fifty. On 14 September, Mr Hall had dinner at home with his wife, Willie Stevens, and a little niece of Mrs Hall's. After dinner, he said, according to his wife and his brother-in-law, that he was going to call on Mrs Mills. There was something about a payment on a doctor's bill. Mrs Mills had had an operation and the Halls had paid for it (Mrs Hall had inherited considerable wealth from her parents). He left the house at about the same time, it came out later, that Mrs Mills left her house, and the two were found murdered, under a crab-apple tree in De Russey's Lane, on the edge of town, some forty hours later. Around the bodies were scattered love letters which the choir singer had written to the minister. No weapons were found, but there were several cartridge shells from an automatic pistol.

The investigation that followed – marked, said one New Jersey lawyer, by 'bungling stupidity' – resulted in the failure of the grand jury to indict anyone. Willie Stevens was questioned for hours, and so was Mrs Hall. The pig woman told her extraordinary story of what she saw and heard in the lane that night, but she failed to impress the grand jurors. Four years went by, and the Hall-Mills case was almost forgotten by people outside of New Brunswick when, in a New Jersey court, one Arthur Riehl brought suit against his wife, the former Louise Geist, for annulment of their marriage. Louise Geist had been, at the time of the murders, a maid in the Hall household. Riehl said in the course of his testimony that his wife had told him 'she knew all about the case but had been given $5,000 to hold her tongue'. This was all that Mr Philip Payne, managing editor of the *Daily Mirror*, nosing around for a big scandal of some sort, needed. His newspaper 'played up' the story until finally, under its goading, Governor Moore of New Jersey appointed Alexander Simpson special prosecutor with orders to reopen the case. Mrs Hall and Willie Stevens were arrested and so was their brother, Henry Stevens, and a cousin, Henry de la Bruyere Carpender.

At a preliminary hearing in Somerville the pig woman, with eager stridency told her story again. About nine o'clock on the night of 14 September she heard a wagon going along Hamilton Road near the farm on which she raised her pigs. Thieves had been stealing her corn and she thought maybe they were at it again. So she saddled her mule, Jenny (soon to become the most famous quadruped in the country), and set off in grotesque pursuit. In the glare of an automobile's headlights in De Russey's Lane, she saw a woman with white hair who was wearing a tan coat, and man with a heavy moustache, who looked like a coloured man. These figures she identified as Mrs Hall and Willie Stevens. Tying her mule to a cedar tree, she started toward the scene on foot and heard voices raised in quarrel: 'Somebody said something about letters.' She now saw three persons (later on she increased this to four), and a flashlight held by one of them illumined the face of a man she identified first as Henry Carpender, later as Henry Stevens, and it 'glittered on something' in the man's hand. Suddenly there was a shot, and as she turned and ran for her mule, there were three more shots; a woman's voice screamed, 'Oh, my! Oh, my! Oh, my!' and the voice of another woman moaned, 'Oh, Henry!' The pig woman rode wildly home on her mule, without investigating further. But she had lost one of her moccasins in her flight, and some three hours later, at one o'clock, she rode her mule back again to see if she could find it. This time, by the light of the moon, she saw Mrs Hall, she said, kneeling in the lane, weeping. There was no one else there. The pig woman did not see any bodies.

Mrs Jane Gibson became, because of her remarkable story, the chief witness for the State, as Willie Stevens was to become the chief witness for the defence. If he and his sister were not in De Russey's Lane, as the pig woman had shrilly insisted, it remained for them to tell the detailed story of their whereabouts and their actions that night after Mr Hall left the house. The grand jury this time indicted all four persons implicated by the pig woman, and the trial began on 3 November 1926.

The first persons Alexander Simpson called to the stand were 'surprise witnesses'. They were a Mr and Mrs John S. Dixon, who lived in North Plainfield, New Jersey, about twelve miles from New Brunswick. It soon became apparent that they were to form part of a net that Simpson was preparing to draw around Willie Stevens. They testified that at about 8.30 on the night of the murders Willie had appeared at their house, wearing a loose-fitting suit, a derby, a wing collar with bow tie, and, across his vest, a heavy gold chain to which was attached a gold watch. He had said that his sister had let him out there from her automobile and that he was trying to find the Parker Home for the Aged, which was at Bound Brook. He stuttered and he told them that he was an epileptic. They directed him to a trolley car and he went stumbling away. When Mrs Dixon identified Willie as her visitor, she walked over to him and took his right hand and shook it vigorously, as if to wring recognition out of him. Willie stared at her, said nothing. When she returned to the stand, he grinned widely. That was one of many bizarre incidents which marked the progress of the famous murder trial. It deepened the mystery that hung about the strange figure of Willie Stevens. People could hardly wait for him to take the stand.

William Carpender Stevens had sat in court for sixteen days before he was called to the witness chair, on 23 November 1926. On that day the trial of Albert B. Fall and Edward L. Doheny, defendants in the notorious Teapot Dome scandal, opened in Washington, but the nation had eyes only for a small, crowded courtroom in Somerville, New Jersey. Willie Stevens, after all these weeks, after all these years, was to speak out in public for the first time. As the *New York Times* said, 'He had been pictured as "Crazy Willie", as a town character, as an oddity, as a butt for all manner of jokes. He had been compared inferentially to an animal, and the hint of an alien racial strain in his parentage had been thrown at him.' Moreover, it had been prophesied that Willie would 'blow up' on the stand, that he would be trapped into contradictions by the 'wily' and 'crafty' Alexander Simpson, that he would be tricked finally into blurting out his guilt. No wonder there was no sound in the courtroom except the heavy tread of Willie Stevens's feet as he walked briskly to the witness stand.

Willie Stevens was an ungainly, rather lumpish man, about five feet ten inches tall. Although he looked flabby, this was only because of his loose-fitting clothes and the way he wore them; despite his fifty-four years, he was a man of great physical strength. He had a large head and a face that would be hard to forget. His head was covered with a thatch of thick, bushy hair, and his heavy black eyebrows seemed always to be arched, giving him an expression of perpetual surprise. This expression was strikingly accentuated by large, prominent eyes which, seen through the thick lenses of the spectacles he always wore, seemed to bulge unnaturally. He had a heavy, drooping, walrus moustache, and his complexion was dark. His glare was sudden and fierce; his smile, which came just as quickly, lighted up his whole face and gave him the wide, beaming look of an enormously pleased child. Born in Aiken, South Carolina, Willie Stevens had been brought to New Brunswick when he was two years old. When his wealthy parents died, a comfortable trust fund was left to Willie. The other children, Frances and Henry, had inherited their money directly. Once, when Mrs Hall was asked if it was not true that Willie was 'regarded as essential to be taken care of in certain things', she replied, 'In certain aspects.' The quality of Willie's mentality, the extent of his eccentricity, were matters the prosecution strove to establish on several occasions. Dr Laurence Runyon, called by the defence to testify that Willie was not an epileptic and had never stuttered, was cross-examined by Simpson. Said the doctor, 'He may not be absolutely normal mentally, but he is able to take care of himself perfectly well. He is brighter than the average person, although he has never advanced as far in school learning as some others. He reads books that are above the average and makes a good many people look like fools.' 'A sort of genius, in a way, I suppose?' said Simpson. To which the doctor quietly replied, 'Yes, that is just what I mean.'

There were all sorts of stories about Willie. One of them was that he had once started a fire in his back yard and then, putting on a fireman's helmet, had doused it gleefully with a pail of water. It was known that for years he had spent most of every day at the firehouse of Engine Company No. 3 in Dennis Street, New Brunswick. He played cards with the firemen, ran errands for them, argued and joked with them, and was a general favourite. Sometimes he went out and bought a steak, or a chicken, and it was prepared and eaten in the firehouse by the firemen and Willie. In the days when the engine company had been a volunteer organization, Willie was an honorary member and always carried, in the firemen's parades, a flag he had bought and presented to the firehouse, an elaborate banner costing sixty or seventy dollars. He had also bought the black-and-white bunting with which the front of the firehouse was draped whenever a member of the company died.

After his arrest, he had whiled away the time in his cell reading books on metallurgy. There was a story that when his sister-in-law, Mrs Henry Stevens, once twitted him on his heavy reading, he said, 'Oh, that is merely the bread and butter of my literary repast.' The night before the trial opened, Willie's chief concern was about a new blue suit that had been ordered for him and that did not fit him to his satisfaction. He had also lost a collar button, and that worried him; Mrs Henry Stevens hurried to the jail before the court convened and brought him another one, and he was happy. At the preliminary hearing weeks before, Simpson had declared with brutal directness that Willie Stevens did indeed look like a coloured man, as the pig woman had said. At this Willie had half risen from his chair and bared his teeth, as if about to leap on the prosecutor. But he had quickly subsided.

For every adult in New Brunswick who had known his frown or his flare-up, there were a dozen children familiar only with his smile and his kindliness. To the younger ones he was a kind of magical plain-clothes Santa Claus who could produce candy from his pocket like rabbits from a hat. He frequently bought clothing for poor children. The record does not show whether he gave them rides in his chauffeur-driven Buick. Willie liked to take long trips alone. Except for the firemen and a few cronies, he avoided adults, but he loved to talk about metallurgy with his intimates. (After the trial he took up botany and entomology, too.) All through the trial Willie Stevens had sat quietly, staring. He had been enormously interested when the pig woman, attended by a doctor and a nurse, was brought in to give her testimony. This was the man who now, on trial for his life, climbed into the witness chair in the courtroom at Somerville. There was an immense stir. Justice Charles W. Parker rapped with his gavel. Mrs Hall's face was strained and white; this was an ordeal she and her family had been dreading for weeks. Willie's left hand gripped his chair tightly; his right hand held a yellow pencil with which he had fiddled all during the trial. He faced the roomful of eyes tensely. His own lawyer, Senator Clarence E. Case, took the witness first. Willie started badly by understating his age ten years. He said he was forty-four. 'Isn't it fifty-four?' asked Case. Willie gave the room his great, beaming smile. 'Yes,' he chortled, boyishly, as if amused by his slip. The spectators smiled. It didn't take Willie long to dispose of the Dixons, the couple who had sworn he stumbled into their house the night of the murder. He answered half a dozen questions on this point with strong emphasis, speaking slowly and clearly: he had worn a derby, he had never had epilepsy, he had never stuttered, he had never had a gold watch and chain. Mr Case held up Willie's old silver watch and chain for the jury to see. When he handed them back, Willie, with fine nonchalance, compared his watch with the clock on the courtroom wall, gave his sister a large reassuring smile, and turned to his questioner with respectful attention. He described, with technical accuracy, an old revolver of his (the murders had been done with an automatic pistol, not a revolver, but a weapon of the same calibre as Willie's). He said he used to fire off the gun on the Fourth of July; remembering these old holidays, his eyes lighted up with childish glee. From this mood he veered suddenly into indignation and anger. 'When was the last time you saw the revolver?' was what set him off. 'The last time I saw it was in this courthouse!' Willie almost shouted. 'I think it was in October 1922, when I was taken and put through a very severe grilling by – I cannot mention every person's name, but I remember Mr Toolan, Mr Lamb, and Detective David, and they did everything but strike me. They cursed me frightfully.' The officers had got him into an automobile 'by a subterfuge', he charged. 'Mr David said he simply wanted me to go out in the country, to ask me a very few questions, that I would not be very long.' It transpired later that on this trip Willie himself had had a question to ask Detective David: would the detective, if they passed De Russey's Lane, be kind enough to point it out to him? Willie had never seen the place, he told the detective, in his life. He said that Mr David showed him where it was.

When Willie got to the night of 14 September 1922 in his testimony his anger and indignation were gone; he was placid, attentive, and courteous. He explained quietly that he had come home for supper that night, had gone to his room afterward, and 'remained in the house, leaving it at 2.30 in the morning with my sister'. Before he went to bed, he said, he had closed his door to confine to his own room the odour of tobacco smoke from his pipe. 'Who objected to that?' asked Mr Case. Willie gave his sudden, beaming grin. 'Everybody,' he said, and won the first of several general laughs from the courtroom. Then he told the story of what happened at 2.30 in the morning. It is necessary, for a well-rounded picture of Willie Stevens, to give it here at some length. 'I was awakened by my sister knocking at my door,' said Willie, 'and I immediately rose and went to the door and she said, "I want you to come down to the church, as Edward has not come home; I am very much worried" – or words to that effect. I immediately got dressed and accompanied her down to the church.

I went through the front door, followed a small path that led directly to the back of the house past the cellar door. We went directly down Redmond Street to Jones Avenue, from Jones Avenue we went to George Street; turning into George Street we went directly down to Commercial Avenue. There our movements were blocked by an immense big freight automobile. We had to wait there maybe half a minute until it went by, going toward New York.

'I am not at all sure whether we crossed right there at Commercial Avenue or went a little further down George Street and went diagonally across to the church. Then we stopped there and looked at the church to see whether there were any lights. There were no lights burning. Then Mrs Hall said, "We might as well go down and see if it could not be possible that he was at the Mills' house." We went down there, down George Street until we came to Carman Street, turned down Carman Street, and got in front of the Mills' house and stood there two or three minutes to see if there were any lights in the Mills' apartment. There were none.' Willie then described, street by street, the return home, and ended with 'I opened the front door with my latchkey. If you wish me, I will show it to you. My sister said, "You might as well go to bed. You can do no more good." With that I went upstairs to bed.' This was the story that Alexander Simpson had to shake. But before Willie was turned over to him, the witness told how he heard that his brother-in-law had been killed. 'I remember I was in the parlour,' said Willie, 'reading a copy of the *New York Times.* I heard someone coming up the steps and I glanced up and I heard my aunt, Mrs Charles J. Carpender, say, "Well, you might as well know it – Edward has been shot."' Willie's voice was thick with emotion. He was asked what happened then. 'Well,' he said, 'I simply let the paper go – that way' (he let his left hand fall slowly and limply to his side) 'and I put my head down, and I cried.' Mr Case asked him if he was present at, or had anything to do with, the murder of Mr Hall and Mrs Mills. 'Absolutely nothing at all!' boomed Willie, coming out of his posture of sorrow, belligerently erect. The attorney for the defence turned, with a confident little bow, to Alexander Simpson. The special prosecutor sauntered over and stood in front of the witness. Willie took in his breath sharply.

Alexander Simpson, a lawyer, a state senator, slight, perky, capable of harsh tongue-lashings, given to sarcasm and innuendo, had intimated that he would 'tie Willie Stevens into knots'. Word had gone around that he intended to 'flay' the eccentric fellow. Hence his manner now came as a surprise. He spoke in a gentle, almost inaudible voice, and his attitude was one of solicitous friendliness. Willie, quite unexpectedly, drew first blood. Simpson asked him if he had ever earned his livelihood. 'For about four or five years,' said Willie, 'I was employed by Mr Siebold, a contractor.' Not having anticipated an affirmative reply, Simpson paused. Willie leaned forward and said, politely, 'Do you wish his address?' He did this in good faith, but the spectators took it for what the *Times* called a 'sally', because Simpson had been in the habit of letting loose a swarm of investigators on anyone whose name was brought into the case. 'No, thank you,' muttered Simpson, above a roar of laughter. The prosecutor now set about picking at Willie's story of the night of 14 September. He tried to find out why the witness and his sister had not knocked on the Mills' door to see if Mr Hall was there. Unfortunately for the steady drumming of questions, Willie soon broke the prosecutor up with another laugh. Simpson had occasion to mention a New Brunswick boarding-house called The Bayard, and he pronounced 'Bay' as it is spelled. With easy politeness, Willie corrected him. 'Biyard,' said Willie. 'Biyard?' repeated Simpson. Willie smiled, as at an apt pupil. Simpson bowed slightly. The spectators laughed again.

Presently the witness made a slip, and Simpson pounced on it like a stooping falcon. Asked if he had not, at the scene of the murder, stood 'in the light of an automobile while a woman on a mule went by', Willie replied, 'I never remember that occurrence.' Let us take up the court record from there. '*Q.* – You would remember if it occurred, wouldn't you? *A.* – I certainly would, but I don't remember of ever being in an automobile and the light from the automobile shone on a woman on a mule. *Q.* – Do you say you were not there, or you don't remember? *A.* – I say positively I was not there. *Q.* – Why did you say you don't *remember*? *A.* – Does not that cover the same thing? *Q.* – No, it don't, because you might be there and not remember it. *A.* – Well, I will withdraw that, if I may, and say I was not there positively.' Willie assumed an air of judicial authority as he 'withdrew' his previous answer, and he spoke his positive denial with sharp decision. Mr Simpson abruptly tried a new tack. 'You have had a great deal of experience in life, Mr Stevens,' he said, 'and have read a great deal, they say, and know a lot about human affairs. Don't you think it sounds rather fishy when you say you got up in the middle of the night to go and look for Dr Hall and went to the house and never even knocked on the door – with your experience of human affairs and people that you met and all that sort of thing – don't that seem rather fishy to you?' There was a loud bickering of attorneys before Willie could say anything to this. Finally Judge Parker turned to the witness and said, 'Can you answer that, Mr Stevens?' 'The only way I can answer it, Your Honour,' said Willie, scornfully, 'is that I don't see that it is at all "fishy".' The prosecutor jumped to something else. 'Dr Hall's church was not your church, was it?' he asked. 'He was not a *Doctor*, sir,' said Willie, once more the instructor. 'He was the Reverend *Mister* Hall.' Simpson paused, nettled. 'I am glad you corrected me on that,' he said. The courtroom laughed again.

The prosecutor now demanded that Willie repeat his story of what happened at 2.30 a.m. He hoped to establish, he intimated, that the witness had learned it 'by rote'. Willie calmly went over the whole thing again, in complete detail, but no one of his sentences was the same as it had been. The prosecutor asked him to tell it a third time. The defence objected vehemently. Simpson vehemently objected to the defence's objection. The Court: 'We will let him tell it once more.' At this point Willie said, 'May I say a word?' 'Certainly,' said Simpson. 'Say all you want.' Weighing his words carefully, speaking with slow emphasis, Willie said, 'All I have to say is I was never taught, as you insinuate, by any person whatsoever. That is my best recollection from the time I started out with my sister to this present minute.' Simpson did not insist further on a third recital. He wanted to know now how Willie could establish the truth of his statement that he was in his room from eight or nine o'clock until his sister knocked on the door at 2.30 a.m. 'Why,' said Willie, 'if a person sees me go upstairs and does not see me come downstairs, isn't that a conclusion that I was in my room?' The court record shows that Mr Simpson replied, 'Absolutely.' 'Well,' said Willie, expansively, 'that is all there was to it.' Nobody but the pig woman had testified to seeing Willie after he went up to his room that night. Barbara Tough, a servant who had been off during the day, testified that she got back to the Hall home about 10 o'clock and noticed that Willie's door was closed (Willie had testified that it wouldn't stay closed unless he locked it). Louise Geist, of the annulment suit, had testified that she had not seen Willie that night after dinner. It was Willie's story against the pig woman's. That day in court he overshadowed her. When he stepped down from the witness chair, his shoulders were back and he was smiling broadly. Headlines in the *Times* the next day said, 'Willie Stevens Remains Calm Under Cross-Examination. Witness a Great Surprise.' There was a touch of admiration, almost of partisanship, in most of the reporters' stories. The final verdict could be read between the lines. The trial dragged on for another ten days, but on 3 December, Willie Stevens was a free man.

He was glad to get home. He stood on the porch at 23 Nichol Avenue, beaming at the house. Reporters had followed him there. He turned to them and said, solemnly, 'It is one hundred and four days since I've been here. And I want to get in.' They let him go.

Mrs Hall died on 19 December 1942 at the age of sixty-eight. Her devoted brother Willie outlived her by only eleven days. They were buried in the same family vault in Greenwood Cemetery, Brooklyn, where Dr Hall had been buried in 1922. Mr Mills, still alive and active at last report, not seeming to have aged at all, according to a friend, has been sexton in a Methodist church in New Jersey for many years, and lives quietly with his son. I see no reason to throw a sharper spotlight upon them now. Nobody in New Brunswick has talked about the Hall-Mills case in many years, a reporter who covered the trial told me. Other scandals and excitements began spreading like witch grass soon after the famous Somerville trial of 1926. Five months later Lindbergh flew the ocean, and names like Sacco and Vanzetti, Ruth Snyder and Judd Gray, Peaches and Daddy Browning pushed the Hall-Mills case out of the papers into the files. Babe Ruth's bat was soon to hit sixty home runs in one season, and the brown derby of Al Smith could be seen bobbing about, on clear days and cloudy, from any part of the country.

Little physical trace of the ancient murder and trial is left anywhere. De Russey's Lane, which Detective David once pointed out to Willie Stevens, is now entirely changed. In the early thirties it was renamed Franklin Boulevard, and where the Rev. Mr Edward W. Hall and Mrs Eleanor Mills lay dead there is now a row of neat brick and stucco houses. The famous crab-apple tree under which the bodies were found disappeared the first week-end after the murders. It was hacked to pieces, roots and all, by souvenir hunters.

The waters of the moon

I HAD broken away from an undulant discussion of kinetic dimentionalism and was having a relaxed moment with a slender woman I had not seen before, who described herself as a chaoticist, when my hostess, an avid disturber of natural balances and angles of repose, dragged me off to meet the guest of honour, a Mr Peifer, editor of a literary review. 'Holds his liquor beautifully,' my hostess said. 'Burns it up, I guess. He's terribly intense.' Peifer was pacing back and forth on a rug, haranguing a trapped etcher whose reluctant eyes kept following him as if he were a tennis rally.

'No, I'm not interested in the ageing American *female* author,' Peifer was saying. 'That's a phenomenon that confounds analysis. The female writer's fertility of invention and glibness of style usually survive into senility, just as her artistic gestation frequently seems to be independent of the nourishment of thought.'

Peifer made three turns of the rug in silence. He had the expression of a chemist absorbed in abstruse formulae. 'I am interested in the male American writer who peters out in his fifties, who has the occupational span of a hockey player. The tempo of our American life may have something to do with it, but there must be a dozen other factors that dry up the flow of ideas and transform a competent prose style into the meagre iterations of a train announcer.'

My hostess finally broke in, and Peifer stopped pacing to shake hands. The etcher seized the opportunity to disappear. 'Mr Thurber is fifty-two,' my hostess said. 'He hasn't written anything since last April.' Peifer looked at me as if I were the precipitate of a moderately successful test-tube experiment. My first name suddenly reminded him of a tangent of his theme. 'Take Henry James,' he said. 'If he had lived in this country, he would probably have spent his middle years raising collies or throwing darts. It is preposterous to assume, however, that region or climate is the important factor. There must be something, though, in the American way of life and habit of thought. I want to get Wylie or Margaret Mead or somebody to do a comprehensive treatise on the subject, looking at it from the viewpoints of marriage, extra-marital relations, the educational system, home environment, the failure of religion, the tyranny of money, and the rich breeding ground of de-composition which I believe is to be found in syphilophobia, prostatitis, early baldness, peptic ulcer, edentulous cases, true and hysterical impotence, and spreading of the metatarsals.' I tried to wrench a tray of Martinis from a man in a white coat, but he would only let me have one. 'Let's go over and sit down on that sofa,' Peifer said. I followed him, glancing ruefully over my shoulder at my lost chaoticist. 'It's a difficult article,' I said. 'If you use names, it's dangerous, and if you don't, it won't be interesting. You can't very well say that Joseph Doakes, after petering out on page 73 of his unfinished novel, *Whatever Gods*, a childlike and feathery permutation of his first book, *Fear Set Free*, is living in sin with his cook and spends his time cutting the pips out of playing cards.'

Peifer took my olive. 'The article is not to be a gossip column,' he said. 'It's to be a scholarly treatise. I am interested in exploring the causes of literary collapse, not in collecting scandalous post-disintegration case histories of quixotic individuals who would no doubt have gone to pieces in precisely the same way had they been milliners or pharmacists' mates.'

'Then, unhappily,' I said, 'you cannot follow the old codgers past the hour of their deterioration, and in so doing you will omit a great deal of fascinating sequelae. You are interested only in causation. You would trace the career of, let us say, Bruce Balliol up to that afternoon in June when he abruptly began to write the middle section of *Love Not the Wind* in the manner of the late Senator Albert J. Beveridge, and realized to his dismay that he was washed up at fifty-six. I would take him through his divorce, his elopement with the hairdresser, and those final baffling years on the peacock ranch.'

A grim man I had never seen before walked up to us, dribbling his Manhattan. 'Cora in the bells and grass,' he said. 'Cora with a cherry half-way to her lips.' The man walked away. 'I like Eve better than Cora,' I said. Peifer apparently didn't know the poem the man had paraphrased. 'You do?' he said, with his laboratory glint. 'You were talking,' I said. 'Go on.' Peifer took a curved briar pipe out of his pocket and rubbed the bowl on his pants leg. He began to chew on the stem of his pipe.

'That was poor old Greg Selby,' I said, 'a perfect specimen for your analysis. He stopped writing suddenly, a fortnight after his fifty-fourth birthday. Bang!' Peifer started. 'Like that,' I said. His felicity of style was the envy and despair of us all, and then abruptly one day he began to write like a doorman cock-eyed on cherry brandy.' 'I never heard of any writer named Greg Selby,' Peifer said. I lifted a Martini from a passing tray. 'He has never published anything,' I said. 'He is going to leave all his work to Harvard, to be published a thousand years from now. Greg's writing has what he calls Projected Meaning. He feels that in another millennium the intellectuals will understand it readily enough. I have never made head or tail of any of his stuff myself, but there is no missing the unique quality of the most exquisite English prose of our time.'

Peifer made figure eights in the air with his pipe. 'He seems a little special,' he said. 'I'm not interested in idiosyncratic variables, except, perhaps, as footnotes.'

'He is a male American writer who petered out in his middle fifties,' I insisted. 'He fits in perfectly.'

'What I have in mind is the published writer of established merit,' my companion said as I stopped another Martini tray, 'but go on. What happened to this man Selby?'

'His first wife, Cora,' I began, 'claimed to have discovered that his last book, *Filiring Gree*, was his next-to-last book, *Saint Tomany's Rain*, written backward. It was insupportable to Greg that his wife should go through his books like a public accountant investigating a bank ledger. He threw her and her Siamese cats out of the house – the macaw wouldn't go. He had not heard the last of her, however. She called him up every few days and in the falsetto of a little child asked him why he didn't dramatize the Little Colonel stories for Margaret O'Brien. She divorced him, finally, and married a minor-league out-fielder.'

'This is really terribly special,' Peifer complained, signalling a tray of highballs.

'Cora was ordinary enough. It was Eve who was special. She was the author of a number of mystery books. You probably remember *Pussy Wants a Coroner*.' Peifer replied, a little pettishly, that he did not read mysteries.

'After her marriage to Greg,' I went on, 'Eve's books took on a curiously Gothic tone; the style was cold and blocky, and the plots had all the flexibility of an incantation. She explained to her alarmed publishers that she was trying to write for the understanding of intellectuals a thousand years ago.' Peifer put his drink on the floor and stood up. 'I presume you would consider Douglas Bryce a published author of established merit, wouldn't you?' I demanded. I had thought the name up fast. 'Well,' Peifer said uneasily. He sat down again.

'Doug,' I said, 'ran out of ideas and his command of sentence construction at the same time, on a Wednesday. He was fifty-eight. That was a long time ago. He died in 1932, on his chinchilla farm, and only the hat-check girl, Dolores, was at his bedside. Nell left him after the Lawrence Stone incident.'

Peifer recrossed his legs restlessly and reached for another highball. 'It would be as hard to find a copy of *The Tenant of the Room* now as it would be to turn up a first edition of *V.V.'s Eyes*,' I told him. '*The Tenant* was Doug's last book. It was a flimsy rehash of his earlier *A Piece in Bloom*. The love story was a little more disgusting, but in general it was a slight rearrangement of the well-worn characters and incidents. Doug had once had a facile and effective style, but the writing in *The Tenant* fell well within the capabilities of a shrewd pin boy.'

I took another Martini. 'Get on with it,' Peifer said.

'Nell once told me that after the failure of *The Tenant*, Doug spent his days making cryptic and vainglorious notes on pieces of Kleenex, doorjambs, the flyleaves of books, and shirt fronts. He would jot down such things as "Translate Lippmann into Latin", "Reply to Shelburne Essays", "Refute Toynbee", "Collaborate with G.B.S.?", "Call Gilbert Miller". Other notes indicated that he planned a history of the New York, New Haven & Hartford in verse, an account of women in sports, to be called *Atalanta to Babe Didrikson*, and a pageant based on the Tristram legends, in which he proposed to star the late Devereux Milburn.'

'I really must go,' Peifer said. He stood up and then resumed iis seat. 'What was the Lawrence Stone incident?' he asked.

'Just before he bought the chinchilla farm, Nell found, scribbled on the bathroom wall, "*The Shore; The Plain; The Mountain*, a riology by Douglas Bryce." Under that he had written "A monunental achievement", which he had signed "Van Wyck Brooks". But he was on to himself at last; he was tired and he was through ınd he knew it. The reservoir of his natural talent had run dry and ıe had been reaching for the waters of the moon. But as I say, he vas on to himself. Under it all he had scrawled, almost illegibly, 'a trilogy wilogy by Brycey-Wycey".'

'Who was this man Stone? And then I must go,' Peifer said. People are beginning to sing.'

'Doug had one more project,' I said. 'He conceived the idea of vriting a long biography of a man picked at random in the street. The book was to be called *Let Twenty Pass.* He stood one day at he corner of Fifth Avenue and Forty-fourth Street, counted off wenty men who walked by going north, and accosted the twentyirst. The twenty-first was a large, preoccupied mining engineer ıamed Lawrence Stone. He called the police and a rather nasty uss was kicked up in the papers. It came out, you remember, that Stone was quite deaf, and his functional disability had twisted Doug's proposal into a shockingly complex plan to seize the major ıetworks. Dolores was passing when Doug accosted Stone, and ıer testimony as to what was actually said cleared Bryce. It was . near thing, though.'

Peifer twisted around on the sofa, slowly and with difficulty, as f invisible blankets hampered his legs. I saw that his unfriendly tare glittered frostily in almost imperceptibly crossed eyes. I vondered I had not noticed before that his liquor, much of it unurned, had left him, in spite of a fluent grasp on his subject, ɔalanced precariously between command and dissolution. His exɪression took away all my pride of invention in the garish show of igures I had conjured up to ornament his theme. I had been careess, too, in the name of the mining engineer, and Peifer had caught ne out. 'I happen to be familiar with Browning,' he said with hrewd dignity, 'and I happen to know how the line that begins 'Let twenty pass" ends.'

I was conscious of a figure at my shoulder. Someone had come to save me. It was the slender lady, my dark lady of chaos, growr a little mistier with the passing of the afternoon and possessec now of the posture of the rose in a summer wind. I stood up, anc Peifer managed it, too. 'Nell,' I said, 'may I present Mr Peifer? He bowed stiffly. 'This is Nell Bryce,' I told him. The game was up, but here I was, kicking field goals by moonlight. 'Peifer here, I said, 'would not have followed Bierce beyond the Rio Grande or Villon through the *porte* of St Denis to see in what caprice o rondeaux their days came to an end.'

'Let's phone the police and plague 'em till hell won't have it, the lady said. It seemed to hurt Peifer like a slap. He bowed, al most too low to sustain the moral advantage he undoubtedly helc over both of us. 'It is a great pity, Madam,' he said, tightly, 'tha your mythical husband had the misfortune to encounter an en gineer named Stone. Ah, what a flaw in the verisilimitude wa there! It is a great pity your husband did not have the luck to en counter an engineer named Costello or McKelway or Shapiro. The dark lady listened to him with the expression of one who i receiving complicated directions in a great, strange town.

Peifer turned a cold, uncertain eye on me. 'Let twenty pass,' h snarled, 'and stone the twenty-first.' The dark lady watched him on a quick opening play, break between guard and centre of mixed quartet. 'Now, how in the God's name' – she had a charm ing diaphragmatic convulsion – 'did he know my husband wa mythical?' It was too long a story to go into. I took her arm and in silence, led her to the telephone to call the police.

Exhibit X

I HAD been a code clerk in the State Department in Washington for four months during the First World War before my loyalty was investigated, if you could call my small, pleasant interview with Mr Shand an investigation. He had no dossier on Thurber, James Grover, except a birth certificate and draft-board deferment papers. In 1918, Americans naïvely feared the enemy more than they feared one another. There was no F.B.I. to speak of, and I had neither been followed nor secretly photographed. A snooping photographer could have caught me taking a code book home to study one night and bringing it back the next day – an act that was indiscreet, and properly regretted when I learned the rules – but a pictorial record of my activites outside the Bureau of Indexes and Archives in Washington would actually have been as innocent as it might have *looked* damning.

It would have shown me in the company of Mrs Nichols, head of the information desk at the State, War, and Navy Building (a psychic lady I had known since I was six); George P. Martin, proprietor of the Post Café, and Mrs Rabbit, his assistant; Frank Farrington, a movie actor who had played the part of a crook named Braine in *The Million Dollar Mystery*; and Jack Bridges, a Los Angeles air-mail flier and Hispano-Suiza expert. I doubt if any such photographs, even one showing me borrowing twenty dollars from Bridges half an hour after meeting him for the first time in my life, would have shaken Mr Shand's confidence in me.

Mr Shand called me to his office about a week before I was to sail for France and the Paris Embassy. He was a tall, quiet, courteous gentleman, and he had only one question to ask me. He wanted to know if all my grandparents had been born in the United States. I said yes, he wished me Godspeed, we shook hands, and I left. That's all there was to it. Waking up at night now and looking back on it, I sometimes wonder how I would have come out of one of those three-men inquisitions the State Department was once caught conducting. Having as great a guilt sense as any congressman, and a greater tendency to confession, it might have taken me hours to dredge up out of my mind and memory all the self-indictments that must have been there. I believed then, and still do, that generals of the Southern Confederacy were, in the main, superior to generals of the Northern armies; I suspected there were flaws in the American political system; I doubted the virgin birth of United States senators; I thought that German cameras and English bicycles were better than ours; and I denied the existence of actual proof that God was exclusively a citizen of the United States. But, as I say, Mr Shand merely asked me about my grandparents, and that was all. I realize now that, as a measure of patriotism, the long existence of my ancestors on American soil makes me more loyal than Virginia Dare or even George Washington, but I didn't give it any thought at the time.

Before I sailed on the s.s. *Orizaba*, a passenger ship converted into an Army transport and looking rather sheepish about it, I was allowed to spend four days in Columbus, Ohio, and my family has preserved, for reasons known only to families, a snapshot taken of me on the last day of my leave. The subject of the photograph is obviously wearing somebody else's suit, which not only convicts him of three major faults in a code clerk – absent-mindedness, carelessness, and peccability – but gives him the unwonted appearance of a saluki who, through some egregious mischance of nature, has exchanged his own ears for those of a barn owl. If this would not be enough to cause a special agent to phone Hoover personally, *regardez*, as the French Sûreté would say excitedly, the figure of this alarming *indiscret*. His worried expression indicates that he has just mislaid a code book or, what is worse, has sold one. Even Mr Hoover's dullest agent could tell that the picture is that of a man who would be putty in the hands of a beautiful, or even a dowdy, female spy. The subject's curious but unmistakable you-ask-me-and-I'll-tell-you look shows that he would babble high confidences to low companions on his third *pernod à l'eau*. This man could even find some way to compromise the Department of Agriculture, let alone the Department of State.

The picture would have aroused no alarm in the old days, however, for it was almost impossible to be a security risk in the State Department in 1918, no matter how you looked. All our code books except one were quaint transparencies dating back to the time when Hamilton Fish was Secretary of State, under President Grant, and they were intended to save words and cut telegraph costs, not to fool anybody. The new code book had been put together so hastily that the word 'America' was left out, and code groups so closely paralleled true readings that 'LOVVE', for example, was the symbol for 'love'.

Whatever slight illusion of secrecy we code clerks may have had was dispelled one day by a dour gentleman who announced that the Germans had all our codes. It was said that the Germans now and then got messages through to Washington taunting us about our childish ciphers, and suggesting on one occasion that our clumsy device of combining two codes, in a desperate effort at deception, would have been a little harder if we had used two other codes, which they named. This may have been rumour or legend, like the story, current at the time, that six of our code books were missing and that a seventh, neatly wrapped, firmly tied, and accompanied by a courteous note, had been returned to one or another of our embassies by the Japanese, either because they had finished with it or because they already had one.

A system of deception as easy to see through as the passing attack of a grammar-school football team naturally produces a cat's-out-of-the-bag attitude. In enciphering messages in one code, in which the symbol for 'quote' was (to make up a group) 'ZOXIL', we were permitted to use 'UNZOXIL' for 'unquote', an aid to perspicuity that gave us code clerks the depressing feeling that our tedious work was merely an exercise in block lettering. The Department may have comforted itself with the knowledge that even the most ingenious and complex codes could have been broken down by enemy cipher experts. Unzoxilation just made it a little easier for them.

Herbert O. Yardley, one-time chief cryptographer of the War Department, warned the government in a book published nearly thirty years ago that the only impregnable codes are those whose pattern is mechanically jumbled in transmission by a special telegraphic method that reassembles the pattern at the point of reception. To prove his point, Yardley revealed how he had broken the toughest Japanese code five years before. The government must have taken his advice. I doubt that we could have got through a second world war shouting, 'ZOXIL Here we come, ready or not UNZOXIL.'

The State Department, in the happy-go-lucky tradition of the time, forgot to visa my special diplomatic passport, and this was to cause a tremendous *brouhaha* later on, when the French discovered I was loose in their country without the signs, seals, and signatures they so devoutly respect. The captain of the *Orizaba* wanted nothing to do with me when I boarded his ship, whether my passport was visaed or not. He had no intention of taking orders from the State Department or carrying its code clerks, and who the hell was Robert Lansing, anyway? He finally let me stay on board after I had bowed and scaped and touched my forelock for an hour, but he refused to have anything at all to do with my trunk. When I received it in Paris, more than a year later, everything in it was covered with the melted chocolate of a dozen Hershey bars I had tucked in here and there.

I had been instructed to report to Colonel House at the Hôtel Crillon when I got to Paris, but I never saw him. I saw instead an outraged gentleman named Auchincloss, who plainly regarded me as an unsuccessfully comic puppet in a crude and inexcusable practical joke. He said bitterly that code clerks had been showing up for days, that Colonel House did not want even one code clerk, let alone twelve or fifteen, and that I was to go on over to the Embassy, where I belonged. The explanation was, I think, as simple as it was monumental. Several weeks before, the State Department in Washington had received a cablegram from Colonel House in Paris urgently requesting the immediate shipment of twelve or fifteen code clerks to the Crillon, where headquarters for American Peace Delegation had been set up. It is plain to me now what must have happened. Colonel House's cablegram must have urgently requested the immediate shipment of twelve or fifteen code books, not code clerks. The cipher groups for 'books' and 'clerks' must have been nearly identical, say 'DOGEC' and 'DOGED', and hence a setup for the telegraphic garble. Thus, if my theory is right, the single letter 'D' sent me to Paris, when I had originally been slated for Berne. Even after forty years, the power of that minuscule slip of the alphabet gives me a high sense of insecurity. A 'D' for a 'C' sent Colonel House clerks instead of books, and sent me to France instead of Switzerland. On the whole, I came off far better, as events proved, than the Colonel did. There I was in Paris, with a lot of jolly colleagues, and there was Colonel House, up to his ears in code clerks, but without any code books, or at least not enough to handle the flow of cablegrams to and from the Crillon when the Peace Conference got under way.

That tiny 'D' was to involve the State Department, the Paris Embassy, the Peace Conference, and, in a way that would have delighted Gilbert and Sullivan, the United States Navy in a magnificent comic opera of confusion. An admiral of the Navy, for some reason (probably because he had a lot of Navy code books), arbitrarily took over, at the Crillon, the State Department's proud prerogative of diplomatic communication, and a code shambles that might have perplexed Herbert Yardley himself developed when cablegrams in Navy codes were dispatched to the State Department in Washington, which could not figure them out and sent back bewildered and frantic queries in State Department codes, which the admiral and his aides could not unravel. The Navy has always been proud of its codes, and the fact that they couldn't be broken by the State Department only went to show how strong they were, but when communication between the Peace Conference and Washington came to a dead stop, the admiral agreed to a compromise. His clerks, young and eager junior lieutenants, would use the State Department codes. This compounded the confusion, since the lieutenants didn't know how to use the strange codes. The dozen State Department clerks Colonel House had turned away and now needed badly were finally sent for, after a month, but even then they were forced to work under the supervision of the Navy. The Great Confusion was at last brought to an end when the desperate State Department finally turned to a newspaperman for help, and assigned him to go and get its stolen power of diplomatic communication and bring it back where it belonged. Not since an American battleship, many years before, in firing a twenty-one-gun salute in honour of the President of France, had accidentally used real shells and blown the bejeezus out of the harbour of Le Havre had the American

Navy so royally loused up a situation. And think of it – a 'DOGEC for a 'DOGED' would have sent me to Berne, where nothing at all ever happened.

The last time I saw the old building, at 5 rue de Chaillot, that housed the chancellery of the American Embassy when I was a code clerk, was in 1937. Near the high grilled door, a plaque proclaimed that Myron T. Herrick was our Ambassador during the First World War, thus perpetuating a fond American misconception and serving as a monument to the era of the Great Confusion. The truth is, as I have already said in an earlier piece in this book, that from December 1914 until after the war, in 1919, an unsung man named William Sharp was our Ambassador to France. This note of bronze fuzziness cheered me in a peculiar way. It was a brave, cock-eyed testament to the enduring strength of a nation that can get more ingloriously mixed up than any other and somehow gloriously come out of it in the end.

As I stood there before the old chancellery, I remembered another visit I had made to 5 rue de Chaillot, in 1925, and for the convenience of the F.B.I., who must already have twenty-three exhibits to fling at me when I am called up before some committee or other, I offer my adventure in 1925 as Exhibit x. Myron Herrick was once more our Ambassador to France, and I was granted an interview with him, or, as Counsellor Sheldon Whitehouse insisted on calling it, an audience. I had given up diplomacy for journalism, as I used to explain it, and I needed material for an article I was writing about Herrick for an American newspaper. I decided I ought to have a little 'art' to go along with the story, such as a photograph of the Ambassador's office, a large, bright, well-appointed room on the second floor, facing the street. I knew I couldn't get official permission to take a picture of the room, but this didn't discourage me. I had discovered that the same old French concierge lived in the same rooms on the ground floor of the chancellery and controlled the opening of the great, grilled door. Remembering that Sunday had always been an off day, with a skeleton staff in charge, I picked out a clear, sunny Sabbath for my exploit. I went to the chancellery and pushed the bell, and the concierge clicked the lock from her room. I went in, said '*Bonjour, Madame*,' went upstairs, photographed the Ambassador's office, came down again, having been challenged by nobody, said '*Bonjour, Madame*' to the concierge, raised my hat politely, and went away.

The Republicans were in charge of the Embassy then, not the Democrats, as in my code-clerk days, but things hadn't changed much. I am a pretty good hand at time exposures, and the photograph came out well. There is still a print of it in the art morgue of an American newspaper, or ought to be, but it is merely a view of a room in the home of whatever French family now lives at 5 rue de Chaillot.

We probably learned a lot during the recent war, and I doubt if tourists with cameras could get into any of our Embassies today. If this belated confession makes it a bit harder for them, anyway, I shall be very happy indeed. I must close now, since somebody is knocking at the door. Why, it's a couple of strange men! Now, what in the world could *they* want with me?

A New Natural History

A Trochee (left) encountering a Spondee.

The Hopeless Quandary.

CREATURES OF THE MEADOW

Left, the Aspic on a stalk of Visiting Fireman. Centre, the Throttle. Right, a Ticket in a patch of Marry-in-Haste. Below, a 99-year lease working slowly toward the surface through the years.

A pair of Martinets.

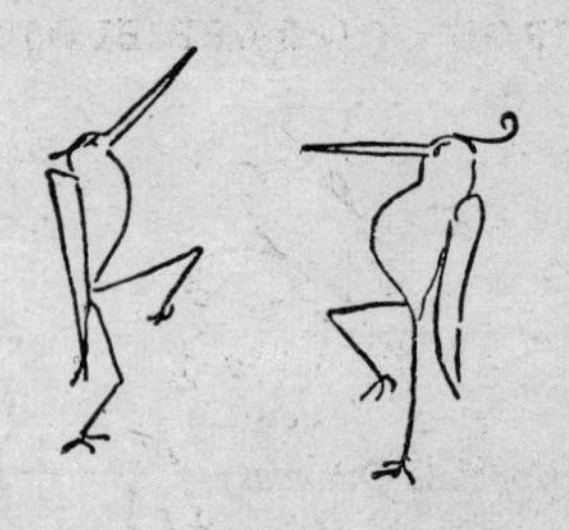

The Hoodwink on a spray of Ragamuffin.

The Bodkin (left) and the Chintz.

A GROUP OF RARE BLOSSOMS AND BUTTERFLIES

Flowers (left to right): Baker's Dozen, Shepherd's Pie, Sailor's Hornpipe, Stepmother's Kiss.
Butterflies (left to right): the Admirable Crichton, the Great Gatsby, the Magnificent Ambersons (male and female), the Beloved Vagabond.

The White-faced Rage (left) and the Blind Rage.

A GROUP OF MORE OR LESS PLEASANT BIRDS

Left to right: the Apothecary, the Night Watchman, the Scoutmaster, and the Barred Barrister.

The Goad.

The male Wedlock (left) cautiously approaching a clump of Devil-May-Care; at right, the female.

A female Shriek (right) rising out of the Verbiage to attack a female Swoon.

The Lapidary in a clump of Merry-Go-Round.

A Garble with an Utter in its claws.

The Dudgeon.

Two widely distributed rodents: the Barefaced Lie (left) and the White Lie.

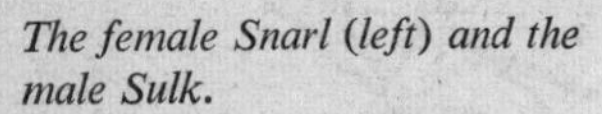

The female Snarl (left) and the male Sulk.

An Upstart rising from a clump of Johnny-Come-Lately. The small rodent (right) is a Spouse.

A GROUP OF BIRDS OF THE WESTERN HEMISPHERE

(Left to right) The Whited Sepulchre; the Misfit; the American Playboy, or Spendthrift, also sometimes called (southern U.S.A.) the Common Blackguard; a Stuffed Shirt; and (above) a Termagant.

The Femur (left) and the Metatarsal.

A GROUP OF SEMI-EDIBLE VEGETABLES

Top: Quench (left) and Arpeggio. Bottom: Therapy (left) and Scabbard.

The Living, or Spitting, Image (left) and the Dead Ringer.

A female Volt with all her Ergs in one Gasket.

The male and female Tryst.

The Early and the Late Riser.

A TRIO OF PREHISTORIC CREATURES

Left to right: the Thesaurus, the Stereopticon, and the Hexameter. The tree is a Sacroiliac.

A Scone (left) and a Crumpet, peering out of the Tiffin.

The Tantamount.

A Serenade (left) about to engage in combat with a Victual.

THREE FRESH-WATER CREATURES

The Qualm. *The Glib.* *The Moot.*

FOUR PLANTS OF THE TEMPERATE ZONE

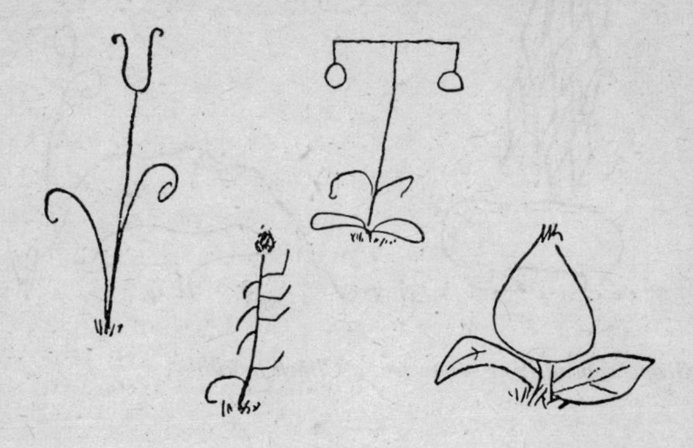

Left to right: Single Standard, False Witness, Double Jeopardy, Heartburn.

The Huff.

A Gloat near a patch of I-Told-You-So.

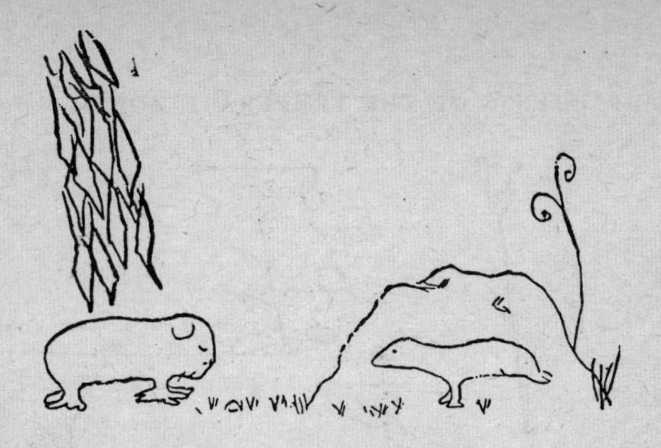

A Grope approaching, unaware, a Clinch in hiding.

The Peeve (or Pet Peeve).

The Troth, Plighted (right) and Unplighted.

Peeve. *The Common Carrier.*

A GROUP OF DESTRUCTIVE INSECTS

The Coal Bin.

The Clock Tick (or Stop Watch).

The Door Latch.

The Tire Tool.

The Window Ledge.

The Ball Bat.

A final note on Chanda Bell

(After reading two or three literary memorials, to this or that lamented talent, written by one critic or another)

THERE were only three of us around Chanda Bell at the end: Charles Vayne, her attorney; Hadley, the butler (if he was a butler); and myself. The others had departed with the beginning of the war, to new dedications, or old hideouts, and the obituaries in the journals after Miss Bell's death were erroneous in claiming that the great, dark house in the East Sixties was, up to the very last, bedlam and carnival. Chanda Bell's famous largesse and *laissez faire* had, naturally enough, attracted the strange and the sublimated from the nooks and crannies of Greenwich Village. I had been particularly pleased to witness the going away of the middle-aged man who rode the tricycle, the schoolteacher who had resigned from the human race to become a bird, and Miss Menta, the disturbingly nude Chilean transcendentalist.

Charles Vayne, as regular and as futile as a clock in an empty

house, showed up once a week with important documents that Chanda Bell would never sign. Some of them were dated as far back as 1924. A year of my friendship with the gifted lady had passed (so long ago!) before I could be sure that I knew what she was trying not to say, but Vayne never knew. Her use of the triple negative, in such expressions as 'not unmeaningless', and her habit of starting sentences in the middle bewildered him, and so did her fondness for surrogate words with ambiguous meanings, like the words in dreams: 'rupture' for 'rapture', 'centaur' for 'sender', 'pressure' for 'pleasure', and 'scorpio' for 'scrofula'. She enjoyed frustrating him, and she made the most of his discomfiture. 'Praise me!' she would say as he handed her a fountain pen and the documents, which she always waved away. 'Praise me!' she would command again. He invariably reacted the same way. It had become a kind of ritual. 'I repeat that I have not read a novel all the way through since *The Crimson Sweater* by Ralph Henry Barbour,' he would say. His expostulations and his entreaties amused her for a while, but then she would poke at him with her cane and drive him off, crying, 'He comes without armour who comes without art!'

Headley, who ushered the attorney in and out every Wednesday afternoon, had one cold, impassive eye and one that he could cause to twinkle. It gave you the chill sense of being, at one and the same time, in the presence of advocate and adversary. His duties in the final months were sparse, consisting mainly of serving Madeira to Chanda Bell and me, or to Chanda Bell and Vayne and me, in the Grey Room, after four o'clock, when she had had her egg and had dressed and was ready to receive. One always stood in her presence, for it was Chanda Bell's conceit to believe that only the uncomfortable are capable of pure attention.

Chanda Bell was fifty-seven when I first bent over her hand, and her mind seemed so keen and agile it was difficult to believe that she could confuse her guests, even her intimates, with one another. But she did. Charles Vayne was sometimes Lord Rudgate an Englishman of dim background and cryptic reference, and sometimes Strephon ('a Jung mad I cussed in the Sprig'). I was alternately Dennis, a deceased painter, who had specialized in gun dogs for the calendars of coal companies, and one McKinnon or

McKenyon, an advertising executive, who had attempted to deflower Miss Bell in a speeding motorboat during the panic of 1907. This was highly exasperating to such scholarly critics as Hudson, van Horne, and Dantes Woodrow, and they never came back after their separate agonized hours in the underwater gloom of the echoing Grey Room.

It is not congenial to me, at this time, to expose in detail how I became lost – if lost I became – in the 'brilliant wilderness' of Chanda Bell's prose, or to re-enact the process of equation, synthesis, and integration by means of which I was able to reveal the subtle affirmation compounded of the double negative of her unmeaning and her unmethod. This was ably – if mistakenly, still ably – set forth in my 'A Note on Chanda Bell'.* Upon its publication she had sent for me, and in the fine years of intellectual intimacy that followed, my faith in her genius was more often reinforced than not. It wasn't until the last few months, when, by design or aberration, she began to discuss herself, between teatime and twilight, as if she were discussing someone else, that the blackest of a critic's ravens, uncertainty of his soundness, came to dwell in my consciousness. It is a terrible thing not to be sure whether one has sought or been sought, not to be able to tell the hunter from the quarry, the sanctuary from the trap.

Chanda Bell had, in fact, commanded me to her salon, but had I not asked for it, had I not commanded the command, by the tribute of my unique and penetrating analysis of her work? She had cause to be grateful, and her summoning me to her side was, in my early opinion, the most natural of acts. Careless and churlish critics, in malice or mischief, had dismissed her bright and tangled intention with such expressions as 'bloom and drool', 'the amorphous richness of a thrown pie', 'as dull as Daiquiris with the commodore of a yacht club', and 'as far to the Right as a soupspoon'. This last was the sheerest nonsense. One might as reasonably have said that she was as far to the Left as a fish fork. The closest she ever came to mentioning politics was one day when, in a rare moment of merriment, she referred to Karl Marx as 'Groucho'. I myself had heard the faint and special obbligato of elfin horns in her work and the laughter in the dusty house, and

* *The Neutral Review*, October 1943.

I alone had seen the swift and single flashing of a naked nymph by moonlight.

It is hard to mark the hour and day when the thunderhead of suspicion first stains the clear horizon of an old admiration, but I came to be drenched, in the horrid mental weather of last autumn, by the downpour of a million doubts and dreads of Chanda Bell. I began to fear that she had perpetrated, in her half-dozen dense, tortured novels, one of the major literary hoaxes of our time and to suspect that she had drawn me into the glittering web of a monstrous deceit, in order to destroy, by proxy and in effigy, the entire critical profession. We would sit in the Grey Room from four till dark – she had permitted me to sit, at last, with the compassionate concession of a queen – and she would pierce my thin armour of hope and prayer with sharp and studied flicks of her sardonic, allusive intelligence. 'You have the scaffold touch of a brain certain,' she told me one afternoon. This was in the best tradition of her infernal dialectic. I could figure, in accordance with her secret code, that I had the scalpel touch of a brain surgeon, or I could take her to mean, in perverted literalness, that I was doomed to die – and was about to – an awful death for my wrong and sinful certainties.

'You have found the figure, Thurber,' she told me one afternoon, 'but have you found the carpet?' This was accompanied by her shrewd, tiny smile. I could not determine whether she meant there was something to find that I had not found, or nothing to find at all, beneath the gleaming surface of her style. The devil of it was that I could not be sure of anything. I spent that night going over *The Huanted Yatch* with a fine-tooth comb, searching for esoteric anagrams, feeling for what she had called 'the carpet'. I scrutinized, investigated, explored, took apart, and put back together again the entire fibre and fabric, uncertain of what shape and texture I was looking for. I read the thing backward, and I even tried to read it upside down and in the mirror of my bureau. I copied out one disturbing sentence and carried it about with me for close study: 'Icing mellow moony on a postgate doves snow and love surrender.' Its once perspicuous feel-meaning deserted me, and its cool loveliness became the chatter of a gibbon in my distraught consciousness. I could no longer tell whether it was beauty or balderdash. If it was balderdash, the book degenerated into the vivid cackling of a macaw, and my critique stood as a monument to a fatuous gullibility.

Toward the end, Chanda Bell began to talk about herself in the third person, as if she were not there in the house but on her way to visit us. 'I've asked her to tea,' she would tell me, 'but it will not astonish me if she fails to appear. Nobody has ever been able to pin her down.' And she would study the effect of this upon me with her hooded gaze. She had lapsed into simple, declarative sentences, and this was a comfort, but I was deeply perturbed by the feeling that her outlandish fantasy and her revelations were new and planned inventions of her cruelty.

'Chanda Bell,' she said one evening, 'had an allowance of two hundred dollars a week while she was still in pigtails. Her father, the millionaire industrialist, doted on the awkward, big-eyed little girl. He would bring her curtsying into the library for his cronies to admire. "By God, she'll be the first woman president of Standard Oil!" he exclaimed one night. He had a stroke when he discovered that she proposed to become a writer. "By God!" he roared. "I would sooner see you operate an unsuccessful house of ill repute!" At fourteen, a dreadful thing occurred. The small son of one of her father's gardeners sold two poems to the *Atlantic Monthly*, entitled "Ruffian Dusk" and "The Strangler of Light". Chanda offered him fifty dollars a week to write poems that she should sign and publish. The little boy coldly rejected the proposition, and his father, a stern Presbyterian, informed Chanda's father of the deal and how it had fallen through. "By God!" the old man roared. "At least she's not guilty of integrity, and that's more than I can say for any Bell in four generations except my grandfather and myself."'

Miss Bell let her reminiscence trail off here, and she watched me from her divan with her penetrating eyes. 'Ah,' I said hopefully, 'but she learned that day the high and holy importance of integrity of trust.' Chanda Bell gave me her sign of dismissal, a languid lift of her left hand. 'You are the critic,' she said. 'I am but the chronicler. Leave me now. You perceive she is not coming.' I rose and bowed. 'Perhaps,' I blurted out, 'there is no Chanda Bell.' But she had closed her eyes and turned away.

The next day, they took her to the hospital. 'I have a panther near my hearth,' she said, the first time they let me call on her. I went to see her twice again, the last time with Charles Vayne, who carried, with polished hopelessness, two bulging briefcases, which the nurse would not permit him to open. Chanda Bell was wandering in a far land, but she contrived a faint smile for each of her visitors. 'Dear Rudgate,' she whispered to Vayne, 'what will become of meaning, thank God, when you are dead?' He tried in silence to make her grip a fountain pen, but she shook her head and turned to me. 'Pretension has no plinth, Dennis,' she said. 'Ah, what a dusty answer. . . .' Her voice and her heart failed, and the most remarkable woman I have ever known was dead.

That night, I called at her house, in the East Sixties. Hadley let me in. I had suspected him for a long time of being joined in dark conspiracy with Chanda Bell to make an end of me. I wondered, as I glared at the cold eye and then at the warm one, whether he might not be a frustrated writer, a bankrupt publisher, or an editor who had suffered a nervous breakdown. I jumped over the amenities of sorrow. 'Her dying request,' I said, 'was that I should examine her papers.'

The eyebrow over his twinkling eye lifted. 'This evening, sir?' he asked.

'Take me to her desk and open it,' I demanded.

There was a full second's pause, then 'Certainly, sir,' he said, and led the way into the Grey Room. 'If I knew what you seek . . .' he began.

I turned on him. 'I think you do!' I snapped. 'I am looking for proof of whether I am an egregious ass or a uniquely perceptive individual. The line is sometimes thinly drawn between a tranquil old age in this city and exile, say, in Nassau.' He seemed genuinely bewildered.

There was nothing in the desk except a large manila envelope, which bore my name on the cover. I tore it open with shaking hands. Inside was a single sheet of white typewriter paper on which there were three carefully drawn squares, one inside another. 'What does it mean?' I asked. 'What is it?'

'If you will permit me, sir,' said Hadley, and he took the paper and studied it. 'That, sir,' he said, finally, 'is what I should describe as a drawing of a plinth.'

I seized him by the shoulder. 'You *are* in on this!' I cried. 'What does it mean? What's behind it? Who are you? What have you two devils been up to all these years? Why should you want to destroy *me*?'

He took a backward step and gaped. He was honestly frightened, or else he was a superb actor. There was no twinkle in his eye. 'I do not understand, sir,' he stammered, or seemed to stammer.

I let go of his shoulder. 'My critical reputation is at stake,' I said. 'Has she ever written an explanation of her writing – perhaps to be sent to some journal or periodical after her death?'

Hadley appeared to frown. 'That, sir, I could not say,' he brought out.

I turned away from him and then whirled back. 'What is the carpet?' I shouted.

He put several feet of the shiny floor between us. 'I do not know what you mean,' he said nervously.

'Would there be papers anywhere else?' I demanded.

He looked about the room. 'Nowhere,' he said hollowly.

I walked over and looked out a window for a long time.

Suddenly, Hadley began to speak. 'She had promised to put me in one of her books,' he said in a tone of sadness, or what came to my ears as a tone of sadness. Then his voice brightened. 'I was to have been the uncharacter of the nonbutler,' he said.

I came back from the window and glared at him.

'Her phrase, sir,' he added hastily.

I lighted a cigarette, inhaled the smoke, and blew it out slowly. 'Didn't you appear in any of her novels?' I asked.

'Oh, but no, sir,' he corrected me proudly. 'I did not appear in *all* of them!'

It was as if Chanda Bell were in the room, her bright, dark eyes taking us both in with a look of veiled amusement. 'It must have made you very happy indeed,' I snarled. 'Not to appear in any of her books was wonderful enough, but not to appear in *all* of them – the final accolade, Hadley, the final accolade.' He acknowledged it with a grave bow. 'What has become of her manuscripts and her letters?' I demanded.

Hadley put on a sad expression. 'She burned them, sir,' he said. 'It was her last act in this house.'

I looked for the last time at the Grey Room – the grey desk, the grey chair, the grey Hadley.

'Perhaps a glass of Madeira, Mr Thurber?' asked the butler. I declined ungraciously and said that I must leave. At the door, with the welcome street so near and desirable, he coughed discreetly. 'Do you wish to take this with you, sir?' It was the drawing of the plinth. I took it without a word. 'If I may say so, sir,' Hadley went on, 'you were the closest of all of them.'

I glared at him, but there was no twinkle. 'How close?' I growled.

'Oh, very close, sir,' he said. 'Very close indeed.' This time I thought I detected the ghost of the twinkle, but I could not be sure. I could not be sure of anything.

It has been eight months since I found the plinth in Chanda Bell's desk. Nothing has happened, but I expect an editor to ring me up any day. 'We've got a remarkable letter or manuscript here, apparently written by Chanda Bell,' he will say. 'Sent to us by her lawyer, in accordance with a request in her will. It isn't signed, but he says she wrote it, all right. Seems she never signed anything. Sort of laughter from beyond the grave, you might say. The old girl exposes her stuff as the merest junk. Proves her point, too. She takes a hell of a crack at your "Note on Chanda Bell". Thought you might want to read the thing and reply to it – we'll print you and her in the same issue. She calls the piece "The Carpet", for some reason. I'll shoot it along.'

No such call has come as yet, but I keep a bag packed, ready at a moment's notice to fly to Zanzibar, or Mozambique, or East Liverpool, Ohio. Meanwhile, I have hit on a new approach to the works of Chanda Bell. I am trying to read them sideways.

There's a time for flags

(Notes of a man who bought a curious Christmas gift)

15 DEC. – Yesterday morning at eleven o'clock I bought an American flag, five feet by three, and a white flagpole, eighteen feet high, surmounted by a bright golden ball, and now I am trying to figure out why. The incongruity of buying a flag and a flagpole in the middle of December as a Christmas present for my wife has begun to disturb me. True, the gesture is not so elaborate as that of the man in the madrigal who gave his true love a partridge in a pear tree, two turtle-doves, and more than a hundred and twenty other gifts, counting the fifes of the eleven fifers and the drums and drumsticks of the twelve drummers, but it is approximately as hard to explain. When did the idea first come to me? Or was it merely an idea? Could it be that I was seized by the stern hand of Compulsion, that dark, unseasonable Urge that impels women to clean house in the middle of the night and men, or at least me, to buy flags in the dead of winter?

As I write this, twenty-four hours have gone by since I bought the large flag and the enormous pole, but unlike every other purchase I have ever made, including my banjo-mandolin and my Cadillac, the emblem and staff show no signs of dwindling to normal proportions in my consciousness. They occupy the whole landscape of my thought. Last night I woke up and thought about the eighteen-foot pole, realizing sharply the measure and magnitude of what I had done. I had bought, for the yard of my home, a flagstaff designed and intended for the grounds of an institution. Nothing smaller than a boys' school with an enrolment of four hundred would think of ordering a pole of that heroic height. A flag for a private residence is supposed to be hung out of an upper-storey window on a five-foot pole. 'Great God,' I said aloud. 'What is happening?' asked my wife, without waking up. It was a good question, a searching wind, a whisper and a rumour . . . a wink of the eye . . . a shake of the head . . . high as his house, they say ... O say ain't you seen ... every heart beats true ... to the red, white, and blues in the night . . . where there's never a post or flag . . . and forever impede Mayhew Wade.

I became furled, at last, in sleep.

16 Dec. – I woke early this morning from a deep dream of flags, and tried to remember when I first got the idea, or when the Compulsion first got me. Did it go back to the quiet years in Washington, D.C., at the turn of the century, when I was fascinated by the miniature flags that came with packs of Sweet Caporal cigarettes? Have I always had a secret desire to command a battleship, or own an office building, or become headmaster of a boy's school with an enrolment of four hundred? Am I intent on blowing psychological taps over the memory of one of those horrible captains of cadets at Ohio State University forty-five years ago? If so, why didn't I buy a bugle? Oh, there must be some simpler explanation. Guilt. That's it. That's what it is. Guilt, the most powerful force in the life and psyche of the individual, more durable than love, deeper than fear. But guilt about what? What have I ever done that demands such a vivid and magnificent symbol of regret? I can think of nothing, except that, as a boy, I sympathized with the cause of the Southern Confederacy and once announced, in Miss MacIlvain's Eighth Grade class at Douglas School, that the South would have won the war if Stonewall Jackson hadn't been killed at the Battle of Chancellorsville. But this sin is surely not black enough to call for so large a flag and so long a pole. I continue to ponder the provenance of the purchase.

17 Dec. – This is exactly what happened. I phoned Jack Howard about three o'clock on the afternoon of 13 December – was it only four days ago? – and asked him if he would go shopping with me. There was a Christmas present I wanted to buy for somebody – a flag. 'A flag?' he asked. 'You mean one of those clips?' 'Not costume jewellery,' I said. 'If I were shopping for that, I'd take a woman with me. I want to buy an American flag. A big flag.' 'Oh?' Jack said, and, after a moment, 'Sure. Fine. Fine. When do you want to go? I can't make it this afternoon.' I arranged for him to pick me up the next morning at ten-thirty at my hotel in the West Forties. I had come to town three days before from my home in Cornwall, Connecticut, to buy a fl— to do my Christmas shopping.

When Jack and I were in a cab the next day, on our way to the famous Annin flag store, at Sixteenth Street and Fifth Avenue, he said, 'They're worried about you at my office – well, not worried exactly, but interested.' I didn't say anything. 'I told Chuck Nelson you were going to buy a flag and he said, "What's he up to?"' Jack laughed. 'All you need to do now,' he went on, 'is to buy a record of "The Stars and Stripes Forever" and they'll have you up before the Un-American Activities Committee.' He was right, and I was frightened. 'I wish you hadn't told everybody,' I said. 'A thing like this can get all over town.' I felt that he was studying my right profile. 'Well, what *are* you up to?' he asked, with a laugh that didn't seem genuine. 'I'm not up to anything,' I said coldly. 'I'm simply going to buy a flag. You don't have to go with me if you don't want to.' 'Forget it,' he said. 'I'll turn up my coat collar and pull down my hat. You call me Joe and I'll call you Sam.' I leaned back in the cab, trying to indicate that I didn't want to talk about it. He began to whistle George M. Cohan's tribute to Old Glory.

Outside of the employees of the store there was only one other person in Annin's when we got there. I realize suddenly as I write this that, in retracing my steps, I have come upon the small and simple solution of the case of the man who bought a flag in December. For some years now I have not been able to see to get around as well as I used to, especially in crowded stores at Christmastime. I remember now a rough experience I had last year in a store filled with fragile crystal and china objects, a store in which I had bought Christmas presents over a period of years. The last time I visited it, I distinctly overhead a clerk say, 'Sweet God, here's that man again!' I retreated from the store without buying anything, and fortunately without breaking anything, but the adventure had left its deep psychic scar. Subsconsciously, since that day I had been seeking an easy, a less perilous, way out of my private shopping problems. My unconscious mind had found the answer. Hardly anyone would be shopping for a Christmas present in Annin's in December. I recall now that a line of verse, written by Clinch Calkins thirty years ago, had been running through my thoughts for months: 'The peril streamed through us like flags.' By an easy process of association, the peril of shopping had been linked up with the word 'flags', and from there it was an even easier step for my mind to pick out the cathedral calm of the Annin store as the perfect place for me to buy my wife's principal Christmas present. The lady who stepped up to wait on us was gracious, competent, and unsuspicious. After all, you must run into all kinds of people in a flag store.

I see now that the flagpole was an afterthought. The five-by-three woollen flag that I decided on came to only five dollars, which didn't seem enough to pay for a gift. 'How about a ten-by-six?' I asked the lady. 'You don't want a ten-by-six flag,' Jack said. 'Not unless you own a skyscraper.' It was then that the idea came to me of buying a pole, halyards and all, to go with the Star-Spangled Banner. 'I would like to look at a flagpole,' I said. 'Certainly,' said the lady, leading the way to the flagpoles. 'Who is this present for?' Jack asked me. 'Eisenhower?' 'It's for my wife; it's for Helen,' I said. I had hold of his left arm and I could feel him shrug, but he didn't say anything. There were flagpoles six feet tall, twelve feet tall, and on up. I finally selected an eighteen-foot pole, which came in three six-foot sections. The price, six times that of the flag, seemed to be suitable for a Christmas gift for one's wife. 'What do you think of it?' I asked Jack. He sighed. 'It's your life,' he said. 'Go ahead. Maybe an eighteen-foot flagpole is what Helen has always wanted.' So I bought the flag and the pole and ordered them to be shipped to Cornwall, Connecticut. When we hailed a cab outside the store, Jack said, 'Let's go somewhere and grab a drink.' 'It's only eleven o'clock,' I told him. 'Let's go somewhere and grab a drink,' he said again, and we did.

18 Dec. 11 a.m. – Now that I know, or think I know, why I bought the flag and the flagpole, I have begun to worry about the effect they will have on my wife. She is used to getting things from me no larger than a woman's hand. I hope the pole doesn't upset her too much, the way the father in Barrie's *Mary Rose* was upset when they told him his daughter had suddenly returned after twenty-five years in Fairyland. 'I have been so occupied all my life with little things' was all that he could say. I don't want Helen to be stunned by a bolt from the red, wh— I mustn't go on like this.

2 p.m. – I finally told Ben Tuller, who does everything about my

place, from shooting crows to finding the coins I drop when I hang my trousers up, that I had bought a present for my wife that would probably arrive at the express office in four or five parts, three of them six feet long, 'I can get a couple of my wife's brothers to help me get it over here,' he said, 'and maybe we can stow it in the garage till Christmas without Mrs Thurber finding out, but I wouldn't count on it. Women have a way of knowing there are flags and flagpoles about. One thing I wanted to ask – ' 'How did you know it was a flag and a flagpole?' I cut in. He stared at me. 'You told me yesterday,' he said. Maybe I am losing my mind. I didn't remember telling him. 'What do you want to know?' I asked. Before replying he gazed out the window for a moment, and then, 'How do you aim to gift-wrap that pole?' he asked. I hadn't thought about that. I simply hadn't thought about it. And even if I could wrap the three six-foot sections, even if there was that much tissue paper and ribbon in the world, Helen wasn't strong enough to unwrap them. 'I'll have to exchange it,' I said. 'Maybe they haven't shipped it yet. I'll exchange it for something else.' 'At *Annin's*?' asked Ben. 'All you could get in place of it, I should think, would be a six-foot pole and maybe four more flags.' I turned, without a word, and walked out of the room.

11.45 p.m. – I can't go on with it. I'm not getting anything done. I just sit here and make occasional notes. A few minutes ago my wife came into my room and said, 'What are you up to?' There was that question again, that note of suspicion. 'I'm planning to overthrow the government,' I said. 'By force, if necessary.' 'Then you'll need your rest,' she said. 'Come on to bed.' As patriotic as she is, like all persons born in Nebraska, she'd be the first to lob a grenade into a congressman's living-room, if I gave the word. She has what has been called 'the strong loyalty of the wife.' I'm going to bed now, but that doesn't mean I'll sleep.

19 Dec. – Well, the cat's out of the bag. This morning I got a letter from Annin & Co., and my wife, who always reads the mail to me, opened it and began to read it aloud. 'No!' I cried, but it was too late. The fat was in the fire. The letter follows, in full, and will serve to authenticate these notes for such of my readers as may have suspected I didn't actually buy a flag and a flagpole but was just making it up:

Dear Sir,

As per the request of our Miss Tal, we are pleased to inform you that the flag and the flagpole are already on their way to you.

We wish to advise you, however, that we have billed you for an additional $3.00, due to the fact that Miss Tal erroneously charged you for the pole without the 22-K Gold Leaf Copper Ball. This additional charge of $3.00 is for the Gold Leaf Copper Ball.

Miss Tal was of the thought and opinion that you wanted the setup as displayed in the store, and the Ball is being shipped with the flag and the flagpole.

We trust that what we have done meets with your entire approval, and, hoping to be of further service to you, we are

Very truly yours,
Annin & Co.
George Jamieson

I told my wife the whole story, beginning with my phone call to Jack Howard. She was wonderful about it. 'I'm really glad to know what it is,' she said. 'Mr Purvis, at the express office, phoned this morning before you were up and said he had two packages for you, one of them more than six feet long, and heavy. I've thought of everything, from a croquet set to a collapsible dog kennel.' She considered a moment. 'The pole isn't luminous at night, is it?' she asked. 'I don't think so,' I said, 'but we could train a spotlight on the flag at night.' 'No, we couldn't,' she said. 'It's going to be evident enough the way it is, what with that twenty-two-carat gold ball.' I began to breathe shallowly. 'Three dollars seems pretty darn reasonable for a twenty-two-carat gold ball,' I said. 'Do you suppose they meant to say three hundred dollars?' My wife sighed. 'Men shouldn't be allowed to shop alone,' she said. 'It's – it's dangerous.' 'No, it isn't,' I protested. 'Well, chaotic then,' she said. I settled for that.

20 Dec. – Last night my wife woke me up long after midnight. It turned out she hadn't been able to get the eighteen-foot pole out of her mind. She had been lying there thinking about a lot of other things, too. 'I was just worrying about what the neighbours will think,' she said. 'I can't very well explain to them why you bought the flag and the pole, because it's too complicated. I understand it, but they wouldn't. They would just think you were facetious, or flippant, and you simply can't kid around about the American flag

in a quiet, reserved New England community like this.' I got up and lighted a cigarette. 'I'm not kidding around,' I said. 'I love the flag. As garish as it is, it has beauty, dignity, and even grandeur, and that is something of a miracle.' 'For heaven's sake,' she said, 'don't tell people it's garish.' 'What has happened to the time of Man,' I demanded, 'when the possession of your country's flag is looked upon as subversive or something?' Helen sighed. 'Well, anyway,' she said, 'we can't put it up in the snow. You'll have to wait till Flag Day. When is Flag Day?' 'April 14th, I think,' I told her. 'No, it's in June,' she said. 'I'm sure it's in June.' We both felt that we had better check on it, that we had better know the day. 'Of course,' Helen went on, 'it didn't help things when you and your daughter put those carbon copies of old letters to Harcourt, Brace in one of Mr Heston's pumpkins last year.' I stamped out my cigarette. 'I know, I know,' I said irritably. 'It didn't come off, but it was one of those things that seem like a good idea at the time. Anyway, we can forget about it until April.' 'June,' said my wife firmly. 'But it might be safer if we waited until the Fourth of July.' 'Maybe it would,' I agreed. 'Not even a senator could find fault with a man who flies the American flag on the Fourth.' I got back in bed. Half an hour later I spoke to her in the dark. 'I was just thinking,' I said, 'I was just thinking that everybody will hear about this and next December Annin's will be just as crowded as every other store on Fifth Avenue. I've killed the goose that laid the golden ball. It's going to be terrible for me.' 'It's going to be wonderful for Annin's,' murmured my wife. I couldn't tell whether she was awake or talking in her sleep.

21 Dec. – This morning I asked Ben Tuller if he had told his wife's brothers about the flag and the flagpole. 'They didn't have to help me.' he said. 'There were only two boxes, and I handled them myself.' My face must have shown relief. 'I wouldn't tell anybody about this,' he said. 'It's between you and me. You can count on that.' I thought he sounded a little aggrieved. 'I never questioned your loyalty,' I assured him. 'Of course, people are bound to see the flagpole sooner or later,' he said. 'We'll face that problem when we come to it,' I told him. 'Where is the stuff now?' 'In the attic,' he said. 'Do you want me to wrap the pole

for you?' 'No,' I said. 'I've decided just to wrap the flag. I can do that myself.' I started out of the room, but turned at the door. 'I suppose I should have married Barbara Frietchie,' I said. Ben made no comment.

Tonight I hope to sleep all the way through to the dawn's early light.

Am not I your Rosalind?

'"A RARE find is an able wife,"' George Thorne recited. 'There are cigarettes in that box, Fred.'

'I got some right here.' Fred Stanton pulled a pack from his pocket.

Thorne walked over, snapped his lighter, and held the flame for his guest. '"A rare find is an able wife,"' he began again. 'She rises early and pays off the servants, and so on, but she invariably mucks up the cocktail hour. I'll stir up some more Martinis for us.' He went over to the bar. 'They'll be up there a good half-hour. Let 'em catch up.'

Stanton watched his host's ritual with bottles, ice, and shaker. 'Lydia always shows her friends over the house, too,' he said, 'even if they've seen everything a hundred times.'

'Pride of possession.' Thorne stirred his mixture thoughtfully. 'These are my jewels, and so on. I gave Ann an old lace fan when we were in Rome before the war. Too fragile to handle, so she's just had it shadow-boxed. That'll take up a good fifteen minutes. Then, there's the Landeck dry point in the hall up there.'

'Thanks.' Stanton studied the cocktail pouring into his glass.

Thorne filled his own glass, set it and the shaker down, and went out into the hall and frowned up the stairs.

'I wouldn't yell at 'em,' Stanton said. 'Women don't like to be yelled at.'

'Ann!' Thorne called. There was no answer, no sound from upstairs. Thorne came back into the room and picked up his glass. 'To the ladies!' he declaimed. 'We can drink with 'em or without 'em.'

'Women like to do things in the house their own way,' Stanton brought out after some thought. 'That's a good cocktail.'

Throne walked over and filled his guest's glass again. 'O.K.?'

'Perfect.'

Thorne refilled his own glass. 'You're over-simplifying a pretty profound difference, Fred. Did you ever see directors at a board meeting exclaiming over a perfectly darling new water cooler or a desk calendar just too cunning for words?'

Stanton stirred uneasily and recrossed his legs. 'How do you shadow-box a fan?' he asked after an obvious search for something to turn the conversation.

'You set it in a deep frame against a rose-coloured background,' Thorne explained. 'Effective and expensive.' He glanced at his wrist watch and went out again to the bottom of the stairs. 'Hey! Girls!' he yelled. 'Ann! It's seven-thirty, for heaven's sake!'

A faint 'Shut up' drifted down from somewhere above. Stanton was sitting on the edge of his chair looking unhappy when his host came back, saying, 'A woman should be yelled at regularly, like an umpire – to paraphrase Noël Coward. Clears the air. Here.'

'Thanks,' said Stanton.

'Ann snaps back – I'll mix some more – but what the hell. Are they dry enough for you? She's got temperament – you know that – but I like it.' He went to the bar after swallowing his drink.

'Lydia's got temperament, too,' Stanton said defensively.

'Seems awful calm and level-headed.' Thorne poured the last measure of gin into the shaker.

'Lydia's got a lot – a lot of variety,' Stanton said, sitting up straighter.

'Oh, sure, sure,' Thorne said, stirring. 'Lydia's a swell gal.'

'Lydia, you know, Lydia' – Stanton's left hand seemed to be trying to pull out of the air an instance of his wife's variety – 'Lydia played Rosalind in her senior-class play when she was in high school,' he said loudly. And, apparently surprised at his outburst, and embarrassed, he lit a cigarette with unnecessary care. 'Oh, that was twenty, twenty-one years ago, in Binghamton. Played only one performance, of course. Every class – '

'For God's sake, this is wonderful!' Thorne cut in. 'This is really wonderful! Ann was Rosalind, too, in *her* senior-class play, in a high school in Nebraska. For God's sake! Hold out your glass.'

'Thanks,' said Stanton. He had the expression of a man who has unwarily touched something old and precious, like an heirloom, and seen it suddenly fall apart.

'Both the girls were born in 1919, so they must have been

ranting and posturing at practically the same time,' Thorne cried.

'I don't know that we better mention it,' Stanton said. 'You know how women are.'

Thorne laughed gleefully. 'What I want to find out is how women *were*, and I got just exactly the right thing. Do you know what a sound mirror is?'

'Have you got one of those wire recorders?' Stanton asked apprehensively. 'You could never get Lydia to talk into it. She'd never do that.'

'Look, you get a hambo high, any hambo, and he'll act.' Thorne chortled.

'After all, this was years ago,' Stanton said.

'Here they come. Leave it to me.' Thorne winked at him.

'If I were you – ' Stanton began.

The two women came down the stairs and into the room laughing and talking.

'You don't know what you got coming to you,' Thorne said.

'Fred, you simply *must* see the perfectly lovely fan George got Ann in Rome!' Lydia cried.

'What's the matter – are the drinks that bad?' Ann asked her husband.

'The drinks are excellent,' Stanton said. 'Excellent.'

Thorne went to the bar, chuckling.

'Has he rigged up a booby trap, or is he just merry and gay?' Ann said to Stanton.

'What's the matter with *you*, Fred?' his wife demanded. 'You look worried. Did Mickey Mantle die, or something?'

'George has been showing off, probably,' Ann said.

Thorne gave each of the women a glass and filled it up.

'No more for me,' Stanton said, raising his hand.

'Come on, we're going to have toasts, old boy. Here.'

'Thanks.' Stanton sighed.

'I was doing that big scene of mine from *A Night at an Inn*,' Thorne told his wife.

'George was all over the stage in college,' Ann said. 'He was picked as the man most likely to flop out of town.' The two women laughed, Thorne grinned, and Stanton shifted in his chair.

'We are poor little hams that have lost our way,' Thorne said, bowing to the women. 'Raise glasses.' Lydia and Ann looked at him. Stanton stared at the floor.

'What are you mumbling about?' Ann said.

'To the two fairest Rosalinds who ever strutted their little hour!'

'George!' Ann made a gavel rap of the name.

Then, suddenly, the two women looked at each other. There was a swift, almost reflex interchange of appraisal. It was as if each had clicked on and off the searching beam of a flashlight.

'Did you play Rosalind, too?' Ann cried.

'I'm afraid I did.' Lydia laughed. They laughed together.

'I think Rosalind is really horribly boring,' Lydia said. She looked at her husband, but he wouldn't meet her eyes.

'It's terribly hard to make her *appealing*,' Ann said. 'She's like Diana of the Crossways in a way. Didn't you *hate* Diana of the Crossways?'

Thorne went around draining the shaker, and moved tentatively to the bar. He could tell that it was all right to mix another round when Ann didn't say anything.

'Mickey Mantle isn't any Tris Speaker, but he's better than DiMaggio for my money,' said Stanton.

'Rosalind is one of the first ten aggressive ladies in literature.' Thorne had no intention of letting Diana or Mantle sidetrack the topic of conversation. 'That's what makes her a hell of a challenge to an actress. Being aggressive, she's also gabby, and that makes it a fat part.'

'George's descriptions are always so charming,' Ann said.

'Any child in her teens could enchant the Parent-Teacher Association by being cute as a little red wagon,' Thorne said.

'Oh, for God's sake, George!' Ann spanked out a cigarette she had just lighted.

'Anybody can be precocious,' Thorne went on. 'The real test comes in the years of maturity.'

'I know what you're up to, but it isn't going to work.' Ann turned to Lydia. 'He has one of those damn recorders, and he thinks he'll get us a little tight and make us perform.'

'You talk into it, turn a gadget, and – zip! – your voice comes out clear and perfect as a bell,' George explained.

'Really?' Lydia said.

'They used 'em in the Air Corps,' Stanton put in. 'Combat reports. Invented for that purpose.'

'George'll do a Jeeter Lester for you at the drop of a hat,' Ann said. 'And that big going-to-pieces scene from *What Price Glory?*'

Lydia, holding out her glass, laughed in a higher key than before. 'Goodness,' she said, 'I haven't done a thing since college.'

'College?' Ann gave her the appraising glance again.

'I don't know why Fred didn't bring it *all* out, in his cups. Lydia gave a little disparaging laugh. 'Yes, I did Nora in *A Doll's House*, and Candida.'

'Well!' Ann made a polite quaver of the exclamation. She held out her glass.

A white-coated coloured man appeared at the dining-room door.

'Herbert, would you ask Florence if she'll give us fifteen minutes more?' Ann said. He nodded and went away.

'There are several makes, all of them hard to get,' Stanton said, and coughed.

'I simply didn't have the time for it in college.' Ann waved it all away lightly with her left hand. 'So many *other* outside activities.'

Lydia brushed from her skirt a thread that was not there. 'Of course,' she said quietly.

Thorne stood grinning at his wife.

'We'll have time for another quick round,' she said. She looked coolly at Lydia. 'The wine can stand a bit more chilling.'

The two women smiled at each other, brightly. Thorne, mixing the Martinis, began to hum, 'I can do anything better than you. Anything you can do, I can do better. . . .'

Over the soup, Stanton wrenched the talk away from acting by launching into a vehement attack on Rube Marquard's record of nineteen straight victories on the mound, attributing the old pitcher's success to the dead baseball of his period. This led into an argument with Thorne as to the exact date of the Oeschger–Cadore twenty-six-inning pitching duel, during which the ladies discovered that they saw precisely eye to eye in the case of an enormous mutual friend who had let herself go with shocking results not only in girth but in intelligence. They were both reminded, in the same instant, of their common incredulity upon encountering a certain blonde whose youth and beauty had been utterly destroyed in less than a year of marriage. The talk joined when the women attacked and the men defended the blonde's husband – a heel, a swell guy, a lush, a drinker of incomparable moderation. It was all amiable enough. Thorne repeated a witticism about marriage that Ann had heard a dozen times, but she laughed merrily with the others.

Over the coffee and brandy in the living-room, the men revealed their secret knowledge of what was going on in the mind of Bulganin, and pointed out how any child could have avoided the blunders of Eden and Mollet. The women, meanwhile, were exchanging candid praises of each other's subtlety of taste in flower arrangement, working in a fleeting counterpoint of small self-deprecations.

Thorne gave one ear to Stanton's fluent breakdown of the first ten ballots that would be cast at the 1960 National Conventions. With the other ear, he sounded the temper of the women, the strength of whose mutual esteem he decided to test with further applications of brandy.

'It'll be a flurry, all right, but it won't be a trend,' Stanton said.

'Hmm?' Thorne had lost the thread of his guest's argument.

'The Kennedy bid,' Stanton explained. 'It'll be like one of those wide end runs that get everybody in the stands to yelling but don't go anywhere.'

The women did not protest when Thorne refilled their glasses. They were now shrewdly exploring the possibility that the enormous woman's vapid stare and slow mental activity might be the result, in part, of persistent overdoses of barbiturates.

'My dear,' Thorne said mockingly, grinning at each one in turn, 'If *I* were married to *that* man, I should *certainly* take – '

'Shut up,' said Ann.

Although the conversation took a dozen different turns, Thorne was careful not to let the mouse of Rosalind get too far away from the cat of his stubborn intention. He filled four or five lulls in the talk with interested questions. How many lines of the play if any, could they remember? Had there been reviews? Had they saved the programmes? How large were their audiences? Why had neither of the girls gone in seriously for a stage career when so many inconsiderable talents had achieved undeserved success? Ann and Lydia waved it all away with little laughs and 'Oh, for heaven's sake!' and 'I haven't the faintest idea,' but Thorne thought he saw the embers of pride glow again in the ashes of old dreams.

Between eleven o'clock and midnight, Stanton made several abortive moves to go, but he finally gave up. One o'clock found him sitting uncomfortably in his chair with the strained expression of a man who has resigned himself to a sleepless night in a hotel taken over by a convention of surgeons. Furthermore, his attempts to rise and his repeated 'Lydia, dear' had had the disturbing effect of bringing out, one after another, George Thorne's imitations of W. C. Fields, Ed Wynn, Al Jolson, Peter Lorre, and Henry Hull as Jeeter Lester.

During these sporadic performances, the smooth surface of Ann Thorne's dutiful attention had developed cracks obvious to her husband's trained eye, which had also discerned Lydia Stanton's polite amusement changing to brave tolerance and deteriorating at last into the restlessness of posture and precise dreaminess of eye that Thorne had been so energetically working to produce. During it all, Thorne had managed to keep the highball glasses constantly refreshed, and the success of this phase of his strategy showed in a glowing relaxation of manner, except in the case of Stanton, and a tendency in the women to use each other's name in every sentence.

'What do you say we run off my Chevalier recording?' Thorne said suddenly.

'He really does do a very good invitation of Chevalier, Lydia,' Ann said.

'We had about six of us here one night after a big party broke up,' Thorne explained. 'Everybody read or recited something into the recorder mike. I remember Tom Sessions read an editorial from the Phi Psi *Shield* – I had one lying around. Well, everybody shot off his mouth except Dot Gardner and Julia Reid. Oh, no – no, indeed – not for them! You wouldn't catch *them* making a fool of themselves. Of course, at three o'clock they elbowed the other hambos aside and took over the mike.'

Stanton cleared his throat. 'Lydia, dear,' he said.

'It was really too wonderful, Lydia,' Ann said, laughing.

'Dot read that Cornford poem – uh – "Autumn Morning in Cambridge"' Thorne said. 'I had a first edition lying around.'

'And what was it Julia did, George?' Ann giggled.

'Lizette Woodworth Reese's, as God is my judge, "Tears".'

'Oh, no!' Lydia shouted. 'That tiny voice, Ann, coming out of that enormous hulk!'

'It was rich,' Thorne said. 'What the hell, it *is* rich! The goddamn thing is preserved for lucky people of the future, digging around in the atomic rubble. Let's play it. My Chevalier imitation, a perfect gem, is thrown in for good measure.'

'Lydia,' Stanton said.

'It's in the library, the recorder is in the library,' Thorne said.

'Come on, Fred.' Lydia took his arm, smiled, and whispered savagely, 'For God's sake, keep your eyes open!'

'Bring your drink, Fred,' Thorne said. 'Let me put some more ice in it.'

'No, thanks,' said Stanton. 'It's fine.' He saw, first the small microphone on the table in the library, and his reluctant eyes followed the cord attached to it as if it were a lighted fuse glittering toward the ominous box at the other end.

'I think you better get Herbert to do it, George,' Ann said. 'Or maybe Fred could – '

Her husband scowled. 'For God's sake, Ann, I've worked this thing a hundred times.'

'I know,' she said, with a look of a woman riding in a car driven by a little boy.

'It's a perfectly wonderful-looking thing,' Lydia said. 'Was it terribly expensive?'

'Around two hundred and fifty bucks,' Thorne said. 'We're in luck. That spool's on here now.'

Stanton was gazing with tidy disapproval at the reproduction of Dufy's *Marne* over the fireplace.

'Are you sure you can make it go without breaking it?' Ann asked.

Thorne did not look at her. 'Here we go!' he yelled.

The machine began to hum, low and menacingly. There was a loud electric whine, a sudden roar, and George's recorded voice bawled from the machine, 'O.K., Herbert? Is it O.K.?'

'Yes, sir, you can go ahead, sir,' the butler's voice bellowed.

'Turn down the volume! For the love of heaven, turn it down!' Ann screamed.

Thorne succeeded at last in finding the knob that controlled the volume. They listened while the solemn voice of Tom Sessions turgidly read an editorial from the Phi Psi *Shield* entitled 'The Meaning of Fraternity in Wartime'. Lydia began to squirm in her chair. She turned on a frosty smile when the voice of her host began a burlesque of Chevalier explaining in English the meaning of *Auprès de Ma Blonde*. During this performance, Thorne modestly left the room, carrying the four highball glasses. He spiked the women's drinks, shooting in only two squirts of soda. He came back in time to hear the voice of Dorothy Gardner reciting, in a curiously uneven mixture of eloquence and uncertainty, the Cornford lyric.

'Sounds like a crippled halfback running through a broken field,' Thorne said.

'Sh-h,' said Lydia. She put her tongue out at the first taste of the powerful highball.

'Go get that seltzer bottle,' Ann commanded.

Thorne grinned and went out to the bar.

'Don't miss this coming now!' Ann cried.

The voice of Julia Reid, exalted, abnormally low, got by 'A rose choked in the grass . . .' and then died. There was a long pause. 'What the hell comes next?' the diseuse demanded. A dim voice that had spoken far from the microphone prompted her. The voice of the unseen, elated lady then went on to finish Miss Reese's sonnet in a tone of almost sepulchral dignity.

'I really think, Lydia – ' Stanton said.

Ann took the seltzer bottle from Thorne and diluted Lydia's drink and her own. 'Turn it off,' she said. The reel was still unwinding, but no voices came from it.

'Wait a second,' Thorne said. 'Don't you want to hear Mark and Ken sing "I Had a Dream, Dear"?' Two male voices began a ragged rendition of the old song in a key too low for them. Ann went over and shut off the machine.

'Well, sir, that was very fine,' Stanton proclaimed loudly. He stood up.

'I'm going to put on a new spool for the gals,' Thorne said. 'Sit down, Fred.'

Ann and Lydia protested quickly, but not, Thorne's ear told him, with sharpness or finality. There was a hint of excitement, an unmistakable eagerness in their chimed 'Oh, no, you're not!'

'I can put on a new one faster than you can say Sarah Bernhardt,' he said.

'I've never heard my own voice,' Lydia said. 'They say you never recognize your own voice.'

'It's because you hear the sound internally, inside your mouth,' Ann explained. 'It's really fascinating.'

'*As You Like It* is right there on the second shelf, Volume Two, the collected comedies,' Thorne said.

'Oh, for heaven's sake,' Ann squealed. 'I haven't looked at that damn play for twenty years!'

Lydia quietly finished her drink.

'There we are,' Thorne said, stepping back and scowling at the sound mirror. 'All ready to shoot. Here, I'll get the book.'

Stanton, eyes closed, hands gripping his chair arms, seemed to be awaiting the impact of a dentist's drill. The women made little arrangements of their hair and skirts. Thorne flipped through the pages of the Shakespeare volume. 'May the best Rosalind win!' He grinned. 'How about this?'

Stanton tightened his grip on the chair. Ann examined her wedding ring. Lydia studied the floor.

'"A lean cheek, which you have not, a blue eye and sunken, which you have not, an unquestionable spirit, which you have not – "'

'For heaven's sake, George, read it straight,' Ann broke in. 'Don't act it.'

'"A beard neglected, which you have not; but I pardon you for that, for simply your having in beard is a younger brother's revenue: then your hose should be ungartered, your bonnet unbanded, your sleeve unbuttoned, your shoe untied and everything about you demonstrating a careless desolation; but you are no such man; you are rather point-device in your accoutrements as loving yourself than seeming the lover of any other."'

'That *awful* speech,' Ann said. 'I hated it.'

'You don't happen to have a copy of *Candida*?' Lydia asked.

'Not fair,' Thorne said. 'Ann never did Candida. How about this passage? "Yes, one, and in this manner. He was to imagine me his love, his mistress; and I set him every day to woo me: at which time would I, being but a moonish youth, grieve, be effeminate, changeable, longing and liking, proud, fantastical, apish, shallow, inconstant, full of tears, full of smiles, for every passion something and for no passion truly anything, as boys and women are for the most part cattle of this colour; would now like him, now loathe him; then entertain him, then forswear him; now weep for him, then spit at him; that I drave my suitor from his mad humour of love to a living humour of madness; which was, to forswear the full stream of the world and to live in a nook merely monastic. And thus I cured him; and this way will I take upon me to wash your liver as clean as a sound sheep's heart, that there shall not be one spot of love in't."'

'Wouldn't you just *know* a man wrote that?' Ann lifted her hands hopelessly.

'It has to be thrown away, you know – parts of that speech.' Lydia sighed, as if it were impossible to explain how to attack this particular passage.

'Oh, let's do it and get it over with, Lydia,' Ann said. 'Do you want to go first?'

'You go ahead, darling.' Lydia waved at Thorne, and he handed his wife the book, pointing at the selected speech. Ann's eyebrows went up when she looked at the page. 'The type is funny,' she announced.

'Read it over a couple of times while I fix a nightcap.' Thorne gathered up all the glasses.

'Just one sip,' Ann said when, a few minutes later, he brought in the fresh highballs.

'Ready?' asked Thorne.

'Roll 'em,' she said.

The machine began to hum. Ann leaned toward the microphone on the edge of the table. Then she leaned back with a shy little run of laughter. 'Heavens, I can't do it in front of people!' Her girlish ripple coagulated when she caught the professional glint of amusement in Lydia's eye. 'All right, George,' Ann said. 'Start the damn thing.'

She seemed to her watchful husband to lunge suddenly, like an unwary boxer. She gave the speech at the very beginning a brisk blow from which it never recovered. The swiftness of her attack was too much for the old lines, and although she slowed down half-way through, the passage could not regain its balance. It faded, brightened unexpectedly, faded again, and collapsed with a dignified whisper at the end. Thorne repressed a wild impulse to jump over and raise his wife's right hand.

Stanton applauded loudly, and all three of her audience called out 'Fine!' and 'Wonderful!'

Ann showed charming dismay. 'Mercy! I was *horrible*!' she wailed. 'You'll murder me, Lydia.'

'You were perfectly fine,' Lydia said.

'Here we go, Lydia!' Thorne shouted. 'Your time has come.'

'Oh, dear, I hate to follow Ann,' Lydia almost whispered. She made an elaborate rite of lifting her highball glass and taking a final sip, and then began to read.

Fred Stanton turned a slow, wondering head toward the source of a voice he had never heard before. It was low, resonant, and strange.

Closing his eyes and pursuing his image of the prize ring, Thorne saw Lydia circle cautiously about the lines, waiting for an opening. She did not find one. Her slow, monotonous tactics went on to the end. It reminded Thorne of the first few rounds of the second Louis–Conn fight.

Thorne led the loud applause this time, Ann shrieked with delight, Stanton said, 'Well, well, well!' and Lydia sat back, covered her eyes with her hand, and shook her head despondently, like a frustrated prima donna whose trunks have gone astray in a small town.

'Well, well, well,' Stanton said again. He got to his feet.

'Sit down, Fred,' Thorne said. 'We got to play it back.'

Worrying the machine as if it were a tangled fishing line, he finally made the necessary shifts and adjustments. 'Quiet! Here we go!' he yelled. The volume was stepped up as high as it would go. 'I set him every day to woo me!' Ann howled from the machine. Thorne made a wild leap and cut the volume down.

'Goddamn it!' Ann said, glaring at him. Then, 'Oh, no,' she whispered, her startled stare disowning the unfamiliar voice that mocked her from the sound mirror. Stanton started to applaud at the end, but Thorne cut him off with 'Sh-h, here comes Lydia!' and moved quickly to the recorder and, as if in an innocent effort to ensure perfection of reproduction, shot up the volume on Lydia's opening line, so that she also bawled it. He turned it down instantly. 'Well,' Lydia said. Then, 'That's not me!' 'Perfect,' Stanton said. Everybody stared fixedly at the machine.

When it was over, Stanton broke through the chatter with a determined 'Very fine, very fine! We must go, Lydia.' 'Can't I sell a nightcap, one nightcap?' Thorne kept saying. But the others moved out of the library, Stanton firmly leading the way. Five minutes later, a high tide of gaiety flooded the front hallway and bore out into the night a bright flotsam of pledge and promise, praise and disclaimer, regrets at parting, and wonder at the swiftness of time.

The Stantons drove in silence until they were a good three hundred yards from the house.

'Well!' Lydia sighed with tired satisfaction, ran up the window, and settled back comfortably. 'I've heard some strange performances in my life, but I never heard anything like that. I sat there biting my lip.' She made a Jane Cowl gesture.

'Yeah,' Stanton said.

'That silly little singsong voice,' she went on. 'Why, she can barely *read*. And the way she kept batting her eyes, trying to look cute and appealing.'

'She doesn't drink very well,' Stanton said. 'She had an awful lot to drink.'

Lydia laughed harshly. '"Invitation of Chevalier!" I thought I would *scream*. I really thought I would *scream*!'

'What was that?' Stanton asked.

'Oh, you didn't get it, of course, sitting there with your eyes closed, a million miles away. You didn't say one word, one single, solitary word, from ten o'clock until we left that house, except "Lydia, dear – Lydia, dear – Lydia, dear," until I thought I would go *out* of my mind.'

'Aw,' Stanton said. He reached for the pack of cigarettes in his pocket.

'I'll light it for you. Keep your hands on the wheel.'

'Light the match toward you,' he said. 'Don't strike it away from you. You always strike it away from you.'

She wasted three matches striking them away from her. 'Slow down,' she said.

He stopped the car. 'I'll light it,' he told her. 'That guy always gets me down. He won't sit still and he won't stop talking. Yammering all over the place.'

'At least he stays awake, at least he knows what's going on.'

'Anyway, you were wonderful,' Stanton said quickly. 'You made Ann look like an amateur. You were marvellous.'

She sighed a hopeless little sigh. 'Well, you either have talent, Fred, or you haven't. She must have been the only girl in that Wyoming school, or wherever it was. You went past that turn again.'

Stanton stopped the car and began to back up. 'What was that goddamn fan like?' he asked.

'It was awful,' she told him. 'And if she said "George got it for me in Rome" once, she said it fifty times. George obviously got it from some Italian street peddler for a few francs. Eighteenth-century, my foot!'

They drove awhile in silence. 'Lire,' Stanton said.

Lydia sniffed. 'I doubt it,' she said.

Back in their living-room, the Thornes were having a short nightcap. 'I wish the hell you wouldn't always act as if I couldn't make anything work,' Thorne said. 'I can do more with my feet than that big dolt can do with his hands. "Better let Fred do it, George. Better get Herbert to do it." For God's sake, lay off, will you? I made the thing work. I always make it work.'

'Shut up, George, and give me some more ice,' Ann said. 'The thing that really got me, though, was that horrible affectation. She sounded like a backward child just learning to read.' She paused and put on a frown that her husband recognized. She wore it when she was hunting for a grievance. She found one. 'If you can make it work so well, why did you turn it up so high people could hear me yelling for three blocks?'

'I cut it down right away, didn't I, and I made her yell even louder.'

Ann laughed. 'That was wonderful. That was really wonderful, George.'

'At your service.' Thorne bowed. 'Come on, let's go with unlighted candle dark to bed. The light that breaks through yonder Eastern window is not the setting sun, my pet.'

They got up and Thorne turned out the lights. 'Does he know *anything*? Has he got a brain in his head?' she demanded.

'Fred? God, no! He has the mind of a turtle.'

'If he'd only yawn and get it over with, instead of working his mouth that way.'

Half-way up the stairs, Ann turned suddenly. Thorne stopped and looked up at her. 'Do you know the most ghastly thing about her?' she asked.

'That moo-cow voice?'

'No. Heaven knows that's bad enough; but can you possibly imagine her in doublet and *hose*? Those *legs*, George, those *legs*!'

Thorne jumped a step, caught up with her, and they went the rest of the way to their bedroom arm-in-arm.

The French Far West

In one of the many interesting essays that make up his book called *Abinger Harvest*, Mr E. M. Forster, discussing what he sees when he is reluctantly dragged to the movies in London, has set down a sentence that fascinates me. It is: 'American women shoot the hippopotamus with eyebrows made of platinum.' I have given that remarkable sentence a great deal of study, but I still do not know whether Mr Forster means that American women have platinum eyebrows or that the hippopotamus has platinum eyebrows or that American women shoot platinum eyebrows into the hippopotamus. At any rate, it faintly stirred in my mind a dim train of elusive memories which were brightened up suddenly and brought into sharp focus for me when, one night, I went to see *The Plainsman*, a hard-riding, fast-shooting movie dealing with warfare in the Far West back in the bloody seventies. I knew then what Mr Forster's curious and tantalizing sentence reminded me of. It was like nothing in the world so much as certain sentences which appeared in a group of French paperback dime (or, rather, twenty-five centime) novels that I collected a dozen years ago in France. *The Plainsman* brought up these old pulp thrillers in all clarity for me because, like that movie, they dealt mainly with the stupendous activities of Buffalo Bill and Wild Bill Hickok; but in them were a unique fantasy, a special inventiveness, and an imaginative abandon beside which the movie treatment of the two heroes pales, as the saying goes, into nothing. In the moving from one apartment to another some years ago, I somehow lost my priceless collection of *contes héroïques du Far-West*, but happily I find that a great many of the deathless adventures of the French Buffalo Bill and Wild Bill Hickok remain in my memory. I hope that I shall recall them, for anodyne, when with eyes too dim to read I pluck finally at the counterpane.

In the first place, it should perhaps be said that in the eighteen-nineties the American dime-novel hero who appears to have been most popular with the French youth – and adult – given to such literature was Nick Carter. You will find somewhere in one of John L. Stoddard's published lectures – there used to be a set in almost every Ohio bookcase – an anecdote about how an American tourist, set upon by *apaches* in a dark *rue* in Paris in the nineties, caused them to scatter in terror merely by shouting, '*Je suis Nick Carter!*' But at the turn of the century, or shortly thereafter, Buffalo Bill became the favourite. Whether he still is or not, I don't know – perhaps Al Capone or John Dillinger has taken his place. Twelve years ago, however, he was going great guns – or perhaps I should say great dynamite, for one of the things I most clearly remember about the Buffalo Bill of the French authors was that he always carried with him sticks of dynamite which, when he was in a particularly tough spot – that is, surrounded by more than two thousand Indians – he hurled into their midst, destroying them by the hundred. Many of the most inspired paperbacks that I picked up in my quest were used ones I found in those little stalls along the Seine. It was there, for instance, that I came across one of my favourties, *Les Aventures du Wild Bill dans le Far-West*.

Wild Bill Hickok was, in this wonderful and beautiful tale, an even more prodigious manipulator of the six-gun than he seems to have been in real life, which, as you must know, is saying a great deal. He frequently mowed down a hundred or two hundred Indians in a few minutes with his redoubtable pistol. The French author of this masterpiece for some mysterious but delightful reason referred to Hickok sometimes as Wild Bill and sometimes as Wild Bird. '*Bonjour, Wild Bill!*' his friend Buffalo Bill often said to him when they met, only to shout a moment later, '*Regardez, Wild Bird! Les Peaux-Rouges!*' The two heroes spent a great deal of their time, as in *The Plainsman*, helping each other out of dreadful situations. Once, for example, while hunting Seminoles in Florida, Buffalo Bill fell into a tiger trap that had been set for him by the Indians – he stepped on to what turned out to be sticks covered with grass, and plunged to the bottom of a deep pit. At this point our author wrote, '"*Mercy me!*" *s'écria Buffalo Bill.*' The great scout was rescued, of course, by none other than Wild Bill, or Bird, who, emerging from the forest to see his old comrade in distress, could only exclaim, '*My word!*'

It was, I believe, in another volume that one of the most interesting characters in all French fiction of the Far West appeared, a certain Major Preston, alias Preeton, alias Preslon (the paperbacks rarely spelled anyone's name twice in succession the same way). This hero, we were told when he was introduced, 'had distinguished himself in the Civil War by capturing Pittsburgh', a feat which makes Lee's invasion of Pennsylvania seem mere child's play. Major Preeton (I always preferred that alias) had come out West to fight the Indians with cannon, since he believed it absurd that nobody had thought to blow them off the face of the earth with cannon before. How he made out with his artillery against the forest skulkers I have forgotten, but I have an indelible memory of a certain close escape that Buffalo Bill had in this same book. It seems that, through an oversight, he had set out on a scouting trip without his dynamite – he also carried, by the way, cheroots and a flashlight – and hence, when he stumbled upon a huge band of redskins, he had to ride as fast as he could for the nearest fort. He made it just in time. 'Buffalo Bill', ran the story, 'clattered across the drawbridge and into the fort just ahead of the Indians, who, unable to stop in time, plunged into the moat and were drowned.' It may have been in this same tale that Buffalo Bill was once so hard pressed that he had to send for Wild Bird to help him out. Usually, when one was in trouble, the other showed up by a kind of instinct, but this time Wild Bird was nowhere to be found. It was a long time, in fact, before his whereabouts were discovered. You will never guess where he was. He

'Vous vous promenez très tard ce soir, mon vieux!'

was ‘taking the baths at Atlantic City under orders of his physician’. But he came riding across the country in one day to Buffalo Bill’s side, and all was well. Major Preeton, it sticks in my mind, got bored with the service in the Western hotels and went ‘back to Philadelphia’. (Philadelphia appears to have been the capital city of the United States at this time.) The Indians in all these tales – and this is probably what gave Major Preeton his great idea – were seldom seen as individuals or in pairs or small groups, but prowled about in well-ordered columns of squads. I recall, however, one drawing (the paperbacks were copiously illustrated) which showed two *Peaux-Rouges* leaping upon and capturing a scout who had wandered too far from his drawbridge one night. The picture represented one of the Indians as smilingly taunting his captive, and the caption read, ‘*Vous vous promenez très tard ce soir, mon vieux!*’ This remained my favourite line until I saw one night in Paris an old W. S. Hart movie called *Le Roi du Far-West*, in which Hart, insulted by a drunken ruffian, turned upon him and said, in his grim, laconic way, ‘*Et puis, après?*’

I first became interested in the French tales of the Far West when, one winter in Nice, a French youngster of fifteen, who, it turned out, devoted all his spending money to them, asked me if I had ever seen a ‘wishtonwich’. This meant nothing to me, and I asked him where he had heard about the wishtonwish. He showed me a Far West paperback he was reading. There was a passage in it which recounted an adventure of Buffalo Bill and Wild Bill, during the course of which Buffalo Bill signalled to Wild Bird ‘in the voice of the wishtonwish’. Said the author in parenthesis which at that time gave me as much trouble as Mr Forster’s sentence about the platinum eyebrows does now, ‘The wishtonwish was seldom heard west of Philadelphia.’ It was some time – indeed, it was not until I got back to America – before I traced the wishtonwish to its lair, and in so doing discovered the influence of James Fenimore Cooper on all these French writers of Far West tales. Cooper, in his novels, frequently mentioned the wishtonwish, which was a Caddoan Indian name for the prairie dog. Cooper erroneously applied it to the whip-poor-will. An animal called the ‘ouapiti’ also figured occasionally in the

French stories, and this turned out to be the wapiti, or American elk, also mentioned in Cooper's tales. The French writer's parenthetical note on the habitat of the wishtonwish only added to the delightful confusion and inaccuracy which threaded these wondrous stories.

There were, in my lost and lamented collection, a hundred other fine things, which I have forgotten, but there is one that will forever remain with me. It occurred in a book in which, as I remember it, Billy the Kid, alias Billy the Boy, was the central figure. At any rate, two strangers had turned up in a small Western town and their actions had aroused the suspicions of a group of respectable citizens, who forthwith called on the sheriff to complain about the newcomers. The sheriff listened gravely for a while, got up and buckled on his gun belt, and said, '*Alors, je vais demander leurs cartes d'identité!*' There are few things, in any literature, that have ever given me a greater thrill than coming across that line.

The Masculine Approach

The candy-and-flowers campaign.

The I'm-drinking-myself-to-death-and-nobody-can-stop-me method.

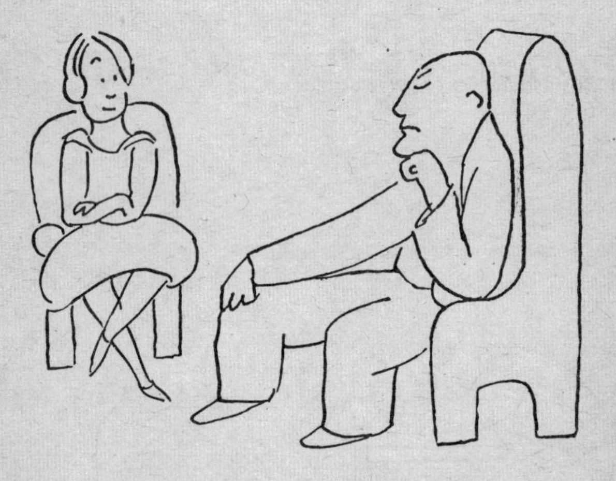

The strong, silent system.

The pawing system.

The strange-fascination technique.

The you'll-never-see-me-again tactics.

The heroic, or dangers-I-have-known, method.

The let-'em-wait-and-wonder plan.

The unhappy-childhood story.

The indifference attitude.

The letter-writing method.

The man-of-the-world, or ordering-in-French, manoeuvre.

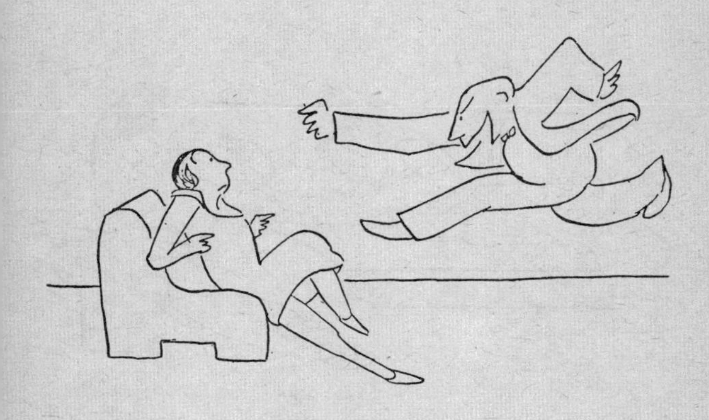

The sweep-'em-off-their-feet method.

The her-two-little-hands-in-huge-ones pass.

The sudden onslaught.

The continental-manners technique.

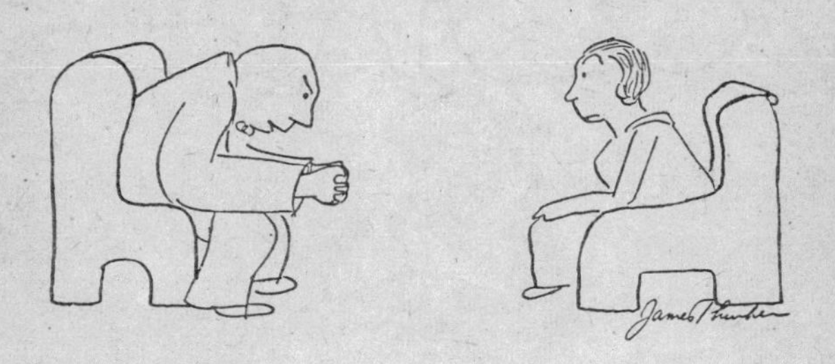

The I'm-not-good-enough-for-you announcement.

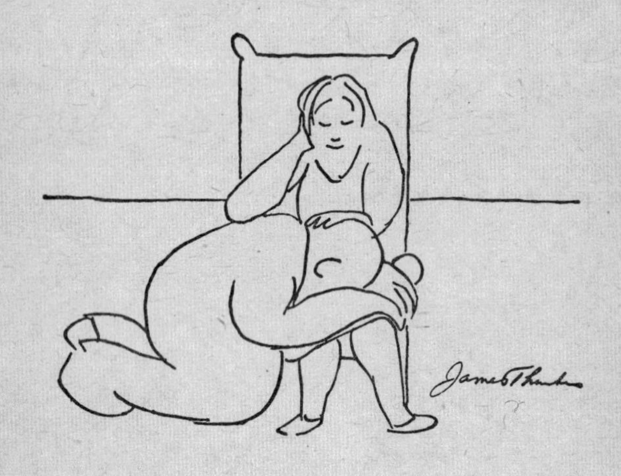

The just-a-little-boy system.

The Harpo Marx attack.

The I-may-go-away-for-a-year-or-two move.

A friend to Alexander

'I HAVE taken to dreaming about Aaron Burr every night,' Andrews said.

'What for?' said Mrs Andrews.

'How do I know what for?' Andrews snarled. 'What for, the woman says.'

Mrs Andrews did not flare up; she simply looked at her husband as he lay on the chaise-longue in her bedroom in his heavy blue dressing-gown, smoking a cigarette. Although he had just got out of bed, he looked haggard and tired. He kept biting his lower lip between puffs.

'Aaron Burr is a funny person to be dreaming about nowadays – I mean with all the countries in the world threatening each other. I wish you would go and see Dr Fox,' said Mrs Andrews, taking her thumb from between the pages of her mystery novel and tossing the book toward the foot of her bed. She sat up straighter against her pillow. 'Maybe haliver oil or B_1 is what you need,' she said. 'B_1 does wonders for people. I don't see why you see *him* in your dreams. *Where* do you see him?'

'Oh, places; in Washington Square or Bowling Green or on Broadway. I'll be talking to a woman in a victoria, a woman holding a white lace parasol, and suddenly there will be Burr, bowing and smiling and smelling like a carnation, telling his stories about France and getting off his insults.'

Mrs Andrews lighted a cigarette, although she rarely smoked until after lunch. 'Who is the woman in the victoria?' she asked.

'What? How do I know? You know about people in dreams, don't you? They are nobody at all, or everybody.'

'You see Aaron Burr plainly enough, though. I mean he isn't nobody or everybody.'

'All right, all right,' said Andrews. 'You have me there. But I don't know who the woman is, and I don't care. Maybe it's Madame Jumel or Mittens Willett or a girl I knew in high school. That's not important.'

'Who is Mittens Willett?' asked Mrs Andrews.

'She was a famous New York actress in her day, fifty years ago or so. She's buried in an old cemetery on Second Avenue.'

'That's very sad,' said Mrs Andrews.

'Why is it?' demanded Andrews, who was now pacing up and down the deep red carpet.

'I mean she probably died young,' said Mrs Andrews. 'Almost all women did in those days.'

Andrews ignored her and walked over to a window and looked out at a neat, bleak street in the Fifties. 'He's a vile, cynical cad,' said Andrews, suddenly turning away from the window. 'I was standing talking to Alexander Hamilton when Burr stepped up and slapped him in the face. When I looked at Hamilton, who do you suppose he was?'

'I don't know,' said Mrs Andrews. 'Who was he?'

'He was my brother, the one I've told you about, the one who was killed by that drunkard in the cemetery.'

Mrs Andrews had never got that story straight and she didn't want to go into it again now; the facts in the tragic case and her way of getting them mixed up always drove Andrews into a white-faced fury. 'I don't think we ought to dwell on your nightmare,' said Mrs Andrews. 'I think we ought to get out more. We could go to the country for week-ends.'

Andrews wasn't listening; he was back at the window, staring out into the street again.

'I wish he'd go back to France and stay there,' Andrews snapped out suddenly the next morning at breakfast.

'Who, dear?' said his wife. 'Oh, you mean Aaron Burr. Did you dream about him again? I don't see why you dream about him all the time. Don't you think you ought to take some Luminal?'

'No,' said Andrews. 'I don't know. Last night he kept shoving Alexander around.'

'Alexander?'

'Hamilton. God knows I'm familiar enough with him to call him by his first name. He hides behind my coat tails every night, or tries to.'

'I was thinking we might go to the Old Drovers' Inn this week-end,' said Mrs Andrews. 'You like it there.'

'Hamilton has become not only my brother Walter but practically every other guy I have ever liked,' said Andrews. 'That's natural.'

'Of course it is,' she said. They got up from the table. 'I do wish you'd go to Dr Fox.'

'I'm going to the zoo,' he said, 'and feed popcorn to the rhinoceros. That makes things seem right, for a little while, anyway.'

It was two nights later at five o'clock in the morning that Andrews bumbled into his wife's bedroom in pyjamas and bare feet, his hair in his eyes, his eyes wild. 'He got him!' he croaked. 'He got him! The bastard got him. Alexander fired into the air, he fired in the air and smiled at him, just like Walter, and that fiend from hell took deliberate aim – I saw him – I saw him take deliberate aim – he killed him in cold blood, the foul scum!'

Mrs Andrews, not quite awake, was fumbling in the box containing the Nembutal while her husband ranted on. She made him take two of the little capsules, between his sobs.

Andrews didn't want to go to see Dr Fox but he went to humour his wife. Dr Fox leaned back in his swivel-chair behind his desk and looked at Andrews. 'Now, just what seems to be the trouble?' he asked.

'Nothing seems to be the trouble,' said Andrews.

The doctor looked at Mrs Andrews. 'He has nightmares,' she said.

'You look a little underweight, perhaps,' said the doctor. 'Are you eating well, getting enough exercise?'

'I'm not underweight,' said Andrews. 'I eat the way I always have and get the same exercise.'

At this, Mrs Andrews sat straighter in her chair and began to talk, while her husband lighted a cigarette. 'You see, I think he's worried about something,' she said, 'because he always has this same dream. It's about his brother Walter, who was killed in a cemetery by a drunken man, only it isn't *really* about him.'

The doctor did the best he could with this information. He cleared his throat, tapped on the glass top of his desk with the fingers of his right hand, and said, 'Very few people are actually *killed* in cemeteries.' Andrews stared at the doctor coldly and said nothing. 'I wonder if you would mind stepping into the next room,' the doctor said to him.

'Well, I hope you're satisfied,' Andrews snapped at his wife as they left the doctor's office a half-hour later. 'You heard what he said. There's nothing the matter with me at all.'

'I'm glad your heart is so fine,' she told him. 'He said it was fine, you know.'

'Sure,' said Andrews. 'It's fine. Everything's fine.' They got into a cab and drove home in silence.

'I was just thinking,' said Mrs Andrews, as the cab stopped in front of their apartment building, 'I was just thinking that now that Alexander Hamilton is dead, you won't see anything more of Aaron Burr.' The cabdriver, who was handing Andrews change for a dollar bill, dropped a quarter on the floor.

Mrs Andrews was wrong. Aaron Burr did not depart from her husband's dreams. Andrews said nothing about it for several mornings, but she could tell. He brooded over his breakfast, did not answer any of her questions, and jumped in his chair if she dropped a knife or spoon. 'Are you still dreaming about that man?' she asked him finally.

'I wish I hadn't told you about it,' he said. 'Forget it, will you?'

'I can't forget it with you going on this way,' she said. 'I think you ought to see a psychiatrist. What does he do now?'

'What does who do now?' Andrews asked.

'Aaron Burr,' she said. 'I don't see why he keeps coming into your dreams now.'

Andrews finished his coffee and stood up. 'He goes around bragging that he did it with his eyes closed,' he snarled. 'He says he didn't even look. He claims he can hit the ace of spades at thirty paces blindfolded. Furthermore, since you asked what he does, he jostles me at parties now.'

Mrs Andrews stood up too and put her hand on her husband's shoulder. 'I think you should stay out of this, Harry,' she said. 'It wasn't any business of yours, anyway, and it happened so long ago.'

'I'm not getting into anything,' said Andrews, his voice rising to a shout. 'It's getting into me. Can't you see that?'

'I see that I've got to get you away from here,' she said. 'Maybe if you slept someplace else for a few nights, you wouldn't dream about him any more. Let's go to the country tomorrow. Let's go to the Lime Rock Lodge.'

Andrews stood for a long while without answering her. 'Why can't we go and visit the Crowleys?' he said finally. 'They live in the country. Bob has a pistol and we could do a little target shooting.'

'What do you want to shoot a pistol for?' she asked quickly. 'I should think you'd want to get away from that.'

'Yeh,' he said, 'sure,' and there was a far-off look in his eyes. 'Sure.'

When they drove into the driveway of the Crowleys' house, several miles north of New Milford, late the next afternoon, Andrews was whistling 'Bye-Bye Blackbird'. Mrs Andrews sighed contentedly and then, as her husband stopped the car, she began looking around wildly. 'My bag!' she cried. 'Did I forget to bring my bag?' He laughed his old, normal laugh for the first time in many days as he found the bag and handed it to her, and then, for the first time in many days, he leaned over and kissed her.

The Crowleys came out of the house and engulfed their guests in questions and exclamations. 'How you been?' said Bob Crowley to Andrews, heartily putting an arm around his shoulder.

'Never better,' said Andrews, 'never better. Boy, is it good to be here!'

They were swept into the house to a shakerful of Bob Crowley's icy Martinis. Mrs Andrews stole a happy glance over the edge of her glass at her husband's relaxed face.

When Mrs Andrews awoke the next morning, her husband lay rigidly on his back in the bed next to hers, staring at the ceiling. 'Oh, God,' said Mrs Andrews.

Andrews didn't move his head. 'One Henry Andrews, an architect,' he said suddenly in a mocking tone. 'One Henry Andrews, an architect.'

'What's the matter, Harry?' she asked. 'Why don't you go back to sleep? It's only eight o'clock.'

'That's what he calls me!' shouted Andrews. '"One Henry Andrews, an architect," he keeps saying in his nasty little sneering voice. "One Henry Andrews, an architect."'

'Please don't yell!' said Mrs Andrews. 'You'll wake the whole house. It's early. People want to sleep.'

Andrews lowered his voice a little. 'I'm beneath him,' he snarled 'I'm just anybody. I'm a man in a grey suit. "Be on your good behaviour, my good man," he says to me, "or I shall have one of my lackeys give you a taste of the riding crop."'

Mrs Andrews sat up in bed. 'Why should he say that to you?' she asked. 'He wasn't such a great man, was he? I mean, didn't he try to sell Louisiana to the French, or something, behind Washington's back?'

'He was a scoundrel,' said Andrews, 'but a very brilliant mind.'

Mrs Andrews lay down again. 'I was in hopes you weren't going to dream about him any more,' she said. 'I thought if I brought you up here – '

'It's him or me,' said Andrews grimly. 'I can't stand this forever.'

'Neither can I,' Mrs Andrews said, and there was a hint of tears in her voice.

Andrews and his host spent most of the afternoon, as Mrs Andrews had expected, shooting at targets on the edge of the wood behind the Crowley studio. After the first few rounds, Andrews surprised Crowley by standing with his back to the huge hulk of dead tree trunk on which the target was nailed, walking thirty paces ahead in a stiff-legged, stern-faced manner, with his revolver held at arm's length above his head, then turning suddenly and firing.

Crowley dropped to the ground, uninjured but scared. 'What the hell's the big idea, Harry?' he yelled.

Andrews didn't say anything, but started to walk back to the tree again. Once more he stood with his back to the target and began stepping off the thirty paces.

'I think they kept their arm hanging straight down,' Bob called to him. 'I don't think they stuck it up in the air.'

Andrews, still counting to himself, lowered his arm, and this time, as he turned at the thirtieth step, he whirled and fired from his hip, three times in rapid succession.

'Hey!' said Crowley.

Two of the shots missed the tree but the last one hit it, about two feet under the target. Crowley looked at his house guest oddly as Andrews began to walk back to the tree again, without a word, his lips tight, his eyes bright, his breath coming fast.

'What the hell?' Crowley said to himself. 'Look, it's my turn,' he called, but Andrews turned, then stalked ahead, unheeding. This time when he wheeled and fired, his eyes were closed.

'Good God Almighty, man!' said Crowley from the grass, where he lay flat on his stomach. 'Hey, give me that gun, will you?' he demanded, getting to his feet.

Andrews let him take it. 'I need a lot more practice, I guess,' he said.

'Not with me standing around,' said Crowley. 'Come on, let's go back to the house and shake up a drink. I've got the jumps.'

'I need a lot more practice,' said Andrews again.

He got his practice next morning just as the sun came up and the light was hard and the air was cold. He had crawled softly out of bed, dressed silently, and crept out of the room. He knew where Crowley kept the target pistol and the cartridges. There would be a target on the tree trunk, just as high as a man's heart. Mrs Andrews heard the shots first and sat sharply upright in bed, crying 'Harry!' almost before she was awake. Then she heard more shots. She got up, put on a dressing gown, and went to the Crowley's door. She heard them moving about in their room. Alice opened the door and stepped out into the hall when Mrs Andrews knocked. 'Is Harry all right?' asked Mrs Andrews. 'Where is he? What is he doing?'

'He's out shooting behind the studio, Bob says,' Alice told her. 'Bob'll go out and get him. Maybe he had a nightmare, or walked in his sleep.'

'No,' said Mrs Andrews, 'he never walks in his sleep. He's awake.'

'Let's go down and put on some coffee,' said Alice. 'He'll need some.'

Crowley came out of the bedroom and joined the women in the hallway. 'I'll need some too,' he said. 'Good morning, Bess. I'll bring him back. What the hell's the matter with him, anyway?' he was down the stairs and gone before she could answer. She was glad of that.

'Come on,' said Alice, taking her arm. They went down to the kitchen.

Mrs Crowley found the butler in the kitchen, just standing there. 'It's all right, Madison,' she said. 'You go back to bed. Tell Clotheta it's all right. Mr Andrews is just shooting a little. He couldn't sleep.'

'Yes, Ma'am,' mumbled Madison, and went back to tell his wife that they said it was all right.

'It can't be right,' said Clotheta, 'shootin' pistols at this time of night.'

'Hush up,' Madison told her. He was shivering as he climbed back into bed.

'I wish dat man would go 'way from heah,' grumbled Clotheta. 'He's got a bad look to his eyes.'

Andrews brightened Clotheta's life by going away late that afternoon. When he and his wife got in their car and drove off, the Crowleys slumped into chairs and looked at each other and said, 'Well.' Crowley got up finally to mix a drink. 'What do you think is the matter with Harry?' he asked.

'I don't know,' said his wife. 'It's what Clotheta would call the shoots, I suppose.'

'He said a funny thing when I went out and got him this morning,' Crowley told her.

'I could stand a funny thing,' she said.

'I asked him what the hell he was doing there in that freezing air with only his pants and shirt and shoes on. "I'll get him one of these nights," he said.'

'Why don't you sleep in my room tonight?' Mrs Andrews asked her husband as he finished his Scotch-and-water nightcap.

'You'd keep shaking me all night to keep me awake,' he said.

'You're afraid to let me meet him. Why do you always think everybody else is better than I am? I can outshoot him the best day he ever lived. Furthermore, I have a modern pistol. He has to use an old-fashioned single-shot muzzle-loader.' Andrews laughed nastily.

'Is that quite fair?' his wife asked after a moment of thoughtful silence.

He jumped up from his chair. 'What do I care if it's fair or not?' he snarled.

She got up too. 'Don't be mad with me, Harry,' she said. There were tears in her eyes.

'I'm sorry, darling,' he said, taking her in his arms.

'I'm very unhappy,' she sobbed.

'I'm sorry, darling,' he said again. 'Don't you worry about me. I'll be all right. I'll be fine.' She was crying too wildly to say anything more.

When she kissed him good night later on she knew it was really good-bye. Women have a way of telling when you aren't coming back.

'Extraordinary,' said Dr Fox the next morning, letting Andrews's dead left hand fall back upon the bed. 'His heart was as sound as dollar when I examined him the other day. It has just stopped as if he had been shot.'

Mrs Andrews, through her tears, was looking at her dead husband's right hand. The three fingers next to the index finger were closed in stiffly on the palm, as if gripping the handle of a pistol. The taut thumb was doing its part to hold that invisible handle tightly and unwaveringly. But it was the index finger that Mrs Andrews's eyes stayed on longest. It was only slightly curved inward, as if it were just about to press the trigger of the pistol. 'Harry never even fired a shot,' wailed Mrs Andrews. 'Aaron Burr killed him the way he killed Hamilton. Aaron Burr shot him through the heart. I knew he would. I knew he would.'

Dr Fox put an arm about the hysterical woman and led her from the room. 'She is crazy,' he said to himself. 'Stark, raving crazy.'

The figgerin' of Aunt Wilma

WHEN I was a boy, John Hance's grocery stood on the south side of Town Street, just east of Fourth, in the Central Market region of Columbus, Ohio. It was an old store even then, fifty-two years ago, and its wide oak floor boards had been worn pleasantly smooth by the shoe soles of three generations of customers. The place smelled of coffee, peppermint, vinegar, and spices. Just inside the door on the left, a counter with a rounded glass front held all the old-fashioned penny candies – gumdrops, liquorice whips, horehounds, and the rest – some of them a little pale with age. On the rear wall, between a barrel of dill pickles and a keg of salt mackerel in brine, there was an iron coffee grinder, whose handle I was sometimes allowed to turn.

Once, Mr Hance gave me a stick of Yucatán gum, an astonishing act of generosity, since he had a sharp sense of the value of a penny. Thrift was John Hance's religion. His store was run on a strictly cash basis. He shared the cost of his telephone with the Hayes Carriage Shop, next door. The instrument was set in a movable wooden cubicle that could be whirled through an opening in the west wall of the store. When I was ten, I used to hang around the grocery on Saturday afternoons, waiting for the telephone to disappear into the wall. Then I would wait for it to swing back again. It was a kind of magic, and I was disappointed to learn of its mundane purpose – the saving of a few dollars a month.

Mr Hance was nearly seventy, a short man with white hair and a white moustache and the most alert eyes that I can remember, except perhaps Aunt Wilma Hudson's. Aunt Wilma lived on South Sixth Street and always shopped at Mr Hance's store. Mr Hance's eyes were blue and capable of a keen concentration that could make you squirm. Aunt Wilma had black agate eyes that moved restlessly and scrutinized everybody with bright suspicion. In church, her glance would dart around the congregation seeking out irreverent men and women whose expressions showed that they were occupied with worldly concerns, or even carnal thoughts, in the holy place. If she lighted on a culprit, her heavy, dark brows would lower, and her mouth would tighten in righteous disapproval. Aunt Wilma was as honest as the day is long and as easily confused, when it came to what she called figgerin', as the night is dark. Her clashes with Mr Hance had become a family legend. He was a swift and competent calculator, and nearly fifty years of constant practice had enabled him to add up a column of figures almost at a glance. He set down his columns swiftly on an empty paper sack with a stubby black pencil. Aunt Wilma, on the other hand, was slow and painstaking when it came to figgerin'. She would go over and over a column of numbers, her glasses far down on her nose, her lips moving soundlessly. To her, rapid calculation, like all the other reckless and impulsive habits of men, was tainted with a kind of godlessness. Mr Hance always sighed when he looked up and saw her coming into his store. He knew that she could lift a simple dollar transaction into a dim and mystic realm of confusion all her own.

I was fortunate enough to be present one day in 1905 when Mr Hance's calculating and Aunt Wilma's figgerin' came together in memorable single combat. She had wheedled me into carrying her market basket, on the ground that it was going to be too heavy for her to manage. Her two grandsons, boys around my own age, had skipped out when I came to call at their house, and Aunt Wilma promptly seized on me. A young'un, as she called everybody under seventeen, was not worth his salt if he couldn't help a body about the house. I had shopped with her before, under duress, and I knew her accustomed and invariable route on Saturday mornings, when Fourth Street, from Main to State, was lined with the stands of truck gardeners. Prices were incredibly low in those days, but Aunt Wilma questioned the cost, the quality, and the measure of everything. By the time she had finished her long and tedious purchases of fresh produce from the country, and we had turned east into Town Street and headed for Mr Hance's store, the weight of the market basket was beginning to pain my arm. 'Come along, child, come along,' Aunt Wilma snapped, her eyes shining with the look of the Middle Western housewife engaged in hard but virtuous battle with the wicked forces of the merchandising world.

I saw Mr Hance make a small involuntary gesture with his right hand as he spied Aunt Wilma coming through the door. He had just finished with a customer, and since his assistant was busy, he knew he was in for it. It took a good half-hour for Aunt Wilma to complete her shopping for groceries, but at length everything she wanted was stacked on the counter in sacks and cans and boxes. Mr Hance set deftly to work with his paper sack and pencil, jotting down the price of each article as he fitted it into the basket. Aunt Wilma watched his expert movements closely, like a hostile baseball fan waiting for an error in the infield. She regarded adroitness in a man as 'slick' rather than skilful.

Aunt Wilma's purchases amounted to ninety-eight cents. After writing down this sum, Mr Hance, knowing my aunt, whisked the paper bag around on the counter so that she could examine his addition. It took her some time, bending over and peering through her glasses, to arrive at a faintly reluctant corroboration of his figgerin'. Even when she was satisfied that all was in order, she had another go at the column of numbers, her lips moving silently as she added them up for the third time. Mr Hance waited patiently, the flat of his hands on the counter. He seemed to be fascinated by the movement of her lips. 'Well, I guess it's all right,' said Aunt Wilma, at last, 'but everything *is* so dear.' What she had bought for less than a dollar made the market basket bulge. Aunt Wilma took her purse out of her bag and drew out a dollar bill slowly and handed it over, as if it were a hundred dollars she would never see again.

Mr Hance deftly pushed the proper keys on the cash register, and the red hand on the indicator pointed to $.98. He studied the cash drawer, which had shot out at him. 'Well, well,' he said, and then, 'Hmm. Looks like I haven't got any pennies.' He turned back to Aunt Wilma. 'Have you got three cents, Mrs Hudson?' he asked.

That started it.

Aunt Wilma gave him a quick look of distrust. Her Sunday suspicion gleamed in her eyes. '*You* owe *me two* cents,' she said sharply.

'I know that, Mrs Hudson,' he sighed, 'but I'm out of pennies. Now, if you'll give me three cents, I'll give you a nickel.'

Aunt Wilma stared at him cautiously.

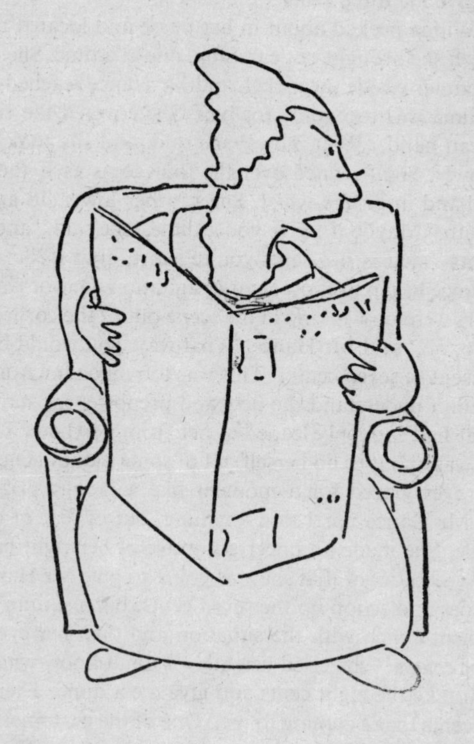

'It's all right if you give him three cents and he gives you a nickel,' I said.

'Hush up,' said Aunt Wilma. 'I'm figgerin'.' She figgered for several moments, her mouth working again.

Mr Hance slipped a nickel out of the drawer and placed it on the counter. 'There is your nickel,' he said firmly. 'Now you just have to give me three cents.'

Aunt Wilma pecked about in her purse and located three pennies, which she brought out carefully, one at a time. She laid them on the counter beside the nickel, and Mr Hance reached for them. Aunt Wilma was too quick for him. She covered the eight cents with a lean hand. 'Wait, now!' she said, and she took her hand away slowly. She frowned over the four coins as if they were a difficult hand in bridge whist. She ran her lower lip against her upper teeth. 'Maybe if I give you a dime,' she said, 'and take the eight cents . . . It is *two* cents you're short, ain't it?'

Mr Hance began to show signs of agitation. One or two amused customers were now taking in the scene out of the corners of their eyes. 'No, no,' said Mr Hance. 'That way, you would be making me a present of seven cents!' This was too much for Aunt Wilma. She couldn't understand the new and preposterous sum of seven cents that had suddenly leaped at her from nowhere. The notion that she was about to do herself out of some money staggered her, and her eyes glazed for a moment like a groggy prizefighter's. Neither Mr Hance nor I said anything, out of fear of deepening the tangle. She made an uncertain move of her right hand and I had the wild thought that she was going to give Mr Hance one of the pennies and scoop up the seven cents, but she didn't. She fell into a silent clinch with the situation and then her eyes cleared. 'Why, of *course*!' she cried brightly. 'I don't know what got into me! You take the eight cents and give me a dime. Then I'll have the two cents that's coming to me.' One of the customers laughed, and Aunt Wilma cut him down with a swift glare. The diversion gave me time to figure out that whereas Mr Hance had been about to gain seven cents, he was now going to lose a nickel. 'That way, *I* would be making *you* a present of *five* cents, Mrs Hudson,' he said stiffly. They stood motionless for several seconds, each trying to stare the other down.

'Now, here,' said Mr Hance, turning and taking her dollar out of the still open cash drawer. He laid it beside the nickel and the pennies. 'Now, here,' he said again. 'You give me a dollar three, but you don't owe me a dollar three – you owe me five cents less than that. There is the five cents.' He snatched it up and handed it to her. She held the nickel between thumb and forefinger, and her eyes gleamed briefly, as if she at last comprehended the peculiar deal, but the gleam faded. Suddenly she handed him his nickel and picked up her dollar and her three cents. She put the pennies back in her purse. 'I've rung up the ninety-eight cents, Mrs Hudson,' said Mr Hance quickly. 'I must put the dollar back in the till.' He turned and pointed at the $.98 on the indicator. 'I tell you what. If you'll give me the dollar, I'll give you the nickel and we'll call it square.' She obviously didn't want to take the nickel or give up the dollar, but she did, finally. I was astounded at first, for here was the penny-careful Mr Hance knocking three cents off a bill, but then I realized he was afraid of losing the dollar and was willing to settle for the lesser of two evils.

'Well,' said Aunt Wilma irritably, 'I'm sure I don't know what you're trying to do.'

I was a timid boy, but I had to plunge into the snarl, if only on behalf of family honour. 'Gee, Aunt Wilma,' I told her, 'if you keep the nickel, he's giving you everything for ninety-five cents.'

Mr Hance scowled hard at me. He was afraid I was going to get him in deeper than he already was. 'It's all right, son,' he said. 'It's all right.' He put the dollar in the till and shoved the drawer shut with a decisive bang, but I wasn't going to give up.

'Gee whizz, Aunt Wilma,' I complained, 'you still owe him three cents. Don't you see that?'

She gave me the pitying glance of a superior and tired intelligence. 'I never owed him three cents in my life,' she said tartly. 'He owes me two cents. You stay out of things you don't understand.'

'It's all right,' said Mr Hance again, in a weary voice. He was sure that if she scrabbled in her purse again for the three pennies, she would want her dollar back, and they would be right where they had started. I gave my aunt a look of disenchantment.

'Now, wait!' she cried suddenly. 'Maybe I have the exact

change! I don't know what's got into me I didn't think of that! I think I have the right change after all.' She put back on the counter the nickel she had been clutching in her left hand, and then she began to peck at the coins in her purse and, after a good minute, arranged two quarters, four dimes, Mr Hance's nickel, and three pennies on the counter. 'There,' she said, her eyes flashing triumph. 'Now you give me my dollar back.'

Mr Hance sighed deeply, rang out the cash drawer by pushing 'No Sale', and handed her the dollar. Then he hastily scraped up the change, deposited each coin in its proper place in the till, and slammed the drawer shut again. I was only ten, and mathematics was not my best study, but it wasn't hard to figure that Mr Hance, who in the previous arrangement had been out three cents, was now out five cents. 'Good day, Mrs Hudson,' he said grimly. He felt my sympathetic eyes on him, and we exchanged a brief, knowing masculine glance of private understanding.

'Good day, Mr Hance,' said Aunt Wilma, and her tone was as grim as the grocer's.

I took the basket from the counter, and Mr Hance sighed again, this time with relief. 'Good-bye, good-bye,' he said with false heartiness, glad to see us on our way. I felt I should slip him the parsley, or whatever sack in the basket had cost a nickel.

'Come on, child,' said Aunt Wilma. 'It's dreadfully late. I declare it's taken hours to shop today.' She muttered plaintively all the way out of the store.

I noticed as I closed the door behind us that Mr Hance was waiting on a man customer. The man was laughing. Mr Hance frowned and shrugged.

As we walked east on Town Street, Aunt Wilma let herself go. 'I never heard of such a thing in all the born days of my life,' she said. 'I don't know where John Hance got his schooling, if he got any. The very idea – a grown man like that getting so mixed up. Why, I could have spent the whole day in that store and he'd never of figgered it out. Let him keep the two cents, then. It was worth it to get out of that store.'

'*What* two cents, Aunt Wilma?' I almost squealed.

'Why, the two cents he still owes me!' she said. 'I don't know what they teach you young 'uns nowadays. Of course he owes me two cents. It come to ninety-eight cents and I give him a dollar. He owed me two cents in the beginning and he still owes me two cents. Your Uncle Herbert will explain it to you. Any man in the world could figger it out except John Hance.'

Mr Punch

LOOKING for a Roman coin I had dropped on the library floor of the house I rented for the winter, I found, on a shelf behind a sofa, two dozen immense bound bolumes of *Punch*. They contained all the copies of the famous British weekly from the year it was founded until 1891, exactly half a century later. I picked out three volumes at random and began idly turning the pages of first one and then another. When the following Tuesday found me still at it, I realized what I was up to: I was getting ready to make some kind of report on Mr Punch of the nineteenth century. If it has been done before, all I can say is that I am doing it again.

Let us begin, then, with the tome which contains the issues from July 1889 to July 1891, and work our way back toward the Civil War. This volume, like all the others, contains some rather heavy introductory notes summarizing what was going on in the world at the time. In this two-year period quite a lot was going on, if you have forgotten. The 'young and impetuous' Kaiser Wilhelm was rattling his sabre and already disturbing the peace of mind of Europe. The volume falls open easily at the double page containing Tenniel's famous cartoon 'Dropping the Pilot' – for it was at this time that Wilhelm got rid of Bismarck. Socialism was raising its troublesome head, so terrifying Mr Punch that he had Tenniel draw a cartoon of a serpent (Socialism) wrapped about the body of an eagle (Trade) and striving to crush the bird's wings (Capital and Labour). The brief, sad romance of Parnell and Captain O'Shea's wife shocked the British Isles and formed a dark foil for the decorous private life of Mr Gladstone, who, past eighty years old, celebrated his golden-wedding anniversary. Tennyson, the poet laureate, became an octogenarian in his turn, and Browning died two years short of the mark. A potato famine was predicted in Ireland and an epidemic of influenza held the world in what I am sure *Punch*, somewhere or other, must have called its grip. A young pianist whom *Punch* laughingly alluded to as 'Paddy Rewski from Irish Poland' gave a concert in London, but *Punch* could not appraise the young man's talents because *Punch* did not attend the concert. *Punch* could report, however, that the life in Marion Crawford's latest novel was real life and that Mr Ibsen's *A Doll's House* was 'unutterably loathsome' and should be removed from the stages of the world.

The harsh effects on the feminine complexion of that new invention, the electric light, gave *Punch* a hundred whimsical ideas, and so did the new and wonderful Eiffel Tower. (One proud London paper wrote, 'The Eiffel Tower is 1000 feet high; the Forth bridge, if stood on end, would be 5280 feet in height.') Mr Edison's phonograph was received with proper respect, *Punch* calling up the spirit of Faraday, who solemnly approved of the device. Montana, the Dakotas, and Washington were admitted to the Union and the government breathed more easily when Sitting Bull was shot dead. Barnum was in London with his great show and Millet's *The Angelus* was sold to an American. A hydrophobia scare led to the muzzling of all the dogs in England and *Punch* came out for the much-abused Pasteur in a drawing with this dialogue between a husband and wife:

'Oh, Joseph! Teddy's just been bitten by a strange dog! Doctor says we'd better take him over to Pasteur *at once*!'

'But, my love, I've just written and published a violent attack upon M. Pasteur, on the score of his cruelty to rabbits! And at *your instigation*, too!'

'Oh, Heavens! Never mind the rabbits *now*! What are all the rabbits in the world compared to *our only child*.'

Among the minor objects of Mr Punch's annoyance during these years were Mr Pinero for an attack on the London music halls, new-fangled barbed-wire fences for interfering with fox hunting, the Americans for coining so much money and so many new words, and Count Tolstoi for a savage assault on tobacco smokers. Of this last *Punch* rhymed, in part:

Tolstoi knew a man who said
He cut off a woman's head;
But, when half the deed was done,
Lo, the murderer's courage gone!
And he finished, 'tis no joke,
Only by the aid of smoke.

Unhorrified by murderers who got a lift from nicotine, Mr Punch could not approve of the use of the weed by ladies, some of whom were apparently going in for cigars:

You're beautiful, but fairer far
You'd be – if only you would let
Your male friends smoke that big cigar
And yield them, too, that cigarette.

Most of the jokes in this volume are about bad cooks, worse painters, errant nursemaids, precocious children, insolent cab-drivers, and nonchalant young blades in ballrooms. I found, somewhat to my surprise, that a great many of these young blades were named Gus. I found, also to my surprise, that the expression 'I'm nuts on', meaning 'I'm crazy about', was used in 1891. And that the Irate-Voice-from-Upstairs joke began seventy years ago (unless what I ran across was just a revival of it):

Stern Voice (*from first-floor landing, temp. 12.10 p.m.*): Alice!
Alice (*softly*): Yes, 'Pa'!
Voice (*with threatening ring in it*): Does that young man in the front parlour take tea or coffee for his breakf—!!?
('Door' – *and he was gone!*)

During the eighties and nineties Mr Henry James (of whom I could find no mention anywhere in *Punch*) was in the midst of his elaborate and delicate examinations of American ladies abroad, but Mr Punch lashed out at them in a simpler manner:

Sir James: And were you in Rome?
American Lady: I guess not. (*To her daughter*) Say, Bella, did we visit Rome?
Fair Daughter: Why, Ma, certainly! Don't you remember? It was in Rome we bought the lisle-thread stockings!
(*American lady is convinced.*)

The American male comes in for it, too:

Young Britisher: Your father's not with you, then, Miss Van Tromp?
Fair New York Millionairess (*one of three*): Why, no – Pa's much too vulgar! It's as much as we can do to stand Ma!

Sometimes *Punch* had at our damsels in verse:

THE AMERICAN GIRL

She 'guesses' and she 'calculates,' she wears all sorts o' collars,
Her yellow hair is not without suspicion of a dye;
Her 'páppa' is a dull old man who turned pork into dollars,
But everyone admits that she's indubitably spry.

She did Rome in a swift two days, gave half the time to Venice,
But vows that she saw everything, although in awful haste;
She's fond of dancing, but she seems to fight shy of lawn tennis,
Because it might endanger the proportions of her waist.

Her manner might be well defined as elegantly skittish;
She loves a Lord as only a Republican can do;
And quite the best of titles she's persuaded are the British,
And well she knows the Peerage, for she's read it through and through.

She's bediamonded superbly and shines like a constellation.
You scarce can see her fingers for the multitude of rings;
She's just a shade too conscious, as it seems, of admiration,
With irritating tendencies to wriggle when she sings.

She owns she is 'Amurican', and her accent is alarming;
Her birthplace is an awful name you pray you may forget;
Yet, after all, we own 'La Belle Américaine' is charming,
So let us hope she'll win at last her longsought coronet.

Phil May, the caricaturist, came back to London in the early nineties after a long stay in Australia, but his work does not appear in this volume. It could have used some. Before I leave this engrossing period of history and humour I must quote a typical Foreigner-in-the-English-Home joke. This one, with its evidence of the nineteenth-century Englishman's fine ear for the German accent, is my favourite of several hundred:

Hostess: Won't you try some of that jelly, Herr Silbermund?

Herr Silbermund (*who has just been helped to pudding*): Ach, zank you, no. I voot 'rahzer pear vix ze ills ve haf zan vly to ozzers ve know not of.'

In the years 1869 to 1871 (our second volume), Mr Punch had a wealth of subjects for his little punning pieces and his big political posters. The Fenians in Ireland and America were raising hell on behalf of the freedom of Erin, and the Alabama claims case was still a sore point between England and America. Harriet Beecher Stowe, having freed the slaves, nosed about in the private life of the late Lord Byron and provided the great scandal of the day in a magazine article revealing the love story of the poet and his half-sister, Augusta Leigh. General Dan Sickles, hero of the Peach Orchard at Gettysburg, who was god-damning up and down the American chancellery in Madrid as our ambassador, informed his government that the Spaniards were sore about our friendly attitude toward the Cuban insurrectionists and might do something about it. On 18 July 1870 the Infallibility of the Pope was declared. On the next day France declared war on Prussia and rushed headlong to defeat, the French *mitrailleuse* proving less deadly than the Prussian needle gun. Disraeli published a novel called *Lothair* and made Bartlett's *Quotations* with a crack about critics being people who have failed in literature and the arts. Oxford beat Harvard in the first crew race ever rowed between the two universities and a small, resolute band of women began to clamour for the right to vote. Darwin's *The Descent of Man* was pie for the wits of *Punch*, and the magazine cried out against the deplorable fact that the word 'reliable', which it described as 'a new and unnecessary American adjective', was creeping into the inviolable English tongue. On top of everything the women of England were affecting the 'Grecian bend', which *Punch* called 'an exaggerated forward inclination of the body, an absurd fashion of the hour'.

I devoted a great deal of my research to hunting down ninety-year-old versions of jokes which are still going the rounds, and I offer my most cherished discovery:

The Curate: O dear, O dear! Drunk again, Jones! *Drunk* again! And in broad daylight, too!

Jones: Lorsh (*hic*)! Whatsh the oddsh! Sh – Sh – Sho am *I*!

You will remember this one, too:

Ticket Collector: Now, then, make haste! Where's your ticket?

Bandsman (*refreshed*): Aw've lost it!

Ticket Collector: Nonsense! Feel in your pockets. Ye cannot hev lost it!

Bandsman: Aw cannot? Why, man, Aw've lost the *big drum*!

Throughout this volume there runs a series of drawings of cute kiddies above the most distressingly cute captions. If the researcher rapidly tires of the pen-and-ink drawings of the famous George Louis Palmella Busson Du Maurier ('the gentle, graceful satirist of modern fashionable life'), it is perhaps mainly because of the gags he is given to illustrate. I select the ickiest of them. A mother is about to give a dose of medicine to a two-year-old girl:

Master George (*whispers*): I say! Kitty! Has mamma been telling you she'd give you 'a lovely spoonful of delicious currant jelly, O so nice, so very nice'?
Kitty: Ess! Cullen' jelly! O so ni', so welly ni'!
Master George: THEN DON'T TAKE IT!

Du Maurier husbands and wives are pictured engaged in what are surely the most depressing conversations ever recorded in the history of civilized man. I quote the first, but not necessarily the worst, of those I come to in my grim notes:

'Well, Dearest, where have you been tonight? "Monday Pops" again?'
'No, Celia, I have spent a most instructive evening with the "Anthropological Society'."
'The "Anthropohowmuch", Darling?'
'The "Anthropo*log*ical," Celia! Are you deaf?'
'How nice! And where do they "Anthropo*lodge*", Duckums?'

I shall end my discussion of this fond old volume with a caption that, for its simplicity and point, rose out of these fusty yellow pages like a little cool wind. I like to think this is one the author of *Trilby* thought up himself. It appears under a drawing of a dowager in a carriage drawn by two horses and surmounted by a coachman and a footman. The lady has just given alms to a poverty-stricken woman whose ragged children are gathered about her knees:

Grateful Recipient: Bless you, my lady! May we meet in Heaven!
Haughty Donor: Good Gracious! Drive on, Jarvis!

It grieves me to report that *Punch* was unable to let it go at that. In parentheses and italics there follows this explanatory line: 'She had evidently read Dr Johnson, who "didn't care to meet certain, people *any*where". Just in case you hadn't caught on.

In the year 1863 (our third and last volume runs from July '63, to July '65) the newly married Edward and Alexandra were cheered everywhere they went. The great Blondin was walking the tightrope in the Crystal Palace and a young woman who imitated him at a small-town carnival fell and broke her neck. The Russians were beating up the Poles, and Schleswig-Holstein was the Czechoslovakia of the year – and of the next. Louis Napoleon announced that 'the improvements brought about by civilization would render war still more destructive'. Disraeli said, 'The condition of Europe is one of very grave character. Let us be sure, if we go to war, first of all that it is a necessary and just war.' The Japanese killed an Englishman named Richardson and 'committed a savage assault' on an English woman and two friends. Garibaldi visited London and the three-hundredth anniversary of Shakespeare's birthday was celebrated. *Punch* was irritated by the clamour in the streets caused by organ grinders and hurdy-gurdy men and hicksters selling watercress and prawns. There is no mention in the volume of what must have been to *Punch* one of the minor events of the early sixties: the battle of Gettysburg.

Mr Punch's snipes and jibes at Abraham Lincoln and the cause of the North are too well known to call for an extended examination, but the researcher will cite two because he wants to append some notes of his own to them:

Instead of *Habeas Corpus* in the United States, which has been suspended, it is now, in the case of the prisoner who is arbitrarily arrested, ABE who has *corpus*. [Researcher's Note: The English government, which was apparently unswayed by *Punch*, suspended the right of habeas corpus in Ireland in 1866.]

LATEST AMERICAN TELEGRAMS (1864)

Grant reduced to grunt.
Sheridan's Rivals successful.
Hunter hunted
Pillow on Sherman's rear.

[Researcher's note: *Encyclopedia Americana* on Pillow, Gideon J., American soldier: 'After 1861 he did not figure in any battle save Murfreesboro, in which he had a courtesy command.' Murfreesboro was fought some twenty months before *Punch*'s little crack.]

You might also be interested in a diatribe printed 21 January 1865, and headed 'To the Yankee Braggarts':

This American crisis is one which is only to be met by the most unmitigated Swagger, and Mr Punch, hastily constituting himself Head Swaggerer to the English Nation, hereby answers the Yankee journals 'with shouts as loud and shrieks as fierce as their own'. [Researcher's note: Somebody had got off some remarks in America about our being able to lick England.] War with England, indeed, you long-faced, wizened, ugly, ignorant Occidentals! Defy the flag that has braved a thousand years the battle and the breeze? Laugh at the Lion and give umbrage to the Unicorn? Bay! Bosh! Shut up! Tremble!

It goes on to say that one Sir Hugh Rose could go over and lick the whole United States. This happened to be the first time I had ever heard of Sir Hugh, but maybe Grant and Lee knew who he was.

The end to all this is well known: Tenniel drew a touching cartoon showing Britannia laying a wreath on Lincoln's bier and Tom Taylor wrote an equally famous and equally touching poem eating all of *Punch*'s nasty words and all of Tenniel's nasty drawings. (This, incidentally, was the year that *Alice in Wonderland* was published, the book that gave Mr Tenniel something really important to do. I find no mention of it in *Punch*.)

Lincoln and the North might be forgiven, but America's pernicious invention of new words wasn't. 'If the pure well of English is to remain undefiled,' said Mr Punch, 'no Yankee should be allowed henceforth to throw mud into it. It is a form of verbal expectoration that is most profane, most destestable.' He gives you an idea of what he has in mind a few pages farther on. Two American ladies are pictured at a dance, with a young beau standing by. Says one of the ladies (under the heading 'Yet Another Americanism'): 'Here, Maria, hold my cloak while I have a fling with stranger.'

American ladies were invariably represented as pretty and well shaped in spite of Mr Punch's purple anger at one Nathaniel Hawthorne, sometime American consul at Liverpool, who had brought out a book about England 'thoroughly saturated with what seems ill-nature and spite' and making a 'savage onslaught upon our women'. Excerpts are quoted, but I have space for only one:

'English girls seemed to me all homely alike. They seemed to be country lasses, of sturdy and wholesome aspect, with coarse-grained, cabbage-rosy cheeks. . . . How unlike the trim little damsels of my native land!' Mr Punch hopes that Mr Hawthorne will go on to write an autobiography, for Mr Punch is 'very partial to essays on the natural history of half-civilized animals'.

I will close this survey with a typical illustrated joke of those years of pain and sorrow. It is labelled 'Gentle Rebuke' and the caption will give you some idea of what the drawing is like:

Old Gentleman: How charmingly that young lady sings! Pray, who composed the beautiful song she has just favoured us with?

Lady of the House: Oh, it is by Mendelssohn.

Old Gentleman: Ah! One of his famous 'Songs without Words', I suppose.

(Moral – Young ladies, when you sing, pronounce your words carefully, and then you will not expose unmusical old gentlemen to making such ridiculous mistakes as the above.)

Has anybody got any bound copies of old almanacs?

The white rabbit caper

(As the boys who turn out the mystery programmes on the air might write a story for children)

FRED FOX was pouring himself a slug of rye when the door of his office opened and in hopped old Mrs Rabbit. She was a white rabbit with pink eyes, and she wore a shawl on her head, and gold-rimmed spectacles.

'I want you to find Daphne,' she said tearfully, and she handed Fred Fox a snapshot of a white rabbit with pink eyes that looked to him like a picture of every other white rabbit with pink eyes.

'When did she hop the hutch?' asked Fred Fox.

'Yesterday,' said old Mrs Rabbit. 'She is only eighteen months old, and I am afraid that some superstitious creature has killed her for one of her feet.'

Fred Fox turned the snapshot over and put it in his pocket. 'Has this bunny got a throb?' he asked.

'Yes,' said old Mrs Rabbit. 'Franz Frog, repulsive owner of the notorious Lily Pad Night Club.'

Fred Fox leaped to his feet. 'Come on, Grandma,' he said, 'and don't step on your ears. We got to move fast.'

On the way to the Lily Pad Night Club, old Mrs Rabbit scampered so fast that Fred Fox had all he could do to keep up with her. 'Daphne is my great-great-great-great-great-granddaughter, if my memory serves,' said old Mrs Rabbit. 'I have thirty-nine thousand descendants.'

'This isn't going to be easy,' said Fred Fox. 'Maybe you should have gone to a magician with a hat.'

'But she is the only one named Daphne,' said old Mrs Rabbit, 'and she lived alone with me on my great carrot farm.'

They came to a broad brook. 'Skip it!' said Fred Fox.

'Keep a civil tongue in your head, young man,' snapped old Mrs Rabbit.

Just as they got to the Lily Pad, a dandelion clock struck twelve, noon. Fred Fox pushed the button on the great green door, on which was painted a white water-lily. The door opened an eighth of an inch, and Ben Rat peered out. 'Beat it,' he said, but Fred Fox shoved the door open, and old Mrs Rabbit followed him into a cool green hallway, softly but restlessly lighted by thousands of fireflies imprisoned in the hollow crystal pendants of an enormous chandelier. At the right there was a flight of green-carpeted stairs, and at the bottom of the steps the door to the cloakroom. Straight ahead, at the end of the long hallway, was the cool green door to Franz Frog's office.

'Beat it,' said Ben Rat again.

'Talk nice,' said Fred Fox, 'or I'll seal your house up with tin. Where's the Croaker?'

'Once a gumpaw, always a gumpaw,' grumbled Ben Rat. 'He's in his office.'

'With Daphne?'

'Who's Daphne?' asked Ben Rat.

'My great-great-great-great-great-granddaughter,' said old Mrs Rabbit.

'Nobody's that great,' snarled Ben Rat.

Fred Fox opened the cool green door and went into Franz Frog's office, followed by old Mrs Rabbit and Ben Rat. The owner of the Lily Pad sat behind his desk, wearing a green suit, green shirt, green tie, green socks, and green shoes. He had an emerald tiepin and seven emerald rings. 'Whong you wong, Fonnxx?' he rumbled in a cold green, cavernous voice. His eyes bulged and his throat began to swell ominously.

'He's going to croak,' explained Ben Rat.

'Nuts,' said Fred Fox. 'He'll outlive all of us.'

'Glunk,' croaked Franz Frog.

Ben Rat glared at Fred Fox. 'You oughta go on the stage,' he snarled.

'Where's Daphne?' demanded Fred Fox.

'Hoong Dangneng?' asked Franz Frog.

'Your bunny friend,' said Fred Fox.

'Nawng,' said Franz Frog.

Fred Fox picked up a cello in a corner and put it down. It was too light to contain a rabbit. The front-door bell rang. 'I'll get it,' said Fred Fox. It was Oliver (Hoot) Owl, a notorious fly-by-night. 'What're you doing up at this hour, Hoot?' asked Fred Fox.

'I'm trying to blind myself, so I'll confess,' said Hoot Owl testily.

'Confess to what?' snapped Fred Fox.

'What can't you solve?' asked Hoot Owl.

'The disappearance of Daphne,' said Fred Fox.

'Who's Daphne?' asked Hoot Owl.

Franz Frog hopped out of his office into the hall. Ben Rat and old Mrs Rabbit followed him.

Down the steps from the second floor came Sherman Stork, carrying a white muffler or something and grinning foolishly.

'Well, bless my soul!' said Fred Fox. 'If it isn't old mid-husband himself! What did you do with Daphne?'

'Who's Daphne?' asked Sherman Stork.

'Fox thinks somebody killed Daphne Rabbit,' said Ben Rat.

'Fonnxx cung brong,' rumbled Franz Frog.

'I *could* be wrong' said Fred Fox, 'but I'm not.' He pulled open the cloakroom door at the bottom of the steps, and the dead body of a female white rabbit toppled furrily on to the cool green carpet. Her head had been bashed in by a heavy blunt instrument.

'Daphne!' screamed old Mrs Rabbit, bursting into tears.

'I can't see a thing,' said Hoot Owl.

'It's a dead white rabbit,' said Ben Rat. 'Anybody can see that. You're dumb.'

'I'm wise!' said Hoot Owl indignantly. 'I know everything.'

'Jeeng Crine,' moaned Franz Frog. He stared up at the chandelier, his eyes bulging and his mammoth mouth gaping open. All the fire flies were frightened and went out.

The cool green hallway became pitch dark. There was a shriek in the black and a feathery 'plump'. The fireflies lighted up to see what had happened. Hoot Owl lay dead on the cool green carpet, his head bashed in by a heavy blunt instrument. Ben Rat, Franz Frog, Sherman Stork, old Mrs Rabbit, and Fred Fox stared at Hoot Owl. Over the cool green carpet crawled a warm red stain, whose source was the body of Hoot Owl. He lay like a feather duster.

'Murder!' squealed old Mrs Rabbit.

'Nobody leaves this hallway!' snapped Fred Fox. 'There's a killer loose in this club!'

'I am not used to death,' said Sherman Stork.

'Roong!' groaned Franz Frog.

'He says he's ruined,' said Ben Rat, but Fred Fox wasn't listening. He was looking for a heavy blunt instrument. There wasn't any.

'Search them!' cried old Mrs Rabbit. 'Somebody has a sap, or a sock full of sand, or something!'

'Yeh,' said Fred Fox. 'Ben Rat is a sap – maybe someone swung him by his tail.'

'You oughta go on the stage,' snarled Ben Rat.

Fred Fox searched the suspects, but he found no concealed weapon. 'You could have strangled them with that muffler,' Fred Fox told Sherman Stork.

'But they were not strangled,' said Sherman Stork.

Fred Fox turned to Ben Rat. 'You could have bitten them to death with your ugly teeth,' he said.

'But they weren't bitten to death,' said Ben Rat.

Fred Fox stared at Franz Frog. 'You could have scared them to death with your ugly face,' he said.

'Bung wung screng ta deng,' said Franz Frog.

'You're right,' admitted Fred Fox. 'They weren't. Where's old Mrs Rabbit?' he asked suddenly.

'I'm hiding in here,' called old Mrs Rabbit from the cloakroom. 'I'm frightened.'

Fred Fox got her out of the cool green sanctuary and went in himself. It was dark. He groped around on the cool green carpet. He didn't know what he was looking for, but he found it, a small object lying in a far corner. He put it in his pocket and came out of the cloakroom.

'What'd you find, shamus?' asked Ben Rat apprehensively.

'Exhibit A,' said Fred Fox casually.

'Sahng plang keeng,' moaned Franz Frog.

'He says somebody's playing for keeps,' said Ben Rat.

'He can say that again,' said Fred Fox as the front door was flung open and Inspector Mastiff trotted in, followed by Sergeant Dachshund.

'Well, well, look who's muzzling in,' said Fred Fox.

'What have we got here?' barked Inspector Mastiff.

'I hate a private nose,' said Sergeant Dachshund.

Fred Fox grinned at him. 'What happened to your legs from the knees down, sport?' he asked.

'Drop dead,' snarled Sergeant Dachshund.

'Quiet, both of you!' snapped Inspector Mastiff. 'I know Ollie Owl, but who's the twenty-dollar Easter present from Schrafft's?' He turned on Fred Fox. 'If this bunny's head comes off and she's filled with candy, I'll have your badge, Fox,' he growled.

'She's real, Inspector,' said Fred Fox. 'Real dead, too. How did you pick up the scent?'

Inspector Mastiff howled. 'The Sergeant thought he smelled a rat at the Lily Club,' he said. 'Wrong again as usual. Who's this dead rabbit?'

'She's my great-great-great-great-great-granddaughter,' sobbed old Mrs Rabbit.

Fred Fox lighted a cigarette. 'Oh, no, she isn't, sweetheart,' he said coolly. 'You are *her* great-great-great-great-great-granddaughter.' Pink lightning flared in the live white rabbit's eyes. 'You killed the old lady, so you could take over her carrot farm,' continued Fred Fox, 'and then you killed Hoot Owl.'

'I'll kill you, too, shamus!' shrieked Daphne Rabbit.

'Put the cuffs on her, Sergeant,' barked Inspector Mastiff. Sergeant Dachshund put a pair of handcuffs on the front legs of the dead rabbit. 'Not *her*, you dumb kraut!' yelped Inspector Mastiff.

It was too late. Daphne Rabbit had jumped through a window pane and run away, with the Sergeant in hot pursuit.

'All white rabbits look alike to me,' growled Inspector Mastiff. 'How could you tell them apart – from their ears?'

'No,' said Fred Fox. 'From their years. The white rabbit that called on me darn near beat me to the Lily Pad, and no old woman can do that.'

'Don't brag,' said Inspector Mastiff. 'Spryness isn't enough. What else?'

'She understood expressions an old rabbit doesn't know,' said Fred Fox, 'like "hop the hutch" and "throb" and "skip it" and "sap".'

'You can't hang a rabbit for her vocabulary,' said Inspector Mastiff. 'Come again.'

Fred Fox pulled the snapshot out of his pocket. 'The white rabbit who called on me told me Daphne was eighteen months old,' he said, 'but read what it says on the back of this picture.'

Inspector Mastiff took the snapshot, turned it over, and read, '"Daphne on her second birthday."'

'Yes,' said Fred Fox. 'Daphne knocked six months off her age. You see, Inspector, she couldn't read the writing on the snapshot, because those weren't her spectacles she was wearing.'

'Now wait a minute,' growled Inspector Mastiff. 'Why did she kill Hoot Owl?'

'Elementary, my dear Mastiff,' said Fred Fox. 'Hoot Owl lived in an oak tree, and she was afraid he saw her burrowing into the club last night, dragging Grandma. She heard Hoot Owl say, "I'm wise. I know everything," and so she killed him.'

'What with?' demanded the Inspector.

'Her right hind foot,' said Fred Fox. 'I was looking for a concealed weapon, and all the time she was carrying her heavy blunt instrument openly.'

'Well, what do you know!' exclaimed Inspector Mastiff. 'Do you think Hoot Owl really saw her?'

'Could be,' said Fred Fox. 'I happen to think he was bragging about his wisdom in general and not about a particular piece of information, but your guess is as good as mine.'

'What did you pick up in the cloakroom?' squeaked Ben Rat

'The final strand in the rope that will hang Daphne,' said Fred Fox. 'I knew she didn't go in there to hide. She went in there to look for something she lost last night. If she'd been frightened, she would have hidden when the flies went out, but she went in there after the flies lighted up again.'

'That adds up,' said Inspector Mastiff grudgingly. 'What was it she was looking for?'

'Well,' said Fred Fox, 'she heard something drop in the dark when she dragged Grandma in there last night and she thought it was a button, or a buckle, or a bead, or a bangle, or a brooch that would incriminate her. That's why she rang me in on the case. She couldn't come here alone to look for it.'

'Well, what was it, Fox?' snapped Inspector Mastiff.

'A carrot,' said Fred Fox, and he took it out of his pocket, 'probably fell out of old Mrs Rabbit's reticule, if you like irony.'

'One more question,' said Inspector Mastiff. 'Why plant the body in the Lily Pad?'

'Easy,' said Fred Fox. 'She wanted to throw suspicion on the Croaker, a well-known lady-killer.'

'Nawng,' rumbled Franz Frog.

'Well, there it is, Inspector,' said Fred Fox, 'all wrapped up for you and tied with ribbons.'

Ben Rat disappeared into a wall. Franz Frog hopped back to his office.

'Mercy!' cried Sherman Stork. 'I'm late for an appointment!' He flew to the front door and opened it.

There stood Daphne Rabbit, holding the unconscious form of Sergeant Dachshund. 'I give up,' she said. 'I surrender.'

'Is he dead?' asked Inspector Mastiff hopefully.

'No,' said Daphne Rabbit. 'He fainted.'

'I never have any luck,' growled Inspector Mastiff.

Fred Fox leaned over and pointed to Daphne's right hind foot. 'Owl feathers,' he said. 'She's all yours, Inspector.'

'Thanks, Fox,' said Inspector Mastiff. 'I'll throw something your way someday.'

'Make it a nice, plump Plymouth Rock pullet,' said Fred Fox, and he sauntered out of the Lily Pad.

Back in his office, Fred Fox dictated his report on the White

Rabbit Caper to his secretary, Lura Fox. 'Period. End of report,' he said finally, toying with the emerald stickpin he had taken from Franz Frog's green necktie when the fireflies went out.

'Is she pretty?' asked Lura Fox.

'Daphne? Quite a dish,' said Fred Fox, 'but I like my rabbits stewed, and I'm afraid little Daphne is going to fry.'

'But she's so young, Fred!' cried Lura Fox. 'Only eighteen months!'

'You weren't listening,' said Fred Fox.

'How did you know she wasn't interested in Franz Frog?' asked Laura Fox.

'Simple,' said Fred Fox. 'Wrong species.'

'What became of the candy, Fred?' asked Lura Fox.

Fred Fox stared at her. 'What candy?' he asked blankly.

Lura Fox suddenly burst into tears. 'She was so soft, and warm, and cuddly, Fred,' she wailed.

Fred Fox filled a glass with rye, drank it slowly, set down the glass, and sighed grimly. 'Sour racket,' he said.

My own ten rules for a happy marriage

NOBODY, I hasten to announce, has asked me to formulate a set of rules for the perpetuation of marital bliss and the preservation of the tranquil American boudoir and inglenook. The idea just came to me one day, when I watched a couple in an apartment across the court from mine gesturing and banging tables and throwing *objets d'art* at each other. I couldn't hear what they were saying, but it was obvious, as the shotput followed the hammer throw, that he and/or she (as the lawyers would put it) had deeply offended her and/or him.

Their apartment, before they began to take it apart, had been quietly and tastefully arranged, but it was a little hard to believe this now, as he stood there by the fireplace, using an andiron to bat back the Royal Doulton figurines she was curving at him from her strongly entrenched position behind the davenport. I wondered what had started the exciting but costly battle, and, brooding on the general subject of Husbands and Wives, I found myself compiling my own Ten Rules for a Happy Marriage.

I have avoided the timeworn admonitions, such as 'Praise her new hat', 'Share his hobbies', 'Be a sweetheart as well as a wife', and 'Don't keep a blonde in the guest room', not only because they are threadbare from repetition, but also because they don't seem to have accomplished their purpose. Maybe what we need is a brand-new set of rules. Anyway, ready or not, here they come, the result of fifty years (I began as a little boy) spent in studying the nature and behaviour, mistakes and misunderstandings, of the American Male (*homo Americansis*) and his Mate.

RULE ONE: Neither party to a sacred union should run down, disparage, or badmouth the other's former girls or beaux, as the case may be. The tendency to attack the character, looks, intelligence, capability, and achievements of one's mate's former friends of the opposite sex is a common cause of domestic discontent. Sweet-heart-slurring, as we will call this deplorable practice, is encouraged by a long spell of gloomy weather, too many highballs, hangovers, and the suspicion that one's spouse is hiding, and finding, letters in a hollow tree, or is intercepting the postman, or putting in secret phone calls from the corner drugstore. These fears almost always turn out to be unfounded, but the unfounded fear, as we all know, is worse than the founded.

Aspersions, insinuations, reflections, or just plain cracks abou old boy friends and girl friends should be avoided at all times Here are some of the expressions that should be especially eschewed: 'That waffle-fingered, minor-league third baseman you latche onto at Cornell'; 'You know the girl I mean – the one with the hip who couldn't read'; 'That old flame of yours with the vocabular of a hoot owl'; and 'You remember her – that old bat who chewe gum and dressed like Daniel Boone.'

This kind of derogatory remark, if persisted in by one or bot parties to a marriage, will surely lead to divorce or, at best, blow on the head with a glass ash tray.

RULE TWO: A man should make an honest effort to get the name of his wife's friends right. This is not easy. The average wife wh was graduated from college at any time during the past thirty years keeps in close touch with at least seven old classmates. These ladies, known as 'the girls', are named, respectively: Mary, Marian, Melissa, Marjorie, Maribel, Madeleine, and Miriam; and all of them are called Myrtle by the careless husband we are talking about. Furthermore, he gets their nicknames wrong. This, to be sure, is understandable, since their nicknames are, respectively: Molly, Muffy, Missy, Midge, Mabby, Maddy, and Mims. The careless husband, out of thoughtlessness or pure cussedness, calls them all Mugs, or, when he is feeling particularly brutal, Mucky.

All the girls are married, one of them to a Ben Tompkins, and as this is the only one he can remember, our hero calls all the husbands Ben, or Tompkins, adding to the general annoyance and confusion.

If you are married to a college graduate, then, try to get the names of her girl friends and their husbands straight. This will prevent some of those interminable arguments that begin after Midge and Harry (not Mucky and Ben) have said a stiff good night and gone home.

RULE THREE: A husband should not insult his wife publicly, at parties. He should insult her in the privacy of the home. Thus, if a man thinks the soufflés his wife makes are as tough as an outfielder's glove, he should tell her so when they are at home, not when they are out at a formal dinner party where a perfect soufflé has just been served. The same rule applies to the wife. She should not regale his men friends, or women friends, with hilarious accounts of her husband's clumsiness, remarking that he dances like a 1907 Pope Hartford, or that he locked himself in the children's rabbit pen and couldn't get out. All parties must end finally, and the husband or wife who has revealed all may find that there is hell to pay in the taxi going home.

RULE FOUR: The wife who keeps saying, 'Isn't that just like a man?' and the husband who keeps saying, 'Oh, well, you know how women are,' are likely to grow farther and farther apart through the years. These famous generalizations have the effect of reducing an individual to the anonymous status of a mere unit in a mass. The wife who, just in time, comes upon her husband about to fry an egg in a dry skillet should not classify him with all other males but should give him the accolade of a special distinction. She might say, for example, 'George, no other man in the world would try to do a thing like that.' Similarly, a husband watching his wife labouring to start the car without turning on the ignition should not say to the gardener or a passer-by, 'Oh, well, you know, etc.' Instead, he should remark to his wife, 'I've seen a lot of women in my life, Nellie, but I've never seen one who could touch you.'

Certain critics of this rule will point out that the specific comments I would substitute for the old familiar generalities do not solve the problem. They will maintain that the husband and wife will be sore and sulky for several days, no matter what is said. One wife, reading Rule Four over my shoulder, exclaimed, 'Isn't that just like a man?' This brings us right back where we started. Oh, well, you know how women are!

RULE FIVE: When a husband is reading aloud, a wife should sit quietly in her chair, relaxed but attentive. If he has decided to read the Republican platform, an article on elm blight, or a blow-by-blow account of a prize fight, it is not going to be easy, but she should at least pretend to be interested. She should not keep swinging one foot, start to wind her wrist-watch, file her fingernails, or clap her hands in an effort to catch a mosquito. The good wife allows the mosquito to bite her when her husband is reading aloud.

She should not break in to correct her husband's pronunciation or to tell him one of his socks is wrong side out. When the husband has finished, the wife should not lunge instantly into some irrelevent subject. It's wiser to exclaim, 'How interesting!' or, at the very least, 'Well, well!' She might even compliment him on his diction and his grasp of politics, elm blight, or boxing. If he should ask some shrewd question to test her attention, she can cry, 'Good heavens!' leap up, and rush out to the kitchen on some urgent fictitious errand. This may fool him, or it may not. I hope, for her sake – and his – that it does.

RULE SIX: A husband should try to remember where things are around the house so that he does not have to wait for his wife to get home from the hairdresser's before he can put his hands on what he wants. Among the things a husband is usually unable to locate are the iodine, the aspirin, the nail file, the French vermouth, his cuff links, studs, black silk socks and evening shirts, the snapshots taken at Nantucket last summer, his favourite recording of 'Kentucky Babe', the borrowed copy of 'The Road to Miltown', the garage key, his own towel, the last bill from Brooks Brothers, his pipe cleaners, the poker chips, crackers, cheese, the whetstone, his new raincoat, and the screens for the upstairs windows.

I don't really know the solution to this problem, but one should be found. Perhaps every wife should draw for her husband a detailed map of the house, showing clearly the location of everything he might need. Trouble is, I suppose, he would lay the map down somewhere and not be able to find it until his wife got home.

RULE SEVEN: If a husband is not listening to what his wife is saying, he should not grunt, 'Okay' or 'Yeah, sure,' or make little affirmative noises. A husband lost in thought or worry is likely not to take in the sense of such a statement as this: 'We're going to the Gordons' for dinner tonight, John, so I'm letting the servants off. Don't come home from the office first. Remember, we both have to be at the dentist's at five, and I'll pick you up there with the car.' Now, an 'Okay' or a 'Yeah, sure' at this point can raise havoc if the husband hasn't really been listening. As usual, he goes all the way out to his home in Glenville – thirteen miles from the dentist's office and seventeen miles from the Gordons' house – and he can't find his wife. He can't find the servants. His wife can't get him on the phone because all she gets is the busy buzz. John is calling everybody he can think of except, of course, the dentist and the Gordons. At last he hangs up, exhausted and enraged. Then the phone rings. It is his wife. And here let us leave them.

RULE EIGHT: If your husband ceases to call you 'Sugarfoot' or 'Candy Eyes' or 'Cutie Fudge Pie' during the first year of your marriage, it is not necessarily a sign that he has come to take you for granted or that he no longer cares. It is probably an indication that he has recovered his normal perspective. Many a young husband who once called his wife 'Tender Mittens' or 'Taffy Ears' or 'Rose Lips' has become austere or important, like a common pleas judge, and he wouldn't want reports of his youthful frivolity to get around. If he doesn't call you Dagmar when your name is Daisy, you are sitting pretty.

RULE NINE: For those whose husbands insist on pitching for the Married Men against the Single Men at the Fourth-of-July picnic of the First M.E. Church, I have the following suggestion: don't sit on the sidelines and watch him. Get lost. George is sure to be struck out by a fourteen-year-old-boy, pull up with a charley horse running to first, and get his teeth knocked out by an easy grounder to the mound. When you see him after the game, tell him everybody knew the little boy was throwing illegal spitballs, everybody saw the first baseman spike George, and everybody said that grounder took such a nasty bounce even Phil Rizzuto couldn't have fielded it. Remember, most middle-aged husbands get to sleep at night by imagining they are striking out the entire batting order of the Yankees.

RULE TEN: A wife's dressing-table should be inviolable. It is the one place in the house a husband should get away from and stay away from, and yet the average husband is drawn to it as by a magnet, especially when he is carrying something wet, oily, greasy or sticky, such as a universal joint, a hub cap, or the blades of a lawn mower. His excuse for bringing these alien objects into his wife's bedroom in the first place is that he is looking for 'an old rag' with which to wipe them off. There are no old rags in a lady's boudoir, but husbands never seem to learn this. They search hampers, closets, and bureau drawers, expecting to find a suitable piece of cloth, but first they set the greasy object on the dressing table. The aggrieved wife may be tempted, following this kind of vandalism, to lock her bedroom door and kick her husband out for good. I suggest, however, a less stringent punishment. Put a turtle in his bed. The wife who is afraid to pick up a turtle should ask Junior to help her. Junior will love it.

Now I realize, in glancing back over these rules, that some of my solutions to marital problems may seem a little untidy; that I have, indeed, left a number of loose ends here and there. For example, if the husbands are going to mislay their detailed maps of household objects, I have accomplished nothing except to add one item for the distraught gentleman to lose.

Then, there is that turtle. Captious critics will point out that a turtle in a husband's bed is not a valid solution to anything, but merely a further provocation. The outraged husband will deliberately trip his wife during their next mixed-doubles match. She will thereupon retaliate by putting salt in his breakfast coffee . . .

Two persons living in holy matrimony, I should have said long before this, must avoid slipping into blasphemy, despond, apathy, and the subjunctive mood. A husband is always set on edge by his mate's 'Far be it from me' or 'Be that as it may'. This can lead to other ominous openings: 'Would God that' and 'Had I only had the good sense to', and the couple is then in the gloomy sub-cellar of the pluperfect subjunctive, a place in which no marriage can thrive. The safest place for a happily wedded pair is the indicative mood, and of its tenses the present is the most secure. The future is a domain of threats and worries, and the past is a wasteland of sorrows and regrets.

I can only hope, in conclusion, that this treatise itself will not start, in any household, a widening gap that can never be closed.

The Race of Life

A PARABLE

This sequence of thirty-five drawings represents the life-story of a man and his wife; or several days, a month, or a year in their life and in that of their child; or their alternately interflowing and diverging streams of consciousness over any given period. It seems to lend itself to a wide variety of interpretations. Anything may be read into it, or left out of it, without making a great deal of difference. Two or three previewers were brought up short by this picture or that – mainly the Enormous Rabbit – and went back and started over again from the beginning. This mars the flow of the sequence by interrupting the increasing tempo of the action. It is better to skip pictures, or tear them out, rather than to begin over again and try to fit them in with some preconceived idea of what is going on.

The Enormous Rabbit, which brought two engravers and a receptionist up short, perhaps calls for a few words of explanation. It can be an Uncrossed Bridge which seems, at first glance, to have been burned behind somebody, or it can be Chickens Counted Too Soon, or a ringing phone, or a thought in the night, or a faint hissing sound. More than likely it is an Unopened Telegram which when opened (see Panel 12) proves not to contain the dreadful news one had expected but merely some such innocuous query as: 'Did you find my silver-rimmed glasses in brown case after party Saturday?'

The snow in which the bloodhounds are caught may be either real snow or pieces of paper torn up.

The Start.

Swinging Along.

Neck and Neck.

Accident.

Water Jump.

The Beautiful Stranger.

The Quarrel.

The Pacemaker.

Spring Dance.

Faster.

The Enormous Rabbit.

Escape.

Top Speed.

Winded.

Quand Même.

Breathing Spell.

The Dive.

Dog Trot.

Down Hill.

Menace.

Up Hill.

Dogs in the Blizzard.

Out of the Storm.

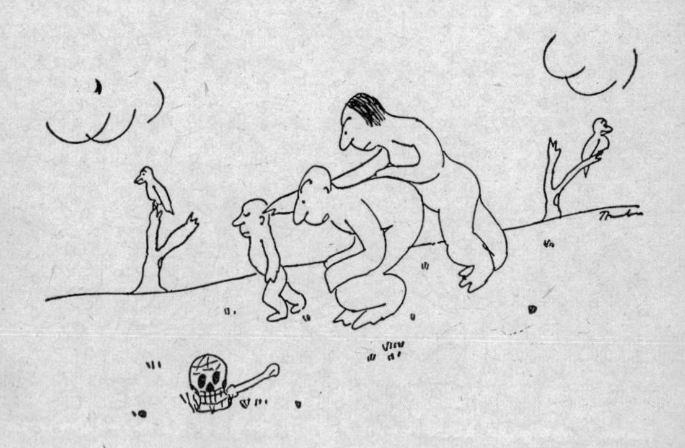

The Skull.

The Water Hole.

The Laggard.

Indians!

War Dance.

Gone!

The Bear.

Sunset.

On Guard.

Dawn: Off Again.

Final Sprint.

The Goal.

The interview

'WONDERFUL place you have here,' said the man from the newspaper. He stood with his host on a rise of ground from where, down a slope to the right, they could see a dead garden, killed by winter, and, off to the left, spare, grim trees stalking the ghost of a brook.

'Everybody says that,' said George Lockhorn. 'Everybody says it's a wonderful place, to which I used to reply "Thank you", or "I'm glad you think so", or "Yes, it is, isn't it?" At fifty-eight, Price, I say what I know. I say that you and the others are, by God, debasing the word wonderful. This bleak prospect is no more wonderful than a frozen shirt. Even in full summer it's no more wonderful than an unfrozen shirt. I will give you the synonyms for wonderful – wondrous, miraculous, prodigious, astonishing, amazing, phenomenal, unique, curious, strange. I looked them up an hour ago, because I knew you would say this is a wonderful place. Apply any of those words to that dahlia stalk down there.'

'I see what you mean,' said Price, who was embarrassed, and began looking in his pockets for something that wasn't there.

'I have known only a few wonderful things in my fifty-eight years,' said Lockhorn. 'They are easy to enumerate, since I have been practising up to toss them off to you casually: the body of a woman, the works of a watch, the verses of Keats, the structure of the hyacinth, the devotion of the dog. Trouble is, I tossed those off casually for the Saint Louis *Post-Dispatch* man, or the Rochester *Times-Union* man. It's cold out here. Shall we go inside?'

'Just as you say,' said the interviewer, who had reached for the copy paper and the pencil in his pocket, but didn't bring them out. 'It's bracing out here, though.'

'You're freezing to death, without your hat and overcoat, and you know it,' said Lockhorn. 'It's late enough for a highball – do you drink cocktails?'

'No, sir. That is, not often,' said Price.

'You're probably a liar,' Lockhorn said. 'Everybody replies to my questions the way they think I want them to reply. You can say that I say "everybody-they"; I hate "everybody-he". "Has everybody brought his or her slate?" a teacher of mine, a great goat of a woman, used to ask us. There is no other tongue in the world as clumsy as ours is – with its back to certain corners. That's been used, too – and don't make notes, or don't let me see you make notes. Never made a note in my life, except after a novel was finished. Plot the chapters out, outline the characters after the book has been published.'

'That is extremely interesting,' said Price. 'What do you do with the notes?'

They had reached the rear of the house now. 'We'll go in the back way,' said Lockhorn. 'I keep them around, tuck them away where my executor can find them if he's on his toes. This is the woodshed. We'll go through the kitchen. Some of my best character touches, some of the best devices, too, are in the notes. Anybody can write a novel, but it takes talent to do notes. We'll go through this door.'

'This is wonderful,' said Price. 'I'm sorry. I mean – '

'Let it stand,' said Lockhorn. 'Wonderful in the sense of being astonishing, curious, and strange. Don't take the chair by the fire,' he added as they reached the living-room. 'That's mine.'

Lockhorn dropped into the chair by the fireplace and motioned his guest into another. 'Can I use that about the notes?' asked Price. 'Mr Hammer wants something new.'

'Make us both a drink,' Lockhorn said. 'That's a bar over there. I drink bourbon, but there's Scotch and rye, too.'

'I'll have bourbon,' said Price.

'Everybody has what I have,' Lockhorn growled. 'I said Scotch, and the *Times-Union* man had Scotch; I said rye, and the *Post-Dispatch* man had rye. No, you can't use that about the notes. Tell it to everybody. Beginning to believe it myself. Have you gained the idea in your half hour here that I am a maniac?'

Price, noisily busy with bottles and glasses, laughed uncomfortably. 'Everybody knows that your methods of work are unusual,' he said. 'May I ask what you are working on now?'

'Easy on the soda,' said Lockhorn. 'Martha will raise hell when she finds me drinking. Just bow at her and grin.'

Price put two frightened squirts of soda in one glass and filled up the other. 'Mrs Lockhorn?' he asked, handing the strong highball to his host.

'What is this man Hammer like?' Lockhorn demanded. 'No, let me tell you. He says "remotely resembles", he says "flashes of insight". He begins, by God, sentences with "moreover". I had an English teacher who began sentences with "too". "Too, there are other factors to be considered." The man says he's read Macaulay, but he never got past page six – Hammer, that is. Should have gone into real estate – subdivision, opening up suburbs, and so on. This English teacher started every class by saying, "None of us can write." Hadn't been for that man, I would have gone into real estate – subdivisions, opening up suburbs, and so on. But he was a challenge. You can say my memoirs will be called *I Didn't Want to Write*.' Lockhorn had almost finished his drink. 'I'll have to see a proof,' he said. 'I'll have to see a proof of your article. Have you noticed that everybody says everything twice? They say everything twice. "Yes, they do," you'll say. "Yes, they do." Only contribution I've made to literature is the discovery of the duplicate statement. "How the hell are you, Bill?" a guy will say, "How the hell are you, anyway?" "Fine," Bill will say. "Just fine".'

'That's very interesting,' said Price, and feeling that his host expected it, he added, 'That's very interesting.'

Lockhorn held out his glass and Price carried it back to the bar. 'The *Times* man, or whoever it was,' Lockhorn went on, 'put down that one of the things I regard as wonderful is the feminine anatomy. You can't get "body of a woman" in the papers. The feminine anatomy is something that can be touched only with the mind, and you'll notice that in my list everything can be touched by the hand. A watch a man never held would not be wonderful.'

'That's true,' said Price, speculating on the actual aspect of devotion.

'There is only one thing I've never told an interviewer,' Lockhorn said, after a pause. 'I've never told any interviewer about the game. "Don't tell the man about the game," Mrs Lockhorn always says. "Promise me you won't tell the man about the game." Let me ask you one thing – why would Martha ask me not to tell you about the game if there were no game?'

'She wouldn't, of course,' said Price, taking a long slow sip of his drink to cover his embarrassment. The two men drank in silence for a while. 'My second wife left me because of the game,' Lockhorn said, 'but you can't print that, because she would deny it, and I would deny it.' Lockhorn took a great gulp of his drink and stared into the fire again. Two minutes of silence went by, during which Price found himself counting the ticks of the clock on the mantelpiece. 'My memory is beginning to slip,' Lockhorn said, 'but if you print that, I'll sue Hammer's pants off. Maybe I'll sue his pants off, anyway. Sunday editors are the worst vermin in the world. If you use that, credit it to Mencken. I don't know why the hell you boys want to interview me. I've said a great many sharp things in my life, but I can't remember which ones are mine and which ones were said by Santayana, or John Jay Chapman, or Bernard DeVoto. You can say my memory is slipping – maybe it will arouse pity. I'm the loneliest man in the United States.' Lockhorn had finished his drink very fast, and he got up and walked to the bar. Price's eyebrows went up as he heard the heavy slug of bourbon chortle into the glass. 'Martha'll be sore as a pup,' Lockhorn said with an owlish grin. 'Just touch your forelock to her. You can't argue with her. She's my fourth wife, you know. The others were Dorothy, Nettie, and Pauline, not necessarily in that order.' He came back to his chair and flopped into it. Price began to listen to the clock again. Lockhorn's head jerked up suddenly. 'Going to call my memoirs *I Had to Write*,' he said. 'You can put that in your piece if you want to.'

When Mrs Lockhorn came into the room, smiling her small, apprehensive smile, Price had just handed his host a seventh highball. 'This is Pricey,' said Lockhorn. Price, who had jumped to his feet, stood bowing and grinning at his hostess. She barely touched him with her smile. 'One for the house,' said Lockhorn, holding up his drink.

'It's early,' said Mrs Lockhorn. 'It isn't five yet.'

'I must be going,' Price said. 'May I make you a drink, Mrs Lockhorn?'

'No, thank you,' she said, in a tone that corked the bottles.

'Nonsense,' said Lockhorn. 'Sit down, Pricey. I've never, by God, known anything like the female time-table. They live by the clock. The purpose of 6 p.m. is to unlock their inhibitions about liquor. Sexual intercourse is for holidays – '

'George!' said Mrs Lockhorn sharply.

Price began to babble. 'Well, I guess it was us men – we men – who actually set a schedule for drinking, with that business about the sun over the yardarm, wasn't it, Mr Lockhorn?'

'Sun over your grandma's thigh,' said Lockhorn irritably, looking at Price but aiming the phrase at his wife. 'Who called tea "the five o'clock"? Women, French women. They don't even believe a man should smoke until he puts on his tuxedo. We are a prisoner of the hours, Pricey, and you know it.' Price flushed and became vastly conscious of his hands.

'Finish your drink,' said Martha Lockhorn to Price. 'My husband is going to finish his, and then I'm afraid he must rest. The new book has taken a great deal out of him.'

'You're goddamn tootin' he's going to finish his,' said Lockhorn, his fingers whitening on his glass, 'and don't third-person me. Sit down, Pricey. We're just getting started.' Price sat stiffly on the edge of his chair. He saw that Mrs Lockhorn, who had moved behind her husband's chair, was trying to communicate with him by a shake of her head and a glance at the bar. 'Don't let 'em third-person you, Pricey,' said Lockhorn sternly. 'Next comes the first person plural – they first-person-plural you to death. Then you might just as well go to bed and die. You might just as well go to bed and die.'

'I hope he hasn't been entertaining you with imprecations all afternoon,' said Mrs Lockhorn.

'Oh, no indeed,' exclaimed Price, picking up his glass and setting it down.

'She loves the happy phrase,' said Lockhorn. 'She spends more time on phrases than most women do on their hips.'

'Don't be tiresome, George,' said Mrs Lockhorn. She turned to Price. 'You see, he has been interviewed constantly,' she told him. 'It seems as if there has been an interviewer here every day since his novel came out. You all want something different, and then it never comes out the way he says it. It's all twisted and ridiculous.'

'I hope to avoid that sin,' said Price, noting that the famous author had closed his eyes but still kept his tight grip on his glass.

'He's terribly tired.' Mrs Lockhorn's voice was lowered to a whisper, as if they were in a sickroom. 'He worked four years on *The Flaw in the Crystal*. Some of the reviews have hurt him deeply.'

'It's selling wonderfully,' whispered Price.

Mrs Lockhorn made a gesture with her hands, but its meaning was lost on him.

The novelist opened his eyes and quickly finished his drink. 'I'll tell you some other wonderful things,' he said. 'A woman crying, children calling over the snow – across the snow – dogs barking at a distance, dogs barking far off at night.' He put his empty glass on the floor and groped in the air for more wonders with his right hand. 'Things I've wanted to do,' he went on. 'You can use this, Pricey. Bat baseballs through the windows of a firescraper from a lower roof across the street, spend – '

'Skyscraper,' said Mrs Lockhorn.

To Price's secret delight his host, after a slow stare at Mrs Lockhorn, repeated with great authority, 'Firescraper.' He winked at Price. 'I want to spend the night in Ovington's,' he said. 'I want to open a pigeon. All my life I've wanted to cut a dove open, looking for the god-damnedest omens in the history of the world. Like the Romans performing the ancient assizes. I want to find two hearts in one of the sons of bitches and go crying through the night, like another Whozis, "Repent, ye sinners, repent. The world is coming to an end."'

'George,' said Mrs Lockhorn, 'the newspapers can't print things like that.'

Lockhorn didn't hear her. He picked up the glass and drank the trickle of ice-water in it. 'Go down, ye sinners, to the sea,' he said, with a wide gesture.

'Talk about your book,' said his wife. 'The newspapers want to know about your book.'

Lockhorn looked at her. 'They are all the same, Pricey,' he said, 'and they differ as the waves differ. Only in height. The blood of the dove, as they say, Pricey. I'll tell you about the book, drunk as I unexpectedly am, or get.'

'He's terribly tired,' cut in his wife.

'Spiritual hope!' bawled Lockhorn, so loudly Price started the ice tinkling in his glass. 'Spiritual hope is my tiny stock in trade, to quote the greatest master of them all.'

Mrs Lockhorn, observing that the newspaperman looked puzzled, said, 'He means Henry James,' and then, to her husband, 'I think he spoke of his *small* trade, George.'

'The greatest master of them all,' said Lockhorn again. 'I always begin with a picture, a visual picture. Woman standing in the doorway with the evening sun in her hair, as Hockett would put it.'

'Hockett?' asked Price, realizing, with a small cold feeling in his stomach, that he was not going to have anything to write.

'Your boss,' said Lockhorn.

'Oh, Hammer,' said Price.

'I beg your pardon?' said Mrs Lockhorn.

The author jiggled what was left of the ice in his glass. 'The women write backwards,' he said, 'beginning with their titles – *Never Dies the Dream, Lonely Is the Hunting Heart.*'

'It's *The Heart Is a Lonely Hunter*,' said his wife, but Lockhorn waved her away.

'I'm tired of the adult world seen through the eyes of a little girl,' he said. 'A woman forgets everything that happens to her after she is fourteen. I, too, have lived in Arcady, Pricey, but I'm tired of viewing the adult world through the great solemn eyes of a sensitive – what is that word like nipper?'

'Moppet?' asked Price.

'Sensitive moppet,' said Lockhorn, closing his eyes, and sinking deeper in his chair.

Price attempted to make a surreptitious note on his copy paper.

'You can't use that,' whispered Mrs Lockhorn. 'He's talking about one of his closest women friends.'

The interviewer put his pencil and paper away as his host opened his eyes again and pointed a finger at him. 'Henry James had the soul of an eavesdropper,' he said. Price gave a laugh that did not sound like his own. 'Everything he got, he got from what he overheard somebody say. No visual sense, and if you haven't got visual sense, what have you got?'

Price stood up as if to go, but Lockhorn waved him down again and grinned at his wife. 'Pricey, here, has invented some remarkable game, Martha,' he said. 'Tell Martha about your game, son. It's all we've talked about all afternoon.'

Price swallowed.

'What sort of game is it?' asked Martha.

'It's nothing, really,' gurgled Price. He stood up again. 'I must be running along,' he said.

'Sit down for a moment,' said Mrs Lockhorn. 'George, you better lie down awhile.'

To Price's astonishment, the novelist got meekly to his feet and started for the door into the hall. He stopped in front of Price and stuck an index finger into his ribs, making a sucking sound with his tongue. 'Is love worse living?' he said, and went out into the hall and closed the door behind him. He began to stomp up the carpeted stairs, shouting, 'Dorothy! Nettie! Martha!'

Price, swallowing again, idiotically wondered whatever became of Pauline.

'As you see, he's really worn out,' said Mrs Lockhorn hastily. 'He's not as young as he used to be, of course, and I wish he'd give up writing. After all, he's written eighteen books and he has a comfortable income.'

From far upstairs Price heard a now faint shouting for the lost Pauline.

'Are you sure you won't have another drink?' asked Mrs Lockhorn, not moving from the edge of her chair.

'A quick one, perhaps,' said Price. 'Just half a glass.'

'Surely,' said Mrs Lockhorn with the hint of a sigh, taking his glass. 'Bourbon?'

'Scotch, if you don't mind,' said Price.

She made it very small, and very weak. 'I know that you will use discretion,' she said. 'George has become a little reckless in some of the things he says, and I hope you were able to tell the truth from the things he just makes up.'

Price finished half his drink. 'I'm afraid I really haven't got anything,' he said miserably. 'Perhaps you could tell me something I could use.'

Mrs Lockhorn looked mysterious. 'There are some wonderful things about the book,' she said. 'I mean about the way he wrote it and what had to be done by the publishers. He had actually written, word for word, a chapter from one of his earlier books into the new one. He hadn't copied it, you understand. It was simply there in his memory, word for word.' Price got out his pencil and paper, but his hostess lifted her hand. 'Oh, mercy!' she said. 'You can't possibly print that. He would be furious if he found it out.'

Price looked puzzled. 'If he found it out?' he asked.

She stood up and Price got to his feet. 'Oh, he doesn't remember writing it,' she said. 'It was just stuck in. The publishers had to take it out. But you mustn't mention it. Please don't even tell Mr Hockett.'

Price set his glass down on the table beside his chair. 'I believe my hat and overcoat – ' he began.

'I'll get them,' she said. 'They must be in the hall closet.'

They went to the closet. There was no sound from upstairs. Price got into his coat, and Mrs Lockhorn went with him to the front door and opened it. 'I'm sorry,' she said. 'I'm afraid it's been something of a wild-goose chase.'

'I'm afraid it has,' said Price, a little grimly.

Mrs Lockhorn gave him her best hostess smile. 'George gets mixed up when he's tired,' she explained, 'or he wouldn't have said "Is love worse living?"'

Price matched her smile with one just as artificial. 'He was quoting one of the most famous lines ever written by James Joyce,' he said. He went out and got into his car. 'Good-bye, Mrs Lockhorn,' he said.

'Good-bye, Mr Pricey,' she called to him. Her smile was gone. 'I'm sorry you didn't have time to tell me about your game.'

'Some other time, maybe,' said Price, whose smile was also gone, and he started the engine.

Mrs Lockhorn closed the front door.

When Price had driven a few hundred yards from the house, he took the copy paper from his pocket and threw it out of the window. Then, suddenly, he reached for his pencil and threw it out of the window, too.

Daguerreotype of a lady

WHEN I first became aware of Mrs Albright in my world – at the age of three or four, I suppose – she was almost seventy, and a figure calculated to excite the retina and linger in the consciousness of any child, Aunt Margery, as everybody called her, was stout and round, and, in the phrase of one of her friends, set close to the ground, like a cabbage. Her shortness was curiously exaggerated by the effect of an early injury. She had fractured her right kneecap in a fall on the ice when she was in her late teens, and the leg remained twisted, so that, when she was standing, she bent over as if she were about to lean down and tie her shoelace, and her torso swayed from side to side when she walked, like the slow pendulum of an ancient clock, arousing sympathy in the old and wonder in the young. I used to marvel at the way she kept her balance, hobbling about in her garden after sundown, with a trowel in one hand and sprinkling-can in the other, her mouth tightening and her eyes closing every now and then when the misery seized her knee. She scorned the support of a cane; canes were for men, who were often feeble and tottery as early as their sixties. It took her a good ten minutes to mount the short staircase that led to the second floor of her home. She would grasp the banister with one hand and, with the other, pull her bad leg up beside her good one, pausing every few steps to catch her breath. She had to come downstairs backward, and this journey was even more laborious and painful. She got up before dawn every morning except Sunday the year around, and she rarely went to bed until after ten o'clock at night.

Aunt Margery was an active woman who got things done, and she did not always carry her cross with meekness and equanimity. She was capable of cursing her bad leg in good, round words that shocked women of more pious vocabulary. In her moments of repose, which were rare enough in a long and arduous lifetime, the gentleness of her face, enhanced by white hair smoothly parted in the middle, belied the energy of her body and the strength of her spirit, but her mouth grew firm, her eyes turned serious or severe, and her will overcame her handicap when she felt called upon, as she often did, to take up some burden too heavy for the shoulders of lesser women, or too formidable for mere menfolks to cope with. Her neighbours often summoned her in an hour of crisis, when there was illness in their homes, or a wife in labour, or a broken bone to set, for she was a natural nurse, renowned for her skill and wisdom and, as we shall see, for many an earthy remedy and forthright practice.

Mrs Albright, born Margery Dangler nearly a hundred and thirty years ago, in a time of stout-hearted and self-reliant women, came West in a covered wagon driven by her father, during the Presidency of Martin Van Buren, when she was only nine. The Danglers, before their westward venture, had lived in Long Branch, in New Jersey – she always used 'in' before a state or county. The family settled for a time in Kokomo, in Indiana, and then retraced its steps to Ohio, to live in Lebanon, in Warren County, Degraff, in Logan County, and Arcanum and Greenville, in Darke County. Shortly after the Civil War, Mrs Albright came to Columbus, where she spent the last forty years of her life in the north half of a two-family frame house at the corner of Fifth Street and Walnut Alley. Her husband had died in Greenville the year the war ended, and she lived with her daughter Belle. When I first knew the neighbourhood, at the turn of the century, Fifth Street was paved with cobblestones and a genial City Council allowed a tall sycamore tree to stand squarely in the middle of the brick sidewalk in front of Mrs Albright's house, dropping its puffballs in season. On the opposite side of the street, the deep-toned clock in the steeple of Holy Cross Church marked, in quarter-hours, the passing of the four decades she lived there. It was a quiet part of town in those days, and the two-storey frame house was one of the serene, substantial structures of my infancy and youth, for all its flimsy shabbiness.

Mrs Albright and her daughter were poor. They took in sewing and washing and ironing, and there was always a roomer in the front room upstairs, but they often found it hard to scrape together ten dollars on the first of the month to pay Mr Lisle, a landlord out of Horatio Alger, who collected his rents in person, and on foot. The sitting-room carpet was faded and, where hot coals from an iron stove had burned it, patched. There was no hot water unless you heated it on the coal stove in the dark basement kitchen, and light was supplied by what Mrs Albright called coal-oil lamps. The old house was a firetrap, menaced by burning coal and by lighted lamps carried by ladies of dimming vision, but these perils, like economic facts, are happily lost on the very young. I spent a lot of time there as a child, and I thought it was a wonderful place, different from the dull formality of the ordinary home and in every difference enchanting. The floors were uneven, and various objects were used to keep the doors from closing: a fieldstone, a paving brick that Mrs Albright had encased in a neat covering made of a piece of carpet, and a conch shell, in which you could hear the roaring of the sea when you held it to your ear. All the mirrors in the house were made of wavy glass and reflected images in fascinating distortions. In the coal cellar, there was what appeared to be an outside toilet moved inside, miraculously connected with the city sewage system; and the lower sash of one of the windows in the sitting-room was flush with the floor – a perfect place to sit and watch the lightning or the snow. Furthermore, the eastern wall of Jim West's livery stable rose less than fifteen feet away from Mrs Albright's back stoop. Against this wall, there was a trellis of moonflowers, which popped open like small white parachutes at twilight in the summertime, and between the trellis and the stoop you could pull up water from a cistern in the veritable oaken bucket of the song. Over all this presided a great lady, fit, it seemed to me, to be the mother of King Arthur or, what was more, of Dick Slater and Bob Estabrook, captain and lieutenant, respectively, in the nickel novels, *Liberty Boys of '76*.

I was reminded of Mrs Albright not long ago when I ran across an old query of Emerson's: 'Is it not an eminent convenience to have in your town a person who knows where arnica grows, or sassafras, or pennyroyal?' Mrs Albright was skilled in using the pharmacopoeia of the woods and fields. She could have brought the great philosopher dozens of roots and leaves and barks, good for everything from ache to agony and from pukin' spells to a knotted gut. She could also have found in the countryside around Concord the proper plants for the treatment of asthma and other bronchial disturbances. She gathered belladonna, Jimson Weed, and digitalis, made a mixture of them, added a solution of saltpetre, put the stuff in a bowl, and set it on fire. The patient simply bent over the bowl and inhaled the fumes. She knew where sour grass grew, which you chew for dyspepsy, and mint, excellent for the naushy, and the slippery elm, whose fragrant inner bark was the favourite demulcent of a hundred years ago – the thing to use for raw throat and other sore tishas. I don't think she ever mentioned goldthread, also known as dodder, but the chances are that she knew it by one or both of its other aliases, devil's-guts and creeping crowfoot.

Mrs Albright's sitting-room was often redolent of spirits of camphor, which could be applied to minor cuts (wet baking soda or cold mashed potato was the stuff for burns); rubbed on the forehead, for headache; used as a gargle or mouthwash, in a mild solution that was never mild enough for me; and sniffed, for attacks of dizzy spells or faintness. Such attacks in Mrs Albright's own case might have been the result of lack of sleep or overwork, but they were never symptoms of the vapours or other feminine weaknesses. A dab of camphor on the back of each hand acted to break affectionate dogs of the habit of licking. Aunt Margery had owned a long line of affectionate dogs, the first of which, Tuney – named after her brother Tunis, who was later killed at Shiloh by a ramrod fired from a nervous Southern farmboy's musket – made the westward trip from Long Branch in the wagon with the Danglers. The last of the line, Cap, a brindle mongrel who looked like a worn carpetbag, caught the secret of vitality from his indomitable mistress and lived to be sixteen, when Aunt Margery, with heavy heart but steady hand, administered the ether that put a merciful end to the miserable burden of his years. That was the year Mrs Albright adopted, fed, and reared a newborn mouse, whose mother had been annihilated in a trap set in the cellar to catch the largest rats I have ever seen. I say annihilated because it was surely the deadliest rat trap in the world, made of a hickory plank, a powerful spring, and a heavy iron ring that could have killed a full-grown cat when it let go.

Once Mrs Albright cornered in the cellar the ugly patriarch of all rats, who had found a safe way to get at the cheese in the trap, and she whammed its life out with a lump of coal.

Shelves in Mrs Albright's sitting-room, where they were handy to get at, held alum, for canker sores; coca butter, for the chest; paregoric, for colic and diarrhoea; laudanum, for pain; balsam apples, for poultices; bismuth, for the bowels; magneeshy (carbonate of magnesium), a light, chalky substance, wrapped in blue paper, that was an antacid and a gentle laxative; and calomel and blue mass, regarded by women of Aunt Margery's generation as infallible regulators of the liver. Blue mass came in the form of pills, and she made it by rubbing up metallic mercury with confection of roses. Blue mass and calomel are no longer found in every house, as they were in Mrs Albright's day, and the free and easy use of paregoric and laudanum, both tinctures of opium, has long been frowned upon by doctors. Your druggist may have heard of balsam apples, alias balsam pears, but unless he is an elderly man, he has probably never seen one. The poultice of today has no source so picturesque as the balsam apple, a warty, oblong West Indian fruit, tropical red or orange in colour. It was used for decoration, too, a hundred years ago and more, and looked nice on a window-sill with love apples turning from green to red. One legend has it, by the way, that the first American tomato was eaten in 1820, by a gentleman of Salem, in New Jersey, a town not far from Long Branch, where Margery Albright was born ten years after this startling and foolhardy act. I was pleased to find out from my pharmacist, Mr Blakely, of Crutch & Macdonald's drugstore, in Litchfield, Connecticut, that folks in small towns and rural regions still favour slippery elm for sore throat. No housewife actually strips the bark from the tree nowadays, the way Mrs Albright did, but slippery-elm lozenges, manufactured by the Henry Thayer Company (founded 1847) from a formula more than ninety years old, are bought by many people in wet or wintry weather. I got a box of the lozenges from Mr Blakely myself and tried a couple. They smelled faintly like fertilizer to my snobbish city nose, but their taste was bland enough and inoffensive. I am sure they soothe the inflamed tishas of the throat. Mr Blakely also said that people from seventy to a hundred years old drop in now and then for blue pills when their liver is kicking up. When I asked him about balsam apples, he told me he knew what they were, but he confessed that he had never seen one. It made me feel old and odd, suddenly, as if I were a contemporary of Aunt Margery's who had lived beyond his time.

Aunt Margery held that cold black coffee – not iced, just cold – was fine for torpor, depression of the spirits, and fatigue. She also used it to disguise the taste of castor oil for timid palates, but she drank the oil straight from the bottle herself, in great, gulping dollops that made me flinch and shudder when I was a boy. For gas on the stomach, and for gentlemen who had brought out the jugs the night before, she made a fizzing mixture of vinegar, sugar, and baking soda. Soda crackers soaked in water were excellent for thinning out the blood in cases that were not severe enough for leeches or the letting of a vein. If you fell down and broke the skin on your elbow or your knee, she kept a sharp look-out for the appearance of proud flesh. In the event of serious injuries, such as gunshot wounds or axe cuts, you had to beware of gangrum. It was easy enough to identify this awful disease as gangrene, but I was well out of my teens before I discovered what 'blue boars' are, or, rather, is. Mrs Albright had described it as a knotted groin, a symptom of the Black Death, at least one siege of which she had survived somewhere in her travels. The true name is 'buboes', from which the word 'bubonic' is derived, and Webster supports Mrs Albright in her definition of the malady as a knotted groin. Then there was cholera morbus, which sounds Asiatic and deadly, but is really no more serious, I found in looking it up the other day, than summer complaint accompanied by green-apple bellyache. If you had the jumpin' toothache, there was nothing better than a large chaw of tobacco. Once, when she was sixteen, Margery Albright was out horseback-riding with a gallant of her acquaintance who bore the gloomy name of Aubrey Hogwood. A jumpin' toothache nearly knocked her from the saddle, and Hogwood, not knowing what the trouble was, paled and stammered when she demanded his tobacco pouch. ('I says to him, "Hogwood," says I, "hand me your pouch."') She took a man-sized helping of the weed and chewed it lustily. The toothache went away, and so did Hogwood. A pallid romantic of queasy stomach, he drifted out of the realistic maiden's life. In Greenville, in Darke County, not long afterward, she married one John Albright, a farmer, whom she was destined to pull out of what I will always think of as the Great Fever.

One day in Darke County, Albright – his wife always called him by his last name – staggered in from the fields, pale and ganted – this was her word for 'gaunt' – and took to his bed with an imposing fever and fits of the shakes that rattled the china in the cupboard. She was not yet thirty at the time, but already a practical nurse of considerable experience, famous in her neighbourhood for her cool presence at sickbeds and her competence as a midwife. She had nursed Albright through a bad case of janders – jaundice to you and me. Her celebrated chills-and-fever medicine, with which she dosed me more than once fifty years after Albright's extremity, failed to do any good. It was a fierce liquid, compounded of the bitterest roots in the world and heavily spiked with quinine, and it seared your throat, burned your stomach, and set your eyes to streaming, but several doses left Albright's forehead still as hot as the bottom of a flatiron. His wife was jubrous – her word for 'dubious' – about his chances of pulling through this strange seizure. Albright tossed all night and moaned and whinkered – a verb she made up herself out of 'whinny' and 'whicker' – and in the morning his temperature had not gone down. She tested his forehead with the flat of her sensitive hand, for she held that thermometers were just pieces of glass used to keep patients' mouths closed while the doctors thought up something to say about conditions that baffled them. The average doctor, in her opinion, was an educated fool, who fussed about a sickroom, fretted the patient, and got in a body's way. The pontifical doctor was likely to be named, in her pungent idiom, a pusgut, and the talkative doctor, with his fluent bedside manner, was nothing more than a whoop in a whirlwind.

In the afternoon of the second day of the Great Fever, John Albright's wife knew what she had to do. She went out into the pasture and gathered a pailful of sheep droppings, which she referred to in the flattest possible terms. Sheep droppings were not the only thing that Mrs Albright looked for in the pasture and the barnyard to assist her ministrations as a natural nurse. Now and then, in the case of a stubborn pregnancy, she would cut a quill from a chicken feather, fill it with powdered tobacco, and blow the contents up one nostril of the expectant mother. This would induce a fit of sneezing that acted to dislodge the most reluctant baby. Albright, whinkering on his bed of pain, knew what she was up to this time, and he began to gag even before the terrible broth was brewing on the kitchen stove. She got it down him somehow, possibly with a firm hand behind his neck and one knee on his stomach. I heard the story of this heroic cure – for cure it was – a dozen times. Albright lay about the house for a day or two, retching and protesting, but before the week was out, he was back at his work in the fields. He died, a few years later, of what his widow called a jaggered kidney stone, and she moved, with her daughter, to Columbus, where she worked for a while as housekeeper of the old American House, a hotel that nobody now remembers. She liked to tell about the tidiest lodger she ever had to deal with, the Honourable Stephen A. Douglas, who kept his room neat as a pin and sometimes even made his own bed. He was a little absent-minded, though, and left a book behind him when he checked out. She could not remember the title of the book or what became of it.

Margery Albright was a woman's woman, who put little faith in the integrity and reliability of the average male. From farm-hand to physician, men were the frequent object of her colourful scorn, especially the mealy-mouthed, and the lazy, the dull, and the stupid, who 'sat around like Stoughton bottles' – a cryptic damnation that charmed me as a little boy. I am happy to report that Webster has a few words to say about Dr Stoughton and the bottle that passed into the workaday idiom of the last century. Stoughton, an earlier Dr Munyon or Father John, made and marketed an elixir of wormwood, germander, rhubarb, orange peel, cascarilla, and aloes. It was used to flavour alcoholic beverages and as a spring tonic for winter-weary folks. It came in a bottle that must have been squat, juglike, and heavy. Unfortunately, my Webster does not have a picture, or even a description, of the old container that became a household word. The dictionary merely says, 'To sit, stand, etc., like a Stoughton bottle: to sit, stand, etc., stolidly and dumbly.' Mrs Albright's figure of speech gave the Stoughton bottle turgid action as well as stolid posture. Only a handful of the husbands and fathers she knew were alert or efficient enough to escape the name of Stoughton bottle.

Aunt Margery lived to be eighty-eight years old, surviving, I am constrained to say, the taking of too much blue mass and calomel. She was salivated, as she called it, at least once a year. This, according to my pharmacist, means that she suffered from mercurial poisoning, as the result of an incautious use of calomel. In spite of everything, her strength and vigour held out to the end, and I can remember no single time that she permitted a doctor to look after her. Her daughter Belle held the medical profession in less contempt, and once, in her fiftieth year, after ailing for several months, she went to see a physician in the neighbourhood. He was greatly concerned about her condition and called a colleague into consultation. The result of their joint findings was a dark prognosis indeed. The patient was given not more than a year to live. When Mrs Albright heard the news, she pushed herself out of her rocking chair and stormed about the room, damning the doctors with such violence that her right knee turned in on her like a flamingo's and she had to be helped back to her chair. Belle recovered from whatever it was that was wrong, and when she died, also at the age of eighty-eight, she had outlived by more than fifteen years the last of the two doctors who had condemned her to death. Mrs Albright never forgave, or long forgot, the mistaken medical men. Every so often, apropos of little or nothing, she would mutter imprecations on their heads. I can remember only two doctors whom she treated with anything approaching respect. She would josh these doctors now and then, when their paths crossed in some sickroom, particularly on the subject of their silly theory that air and water were filled with invisible agencies of disease. This, to a natural nurse who had mastered the simple techniques of barnyard and pasture, was palpable nonsense. 'How, then,' Dr Rankin asked her once, 'do you account for the spread of an epidemic?' 'It's just the contagion,' said Mrs Albright. The doctor gave this a moment of studious thought. 'It's just possible,' he said, 'that we may both be right.'

Dr Dunham, one of her favourites – if I may use so strong a word – arrived late at a house on Parsons Avenue on the night of 8 December 1894. I had got there ahead of him, with the assistance of Mrs Albright. 'You might have spared your horse,' she snapped when he finally showed up. 'We managed all right without you.' But she was jubrous about something, and she decided to take it up with the doctor. 'He has too much hair on his head for a male child,' she told him. 'Ain't it true that they don't grow up to be bright?' Dr Dunham gave the matter his usual grave consideration. 'I believe that holds good only when the hair is thicker at the temples than this infant's,' he said. 'By the way, I wouldn't discuss the matter with the mother.' Fortunately for my own peace of mind, I was unable to understand English at the time. It was a source of great satisfaction to Margery Albright, and not a little surprise, when it became evident, in apt season, that I was going to be able to grasp my mother tongue and add, without undue effort, two and two. I have had my own jubrous moments, however. There was the time when, at forty-three, I sweated and strained to shove an enormous bed nearer the lamp on a small table, instead of merely lifting the small table and placing it nearer the enormous bed. There have been other significant instances, too, but this is the story of Aunt Margery Albright.

I remember the time in 1905 when the doctors thought my father was dying, and the morning someone was wise enough to send for Aunt Margery. We went to get her in my grandfather's surrey. It was an old woodcut of a morning. I can see Mrs Albright, dressed in her best black skirt and percale blouse (she pronounced it 'percal'), bent over before the oval mirror of a cherry wood bureau, tying the velvet ribbons of an antique bonnet under her chin. People turned to stare at the lady out of Lincoln's day as we helped her to the curb. The carriage step was no larger than the blade of a hoe, and getting Aunt Margery, kneecap and all, into the surrey was an impressive operation. It was the first time she had been out of her own dooryard in several years, but she didn't enjoy the April drive. My father was her favourite person in the world, and they had told her he was dying. Mrs Albright's encounter with Miss Wilson, the registered nurse on the case, was a milestone in medical history – or, at least, it was for me. The meeting between the starched young lady in white and the bent old woman in black was the meeting of the present and the past, the newfangled and the old-fashioned, the ritualistic and the instinctive, and the shock of antagonistic schools of thought clashing sent out cold sparks. Miss Wilson was coolly disdainful, and Mrs Albright plainly hated her crisp guts. The patient, ganted beyond belief, recognized Aunt Margery, and she began to take over, in her ample, accustomed way. The showdown came on the third day, when Miss Wilson returned from lunch to find the patient propped up in a chair before a sunny window, sipping, of all outrageous things, a cup of cold coffee, held to his lips by Mrs Albright, who was a staunch believer in getting a patient up out of bed. All the rest of her life, Aunt Margery, recalling the scene that followed, would mimic Miss Wilson's indignation, crying in a shrill voice, 'It shan't be done!' waving a clenched fist in the air, exaggerating the young nurse's wrath. 'It shan't be done!' she would repeat, relaxing at last with a clutch at her protesting kneecap and a satisfied smile. For Aunt Margery won out, of course, as the patient, upright after many horizontal weeks, began to improve. The doctors were surprised and delighted, Miss Wilson tightly refused to comment, Mrs Albright took it all in her stride. The day after the convalscent was able to put on his clothes and walk a little way by himself, she was hoisted into the surrey again and driven home. She enjoyed the ride this time. She asked the driver to stop for a moment in front of the marble house at Washington and Town, built by Dr S. B. Hartman out of the profits of Peruna, a tonic far more popular than Dr Stoughton's, even if the bottle it came in never did make Webster's Dictionary.

The old frame house in Columbus and the old sycamore tree that shaded it disappeared a long time ago, and a filling station now stands on the north-west corner of Fifth Street and Walnut Alley, its lubricating pit about where Mrs Albright's garden used to be. The only familiar landmark of my youth is the church across the way, whose deep-toned clock still marks the passing of the quarter hours as tranquilly as ever. When Belle died in 1937, in another house on Fifth Street, the family possessions were scattered among the friends who had looked after her in her final years. I sometimes wonder who got the photograph album that had been promised to me; the card table, bought for a dollar or two before the Civil War, but now surely an antique of price and value; the two brown plaster-of-Paris spaniels that stood on either end of the mantel in Mrs Albright's bedroom; and the muddy colour print that depicted the brave and sturdy Grace Darling pulling away from a yellow lighthouse on her famous errand of mercy. I have no doubt that some of the things were thrown away: the carpet-covered brick, the fieldstone, the green tobacco tin that Aunt Margery used for a button box, and the ragbag filled with silk cuttings for the crazy quilts she made. Who could have guessed that a writer living in the East would cherish such objects as these, or that he would have settled for one of the dark and wavy mirrors, or the window sash in the sitting-room that was flush with the floor?

I sometimes wonder, too, what has happened to the people who used to call so often when Aunt Margery was alive. I can remember all the tenants of the front room upstairs, who came and went: Vernie, who clerked in a store; the fabulous Doc Marlowe, who made and sold Sioux Liniment and wore a ten-gallon hat with kitchen matches stuck in the band; the blonde and mysterious Mrs Lane, of the strong perfume and the elegant dresses; Mr Richardson, a guard at the penitentiary, who kept a gun in his room; and a silent, thin, smiling man who never revealed his business and left with his rent two weeks in arrears. I remember Dora and Sarah Koontz, daughters of a labourer, who lived for many years in the other half of the two-family house, and the visitors who dropped in from time to time: Mr Pepper and his daughter Dolly, who came to play cards on summer evenings; Mrs Straub, who babbled of her children – her Clement and her Minna; Joe Chickalilli, a Mexican rope thrower; and Professor Fields, a Stoughton bottle if there ever was one, who played the banjo and helped Doc Marlowe sell the liniment that Mrs Albright and Belle put up in bottles; and the Gammadingers and their brood, who lived on a farm in the Hocking Valley. Most of them were beholden to Mrs Albright for some service or other in time of trouble, and they all adored her.

When Margery Albright took to her bed for the last time – the bed in the front room downstairs, where she could hear people talking and life stirring in the street outside her window – she gave strict orders that she was not to be 'called back'. She had seen too much of that, at a hundred bedsides, and she wanted to die quietly, without a lot of unseemly fuss over the natural ending of a span of nearly ninety complete and crowded years. There was no call, she told her daughter, to summon anybody. There was nothing anybody could do. A doctor would just pester her, and she couldn't abide one now. Her greatest comfort lay in the knowledge that her plot in Green Lawn Cemetery had been paid for, a dollar at a time, through the years, and that there was money enough for a stone marker, tucked away in a place her daughter knew about. Mrs Albright made Belle repeat to her the location of this secret and precious cache. Then she gave a few more final instructions and turned over in bed, pulling her bad leg into a comfortable position. 'Hush up!' she snapped when her daughter began to cry. 'You give a body the fidgets.'

Women who were marked for death, Aunt Margery had often told me, always manifested, sooner or later, an ominous desire to do something beyond the range of their failing strength. These ladies in the very act of dying fancied, like Verdi's Violetta, that life was returning in full and joyous tide. They wanted to sit up in bed and comb their hair, or alter a dress, or bathe the cat, or change the labels on the jam jars. It was an invariable sign that the end was not far off. Old Mrs Dozier, who had insisted on going to the piano to play 'Abide with Me', collapsed with a discordant jangle on the keys and was dead when they carried her back to the bed. Mrs Albright's final urge, with which her ebbing sense no doubt sternly dealt, might easily have been to potter about in her garden, since it was coming summer and the flowers needed constant attention. It was a narrow plot, occasionally enlivened with soil from the country, that began with an elephant ear near the rickety wooden fence in front and extended to the trellis of moonflowers against the wall of Jim West's stable. It was further shaded by her own house and the Fenstermakers', and it caught only stingy glimpses of the sun, but, to the wonder of the jubrous, it sustained for forty summers Canterbury bells and bluebells, bleeding hearts and fuchsias, asters and roses. There were tall stalks of asparagus, raised for ornament, and castor-oil plants six feet high (I doubt that she made the castor oil that she disguised in coffee for timid palates and drank neat from the bottle herself, but I have no doubt she could have). 'This garden,' said Dr Sparks, pastor of the old Third Street Methodist Church, one day, 'is a testament of faith.' 'It takes faith, and it takes work, and it takes a lot of good, rich manure,' said Mrs Albright, far and away the most distinguished manurist of her time.

Since there had to be services of some kind, in accordance with a custom that irked her, Mrs Albright would have preferred a country parson, who rode a horse in any weather and could lend a hand at homely chores, if need be. She liked what she called a man of groin, who could carry his proper share of the daily burden and knew how to tell a sow from a sawbuck. City ministers, in her estimation, were delicate fellows, given to tampering with the will of God, and with the mysteries of life after death, which the Almighty would have cleared up for people Himself if He had had a mind to. It was her fancy that urban reverends were inclined to insanity, because of their habit of studying. 'Studying,' in Mrs Albright's language, meant that form of meditation in which the eyes are lifted up. The worst cases let their gaze slowly follow, about a room, the juncture of ceiling and walls, and once a pastor developed this symptom, he was in imminent danger of going off his worshipful rocker. Such parsons, whether they studied or not, made Mrs Albright uneasy, except for the Reverend Stacy Matheny, a first cousin of my mother's. He had been born on a farm in Fairfield County, and he knew how to hitch a horse, split a rail, and tell a jaybird from a bootjack. Mrs Albright wanted him to read her funeral service because he was a man of few words, and he would get it over with and not whinker all afternoon, keeping people away from their jobs. Aunt Margery never discussed religion with me or with anyone else. She seemed to take it for granted that the Lord would find a fitting place in Heaven for women who devoted their lives to good works, and she let it go at that. Tales of ghosts and haunted houses annoyed her. Earthbound spirits, in her pragmatic view, had no business puttering about among the living. A certain house in Kokomo, she told me once when I was ten, was supposed to be haunted by a woman, but her ghost was laid by a peremptory command from the great nurse. 'I never seen her myself,' she told me, 'but I went into the room they said she haunted, and I says, "Rest, Mrs Detweiler," says I.' As I remember the tale after more than fifty years, the ghost of Mrs Detweiler rested. Women, in any shape or form, were accustomed to obey Margery Albright's commands.

The Reverend Stacy Matheny compared the late Margery Albright to the virtuous woman of Proverbs, who rose while it was yet night, worked willingly with her hands, and ate not the bread of idleness. The original lady of the tribute was, of course, far richer in worldly goods than Mrs Albright, whose clothing was not silk and purple, but in trait and toil and temper they were rare and similar examples of that noble breed of women the French call *brave et travailleuse*. I wished that some closer student of Aunt Margery could have taken over those final rites, whose formality would have annoyed the great lady as much as the lugubrious faces of her friends and neighbours. Somebody should have told how she snatched up a pair of scissors one day and cut a hornet in two when it lighted on the head of a sleeping baby; and how she took an axe and chopped off the head of a savage outlaw cat that killed chickens, attacked children, and, blackest sin of all, disturbed the sleep of a woman patient; and about the time she whipped off her calico blouse, put it over the eyes of a frightened horse, and led him out of a burning barn while the menfolks, at a safe distance, laughed at her corset cover and cheered her courage. But it would have taken all afternoon to do even faint justice to the saga of Mrs Albright, born Margery Dangler, nearly a hundred and thirty years ago, in Long Branch, in New Jersey, who departed this earthly scene 6 June 1918 in the confident hope – as old epitaphs used to say – of the blessed resurrection and the life eternal. It seemed to me, standing there in the dim parlour of the old frame house, that something as important as rain had gone out of the land.

The services came to a close with the singing of 'No Night There' by two tearful women, who sang it as only middle-aged Methodist females in Ohio can sing a hymn – upper register all the way, nasal, tremulous, and loud. Mrs Albright, I reflected would enjoy the absence of night in Paradise only because ever lasting light would give her more time to look after people and to get things done. I still like to believe, after all these years, tha chalcedony is subject to cleaning, and that a foolish angel falls now and then and breaks a wing, for glory, as mere reward o labours ended, would make Margery Albright uncomfortable and sad. I trust that Providence has kept this simple truth in mind.

A call on Mrs Forrester

(*After rereading, in my middle years, Willa Cather's* A Lost Lady *and Henry James's* The Ambassadors)

I DROPPED off a Burlington train at Sweet Water one afternoon last fall to call on Marian Forrester. It was a lovely day. October stained the hills with quiet gold and russet, and scarlet as violent as the blood spilled not far away so many years ago along the banks of the Little Big Horn. It had been just such a day as this when I was last in Sweet Water, fifteen years before, but the glory of the earth affected me more sharply now than it had when I was mid-way through my confident thirties. October weather, once a plentiful wine, had become a rare and precious brandy and I took my time savouring it as I walked out of the town toward the Forrester house. Sweet Water has changed greatly since the days when Frank Ellinger stepped down from the Burlington and everybody in the place knew about it. The town is large and wealthy now and, it seemed to me, vulgar and preoccupied. I was afflicted with a sense of having come into the presence of an old uncle, declining in the increase of his fortune, who no longer bothered to identify his visitors. It was a relief to leave the town behind, but as I approached the Forrester house I felt that the lines of my face were set in grave resolution rather than in high anticipation. It was all so different from the free, lost time of the lovely lady's 'bright occasions' that I found myself making a little involuntary gesture with my hand, like one who wipes the tarnish from a silver spoon, searching for a fine, forgotten monogram.

I first met Marian Forrester when I was twenty-seven, and then again when I was thirty-six. It is my vanity to believe that Mrs Forrester had no stauncher admirer, no more studious appreciator. I took not only her smallest foible but her largest sin in my stride; I was as fascinated by the glitter of her flaws as by the glow of her perfections, if, indeed, I could tell one radiance from the other. There was never anything reprehensible to me in the lady's ardent adventures, and even in her awfulest attachment I persisted in seeing only the further flowering of a unique and privileged spirit. As I neared her home, I remembered a dozen florid charities I had invented to cover her multitude of frailties: her dependence on money and position, her admiration of an aristocracy half false and half imaginary, her lack of any security inside herself, her easy loneliness. It was no use, I was fond of telling myself, to look for the qualities of the common and wholesome morning glory in the strange and wanton Nicotiana. From the darkest earth, I would add, springs ever the sweetest rose. A green isle in the sea, if it has the sparkling fountain, needs not the solemn shrine, and so forth and so on.

I had built the lady up very high, as you see. I had commanded myself to believe that emotional literacy, a lively spirit, and personal grace, so rarely joined in American females, particularly those who live between Omaha and Denver, were all the raiment a lady needed. As I crossed the bridge, with the Forrester house now in full view, I had, all of a sudden, a disturbing fancy. There flashed into my consciousness a vivid vision of the pretty lady, seated at her dressing-table, practising in secrecy her little arts, making her famous ear-rings gleam with small, studied turnings of her head, revealing her teeth for a moment in a brief, mocking smile, and, unhappiest picture of all, rehearsing her wonderful laughter.

I stopped on the bridge and leaned against the rail and felt old and tired. Black clouds had come up, obscuring the sun, and they seemed to take the mushroom shape of atomic dust, threatening all frail and ancient satisfactions. It began to rain.

I wondered what I would say to Marian Forrester if she appeared at the door in one of her famous, familiar postures – *en déshabillé*, her hair down her back, a brush in her hand, her face raised in warm, anachronistic gaiety. I tried to remember what we had ever talked about, and could think only of the dreadful topic of grasping women and eligible men. We had never discussed any book that I could recall, and she had never mentioned music. I had another of my ungallant fancies – a vision of the lovely lady at a concert in the town, sitting with bright eye and deaf ear, displaying a new bonnet and gown, striving, less subtly than of old, to capture the attention of worried and oblivious gentlemen. I recalled with sharp clarity a gown and bonnet she had once worn, but for the life of me I could not put a face between them. I caught the twinkle of ear-rings, and that was all.

The latest newspaper lying open on a chair, a note stuck in a milk bottle on the back porch, are enough to indicate the pulse of a living house, but there would not even be these faint signs of today and tomorrow in Marian Forrester's house, only the fibrillation of a yesterday that had died but would not stay dead. There would be an old copy of *Ainslee's* on the floor somewhere, a glitter of glass under a broken windowpane, springs leaking from a ruptured sofa, a cobweb in a chandelier, a dusty etching of Notre-Dame unevenly hung on the wall, and a stopped clock on the marble mantel above a cold fireplace. I could see the brandy bottle, too, on a stained table, wearing its cork drunkenly.

Just to the left of the front door, the big hall closet would be filled with relics of the turn of the century – the canes and guns of Captain Forrester, a crokinole board, a diavolo, a frivolous parasol, a collection of McKinley campaign buttons, a broken stereopticon, a table-tennis net, a toppled stack of blue poker chips and a scatter of playing cards, a wood-burning set, and one of those large, white, artificial Easter eggs you put to your eye and, squinting into it, behold the light that never was, in a frosty fairyland. There would be a crack in the crusty shell, and common daylight would violate the sanctuary of the yellowed and tottery angels. You could find, in all the litter, as measuring sticks of calamity, nothing longer than an envelope firmly addressed in a gentleman's hand, a cancelled cheque, a stern notice from the bank.

The shade of one upstairs window was pulled all the way down, and it suddenly had the effect of making the house appear to wink, as if it were about to whisper, out of the corner of its door, some piece of scandal. If I went in, I might be embarrassed by the ungainly sounds of someone moving about upstairs after the lady had descended, sounds that she would cover by riffling nervously through a dozen frilly seasons of her faded past, trying, a little shrilly, to place me among the beaux in some half-remembered ballroom. I was afraid, too, that I might encounter in some dim and dusty mirror a young man frowning disapproval of an older self come to make a judgement on a poor lady not for her sake and salvation but, in some strange way, for his own. And what if she brought out, in the ruins of her famous laughter, what was left of the old disdain, and fixed me shrewdly for what I was, a frightened penitent, come to claim and take away and burn the old praises he had given her? I wouldn't succeed, of course, standing there in my unbecoming middle years, foolishly clutching reasons and arguments like a shopper's husband loaded down with bundles. She would gaily accuse me of being in love with another and, with the ghost of one of her poses of charming bewilderment, would claim a forfeit for my cruelty and insist that I sit down and have a brandy. I would have one – or several – and in the face of my suspicions of the presence of a man upstairs, my surrender would compromise the delicacy of my original cool intentions, and the lost individual would be, once again, as always in this house, myself. I wondered, standing there in the rain, how it would all come out.

She would get the other lady's name out of me easily enough when the brandy began to ebb in the bottle, and, being Marian Forrester, for whom jealousy was as simple as a reflex, she would be jealous of the imaginary relations of a man she could not place, with a woman she had never heard of. I would then confess my love for Mme de Vionnet, the lady of the lilacs, of Gloriani's bright Sunday garden, of the stately house in the Boulevard Malesherbes, with its cool parlour and dark medallions. I would rise no doubt to the seedy grandiloquence of which I am capable when the cognac is flowing, and I could hear her pitiless comment. 'One of those women who have something to *give*, for heaven's sake!' she would say. 'One of those women who save men, a female whose abandon might possibly tiptoe to the point of tousling her lover's hair, a woman who at the first alarm of a true embrace would telephone the gendarmes.' 'Stop it!' I heard myself shout there in the rain. 'I beg you to remember it was once said of Mme de Vionnet that when she touched a thing, the ugliness, God knows how, went out of it.' 'How sweet!' I could hear

Mrs Forrester go on. 'And yet, according to you, she lost her lover, for all her charm, and to a snippet of an applecheek from New England. Did the ugliness go out of *that*? And if it did, what did the poor lady do with all the prettiness?'

As I stood there in the darkening afternoon, getting soaked, I realized sharply that in my fantasy I had actually been handing Marian Forrester stones to throw at the house in Paris, and the confusion in my viewpoint of the two ladies, if up to that moment I had had a viewpoint, overwhelmed me. I figured what would happen as the shadows deepened in the Forrester house, and we drank what was left of the brandy out of ordinary tumblers – the *ballons* of the great days would long since have been shattered. Banter would take on the sharp edge of wrangling, and in the end she would stand above me, maintaining a reedy balance, and denounce the lady of the lilacs in the flat terms she had overheard gentlemen use so long ago over their cigars and coffee in the library. I would set my glass down on the sticky arm of the chair and get up and stalk out into the hall. But though she had the last word, she would not let me have the last silence, the gesture in conclusion. She would follow me to the door. In her house, by an ancient rule, Marian Forrester always had the final moment – standing on the threshold, her face lifted, her eyes shining, her hand raised to wave good-bye. Yes, she would follow me to the door, and in the hall – I could see it so clearly I shivered there on the bridge – something wonderful would happen. With the faintest of smiles and the slightest of murmurs, I would bow to my hostess, open the door, and walk not out into the rain but into that damn closet, with its junk and clutter, smashing the Easter egg with my shoe, becoming tangled in the table-tennis net, and holding in my hand, when I regained my balance, that comic parasol. Mme de Vionnet would ignore such a calamity; she would pretend not to see it, on the ground that a hostess is blind – a convention that can leave a man sitting at table with an omelet in his lap, unable to mention it, forced to go on with the conversation. But Marian would laugh, the lost laugh of the bright occasions, of the day of her shameless passion in the snow, and it would light the house like candles, reducing the sounds upstairs, in some miraculous way, to what they really were, the innocent creaking of the old floorboards. 'What's all this about saving men?' I would cry. 'Look who's talking!' And, still holding the parasol, I would kiss her on the cheek, mumble something about coming back some day, and leave, this time by the right door, finding, as I went to rejoin myself at the bridge, a poker chip in the cuff of my trousers.

It seems like a long time ago, my call on Mrs Forrester. I have never been back. I didn't even send her a Valentine last February. But I did send a pretty book of impeccable verses to Mme de Vionnet, writing in the inscription something polite and nostalgic about '*ta voix dans le Bois de Boulogne*'. I did this, I suppose, out of some obscure guilt sense – these things are never very clear to any man, if the truth were told. I think the mental process goes like this, though. Drinking brandy out of a water glass in the amiable company of a lady who uses spirits for anodyne and not amenity, a timid gentleman promises his subconscious to make up for it later on by taking a single Malaga before *déjeuner à midi* with a fastidious lady, toying with aspic, discussing Thornton Wilder, praising the silverpoint in the hall on the way out, and going home to lie down, exhausted but somehow purified.

I will carry lilacs, one of these summers, to the house on the Boulevard Malesherbes, and take Mme de Vionnet to a matinée of *Louise*, have a white port with her at one of the little terraces at the quietest corner of the Parc Monceau, and drop her at the door well before the bold moon has begun to wink at the modest twilight. Since, in the best Henry James tradition, I will get nothing out of this for myself, it ought to make up for something. I could do worse than spend my last summers serenely, sipping wine, clop-clopping around town, listening to good music, kissing a lady's hand at her door, going to bed early, and getting a good night's sleep. A man's a fool who walks in the rain, drinks too much brandy, risks his neck floundering around in an untidy closet. Besides, if you miss the six-fifteen, the eastbound Burlington that has a rendezvous with dusk in Sweet Water every day except Sundays and holidays, you have to wait till midnight for the next train east. A man could catch his death, dozing there in that cold and lonesome station.

There's no place like home

IF you are thinking about going abroad and want to preserve your ardour for travelling, don't pore over a little book called *Collins' Pocket Interpreters: France*, which I picked up in London. Written especially to instruct the English how to speak French in the train, the hotel, the quandary, the dilemma, etc., it is, of course, equally useful – I might also say equally depressing – to Americans. I have come across a number of these helps-for-travellers, but none that has the heavy impact, the dark, cumulative power of Collins's. A writer in a London magazine, not so many years ago, mentions a phrase book got out in the era of Imperial Russia which contained this one magnificent line: 'Oh dear, our postillion has been struck by lightning!' But that fantastic piece of disaster, while charming and provocative – though, I daresay, quite rare even in the days of the Tsars – is to Mr Collins's modern, workaday disasters as Fragonard is to George Bellows, or Sarah Orne Jewett to William Faulkner. Let us turn the pages of this appalling little volume.

Each page has a list of English expressions, one under the other, which gives them the form of verse. The French translations are run alongside. Thus, on the first page, under 'The Port of Arrival', we begin (quietly enough) with 'Porter, here is my baggage!' – '*Porteur, voici mes bagages!*' From then on disaster follows fast and follows faster until in the end, as you shall see, all hell breaks loose. The volume contains three times as many expressions to use when one is in trouble as when everything is going all right. This, my own experience has shown, is about the right ratio, but God spare me from some of the difficulties for which the traveller is prepared in Mr Collins's melancholy narrative poem. I am going to leave out the French translations because, for one thing, people who get involved in the messes and tangles we are coming to invariably forget their French and scream in English, anyway. Furthermore, the French would interrupt the fine, free flow of the English and spoil what amounts to a dramatic tragedy of an overwhelming and original kind.

The phrases, as I have said, run one under the other, but herein I shall have to run them one after the other (you can copy them down the other way, if you want to).

Trouble really starts in the canto called 'In the Customs Shed'. Here we have: 'I cannot open my case.' 'I have lost my keys.' 'Help me to close this case.' 'I did not know that I had to pay.' 'I don't want to pay so much.' 'I cannot find my porter.' 'Have you seen porter 153?' That last query is a little master-stroke of writing, I think, for in those few words we have a graphic picture of a tourist lost in a jumble of thousands of bags and scores of customs men, looking frantically for one of at least a hundred and fifty-three porters. We feel that the tourist will not find porter 153, and the note of frustration has been struck.

Our tourist (accompanied by his wife, I like to think) finally gets on the train for Paris – having lost his keys and not having found his porter – and it comes time presently to go to the dining-car, although he probably has no appetite, for the customs men, of course, have had to break open that one suitcase. Now, I think, it is the wife who begins to crumble: 'Someone has taken my seat.' 'Excuse me, sir, that seat is mine.' 'I cannot find my ticket!' 'I have left my ticket in the compartment.' 'I will go and look for it.' 'I have left my gloves (my purse) in the dining-car.' Here the note of frenzied disintegration, so familiar to all travellers abroad, is sounded. Next comes 'The Sleeper', which begins, ominously, with 'What is the matter?' and ends with 'May I open the window?' 'Can you open this window, please?' We realize, of course, that *nobody* is going to be able to open the window and that the tourist and his wife will suffocate. In this condition they arrive in Paris, and the scene there, on the crowded station platform, is done with superb economy of line: 'I have left something in the train.' 'A parcel, an overcoat.' 'A mackintosh, a stick.' 'An umbrella, a camera.' 'A fur, a suitcase.' The travellers have now begun to go completely to pieces, in the grand manner.

Next comes an effective little interlude about an aeroplane trip, which is one of my favourite passages in this swift and sorrowful tragedy: 'I want to reserve a place in the plane leaving tomorrow morning.' 'When do we start?' 'Can we get anything to eat on board?' 'When do we arrive?' 'I feel sick.' 'Have you any paper bags for air-sickness?' 'The noise is terrible.' 'Have you any cotton wool?' 'When are we going to land?' This brief masterpiece caused me to cancel an air trip from London to Paris and go the easy way, across the Channel.

We now come to a section called 'At the Hotel', in which things go from worse to awful: 'Did you not get my letter?' 'I wrote to you three weeks ago.' 'I asked for a first-floor room.' 'If you can't give me something better, I shall go away.' 'The chambermaid never comes when I ring.' 'I cannot sleep at night, there is so much noise.' 'I have just had a wire. I must leave at once.' Panic has begun to set in, and it is not appeased any by the advent of 'The Chambermaid': 'Are you the chambermaid?' 'There are no towels here.' 'The sheets on this bed are damp.' 'This room is not clean.' 'I have seen a mouse in the room' 'You will have to set a mouse trap here.' (I am sure all you brave people who are still determined to come to France will want to know how to say 'mouse trap' in French: it's *souricière*; but you better bring one with you.) The bells of hell at this point begin to ring in earnest: 'These shoes are not mine.' 'I put my shoes here, where are they now?' 'The light is not good.' 'The bulb is broken.' 'The radiator is too warm.' 'The radiator doesn't work.' 'It is cold in this room.' 'This is not clean, bring me another.' 'I don't like this.' 'I can't eat this. Take it away!'

I somehow now see the tourist's wife stalking angrily out of the hotel, to get away from it all (without any shoes on), and, properly enough, the booklet seems to follow her course – first under 'Guides and Interpreters': 'You are asking too much.' 'I will not give you any more.' 'I shall call a policeman.' 'He can settle this affair.' Then under 'Inquiring the Way': 'I am lost.' 'I was looking for—' 'Someone robbed me.' 'That man robbed me.' 'That man is following me everywhere.' She rushes to 'The Hairdresser', where, for a change, everything goes quite smoothly until: 'The water is too hot, you are scalding me!' Then she goes shopping, but there is no surcease: 'You have not given me the right change.' 'I bought this two days ago.' 'It doesn't work.' 'It is broken.' 'It is torn.' 'It doesn't fit me.' Then to a restaurant for a snack and a reviving cup of tea: 'This is not fresh.' 'This piece is too fat.' 'This doesn't smell very nice.' 'There is a mistake in the bill.'

'While I was dining someone has taken my purse.' 'I have left my glasses (my watch) (a ring) in the lavatory.' Madness has now come upon her and she rushes wildly out into the street. Her husband, I think, has at the same time plunged blindly out of the hotel to find her. We come then, quite naturally, to 'Accident', which is calculated to keep the faint of heart – nay, the heart of oak – safely at home by his own fireside: 'There has been an accident!' 'Go and fetch a policeman quickly.' 'Is there a doctor near here?' 'Send for the ambulance.' 'He is seriously injured.' 'She has been run over.' 'He has been knocked down.' 'Someone has fallen in the water.' 'The ankle, the arm.' 'The back, a bone.' 'The face, the finger.' 'The foot, the head.' 'The knee, the leg.' 'The neck, the nose.' 'The wrist, the shoulder.' 'He has broken his arm.' 'He has broken his leg.' 'He has a sprained ankle.' 'He has a sprained wrist.' 'He is losing blood.' 'He has fainted.' 'He has lost consciousness.' 'He has burnt his face.' 'It is swollen.' 'It is bleeding.' 'Bring some cold water.' 'Help me to carry him.' (Apparently, you just let *her* lie there, while you attend to him – but, of course, she was merely run over, whereas he has taken a terrific tossing around.)

We next see the husband and wife back in their room at the dreary hotel, both in bed, and both obviously hysterical. This scene is entitled 'Illness': 'I am feeling very ill, send for the doctor.' 'I have pains in —' 'I have pains all over.' 'The back, the chest.' 'The ear, the head.' 'The eyes, the heart.' 'The joints, the kidneys.' 'The lungs, the stomach.' 'The throat, the tongue.' 'Put out your tongue.' 'The heart is affected.' 'I feel a pain here.' 'He is not sleeping well.' 'He cannot eat.' 'My stomach is out of order.' 'She is feverish.' 'I have caught a cold.' 'I have caught a chill.' 'He has a temperature.' 'I have a cough.' 'Will you give me a prescription?' 'What must I do?' 'Must I stay in bed?' 'I feel better.' 'When will you come and see me again?' 'Biliousness, rheumatism.' 'Insomnia, sunstroke.' 'Fainting, a fit.' 'Hoarseness, sore throat.' 'The medicine, the remedy.' 'A poultice, a draught.' 'A tablespoonful, a teaspoonful.' 'A sticking plaster, senna.' 'Iodine.' The last suicidal bleat for iodine is, to me, a masterful touch.

Our couple finally get on their feet again, for travellers are tough – they've got to be – but we see under the next heading, 'Common Words and Phrases', that they are left forever punch-drunk and shattered: 'Can I help you?' 'Excuse me.' 'Carry on!' 'Look here!' 'Look down there!' 'Look up there!' 'Why, how?' 'When, where?' 'Because.' 'That's it!' 'It is too much, it is too dear.' 'It is very cheap.' 'Who, what, which?' 'Look out!' Those are Valkyries, one feels, riding around, and above, and under our unhappy husband and wife. The book sweeps on to a mad operatic ending of the tragedy, with all the strings and brasses and woodwinds going full blast: 'Where are we going?' 'Where are you going?' 'Come quickly and see!' 'I shall call a policeman.' 'Bring a policeman! 'I shall stay here.' 'Will you help me?' 'Help! Fire!' 'Who are you?' 'I don't know you.' 'I don't want to speak to you.' 'Leave me alone.' 'That will do.' 'You are mistaken.' 'It was not I.' 'I didn't do it.' 'I will give you nothing.' 'Go away now!' 'It has nothing to do with me.' 'Where should one apply?' 'What must I do?' 'What have I done?' 'I have done nothing.' 'I have already paid you.' 'I have paid you enough.' 'Let me pass!' 'Where is the British consulate?' The oboes take that last, despairing wail, and the curtain comes down.

So you're going to France?

The lady on the bookcase

ONE day some twenty years ago an outraged cartoonist, four of whose drawings had been rejected in a clump by the *New Yorker*, stormed into the office of the late Harold Ross, editor of the magazine. 'Why is it,' demanded the cartoonist, 'that you reject my work and publish drawings by a fifth-rate artist like Thurber?' Ross came quickly to my defence like the true friend and devoted employer he was. 'You mean third-rate,' he said quietly, but there was a warning glint in his steady grey eyes that caused the discomfited cartoonist to beat a hasty retreat.

With the exception of Ross, the interest of editors in what I draw has been rather more journalistic than critical. They want to know if it is true that I draw by moonlight, or under water, and when I say no, they lose interest until they hear the rumour that I found the drawings in an old trunk or that I do the captions while my nephew makes the sketches.

One day I was shoving some of my originals around on the floor (I didn't draw on the floor; I was just shoving the originals around) and they fell, or perhaps I pushed them, into five separate and indistinct categories. I have never wanted to write about my drawings, and I still don't want to, but it occurred to me that it might be a good idea to do it now, when everybody is busy with something else, and get it over quietly.

Category No. 1, then, which may be called the Unconscious or Stream of Nervousness Category, is represented by 'With you I have known peace, Lida, and now you say you're going crazy' and the drawing entitled with simple dignity, 'Home'. These drawings were done while the artist was thinking of something else (or so he has been assured by experts) and hence his hand was guided by the Unconscious which, in turn, was more or less influenced by the Subconscious.

Students of Jung have instructed me that Lida and the House-Woman are representations of the *anima*, the female essence or directive which floats around in the ageless universal Subconscious

'With you I have known peace, Lida, and now you say you're going crazy.'

Home.

of Man like a tadpole in a cistern. Less intellectual critics insist that the two ladies are actual persons I have consciously known. Between these two schools of thought lies a discouragingly large space of time extending roughly from 1,000,000 B.C. to the middle nineteen-thirties.

Whenever I try to trace the true identity of the House-Woman, I get to thinking of Mr Jones. He appeared in my office one day twelve years ago, said he was Mr Jones, and asked me to lend him 'Home' for reproduction in an art magazine. I never saw the drawing again. Tall, well-dressed, kind of sad-looking chap, and as well spoken a gentleman as you would want to meet.

Category No. 2 brings us to Freud and another one of those discouragingly large spaces – namely, the space between the Concept of the Purely Accidental and the Theory of Haphazard Determination. Whether chance is capricious or we are all prisoners of pattern is too long and cloudy a subject to go into here. I shall consider each of the drawings in Category No. 2, explaining what happened and leaving the definition of the forces involved up to you. The seal on top of the bed, then ('All right, have it your way – you heard a seal bark'), started out to be a seal on a rock. The rock, in the process of being drawn, began to look like the head of a bed, so I made a bed out of it, put a man and wife in the bed, and stumbled on to the caption as easily and unexpectedly as the seal had stumbled into the bedroom.

The woman on top of the bookcase ('That's my first wife up there, and this is the *present* Mrs Harris') was originally designed to be a woman crouched on the top step of a staircase, but since the tricks and conventions of perspective and planes sometimes fail me, the staircase assumed the shape of a bookcase and was finished as such, to the surprise and embarrassment of the first Mrs Harris, the present Mrs Harris, the male visitor, Mr Harris, and me. Before the *New Yorker* would print the drawing, they phoned me long distance to inquire whether the first Mrs Harris was alive or dead or stuffed. I replied that my taxidermist had advised me that you cannot stuff a woman, and that my physician had informed me that a dead lady cannot support herself on all fours. This meant, I said, that the first Mrs Harris was unquestionably alive.

'All right, have it your way – you heard a seal bark!'

'That's my first wife up there, and this is the present *Mrs Harris.'*

The man riding on the other man's shoulders in the bar ('For the last time – you and your horsie get away from me and stay away!') was intended to be standing alongside the irate speaker, but I started his head up too high and made it too small, so that he would have been nine feet tall if I had completed his body that way. It was but the work of thirty-two seconds to put him on another man's shoulders. As simple or, if you like, as complicated as that. The psychological factors which may be present here are, as I have indicated, elaborate and confused. Personally, I like Dr Claude Thornway's theory of the Deliberate Accident or Conditioned Mistake.

Category No. 3 is perhaps a variant of Category No. 2; indeed, they may even be identical. The dogs in 'The father belonged to some people who were driving through in a Packard' were drawn in a captionless spot, and the interior with figures just sort of grew up around them. The hippopotamus in 'What have you done with Dr Millmoss?' was drawn to amuse my small daughter. Something about the creature's expression when he was completed convinced me that he had recently eaten a man. I added the hat and pipe and Mrs Millmoss, and the caption followed easily enough. Incidentally, my daughter, who was two years old at the time, identified the beast immediately. 'That's a hippotomanus,' she said. The *New Yorker* was not so smart. They described the drawing for their files as follows: 'Woman with strange animal.' The *New Yorker* was nine years old at the time.

Category No. 4 is represented by perhaps the best known of some fifteen drawings belonging to this special grouping, which may be called the Contributed Idea Category. This drawing ('*Touché!*') was originally done for the *New Yorker* by Carl Rose, caption and all. Mr Rose is a realistic artist, and his gory scene distressed the editors, who hate violence. They asked Rose if he would let me have the idea, since there is obviously no blood to speak of in the people I draw. Rose graciously consented. No one who looks at '*Touché!*' believes that the man whose head is in the air is really dead. His opponent will hand it back to him with profuse apologies, and the discommoded fencer will replace it on his shoulders and say, 'No harm done, forget it.' Thus the old

'For the last time – you and your horsie get away from me and stay away!'

'The father belonged to some people who were driving through in a Packard.'

controversy as to whether death can be made funny is left just where it was before Carl Rose came along with his wonderful idea.

Category No. 5, our final one, can be called, believe it or not, the Intentional or Thought-Up Category. The idea for each of these two drawings just came to me and I sat down and made a sketch to fit the prepared caption. Perhaps, in the case of 'Well, I'm disenchanted, too. We're all disenchanted', another one of those Outside Forces played a part. That is, I may have overheard a husband say to his wife, on the street or at a party, 'I'm disenchanted.' I do not think this is true, however, in the case of the rabbit-headed doctor and his woman patient. I believe that the scene and its caption came to me one night in bed. I *may* have got the idea in a doctor's office or a rabbit hutch, but I don't think so.

As my eyesight grew dimmer, the paper I drew on grew larger, and even though I used a heavy black crayon, the fine Ohio clarity of my work diminished. In one of my last drawings I had to make the eyes of a young lady so large that it was easy to arrive at the caption: 'Where did you get those big brown eyes and that tiny mind?' Seven years ago I shifted to luminous white crayon on dead black paper, and then finally gave up drawing altogether for writing, meditation, and drinking.

Most of my originals have disappeared, mysteriously or otherwise. Thirty were never heard of again after a show in Los Angeles. Several pretty girls with big brown eyes and minds of various sizes have swiped a dozen or so of the scrawls, and a man I loved, now dead, told me one day he had taken seven drawings from my office desk to give to some friends of his in California. That is what became of Dr Millmoss, among others. My favourite loss, however, occurred at the varnishing, or vanishing, of a show of my drawings in London in 1937. Seems that someone eased a portfolio of two dog drawings. I'm mighty proud of that, and I like to think that Scotland Yard was duly informed of the incident. Theft is an even higher form of praise than emulation, for it carries with it the risk of fine and imprisonment, or, in the case of my 'work', at least a mild dressing down by the authorities.

'Touché!'

'Well, I'm disenchanted, too. We're all disenchanted.'

If you should ever run across 'Home' or 'What have you done with Dr Millmoss?' write to me, not to J. Edgar Hoover. We are equally busy, but he would only be puzzled, and possibly irked. So much for my drawings, wherever they are.

'What have you done with Dr Millmoss?'

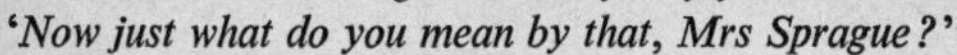

'You said a moment ago that everybody you look at seems to be a rabbit. 'Now just what do you mean by that, Mrs Sprague?'

'Where did you get those big brown eyes and that tiny mind?'

A Miscellany

Destinations.

'I love the idea of there being two sexes, don't you?'

'Unhappy woman!'

'My wife wants to spend Halloween with her first husband.'

'It's a strange mood she's in, kind of a cross between Baby Doll and Elizabeth Barrett Browning.'

'I beg to differ with you!'

'I don't want any part of it!'

'Miss Gorce is in the embalming game.'

'Every day is Arbor Day to Mr Chisholm.'

'Le cœur a ses raisons, Mrs Bence, que la raison ne connaît pas.'

'And this is the little woman.'

'Why, Mr Spears, how cute you look!'

'He's so charming it gives you the creeps.'

'He doesn't know anything except facts.'

'Mush!'

'No, I won't apologize – and neither will your father.'

'Don't you want to greet the rosy-fingered dawn?'

Do you want to make something out of it?

Or, if you put an 'O' on 'Understo', you'll ruin my 'Thunderstorm'

I'M probably not the oldest word-game player in the country and I know I'm not the ablest, but my friends will all testify that I'm the doggedest. (We'll come back to the word 'doggedest' later on.) I sometimes keep on playing the game, all by myself, after it is over and I have gone to bed. On a recent night, tossing and spelling, I spent two hours hunting for another word besides 'phlox' that has 'hlo' in it. I finally found seven: 'matchlock', 'decathlon', 'pentathlon', 'hydrochloric', 'chlorine', 'chloroform', and 'monthlong'. There are more than a dozen others, beginning with 'phlo', but I had to look them up in the dictionary the next morning, and that doesn't count.

By 'the game', I mean Superghosts, as some of us call it, a difficult variation of the familiar parlour game known as Ghosts. In Ghosts, as everybody knows, one of a group of sedentary players starts with a letter, and the spelling proceeds clockwise around the group until a player spells a word of more than three letters, thus becoming 'a third of a ghost', or two-thirds, or a whole ghost. The game goes on until everyone but the winner has been eliminated. Superghosts differs from the old game in one small, tricky, and often exacerbating respect: The rules allow a player to *prefix* a letter to the word in progress, thus increasing the flexibility of the indoor sport. If 'busines' comes to a player, he does not have to add the final 's'; he can put an 'n' in front, and the player who has to add the 'e' to 'unbusinesslik' becomes part of a ghost. In a recent game in my league, a devious gentleman boldly stuck an 'n' in front of 'sobsiste', stoutly maintaining the validity of 'unsobsisterlike', but he was shouted down. There is a lot of shouting in the game, especially when it is played late at night.

Starting words in the middle and spelling them in both directions lifts the pallid pastime of Ghosts out of the realm of children's parties and ladies' sewing circles and makes it a game to test the mettle of the mature adult mind. As long ago as 1930, aficionados began to appear in New York parlours, and then the game waned, to be revived, in my circle, last year. The Superghost aficionado is a moody fellow, given to spelling to himself at table, not listening to his wife, and staring dully at his frightened children, wondering why he didn't detect, in yesterday's game, that 'cklu' is the guts of 'lacklustre', and priding himself on having stumped everybody with 'nehe', the middle of 'swineherd'. In this last case, 'bonehead' would have done, since we allow slang if it is in the dictionary, but 'Stonehenge' is out, because we don't allow proper nouns. All compound and hyphenated words are privileged, even 'jack-o'-lantern' and 'love-in-a-mist', but the speller must indicate where a hyphen occurs.

Many people, who don't like word games and just want to sit around and drink and talk, hate Superghosts and wish it were in hell with Knock, Knock, Who's There? The game is also tough on bad spellers, poor visualizers, mediocre concentrators, ladies and gentlemen of small vocabulary, and those who are, to use a word presently popular with the younger drinking set, clobbered. I remember the night a bad speller, female, put an 'm' on 'ale', thinking, as she later confessed, that 'salamander' is spelled with two 'e's. The next player could have gone to 'alemb' – the word 'alembic' turns up a lot – but he made it 'alema' and was promptly challenged. (You can challenge a player if you think he is bluffing.) What the challenged player had in mind was 'stalemate'. The man who had challenged him got sore, because he hadn't thought of 'stalemate', and went home. More than one game has ended in hard feelings, but I have never seen players come to blows, or friendships actually broken.

I said we would get back to 'doggedest', and here we are. This word, if it is a word, caused a lot of trouble during one game, when a lady found 'ogged' in her lap, refused to be bogged, dogged, fogged, jogged, or logged, and added an 'e'. She was challenged and lost, since Webster's unabridged dictionary is accepted as the final judge and authority, and while it gives 'doggedly' and 'doggedness', it doesn't give 'doggedest'. She could also have got out of 'ogged' with an 'r' in front, for 'frogged' is a good word, and also what might be called a lady's word, but she stuck doggedly to 'doggedest'. Then there was the evening a dangerous and exasperating player named Bert Mitchell challenged somebody's 'dogger'. The challenged man had 'doggerel' in mind, of course, but Mitchell said, in his irritating voice, 'You have spelled a word. "Dogger" is a word,' and he flipped through the unabridged dictionary, which he reads for pleasure and always has on his lap during a game. 'Dogger' is indeed a word, and quite a word. Look it up yourself.

When I looked up 'dogger' the other day, I decided to have a look at 'dog', a word practically nobody ever looks up, because everybody is smugly confident that he knows what a dog is. Here, for your amazement, are some dogs other than the carnivorous mammal:

The hammer in a gunlock. Any of various devices, usually of simple design, for holding, gripping, or fastening something; as: *a* Any of various devices consisting essentially of a spike, rod, or bar of metal, as of iron, with a ring, hook, claw, lug, or the like, at the end, used for gripping, clutching, or holding something, as by driving or embedding it in the object, hooking it to the object, etc. See RAFT DOG, TOE DOG. *b* Specif., either of the hooks or claws of a pair of sling dogs. See CRAMPON. *c* An iron for holding wood in a fireplace; a firedog; an andiron. *d* In a lathe, a clamp for gripping the piece of work and for communicating motion to it from the faceplate. A *clamp dog* consists of two parts drawn together by screws. A *bent-tail dog* has an L-shaped projection that enters a slot in the faceplate for communicating motion. A *straight-tail dog* has a projecting part that engages with a stud fastened to or forming part of the faceplate. A *safety dog* is one equipped with safety setscrews. *e* Any of the jaws in a lathe chuck. *f* A pair of nippers or forceps. *g* A wheeled gripping device for drawing the fillet from which coin blanks are stamped through the opening at the head of the drawbench. *h* Any of a set of adjusting screws for the bed tool of a punching machine. *i* A grapple for clutching and raising a pile-driver monkey or a well-boring tool. *j* A stop or detent; a click or ratchet. *k* A drag for the wheel of a vehicle. *l* A steel block attached to a locking bar or tappet of an interlocking machine, by which locking between bars is accomplished. *m* A short, heavy, sharp-pointed, steel hook with a ring at one end. *n* A steel toothlike projection on a log carriage or on the endless chain that conveys logs into the sawmill.

And now, unless you have had enough, we will get back to Superghosts, through the clanging and clatter of all those dogs. The game has a major handicap, or perhaps I should call it blockage. A player rarely gets the chance to stick the others with a truly tough word, because someone is pretty sure to simplify the word under construction. Mitchell tells me that he always hopes he can get around to 'ug-ug' or 'ach-ach' on his way to 'plug-ugly' and 'stomach-ache'. These words are hyphenated in my Webster's, for the old boy was a great hyphenator. (I like his definition of 'plug-ugly'; 'A kind of city rowdy, ruffian, or disorderly tough; – a term said to have been originated by a gang of such in Baltimore.') In the case of 'ug', the simplifiers usually go to 'bug', trying to catch someone with 'buggies', or they add an 'l' and the word ends in 'ugliness'. And 'ach' often turns into 'machinery', although it could go in half a dozen directions. Since the simplifiers dull the game by getting into easy words, the experts are fond of a variant that goes like this: Mitchell, for example, will call up a friend and say, 'Get out of "ightf" twenty ways'. Well, I tossed in bed one night and got ten: 'rightful', 'frightful', 'delightful', 'nightfall', 'lightfoot', 'straightforward', 'eightfold', 'light-fingered', 'tight-fisted', and 'tight-fitting'. The next day, I thought of 'light-face', 'right-footed', and 'night-flowering', and came to a stop. 'Right fielder' is neither compounded nor hyphenated by Webster, and I began to wonder about Mitchell's twenty 'ightf's. I finally figured it out. The old devil was familiar with the ten or more fish and fowl and miscellaneous things that begin with 'nightf'.

It must have been about 1932 that an old player I know figured that nothing could be got out of 'dke' except 'handkerchief', and then, in a noisy game one night this year, he passed that combination on to the player at his left. This rascal immediately made it 'dkee'. He was challenged by the lady on *his* left and triumphantly announced that his word was 'groundkeeper'. It looked like an ingenious escape from 'handkerchief', but old Webster let the fellow down. Webster accepts only 'groundman' and 'groundsman', thus implying that there is no such word as 'groundkeeper'.

Mitchell threw 'abc' at me one night, and I couldn't get anything out of it and challenged him. 'Dabchick,' he said patronizingly, and added blandly, 'It is the little grebe.' Needless to say, it *is* the little grebe.

I went through a hundred permutations in bed that night without getting anything else out of 'abc' except a word I made up, which is 'grabcheck', one who quickly picks up a tab, a big spender, a generous fellow. I have invented quite a few other words, too, which I modestly bring to the attention of modern lexicographers, if there are any. I think of dictionary-makers as being rigidly conventional gentlemen who are the first to put the new aside. They probably won't even read my list of what I shall call bedwords, but I am going to set it down anyway. A young matron in Bermuda last spring told me to see what I could do with 'sgra', and what I did with it occupied a whole week-end. Outside of 'disgrace' and 'grosgrain', all I could find were 'cross-grained' and 'misgraff', which means to misgraft (obsolete). I found this last word while looking, in vain, for 'misgrade' in the dictionary. Maybe you can think of something else, and I wish you luck. Here, then, in no special order, are my bedwords based on 'sgra'.

PUSSGRAPPLE. A bickering, or minor disturbance; an argument or dispute among effeminate men. Also, less frequently, a physical struggle between, or among, women.

KISSGRANNY. 1. A man who seeks the company of older women, especially older women with money; a designing fellow, a fortune hunter. 2. An over-affectionate old woman, a hugmoppet, bunnytalker.

GLASSGRABBER. 1. A woman who disapproves of, or interferes with, her husband's drinking; a kill-joy, a shushlaugh, a douselight. 2. A man who asks for another drink at a friend's house, or goes out and gets one in the kitchen.

BLESSGRAVY. A minister or cleric; the head of a family; one who says grace. Not to be confused with praisegravy, one who extols a woman's cooking, especially the cooking of a friend's wife; a gay fellow, a flirt, a seducer. *Colloq.*, a brakvow, a shrugholy.

CUSSGRAVY. A husband who complains of his wife's cooking, more especially a husband who complains of his wife's cooking in the presence of guests; an ill-tempered fellow, a curmudgeon. Also, sometimes, a peptic-ulcer case.

MESSGRANTER. An untidy housekeeper, a careless housewife. Said of a woman who admits, often proudly, that she has let herself go; a bragdowdy, a frumpess.

HISSGRAMMAR. An illiterate fellow, a user of slovenly rhetoric, a father who disapproves of booklearning. Also, more rarely, one who lisps, a twisttongue.

CHORUSGRABLE. *Orig.* a young actress, over-confident of her ability and her future; a snippet, a flappertigibbet. *Deriv.* Betty Grable, an American movie actress.

PRESSGRAPE. One who presses grapes, a grape presser. Less commonly, a crunchberry.

PRESSGRAIN. 1. A man who tries to make whisky in his own cellar; hence, a secret drinker, a hidebottle, a sneakslug. 2. One who presses grain in a grain presser. *Arch.*

DRESSGRADER. A woman who stares another woman up and down, a starefrock; hence, a rude female, a hobbledehoyden.

FUSSGRAPE. 1. One who diets or toys with his food, a light eater, a person without appetite, a scornmuffin, a shuncabbage. 2. A man, usually American, who boasts of his knowledge of wines, a smugbottle.

BASSGRAVE. 1. Cold-eyed, unemotional, stolid, troutsolemn. 2. The grave of a bass. *Obs.*

LASSGRAPHIC. Of, or pertaining to, the vivid description of females; as, the guest was so lassgraphic his host asked him to change the subject or get out. Also said of fathers of daughters, more rarely of mothers.

BLISSGRAVE. Aged by marriage. Also sometimes, discouraged by wedlock, or by the institution of marriage.

GLASSGRAIL. A large nocturnal moth. Not to be confused with smack-window, the common June bug, or bangsash.

HOSSGRACE. Innate or native dignity, similar to that of the thoroughbred hoss. *Southern U.S.*

BUSSGRANITE. Literally, a stonekisser; a man who persists in trying to win the favour or attention of cold, indifferent, or capricious women. Not to be confused with snatchkiss, a kitchen lover.

TOSSGRAVEL. 1. A male human being who tosses gravel, usually at night, at the window of a female human being's bedroom, usually that of a young virgin; hence, a lover, a male sweetheart, and an eloper. 2. One who is suspected by the father of a daughter of planning an elopement with her, a grablass.

If you should ever get into a game of Superghosts with Mitchell by the way, don't pass 'bugl' on to him, hoping to send him into 'bugling'. He will simply add an 'o', making the group 'buglo', which is five-sevenths of 'bugloss'. The word means 'hawkweed', and you can see what Mitchell would do if you handed him 'awkw', expecting to make him continue the spelling of 'awkward'. Tough guy, Mitchell. Tough game, Superghosts. You take it from here. I'm tired.

The whip-poor-will

THE night had just begun to get pale around the edges when the whip-poor-will began. Kinstrey, who slept in a back room on the first floor, facing the meadow and the strip of woods beyond, heard a blind man tapping and a bugle calling and a woman screaming 'Help! Police!' The sergeant in grey was cutting open envelopes with a sword. 'Sit down there, sit down there, sit down there!' he chanted at Kinstrey. 'Sit down there, cut your throat, cut your throat, whip-poor-will, whip-poor-will, whip-poor-will!' And Kinstrey woke up.

He opened his eyes, but lay without moving for several minutes, separating the fantastic morning from the sounds and symbols of his dream. There was the palest wash of light in the room. Kinstrey scowled through tousled hair at his wristwatch and saw that it was ten minutes past four. 'Whip-poor-will, whip-poor-will, whip-poor-will!' The bird sounded very near – in the grass outside the window, perhaps. Kinstrey got up and went to the window in his bare feet and looked out. You couldn't tell where the thing was. The sound was all around you, incredibly loud and compelling and penetrating. Kinstrey had never heard a whip-poor-will so near at hand before. He had heard them as a boy in Ohio in the country, but he remembered their call as faint and plaintive and far away, dying before long somewhere between the hills and the horizon. You didn't hear the bird often in Ohio, it came back to him, and it almost never ventured as close to a house or barn as this brazen-breasted bird murdering sleep out there along the fence line somewhere. 'Whip-poor-will, whip-poor-will, whip-poor-will!' Kinstrey climbed back into bed and began to count; the bird did twenty-seven whips without pausing. His lungs must be built like a pelican's pouch, or a puffin or a penguin or pemmican or a paladin. . . . It was bright daylight when Kinstrey fell asleep again.

At breakfast, Madge Kinstrey, looking cool and well rested in her white piqué house coat, poured the coffee with steady authority. She raised her eyebrows slightly in mild surprise when Kinstrey mentioned the whip-poor-will the second time (she had not listened the first time, for she was lost in exploring with a long, sensitive finger an infinitesimal chip on the rim of her coffee cup).

'Whip-poor-will?' she said, finally. 'No, I didn't hear it. Of course, my room is on the front of the house. You must have been slept out and ready to wake up anyway, or you wouldn't have heard it.'

'Ready to wake up?' said Kinstrey. 'At four o'clock in the morning? I hadn't slept three hours.'

'Well, I didn't hear it,' said Mrs Kinstrey. 'I don't listen for night noises; I don't even hear the crickets or the frogs.'

'Neither do I,' said Kinstrey. 'It's not the same thing. This thing is loud as a fire bell. You can hear it for a mile.'

'I didn't hear it,' she said, buttering a piece of thin toast.

Kinstrey gave it up and turned his scowling attention to the headlines in the *Herald Tribune* of the day before. The vision of his wife sleeping quietly in her canopied four-poster came between his eyes and the ominous headlines. Madge always slept quietly, almost without moving, her arms straight and still outside the covers, her fingers relaxed. She did not believe anyone had to toss and turn. 'It's a notion,' she would tell Kinstrey. 'Don't let your nerves get the best of you. Use your will power.'

'Um, hm,' said Kinstrey aloud, not meaning to.

'Yes, sir?' said Arthur, the Kinstreys' coloured butler, offering Kinstrey a plate of hot blueberry muffins.

'Nothing,' said Kinstrey, looking at his wife. 'Did you hear the whip-poor-will, Arthur?'

'No, sir, I didn't,' said Arthur.

'Did Margaret?'

'I don't think she did, sir,' said Arthur. 'She didn't say anything about it.'

The next morning the whip-poor-will began again at the same hour, rolling out its loops and circles of sound across the new day. Kinstrey, in his dreams, was beset by trios of little bearded men rolling hoops at him. He tried to climb up on to a gigantic Ferris wheel whose swinging seats were rumpled beds. The round cop with wheels for feet rolled toward him shouting, 'Will power will, will power will, whip-poor-will!'

Kinstrey opened his eyes and stared at the ceiling and began to count the whips. At one point the bird did fifty-three straight, without pausing. I suppose, like the drops of water or the bright light in the third degree, this could drive you nuts, Kinstrey thought. Or make you confess. He began to think of things he hadn't thought of for years: the time he took the quarter from his mother's pocket-book, the time he steamed open a letter addressed to his father; it was from his teacher in the eighth grade. Miss – let's see – Miss Willpool, Miss Whippoor, Miss Will Power, Miss Wilmott – that was it.

He had reached the indiscretions of his middle twenties when the whip-poor-will suddenly stopped, on 'poor', not on 'will'. Something must have frightened it. Kinstrey sat up on the edge of the bed and lighted a cigarette and listened. The bird was through calling, all right, but Kinstrey couldn't go back to sleep. The day as bright as a flag. He got up and dressed.

'I thought you weren't going to smoke cigarettes before breakfast any more,' said Madge later. 'I found four stubs in the ashtray in your bedroom.'

It was no use telling her he had smoked them before going to bed; you couldn't fool Madge; she always knew. 'That goddamn bird woke me up again,' he said, 'and this time I couldn't get back to sleep.' He passed her his empty coffee cup. 'It did fifty-three without stopping this morning,' he added. 'I don't know how the hell it breathes.'

His wife took his coffee cup and set it down firmly. 'Not three cups,' she said. 'Not with you sleeping so restlessly the way it is.'

'You didn't hear it, I suppose?' he said.

She poured herself some more coffee. 'No,' she said, 'I didn't hear it.'

Margaret hadn't heard it, either, but Arthur had. Kinstrey talked to them in the kitchen while they were clearing up after breakfast. Arthur said that it 'wuk' him but he went right back to sleep. He said he slept like a log – must be the air off the ocean. As for Margaret, she always slept like a log; only thing ever kept her awake was people a-hoopin' and a-hollerin'. She was glad she didn't hear the whip-poor-will. Down where she came from, she said, if you heard a whip-poor-will singing near the house, it meant there was going to be a death. Arthur said he had heard about that, too; must have been his grandma told him, or somebody.

If a whip-poor-will singing near the house meant death, Kinstrey told them, it wouldn't really make any difference whether you heard it or not. 'It doesn't make any difference whether you see the ladder you're walking under,' he said, lighting a cigarette and watching the effect of his words on Margaret. She turned from putting some plates away, and her eyes widened and rolled a little.

'Mr Kinstrey is just teasin' you, Mag,' said Arthur, who smiled and was not afraid. Thinks he's pretty smart, Kinstrey thought. Just a little bit too smart, maybe. Kinstrey remembered Arthur's way of smiling, almost imperceptibly, at things Mrs Kinstrey sometimes said to her husband when Arthur was just coming into the room or just going out – little things that were none of his business to listen to. Like 'Not three cups of coffee if a bird keeps you awake.' Wasn't that what she had said?

'Is there any more coffee?' he asked, testily. 'Or did you throw it out?' He knew they had thrown it out; breakfast had been over for almost an hour.

'We can make you some fresh,' said Arthur.

'Never mind,' said Kinstrey. 'Just don't be so sure of yourself. There's nothing in life to be sure about.'

When, later in the morning, he started out the gate to walk down to the post office, Madge called to him from an upstairs window. 'Where are you going?' she asked, amiably enough. He frowned up at her. 'To the taxidermist's,' he said, and went on.

He realized, as he walked along in the warm sunlight, that he had made something of a spectacle of himself. Just because he hadn't had enough sleep – or enough coffee. It wasn't his fault, though. It was that infernal bird. He discovered, after a quarter of a mile, that the imperative rhythm of the whip-poor-will's call was running through his mind, but the words of the song were new: fatal bell, fatal bell, fa-tal bell. Now, where had that popped up from? It took him some time to place it; it was a fragment from *Macbeth.* There was something about the fatal bellman crying in the night. 'The fatal bellman cried the livelong night' – something like that. It was an owl that cried the night Duncan was murdered. Funny thing to call up after all these years; he hadn't read the play since college. It was that fool Margaret talking about the whip-poor-will and the old superstition that if you hear the whip-poor-will singing near the house, it means there is going to be a death. Here it was the middle of the twentieth century, and people still believed in stuff like that.

The next dawn the dream induced by the calling of the whip-poor-will was longer and more tortured – a nightmare filled with dark perils and heavy hopelessness. Kinstrey woke up trying to cry out. He lay there breathing hard and listening to the bird. He began to count: one, two, three, four, five . . .

Then suddenly, he leaped out of bed and ran to the window and began yelling and pounding on the windowpane and running the blind up and down. He shouted and cursed until his voice got hoarse. The bird kept right on going. He slammed the window down and turned away from it, and there was Arthur in the doorway.

'What is it, Mr Kinstrey?' said Arthur. He was fumbling with the cord of a faded old bathrobe and trying to blink the sleep out of his eyes. 'Is anything the matter?'

Kinstrey glared at him. 'Get out of here!' he shouted. 'And put some coffee on. Or get me a brandy or something.'

'I'll put some coffee on,' said Arthur. He went shuffling away in his slippers, still half-asleep.

'Well,' said Madge Kinstrey over her coffee cup at breakfast, 'I hope you got your tantrum over and done with this morning. I never heard such a spectacle – squalling like a spoiled brat.'

'You can't hear spectacles,' said Kinstrey, coldly. 'You see them.'

No, you don't, thought Kinstrey, you never have; never have, nev-er have, nev-er have. Would he ever get that damned rhythm out of his head? It struck him that perhaps Madge had no subconscious. When she lay on her back, her eyes closed; when she got up, they opened, like a doll's. The mechanism of her mind was as simple as a cigarette box; it was either open or it was closed, and there was nothing else, nothing else, nothing else. . . .

The whole problem turns on a very neat point, Kinstrey thought as he lay awake that night, drumming on the headboard with his fingers. William James would have been interested in it; Henry, too, probably. I've got to ignore this thing, get adjusted to it, become oblivious of it. I mustn't fight it, I mustn't build it up. If I get to screaming at it, I'll be running across that wet grass out there in my bare feet, charging that bird as if it were a trench full of Germans, throwing rocks at it, giving the Rebel yell or something, for God's sake. No. I mustn't build it up. I'll think of something else every time it pops into my mind. I'll name the old Cub infield to myself, over and over: Steinfeld to Tinker to Evers to Chance, Steinfeld to Tinker to Evers . . .

Kinstrey did not succeed in becoming oblivious of the whip-poor-will. Its dawn call pecked away at his dreams like a vulture at a heart. It slowly carved out a recurring nightmare in which Kinstrey was attacked by an umbrella whose handle, when you clutched it, clutched right back, for the umbrella was not an umbrella at all, but a raven. Through the gloomy hallways of his mind rang the Thing's dolorous cry: nevermore, nevermore, nevermore, whip-poor-will, whip-poor-will . . .

One day, Kinstrey asked Mr Tetford at the post office if the whip-poor-wills ever went away. Mr Tetford squinted at him. 'Don't look like the sun was brownin' you up none,' he said. 'I don't know as they ever go away. They move around. I like to hear 'em. You get used to 'em.'

'Sure,' said Kinstrey. 'What do people do when they can't get used to them, though – I mean old ladies or sick people?'

'Only one's been bothered was old Miss Purdy. She darn near set fire to the whole island tryin' to burn 'em out of her woods. Shootin' at 'em might drive 'em off, or a body could trap 'em easy enough and let 'em loose somewheres else. But people get used to 'em after a few mornings.'

'Oh sure,' said Kinstrey. 'Sure.'

That evening in the living-room, when Arthur brought in the coffee, Kinstrey's cup cackled idiotically in its saucer when he took it off the tray.

Madge Kinstrey laughed. 'Your hand is shaking like a leaf,' she said.

He drank all his coffee at once and looked up savagely. 'If I could get one good night's sleep, it might help,' he said. 'That damn bird! I'd like to wring its neck.'

'Oh come, now,' she said, mockingly. 'You wouldn't hurt a fly. Remember the mouse we caught in the Westport house? You took it out in the field and let it go.'

'The trouble with you – ' he began, and stopped. He opened the lid of a cigarette box and shut it, opened and shut it again, reflectively. 'As simple as that,' he said.

She dropped her amused smile and spoke shortly. 'You're acting like a child about that silly bird,' she said. 'Worse than a child. I was over at the Barrys' this afternoon. Even their little Ann didn't make such a fuss. A whip-poor-will frightened her the first morning, but now she never notices them.'

'I'm not frightened, for God's sake!' shouted Kinstrey. 'Frightened or brave, asleep or awake, open or shut – you make everything black or white.'

'Well,' she said, 'I like that.'

'I think the bird wakes you up, too,' he said. 'I think it wakes up Arthur and Margaret.'

'And we just pretend it doesn't?' she asked. 'Why on earth should we?'

'Oh, out of some fool notion of superiority, I suppose. Out of – I don't know.'

'I'll thank you not to class me with the servants,' she said coldly. He lighted a cigarette and didn't say anything. 'You're being ridiculous and childish,' she said, 'fussing about nothing at all, like an invalid in a wheel chair.' She got and started from the room.

'Nothing at all,' he said, watching her go.

She turned at the door. 'Ted Barry says he'll take you on at tennis if your bird hasn't worn you down too much.' She went on up the stairs, and he heard her close the door of her room.

He sat smoking moodily for a long time, and fell to wondering whether the man's wife in *The Raven* has seen what the man had seen perched on the pallid bust of Pallas just above the chamber door. Probably not, he decided. When he went to bed, he lay awake a long while trying to think of the last line of *The Raven.* He couldn't get any farther than 'Like a demon that is dreaming', and this kept running through his head. 'Nuts,' he said at last, aloud, and he had the oddly disturbing feeling that it wasn't he who had spoken but somebody else. . . .

Kinstrey was not surprised that Madge was a little girl in pigtails and a play suit. The long grey hospital room was filled with poor men in will chairs, running with long, sensitive fingers around the rims of empty coffee cups. 'Poor Will, poor Will,' chanted Madge, pointing her finger at him. 'Here are your spectacles, here are your spectacles.' One of the six men was Arthur, grinning at him, grinning at him and holding him with one hand, so that he was powerless to move his arms or legs. 'Hurt a fly, hurt a fly,' chanted Madge. 'Whip him now, whip him now!' she cried, and she was the umpoor in the high chair beside the court, holding a black umbrella over her head: love thirty, love forty, forty-one, forty-two, forty-three, forty-four. His feet were stuck in the wet concrete on his side of the net and Margaret peered over the net at him, holding a skillet for a racquet. Arthur was pushing him down now, and he was caught in the concrete from head to foot. It was Madge laughing and counting over him: refer-three, refer-four, refer-five, refer-will, repoor-will, whip-poor will, whip-poor-will, whip-poor-will. . . .

The dream still clung to Kinstrey's mind like a cobweb as he stood in the kitchen in his pyjamas and bare feet, wondering what he wanted, what he was looking for. He turned on the cold water in the sink and filled a glass, but only took a sip, and put it down. He left the water running. He opened the breadbox and took out half a loaf wrapped in oiled paper, and pulled open a drawer. He took out the bread knife and then put it back and took out the long, sharp carving knife. He was standing there holding the knife in one hand and the bread in the other when the door to the dining-room opened. It was Arthur. 'Who do you do first?' Kinstrey said to him, hoarsely. . . .

The Barrys, on their way to the beach in their station wagon, drove into the driveway between the house and the barn. They were surprised to see that, at a quarter to eleven in the morning, the Kinstry servants hadn't taken in the milk. The bottle, standing on the small back porch, was hot to Barry's touch. When he couldn't rouse anyone, pounding and calling, he climbed up on the cellar door and looked in the kitchen window. He told his wife sharply to get back in the car. . . .

The local police and the state troopers were in and out of the house all day. It wasn't every morning in the year that you got called out on a triple murder and suicide.

It was just getting dark when Troopers Baird and Lennon came out of the front door and walked down to their car, pulled up beside the road in front of the house. Out in back, probably in the little strip of wood there, Lennon figured, a whip-poor-will began to call. Lennon listened a minute. 'You ever hear the old people say a whip-poor-will singing near the house means death?' he asked.

Baird grunted and got in under the wheel. Lennon climbed in beside him. 'Take more'n a whip-poor-will to cause a mess like that,' said Trooper Baird, starting the car.

The ordeal of Mr Matthews

'THE practice of wit as a fine art is one with the carriage horse and the dulcimer,' I said to the businessman who got stuck with me at a party in the country one afternoon. The sounds of modern teatime – gabble and loud laughter – drifted into the small study where I had found him sitting down over a back-copy of *Life*. 'For one thing,' I went on, 'the appointments, the accoutrements, the accessories have vanished like the snows of the famous ballade.'

'My name is Matthews,' he said, and shifted a glass of ale from his right hand to his left. We shook hands.

'Where now, Matthews,' I demanded, 'are the long draperies, the bright chandeliers, the shining floors, the high ceilings, the snuffbox, the handkerchief stuck in the sleeve with careless care, the perfect bow from the waist, the formal but agile idiom?'

'Set-up is different today,' Matthews said.

'Gone,' I told him. 'Lost in the oblivious plangency of our darkening era, crumbled of their lustre, save for a sparkle here, a twinkle there, in the remembered dust of the stately centuries.'

Matthews put the copy of *Life* on the floor and got up. 'Think I'll have some more of this ale,' he said.

To my surprise, he came back a minute later, with an uncapped bottle and the dogged expression of a man determined to make out the meaning of voices heard dimly beyond a wall.

'The high tradition of wit in court and chancellery,' I resumed, 'died, I suppose, with Joseph Choate. His weapon was a sabre, not a rapier, but even the clangour of that bold steel did not linger in London Town to inspire with its faraway echoes Walter Page and Joseph Kennedy.'

'Lots of energy, Joe Kennedy,' Matthews said, 'Tackle anything, handle it well.'

'Choate lived to see the lights diminish, the magnificence dwindle, and the men decline,' I said. 'He saw the thrust lose its deftness until there was no longer need for skilful parry and riposte. The querulous and the irritable then had their day, giving way, in our land and time, to the wisecrack and the gag, the leg-pull and the hotfoot, the gimmick and the switcheroo.'

Matthews grunted and sought sanctuary in the close examination of a cigar.

'For the exercise of wit in the grand manner,' I told him, 'for the slash supreme, the stab sublime, or, if you prefer Untermeyer, the devastating crusher, one has to go back to the golden age of John Wilkes and Benjamin Disraeli.'

Matthews lighted his cigar. 'What'd you say it was Sam Untermyer said?' he asked.

'Not Sam,' I said. 'Louis.'

A woman appeared at the door of the study. 'Have you seen Nora?' Matthews asked her.

'She's in the dining-room with Ed and Carl, having fun and laughs. Don't you want a drink, Mr Thurber?'

'I'm on the wagon,' I said. Matthews looked at me as if he didn't believe it. The woman went away. 'Who was that?' I asked.

'Our hostess,' he said simply. He tried a sudden tack. 'Ed's certainly brought that business of his up from nowhere.'

I quickly bypassed the looming discussion of Ed's acumen and went on talking. 'Both Wilkes and Disraeli enjoyed, of course, those unique advantages of décor and deportment which were so conducive and becoming to the brilliant verbal duel. Wilkes, for example, had that most superb of foils, that greatest straight man in the history of wit, Lord Sandwich, almost always at his side in resplendent assemblages. At one of these, with all the important ears in town cocked, Sandwich accosted Wilkes with "You will die of a pox, sir, or on the gallows," to which Wilkes replied, "That depends, sir, on whether I embrace your mistress or your principles."'

Matthews turned his glass in his hand. 'Had 'em more openly in those days, of course – mistresses,' he said.

'Disraeli also had the luck of the witty,' I said. 'A lady once asked him at a reception if he could tell her the difference between a misfortune and a calamity. While all London listened, the great man replied, "If Mr Gladstone were to fall into the Thames it would be a misfortune. If someone pulled him out it would be a calamity."'

'Great deal of bickering among the English in those days,' Matthews said. 'Still is,' he added after a moment. I made an impatient gesture.

'The Disraeli woman,' I went on, 'with her eager interest in definition, is extinct. The curiosity of the American woman, cabined and confined, rarely takes provocative or stimulating shape. It is all but impossible, for instance, to conceive of a lady upping to Swope, say, at the bar in "21", with a question calculated to evoke an immortal reply. For one thing, the cramped and noisy setting is distinctly unpropitious, since it is far removed indeed from the resplendent assemblage, with its gracious and convenient lulls in conversation. One would have to say to our hypothetical lady, "How's that?" or "I beg your pardon?" and the precise timing so essential to the great retort would be irreparably ruined.'

A woman came into the study with a cocktail in her hand.

'Don't you think we ought to be getting along, Nora?' Matthews asked.

'Nonsense,' she said. 'It's early.'

'This is Mr Thurber,' he told her. 'My wife,' I stood up. 'Mr Thurber has been telling a story about Gerard Swope.'

'Not Gerard,' I said. 'Herber Bayard.'

'Oh,' said Matthews.

'That's nice,' said his wife, and she went away.

'Only yesterday,' I said, sitting down, 'my secretary straightened up the room I work in – and an imposing task it was, to be sure. She separated answered and unanswered mail, soiled handkerchiefs and telegrams, dog drawings and razor blades, and in the process she came up with a folder of news clippings marked "Things You Said".'

'Things you said yourself, eh?' Matthews's eyes narrowed a little.

'Well, so the record shows.' I sighed. 'It all supports our theory of the changing set-up, the deterioration of the players and the scene, the passing of the ancient glories. I have the contents of the folder fairly well in mind. They're skimpy enough, God knows. The first item is a clipping from the Chicago *Sun*.'

'Field,' said Matthews. 'Big operator.'

'It seems that Freddy Wakeman, the millionaire novelist, told the *Sun*'s Spectorsky an anecdote about me when I was in Bermuda. A dewy young thing came up to me in a bar in Somerset, the story goes, and asked me why I had sold a certain piece of mine to the movies. Quick as a flash, I answered, "M-o-n-e-y".'

'Government probably got most of it,' Matthews said.

The man was beginning to make me nervous. 'The point is not in the financial transaction itself,' I said testily. 'The point is in the pay-off at the bar down there in Somerset. I spelled it out. There is no surer way to blunt the crusher and destroy the devastation.'

'You don't have any recollection of the incident, eh?' Matthews asked shrewdly.

'None,' I said. 'Of course, I was fifty-one at the time, and perhaps a little cock-eyed. If I spelled out the pay-off, it is an indictment of my slowing mind or a proof of my decrepitude.'

Matthews sat forward in his chair, as if poised for flight. 'How big a folder'd you say this was?' he asked.

'Sparse,' I snapped. 'It won't detain you long. Why don't you get some more ale?'

'I believe I will,' he said, and went away.

When Matthews came back, I began again. 'Well, it seems I came out of this movie theatre with a group of friends – I always attend the cinema in the bosom of my circle – and one of them said, "I think that picture stinks," to which I instantly replied, "I didn't think it was that good."' I got out a cigarette and lighted it.

'My wife and daughter are crazy about this James Mason,' Matthews said.

'The anecdote limps so obviously that I feel myself, now and then, attempting to repair or recap it.' I went on. 'Like this, for example: "If a picture worse than stinks," put in Louis Sobol, who was also there, "metrofaction may be said to have set in."'

'What was that?' asked Matthews.

I exhaled slowly. 'Nothing,' I said. 'But if you have already been blinded by the brilliance, shade your mental eyes against what is still to come. In the summer of 1946, some months after the movie episode, a sensitive *Time* reporter got me on the long-distance phone to chat about the I.C.C. He said, "Do you know Jo Davidson?"'

'No,' said Matthews, 'I don't.'

'The reporter asked *me* that,' I snarled. 'The files of *Time*, forever antic and forever wrong, reveal that I shot back, "I met him once. He has a beard."'

Matthews shifted his glass to his left hand and adjusted his tie.

'The *Time* man omitted to report, for some obscure reason, that I thought Mr Davidson was head of the Interstate Commerce Commission. It's too bad, because Timen and Tiwomen – in fact, the whole lucempire – would still be laughing.'

'Never miss an issue of *Time* if I can help it,' Matthews said.

'As keen as my famous Davidson quip was,' I said, 'I was to top it in that same remarkable year. A few months later, Earl Wilson, the sympathetic columnist of the New York *Post*, called on me at my office in the city. When he came in, I was drinking black coffee. My greeting was what I can only describe as a staggeroo. "I'm having some formaldehyde," I'm supposed to have said. "Will you join me?"'

Matthews took out another cigar and gave it a squirrelly inspection.

'Well, sir, to get on with the folder,' I began again, 'it seems that I came out of a movie theatre last July after seeing a picture based rather insecurely on a piece I wrote years ago. On this occasion, the story goes, I emerged in the company of a distinguished group of New York cognoscenti. "Did anybody catch the name of that picture?" I asked drolly. Bennett Cerf, a wit in his own right, and in several other persons', printed my comment in his column. The town is still chuckling.'

Matthews lighted his cigar and seemed to be trying to hide behind it.

'The most recent and, you will be glad to hear, the final item in the folder,' I said, 'appeared in an issue of the *Hollywood Reporter*. I think I can quote it exactly. "His" – mine, that is – "favourite line about Hollywood is 'Look what they did to Maurice Costello'." I take it that one repeats one's favourite line as one rereads one's favourite book. The appalling thought has occurred to me that at some part or other I may have repeated the line several times to the same person. I wonder that no one has shouted at me, "Will you, for the love of God, stop saying that!"'

'What's going on in here? Are you two fighting?' It was Nora back again, with a fresh cocktail.

'No,' I said. 'You overheard an inner quote.'

'Some woman yelled at him at a party,' Matthews explained.

'The wretch!' cried Nora.

'We must be charitable,' I said. 'After all, she had been through a lot.'

'Nora 'don't you think – ' Matthews began.

'It's the shank of the afternoon,' she said, and left the room. Matthews finished his ale and puffed at his cigar. He was getting fidgety.

'So endeth,' I sighed, 'the paltry, the pathetic folder.'

Matthews's elbows seemed about to lift him out of his chair, but he relaxed when I began again.

'One of my colleagues is reported to have watched, on a Long Island estate, the transplanting of a great elm. "This little job," his host told him, "is costing me two hundred thousand dollars." "Shows what God could do if he had money," my friend commented. He modestly disclaims the observation, but the point I want to make is this. If it had been hung on me, the story would go: "'This little job is costing me two hundred thousand dollars.' 'That,' remarked Thurber, 'is a lot of money.'" 'I resent, Matthews,' I added angrily, 'what has all the appearance of a conspiracy to place on my shoulders the mantle of Calvin Coolidge.'

Matthews frowned for a long moment. 'Things you really said never got printed, eh?' he shrewdly inquired.

I laughed modestly and put on an expression of feigned embarrassment. 'Well, they don't exactly ripple off my tongue,' I said. 'I'm no Jack Warner. But as a matter of fact, since you ask, there *was* one. This happened – oh, fifteen years ago. I had completely forgotten about it until something reminded me of it about six months ago. A tall, thin, serious-looking man came into the reception-room of the magazine I worked for and asked for me. He told me he represented a publisher of high-priced special editions. He said his firm had hit on the idea of having me do new illustrations for *Alice in Wonderland.* I said, "Let's keep the Tenniel drawings and I'll rewrite the story." The chap bowed and went away.'

Matthews scowled. 'Fellow thought you were an artist instead of a writer, eh?' he brought out finally.

'Precisely,' I said. 'Well, as it happened, there was no one but this man and me in the reception-room at the time. I never have any luck that way. However, I sauntered into the office of a colleague and told him what I had said. Weeks went by, then months, and years, but no one ever spoke to me about the incident. My colleague, absorbed with some problem of his own, had apparently not listened to what I told him. The tall, thin man obviously never repeated the bit of dialogue, either.'

'Turned down, probably disappointed,' said Matthews.

'When I was reminded of the incident six months ago,' I went on, 'I told it to a writer friend of mine. He put it in the first act of a play he was writing, giving me credit by name and retelling the story perfectly.'

'What play was that?' said Matthews.

'It was never produced,' I said.

Matthews pushed himself up out of his chair, mumbled something about have to see Ed, and walked away – swiftly, I thought, for a man of his bulk. He had pretty well worn me out.

A middle-aged woman flounced into the room and sat down in the chair he had left. 'What do you know about Putney?' she yelped.

'Everything,' I lied, hastily, but it was no good. She told me about Putney until it was time to leave.

Another woman came up to me before I could find my hostess or my hat. 'John Matthews has been telling us a perfectly wonderful story, Mr Thurber,' she squealed, 'about how you absolutely refused to rewrite *Alice in Wonderland*, in spite of all the money they offered you.'

'M-o-o-l-a,' I said, coldly.

'Well, I think it was perfectly wonderful of you, I really do!'

'It was nothing at all,' I said. 'Anybody would have done the same thing.'

She shrieked, 'You're much too modest, Mr Thurber, really!'

'I'm not modest, Madam!' I snarled. 'I'm simply too g-o-d-d-a-m-n unlucky for words.' I felt my wife's firm, familiar grip on my arm.

'Come on,' she said. 'It's time to go. I said good-bye to Harriet for you.' She found my hat and we went out and got in the car.

'What were you shouting at Ida Barlow for?' she asked, starting the engine.

'Madam,' I said, 'if a man shouts at Ida Barlow, he makes an ass of her, but if he does not shout at Ida Barlow, he makes an ass of himself. Ask me anything and I'll give you a come back.'

'How did you manage not to fall off the wagon?' she asked. 'I was sure you were going to when I saw you were stuck with John Matthews.'

'Putney anything else would have been as bad,' I said. She glanced at me with a hint of concern. 'Ask me why I didn't fall off the wagon,' I demanded.

She sighed. 'All right, why didn't you fall off the wagon?'

'They didn't have any formaldehyde,' I chortled.

It didn't strike her as funny, for some reason, but I had to laugh. I laughed most of the way home.

Lavender with a difference

BELINDA WOOLF telephoned my mother at the Southern Hotel in Columbus one morning ten years ago, and apologized, in a faintly familiar voice, for never having run in to call on her. Something always seemed to turn up, she declared, to keep her from dropping by for a visit, and she was sorry. 'I've thought of you, Mrs Thurber,' said Belinda. 'I've thought of you every day since I worked for you on Champion Avenue. It's been a long time, hasn't it?' It certainly had. Belinda Woolf was only twenty-three years old when she came to work for us as cook in the spring of 1899, and she was seventy-three when she finally got around to calling her former employer. Half a century had gone by since my mother had heard her voice. Belinda had thought of telephoning for more than eighteen thousand days but, as she indicated, more than eighteen thousand things had turned up to prevent her.

About a year after Belinda's appearance out of the past, I went to Columbus, and my mother and I drove out to see her. She was then the wife of Joe Barlow, master carpenter of the Neil House, where Charles Dickens used to stay, during his western trips a hundred years ago. In fifty years Belinda had not wandered very far. She was living only two blocks from our old house on South Champion Avenue. The weather was warm, and we sat on the veranda and talked about a night in 1899 that we all remembered. It was past midnight, according to an old clock in the attic of my memory, when Belinda suddenly flung open a window of her bedroom and fired two shots from a ·32-calibre revolver at the shadowy figure of a man skulking about in our back yard. Belinda's shooting frightened off the prowler and aroused the family. I was five years old, going on six, at the time, and I had thought that only soldiers and policemen were allowed to have guns. From then on I stood in awe, but not in fear, of the lady who kept a revolver under her pillow. 'It was a lonesome place, wasn't it?' said Belinda, with a sigh. 'Way out there at the end of nowhere.' We sat for a while without talking, thinking about the lonesome place at the end of nowhere.

No. 921 South Champion Avenue is just another house now, in a long row of houses, but when we lived there in 1899 and 1900, it was the last house on the street. Just south of us the avenue dwindled to a wood road that led into a thick grove of oak and walnut trees, long since destroyed by the southward march of asphalt. Our nearest neighbour on the north was fifty yards away, and across from us was a country meadow that ticked with crickets in the summertime and turned yellow with golden rod in the fall. Living on the edge of town, we rarely heard footsteps at night, or carriage wheels, but the darkness, in every season, was deepened by the lonely sound of locomotive whistles. I no longer wonder as I did when I was six, that Aunt Mary Van York, arriving at dusk for her first visit to us, looked about her disconsolately, and said to my mother, 'Why in the world do you want to live in this godforsaken place, Mary?'

Almost all my memories of the Champion Avenue house have as their focal point the lively figure of my mother. I remember her tugging and hauling at a burning mattress and finally managing to shove it out a bedroom window on to the roof of the front porch, where it smouldered until my father came home from work and doused it with water. When he asked his wife how the mattress happened to catch fire, she told him the peculiar truth (all truths in that house were peculiar) – that his youngest son, Robert, had set it on fire with a buggy whip. It seemed he had lighted the lash of the whip in the gas grate of the nursery and applied it to the mattress. I also have a vivid memory of the night my mother was alone in the house with her three small sons and set the oil-splashed bowl of a kerosene lamp on fire, trying to light the wick, and herded all of us out of the house, announcing that it was going to explode. We children waited across the street in high anticipation, but the spilled oil burned itself out and, to our bitter disappointment, the house did not go up like a skyrocket to scatter coloured balloons among the stars. My mother claimed that my brother William, who was seven at the time, kept crying, 'Try it again, Mama, try it again,' but she was a famous hand at ornamenting a tale, and there is no way of telling whether he did or not.

My brightest remembrance of the old house goes back to the confused and noisy second and last visit of Aunt Mary, who had ut her first visit short because she hated our two dogs – Judge, an rritable old pug, and Sampson, a restless water spaniel – and they ated her. She had snarled at them and they had growled at her all uring her stay with us, and not even my mother remembered how he persuaded the old lady to come back for a week-end, but she id, and, what is more, she cajoled Aunt Mary into feeding 'those readful brutes' the evening she arrived.

In preparation for this seemingly simple act of household routine, ny mother had spent the afternoon gathering up all the dogs of he neighbourhood, in advance of Aunt Mary's appearance, and utting them in the cellar. I had been allowed to go with her on er wonderful forays, and I thought that we were going to keep ll the sixteen dogs we rounded up. Such an adventure does ot have to have logical point or purpose in the mind of a six-year-old, and I accepted as a remarkable but natural phenomenon ny mother's sudden assumption of the stature of Santa Claus.

She did not always let my father in on her elaborate pranks, but he came home that evening to a house heavy with tension and suspense, and she whispered to him the peculiar truth that there were a dozen and a half dogs in the cellar, counting our Judge and Sampson. 'What are you up to now, Mame?' he asked her, and she said she just wanted to see Aunt Mary's face when the dogs swarmed up into the kitchen. She could not recall where she had picked up all of the dogs, but I remembered, and still do, that we had imprisoned the Johnsons' Irish terrier, the Eiseles' shepherd, and the Mitchells' fox terrier, among others. 'Well, let's get it over with, then,' my father said nervously. 'I want to eat dinner in peace, if that is possible.'

The big moment finally arrived. My mother, full of smiles and insincerity, told Aunt Mary that it would relieve her of a tedious chore – and heaven knows, she added, there were a thousand steps to take in that big house – if the old lady would be good enough to set down a plate of dog food in the kitchen at the head of the cellar stairs and call Judge and Sampson to their supper. Aunt Mary growled and grumbled, and consigned all dogs to the fires of hell, but she grudgingly took the plate, and carried it to the kitchen, with the Thurber family on her heels. 'Heavenly days!' cried Aunt Mary. 'Do you make a ceremony out of feeding these brutes?' She put the plate down and reached for the handle of th door.

None of us has ever been able to understand why bedlam hadn broken loose in the cellar long before this, but it hadn't. The dog were probably so frightened by their unique predicament tha their belligerence had momentarily left them. But when the doo opened and they could see the light of freedom and smell the lur of food, they gave tongue like a pack of hunting hounds. Aun Mary got the door half-way open and the bodies of three of th largest dogs pushed it the rest of the way. There was a snarling barking, yelping swirl of yellow and white, black and tan, grey an brindle, as the dogs tumbled into the kitchen, skidded on th linoleum, sent the food flying from the plate, and backed Aun Mary into a corner. 'Great God Almighty!' she screamed. 'It's dog factory!' She was only five feet tall, but her counter-attac was swift and terrible. Grabbing a broom, she opened the bac door and the kitchen windows, and began to beat and flail at th army of canines, engaged now in half a dozen separate battle over the scattered food. Dogs flew out the back door and leape through the windows, but some of them ran upstairs, and three o four others hid under sofas and chairs in the parlour. The indig-nant snarling and cursing of Judge and Sampson rose above eve the laughter of my mother and the delighted squeals of her chil-dren. Aunt Mary whammed her way from room to room, driving dogs ahead of her. When the last one had departed and the upse house had been put back in order, my father said to his wife, 'Well, Mame, I hope you're satisfied.' She was.

Aunt Mary, toward the end of her long life, got the curious notion that it was my father and his sons, and not my mother, who had been responsible for the noisy flux of 'all those brutes'. Years later, when we visited the old lady on one of her birthdays, she went over the story again, as she always did, touching it up with distortions and magnifications of her own. Then she looked at the male Thurbers in slow, rueful turn, sighed deeply, gazed sympathetically at my mother, and said, in her hollowest tone, 'Poor Mary!'

Only a few months after poor Mary borrowed the neighbours' dogs, she 'bought' the Simonses' house. It was a cold, blocky house, not far from ours, and its owner had been trying to sell it for a long time. The thing had become a standing joke among the Frioleras, a club of young married couples to which the Simonses and my father and mother belonged. It was generally believed that Harry and Laura would never get the big, damp place off their hands. Then, late one dark afternoon, a strange and avid purchaser showed up. It was my mother, wearing dark glasses, her hair and eyebrows whitened with flour, her cheeks lightly shadowed with charcoal to make them look hollow, and her upper front teeth covered with the serrated edge of a soda cracker. On one side of her, as she pressed the doorbell of the Simonses' house, stood a giggling cousin of hers, named Belle Cook, and I was on her other side; we were there to prevent a prolonged scrutiny of the central figure of our trio. Belle was to pose as my mother's daughter, and I was to be Belle's son. Simons had never met Miss Cook, and my mother was confident that he wouldn't recognize me. His wife, Laura, would have penetrated her friend's disguise at once, or, failing that, she would surely have phoned the police, for the weird visitor seemed, because of her sharp, projecting teeth, both demented and about to spring, but my mother had found out that Laura would not be home. When she made herself up, an hour before, I had watched her transformation from mother to witch with a mixture of wonder and worry that lingered in my memory for years.

Harry Simons, opening his front door on that dark evening in the age of innocence, when trust flowered as readily as suspicion does today, was completely taken in by the sudden apparition of an eccentric elderly woman who babbled of her recently inherited fortune and said she had passed his house the day before and fallen in love with it. Simons was a big, jovial, sanguine man, expert at business deals in a lighted office, but a set-up for my mother's deviltry at dusk. When she praised every room she stumbled into and every object she bumped against – she wouldn't take off her dark glasses in the lamplit gloom – a wild hope must have glazed his eye, disarming his perception. He admitted later, when the cat was out of the bag, that Belle's idiotic laughter, and mine, at everything that was said had disturbed him, especially when it was provoked by my mother's tearful account of the sad death of her mythical husband, a millionaire oil-man. But idiocy in a family is one thing, and money is another. Mrs Prentice, or Douglas, or whatever she called herself, was rolling in money that day. She upped Simons' asking price for the house by several thousand dollars, on the ground that she wouldn't think of paying as little as ten thousand for such a lovely place. When she found out that the furniture was for sale, she upped the price on that, too, promising to send her cheque through her lawyers the next day. By this time, she was overacting with fine abandon, but the overwhelmed Simons was too far gone in her land of fantasy for reality to operate. On her way out of the house, she picked up small portable things – a vase, a travelling clock, a few books – remarking that, after all, they now belonged to her. Still Simons' wits did not rally, and all of a sudden the three of us were out in the street again – my mother who had been my grandmother, her cousin who had been my mother, and me. I feel that this twisted hour marked the occupation of my mind by a sense of confusion that has never left it.

My father was home from work when we got back, and he gasped at the sight of his wife, even though she had thrown away her cracker teeth. When these latest goings-on were explained to him, he was all for taking his friend's possessions over to his unsold house and returning them, with nervous apologies. But my mother had another idea. That night she gift-wrapped, separately, the vase, the clock, and the books, and they were delivered to Simons' door the next morning, before he set out for his office, each 'present' containing a card that read, 'To Harry Simons from Mame Thurber with love.' It was not my mother's most subdued performance, but it was certainly one of her outstanding triumphs. The Frioleras laughed about it for years. There had been fifty of them when the club was founded in 1882. At one of their parties fifty years ago – they played pedro and euchre in the winter and went on picnics and bicycle trips in the summer – my father asked his wife, apropos of what prank I do not know, 'How long do you expect to keep up this kind of thing, Mame?' She thought a moment and replied, 'Why, until I'm eighty, I suppose.'

Mary Agnes Thurber, eldest of the six children of William and Katherine Fisher, was eighty years old in January 1946, and I went to Columbus for a birthday party that brought together scores of her relatives. The day after the event, a columnist in one of the Columbus papers recklessly described her as 'a bit of lavender and old lace'. She was indignant. 'Why, he doesn't even know about the time I threw those eggs!' she exclaimed. I didn't know about it, either, but I found out. At a meeting, a few months before of one of the several women's clubs she belonged to, she had gone to the kitchen of her hostess's house, carefully removed a dozen eggs from a cardboard container, and returned to the living-room to reactivate a party that she felt was growing dull. Balancing the box on the palm of her hand, like a halfback about to let go a forward pass, she cried, 'I've always wanted to throw a dozen eggs, and now I'm going to do it!' The ladies gathered in the room squealed and scattered as the carton sailed into the air. Then it drifted harmlessly to the floor. Lavender and old lace, in their conventional and symbolic sense, were not for Mary Thurber. It would be hard for me to say what was. She never wore black. 'Black is for old ladies,' she told me scornfully.

In 1884, when Mamie Fisher got out of high school, she wanted to go on the stage, but her unladylike and godless urge was discouraged by her family. Aunt Melissa warned her that young actresses were in peril not only of hellfire but of lewd Shakespearian actors, skilled in the arts of seduction, and she pointed out that there was too much talk about talent in the world, and not enough about virtue. She predicted that God's wrath would be visited, in His own time, upon all theatres, beginning, like as not, with those in Paris, France. Mamie Fisher listened with what appeared to be rapt and contrite attention. Actually, she was studying Aunt Melissa's voice, so that she could learn to imitate it.

Deprived of a larger audience, the frustrated comedienne performed for whoever would listen, and once distressed a couple of stately guests in her father's home by descending the front stairs in her dressing-gown, her hair tumbling and her eyes staring, to announce that she had escaped from the attic, where she was kept because of her ardent and hapless love for Mr Briscoe, the postman. An entry in her diary of that period, dated Monday, 14 May 1888, would have puzzled the shocked visitors:

Went over to Flora's to talk over yesterday's visit. I tell you tha Ira D. is cute, but I do not like him very well – he is a perfect gentleman only he will insist on kissing me every time and I will not allow it. I ca truthfully say I never kissed a fellow in all my life but once, and tha was Charlie Thurber at the depot a few years ago.

Those of her relatives who drew no sharp line between life and art, the gifted and the mad, and consoled themselves with the hope that marriage would settle her down, could not have been more mistaken. Even the birth of her third son, in 1896, had littl effect on her merry inventions, and her aunts must have been re lieved when we left Champion Avenue and moved to Washington D.C., in 1901. They probably thought of Washington, in thos years, as a city of inviolable decorum, but it was there that we me a young Cleveland newspaperman named George Marvin, whos gaiety was to enrich our lives. He was a superior wag, with a round, mobile face, a trick of protruding his large eyeballs tha entranced the Thurber boys, and a gift of confusion that matched my mother's. Uncivil clerks and supercilious shoppe proprietors in the nation's capital came to regret their refusal to sell Marvin and my mother one dish of ice-cream with two spoons, or a single glove for the left hand, or one shoe. The mild, soft-spoken Jekylls from the Middle West would be transformed into Mr and Mrs Hyde, to the consternation of the management. 'Senator Beveridge will hear about this!' Marvin would shout, and they would stalk out of the shoppe, in high and magnificent dudgeon. But it was when we were all back in Columbus two years later that these comics reached their heights. Their finest hour arrived one day at Memorial Hall, during a lecture given by a woman mental healer whose ability and sincerity my mother held in low esteem. She has always been a serious and devoted student of psychotherapy, even when it was known and practised under foolish and flowery names, and she learned long ago to detect tommyrot. Arriving after the lecture had begun, our cut-ups found an empty wheel-chair in the lobby, and my mother, bundled up in it, was rolled down the aisle by her confederate. The lady on the platform had reached a peroration of whoosh, during which she chanted that if you had done it before, you could do it again, whatever it was, and other candy-coated inspiration to that effect. At the peak of this marshmallow mentation, my mother leaped from the chair, crying that she had walked before and could do it again. Some ten or twenty persons of the two hundred present must have recognized her, but the others were caught between cheers and consternation. The lecturer shouted, 'Hallelujah, sister!' and at this point Marvin increased the confusion by bulging out his eyes, dropping his jaw, and mumbling that what he had done before he was now doing again; namely, losing his grip on reality. The crisis ended when a querulous man shouted, 'Hey, that's my wheelchair!' and the culprits made good their escape.

The career of almost any actress is marked by open dates and, in the end, a long period of retirement. Who heard of the late Julia Marlowe in her last twenty years? But my mother's crowded calendar shows no season of repose, and the biographer is overwhelmed by instances and can only select a few more. There was the time she went back to Washington, in her sixties, wearing a red rose so the woman she was going to meet could identify her; they hadn't seen each other for thirty years. The train being early, or her hostess late, she pinned the rose on a sleeping dowager, twenty years her senior, who was sitting on a bench in the railway terminal, and watched at a distance the dismay of her friend when she finally arrived and the irritability of the sleeper awakened by a cry of 'Why, Mame Thurber, how are you? You're looking just fine.' And there was the occasion, not long ago, when she deflated a pompous gentleman, overproud of his forebears, who made the mistake of asking her how far back she had traced her own ancestry. 'Until I came to a couple of horse thieves,' she said with a troubled sigh. 'Do you mean a father and son?' the shocked man asked. 'Or was it a couple of brothers?' My mother sighed again. 'It was much worse than that,' she said. 'A man and his wife. You see, it runs in both sides of the family.' A hundred other hours and moments I leave to the record of another year.

With all this to take up her time, Mrs Charles Thurber nevertheless managed to run her home like any other good housewife, hovering over the cook when we had one, following the cleaning woman around with pail and cloth of her own, and rearing three sons who were far from being mother's helpers. She was famous for her pastry and, after long study and practice, learned to make the best chocolate creams in the world. Two or three professional candy men tried to catch her secret, watching her at work like a child watching a magician, and with just about as little profit. She made her last twenty pounds of chocolates when she was eighty, and then turned to writing a cookbook of her own recipes.

I found, in going over her letters, that time hasn't dulled their sparkle. In one, dated 26 December 1949, she told, in fine full detail, the story of her 1933 search for Miss Bagley, which has become a family saga. Miss Annette Bagley, known to her intimates as Anna, wandered from her home in England more than sixty years ago to become a home-to-home sewing woman in Columbus. She and my mother became great friends, and then, one morning in the spring of 1895, Miss Bagley, at the age of thirty-four, took a train to Boston, where she planned to open a dressmaking shop. For several years my mother's fond letters were promptly answered, but about the turn of the century, two of them were returned by the Boston post office. Miss Bagley had dropped out of sight, leaving no forwarding address, and it wasn't until 1913 that she was heard from again. The floods of that year had inundated Columbus, and she sent a worried telegram from Boston. My mother replied, by wire, that all her friends were safe, and Miss Bagley apparently received this telegram at the Western Union office in which she had dispatched her own, but a letter my mother instantly sent to the old address was returned, like the others. Twenty silent years went by.

In 1933, Mary Thurber took up the quest again, writing to the postmasters of Boston and surrounding towns, and inventing a story about the settlement of an estate. 'Money', she wrote me in the 1949 letter, 'always increases people's interest.' It greatly increased the interest of an Anna Bagley in Malden, Massachusetts, who turned out to be the wrong one, and with whom my mother exchanged a brief and cloudy correspondence. Then she came East to take up the search in person. She was sixty-seven and she knew that Miss Bagley, if she was alive, was seventy-two. In Boston my mother set out on the old, dim trail like a trained researcher, looking up outdated phone books and directories at the Chamber of Commerce. The most recent record of Annette Bagley she could find placed her friend in Malden in 1925, so she went to

Malden. Miss Bagley was not at the address listed, and the woman who lived there had never heard of her. My mother did what any good reporter would have done: she looked up old residents of the neighbourhood and called on the older druggists and grocers. She learned that Annette Bagley had left that Malden house about seven years before. Someone seemed to remember that the old lady had moved to Everett Street. This street turned out to be only a block long, and my mother rang all its doorbells without success. Nobody knew anything about Miss Bagley. Then a druggist suggested that her quarry might have moved not to Everett Street but to the town of Everett, which is only a few miles from Malden. My mother transferred her pattern of search to Everett, and it was in that Boston suburb that the trail become warm. She found Annette Bagley listed in a three-year-old directory, but the elusive dressmaker was no longer at the address given. Neighbours, however, thought she had not gone far away, so her tracer continued questioning druggists and grocers and elderly people she stopped on the street. At twilight of the second day of her search, she came upon a small dressmaking shop on a side street. 'I looked through the window,' my mother wrote, 'and there she was, sitting and sewing with her back to me.' Thirty-eight years had made a great difference in the two friends, and it wasn't until my mother asked the old lady if she had ever lived in Columbus, Ohio, that Annette Bagley recognized her.

The reason for her years of hiding was simple enough. She did not want her Columbus friends to know that her dream of a big and flourishing dressmaking establishment of her own had failed to come true. 'I took her to dinner in Boston,' my mother wrote, 'and then to a movie. It was hard for her to believe that my oldest son, William, was forty, for when she had seen him last he was only two. I'm not sure about the movie, but I think it was *It Happened One Night*, or *One Sunday Afternoon*, or something like that.' It isn't often that my memory outdoes my mother's, but I have always remembered the name of that movie since she first told me the story of her celebrated search for Annette Bagley twenty-four years ago. It was called *I Loved You Wednesday*.

In New York, which my mother visited often, she liked to escape from her sons and see the sights of the city on her own. One morning some twenty-five years ago, she reached the second floor of the famous Wendel house on Fifth Avenue, but her tour of inspection was interrupted. 'I was just going by and I thought I would drop in,' she told me. On that visit she made a tour of Greenwich Village by herself, but asked me to take her to what she called 'the Tony's' and the "21",' whose fame she had somehow heard about. At 'the Tony's' she was fortunate enough to meet one of her idols, the late Heywood Broun, and she enchanted him by casting an offhand horoscope for him that turned out to be a recognizable portrait, done in the bold colours of both virtue and shortcoming. She had always had a lot of fun monkeying around with the inexact sciences (she corresponded with Evangeline Adams, and once had Professor Coué out to dinner at our house, in Columbus) and I am sure that she must have dipped into Dianetics. She embarrassed my father one time, in an impish numerology phase, by making him return a set of ominously numbered automobile licence plates and exchange it for a safer one. In 1940, when she entered Columbia Presbyterian Medical Centre for a major operation that she took in her stride, she demanded to know the date of birth of her distinguished surgeon before she would let him operate. He solemnly gave it to her, and was pleased to learn that he had been engaged for thirty years in a profession for which his signs clearly fitted him. Later, he was astonished by her familiarity with medicine and surgery, and told her one day that she had the sound implementation of a nurse. 'Of course,' my mother said. 'I'm Capricorn with the moon in Sagittarius.'

The day she was discharged from the hospital, she decided to visit the World's Fair, and she did, in spite of heat and humidity. In a bus on the way back, she found that she had exceeded her strength, and she asked the bus driver to take her pulse. He took it with one hand, continuing to drive with the other, and reported that it was a little high but nothing to worry about. I am sure she got the bus driver's date of birth. She remembered the birthdays of literally hundreds of men and women. She once sent me a clipping of an Earl Wilson column in which he had given Dorothy Parker's birthday as 23 August. 'Dorothy Parker's birthday is August 22nd,' my mother wrote. 'August 23rd is Helen Gude's birthday.' A few years ago I phoned her in Columbus and asked her if she remembered her surgeon's birthday. 'Why, certainly,' she said. 'He was born on the 30th of March. My Columbus surgeon is also Aries – April 1st.'

When my mother came to New York in 1947, I found that she had made a date for tea at the Algonquin with an old friend of my father's, Charles Dewey Hilles. She said that she herself hadn't seen him for 'a long time'. Mr Hilles, a celebrated Ohio Republican, died eight years ago, and his long obituaries told of his having been, among many other things, an Assistant Secretary of the Treasury under Taft, Chairman of the Republican National Committee from 1912 to 1916, and a member of dozens of boards of directors. I had the good luck to be asked to the Ohio tea party, along with the late John McNulty, for many years a reporter on Columbus newspapers. We had a jolly time, and various ancient facts and forgotten dates were brought up. It came out that my mother was a year older than Mr Hilles. 'When was it,' I finally asked, 'that you two last met?' My mother thought about this and said, 'Well, Mr Hilles was secretary to the superintendent of the Boys' Industrial School at Lancaster, Ohio. Let me see – yes, it must have been in 1888.' My mother was twenty-two in 1888, and Mr Hilles, of course, was only twenty-one. Now, no elderly man of high and varied achievement likes to be reminded of his juvenile beginnings, and it was obvious to us all that my mother's grasp of her friend's later career was tenuous. McNulty saved the situation. 'Eighteen-eighty-eight,' he said, 'was the year the owls were so bad.' What Mr Hilles must have approached as something of an ordeal turned out to be fun for him. He had said he would have to take a 3.30 train, but he stayed until 5.30. Heywood Broun, on the night my mother read his horoscope offhand, had not only missed one train for Boston, but two.

Mary Thurber died on 20 December 1955, within three weeks of her ninetieth birthday, the oldest and the last of her generation of Fishers. At the funeral the last survivor of the old Friolera Club, founded nearly seventy-five years before, had something memorable to say to me. 'You know,' she said, 'even if Mame had been the first to go, she would have outlived us all.' There is no epitaph she would have liked better than that.

The Last Flower A PARABLE IN PICTURES

FOR ROSEMARY

In the wistful hope that her ***world*** *will be better than mine*

World War XII, as everybody knows,

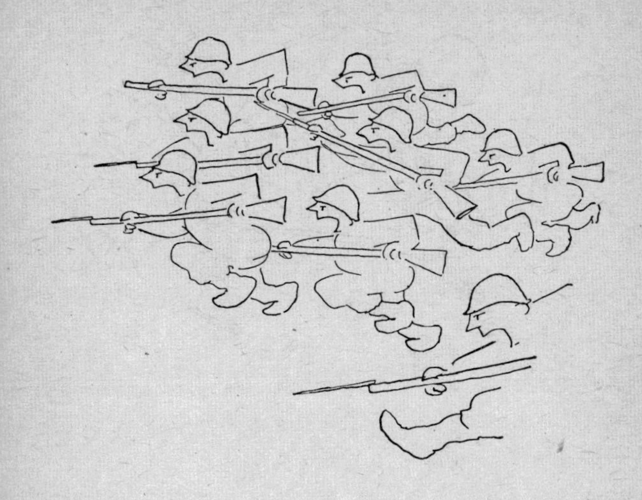

Brought about the collapse of civilization

Towns, cities, and villages disappeared from the earth

All the groves and forests were destroyed

And all the gardens

And all the works of art

Men, women, and children became lower than the lower animals

Discouraged and disillusioned, dogs deserted their fallen masters

Emboldened by the pitiful condition of the former lords of the earth, rabbits descended upon them

Books, paintings, and music disappeared from the earth, and human beings just sat around doing nothing

Years and years went by

Even the few Generals who were left forgot what the last war had decided

Boys and girls grew up to stare at each other blankly, for love had passed from the earth

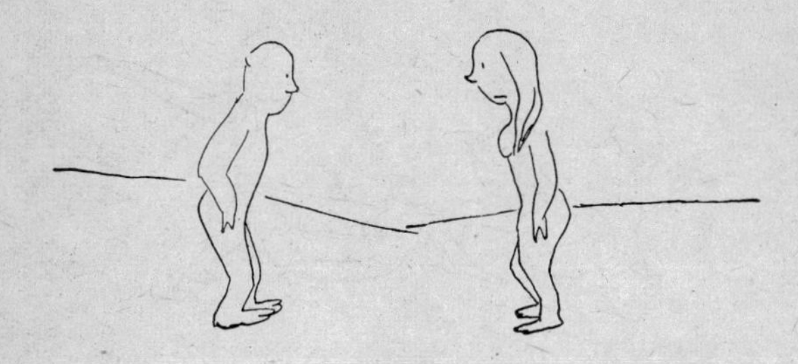

One day a young girl who had never seen a flower chanced to come upon the last one in the world

She told the other human beings that the last flower was dying

The only one who paid any attention to her was a young man she found wandering about

Together the young man and the girl nurtured the flower and it began to live again

One day a bee visited the flower, and a Hummingbird

Before long there were two flowers, and then four, and then a great many

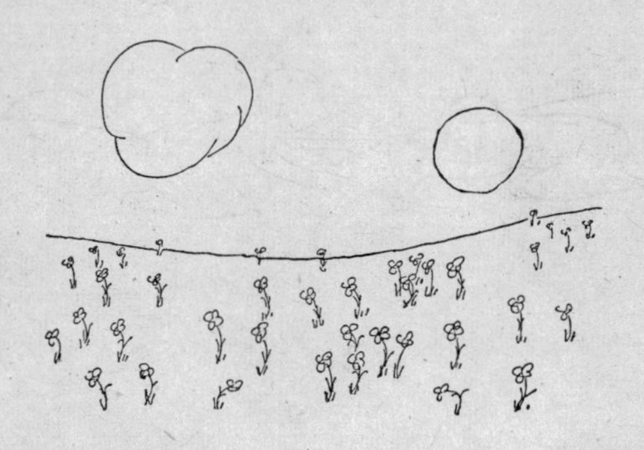

Groves and forests flourished again

The young girl began to take an interest in how she looked

The young man discovered that touching the girl was pleasurable

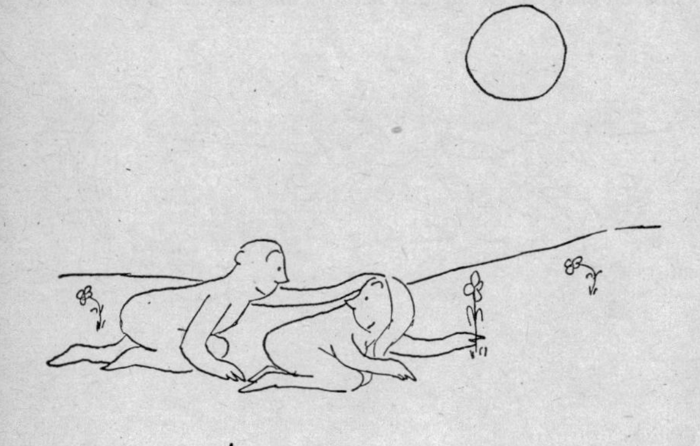

Love was reborn into the world

Their children grew up strong and healthy and learned to run and laugh

Dogs came out of their exile

The young man discovered, by putting one stone upon another, how to build a shelter

Pretty soon everybody was building shelters

Towns, cities, and villages sprang up

Song came back into the world

And troubadours and jugglers

And tailors and cobblers

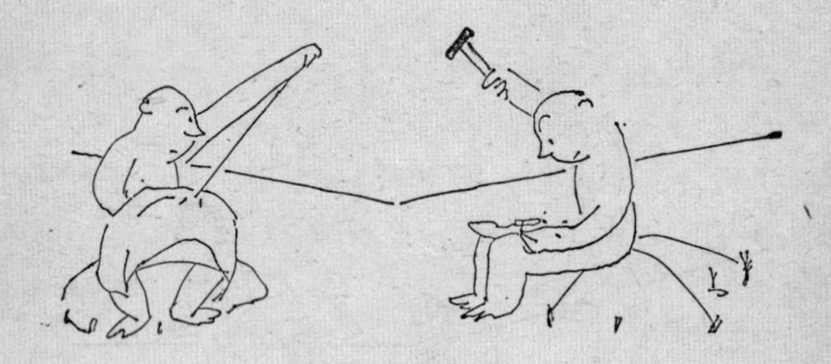

And painters and poets

And sculptors and wheelwrights

And soldiers

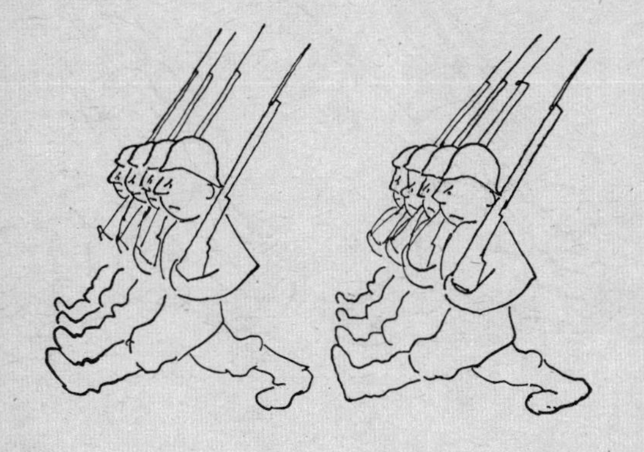

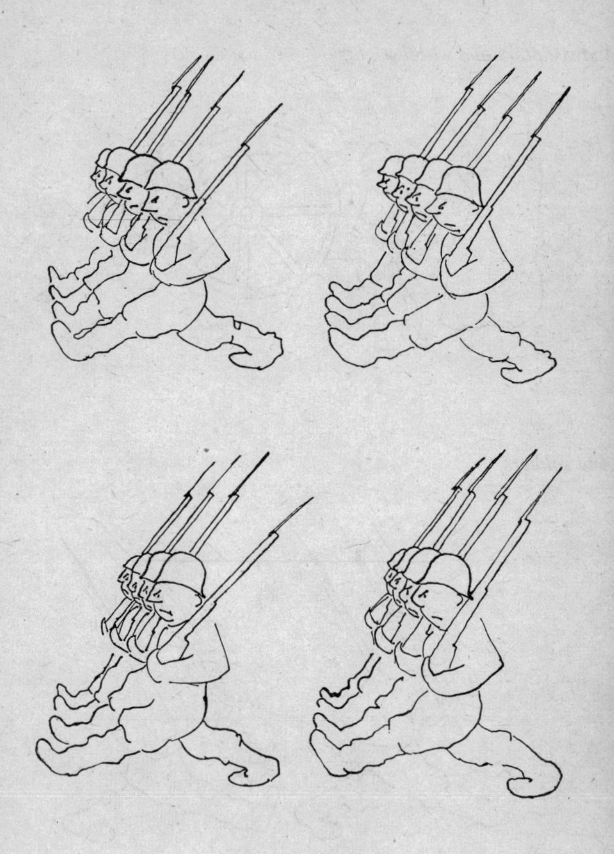

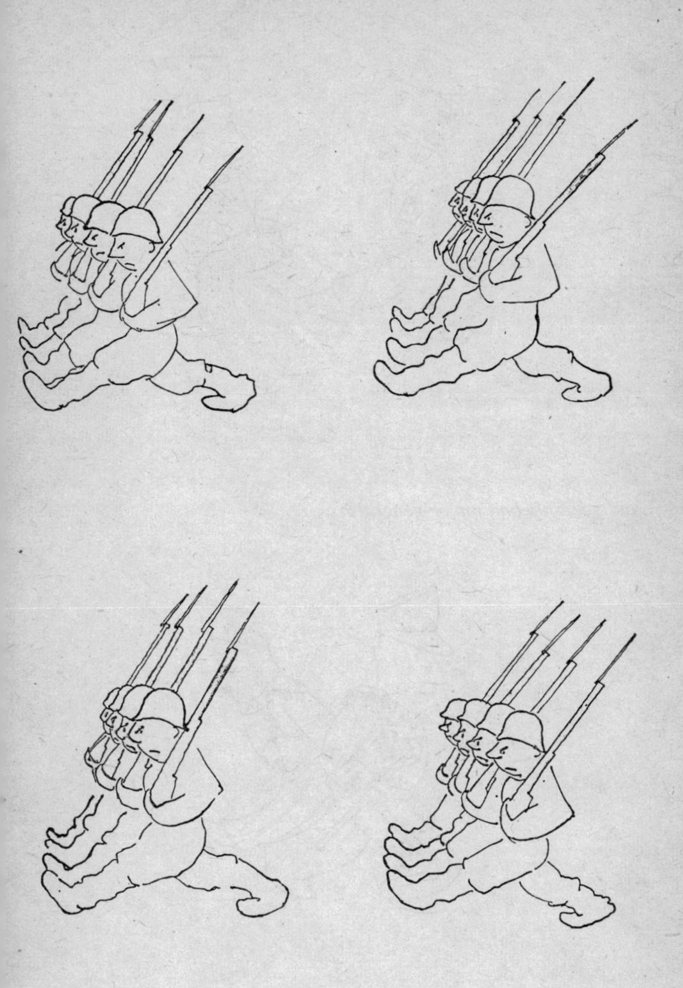

And lieutenants and captains

And generals and major-generals

And liberators

Some people went one place to live, and some another

Before long, those who went to live in the valleys wished they had gon[e] to live in the hills

And those who had gone to live in the hills wished they had gone to liv[e] in the valleys

The liberators, under the guidance of God, set fire to the discontent

So presently the world was at war again

This time the destruction was so complete . . .

That nothing at all was left in the world

Except one man

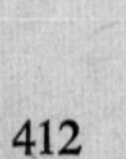

And one woman

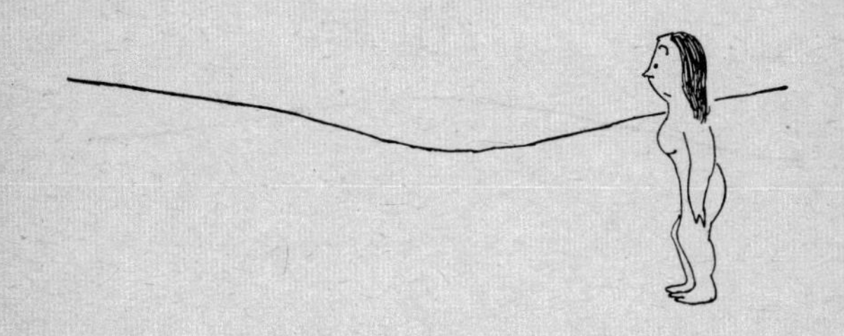

And one flower